GRIDLOCK

GRIDLOCK

BYRON L. DORGAN

AND

DAVID HAGBERG

A TOM DOHERTY ASSOCIATES BOOK

NEW YORK

GRIDLOCK

Copyright © 2013 by Byron L. Dorgan and David Hagberg

A Forge Book
Published by Tom Doherty Associates, LLC
175 Fifth Avenue
New York, NY 10010

www.tor-forge.com

Forge® is a registered trademark of Tom Doherty Associates, LLC.

Library of Congress Cataloging-in-Publication Data

Dorgan, Byron L.
    Gridlock / Byron L. Dorgan and David Hagberg.—First Edition.
      p. cm.
    "A Tom Doherty Associates book."
    ISBN 978-0-7653-2738-3 (hardcover)
    ISBN 978-1-4299-4942-2 (e-book)
    1. Energy security—United States—Fiction.   2. Energy industries—Political aspects—United States—Fiction.   3. Energy industries—Government policy—United States—Fiction.   4. Terrorism—Prevention—United States—Fiction. I. Hagberg, David.   II. Title.
PS3604.O7365G75 2013
813'.6—dc23

2013003645

Forge books may be purchased for educational, business, or promotional use. For information on bulk purchases, please contact Macmillan Corporate and Premium Sales Department at 1-800-221-7945 extension 5442 or write specialmarkets@macmillan.com.

First Edition: July 2013

Printed in the United States of America

0 9 8 7 6 5 4 3 2 1

To Kim, my inspiration!

—BYRON DORGAN

For Lorrel as always
—DAVID HAGBERG

ACKNOWLEDGMENTS

A special thanks to Mel Berger at William Morris Endeavor (WME) for his role in helping make this project a reality. He is a superb agent and a good friend.

And my appreciation goes to Tom Doherty and Bob Gleason at Tor Books, who were so supportive of this book and the book that preceded it, *Blowout*. Tom and Bob love the world of books, and their leadership in publishing novels that make people think about the world around them is inspiring.

Finally thanks to my coauthor, David Hagberg. He is a creative thinker and talented writer, and it's clear to me why he has had such a long and successful career as a novelist. It's been a great privilege to work with him.

AUTHORS' NOTE

What we have written here about America's power grid and 120-plus control centers is not quite accurate. We've distorted some elements of the complex system so as not to make this story a blueprint for a terrorist attack. Unfortunately, though, such a thing is well within the realm of possibility. At any moment. And if it happens the United States will be in serious trouble; more trouble than could be imagined . . . a thousand, ten thousand times worse than 9/11.

GRIDLOCK

Prologue

Along the Iran-Turkmenistan Border

LIEUTENANT MOSHEN HAMIDI, the slighter of the two men dressed in winter camos, raised his hand for his partner to pull up so that he could recheck the GPS receiver for the third time in less than a half hour. They were in the foothills one hundred kilometers north of Mashad and within a kilometer or two of their rendezvous point. The night was bitterly cold and dark under a deeply overcast sky, no lights from any civilization in any direction. They could have been on the moon.

He was twenty-seven, short even for an Iranian, with the dark good looks that his wife of five years still found devastating, and a quick mind that had put him on the fast track through university and then basic training at VEVAK, the Ministry of Intelligence and National Security's School One outside of Tehran. He'd specialized at first in communications services including methods of encryption, until a supervisor had noticed that Hamidi was good with his hands, very good, and in personal combat exercises he never lost. From the start he became known as the dark ghost, because he was too elusive ever to be reached by a knife or club or fist, but when he struck it was with an almost otherworldly speed and force.

And he never showed fear until this mission, which was classified top secret.

"Failure is not an option," Colonel Dabir had warned two days ago.

They had met in civilian clothes downtown at a coffee bar that was never frequented by anyone in government. Hamidi had not questioned his orders, but the colonel had told him in a lowered voice that the need-to-know list was extremely small. The nature of the mission was such that no blame could ever come back to anyone in the republic, not even to anyone in VEVAK.

"Take one man with you, but he is to be told nothing except that you are meeting with a Russian intelligence officer who will bring a computer thumb drive to the border, for which you will pay him one million dollars U.S. When you have it you will return back here to Mashad, to this very place, where I will be waiting."

"Am I to be told what is on this thumb drive?"

"Only that it is potentially more important than your life, or mine, and the sooner you bring it to me the sooner I can send it out of the country to a client."

The colonel was nominally in charge of Section One, which dealt only with Israeli matters, but everyone suspected that some years ago he had carved out his own Special Operations Section that answered directly to President Ahmadinejad and no one else. And right now, with the troubles between the president and Ayatollah Ali Khamenei, the colonel's position was precarious.

"Succeed and you will make captain."

"And if I fail?"

"You do not want to consider the consequences, for you and your wife and child," the colonel had warned.

They had driven from Mashad late last night, stopping just outside of the small border settlement of Kabud Gombad and going the rest of the way on foot. It was nearly two in the morning and a light breeze had sprung up making the spring morning feel even colder.

"Are we close, Lieutenant?" Sergeant Ali Alani asked. He was twenty-four and built like a short, dark, very dangerous military weapon, which he was. He complained constantly, never smiled, never cracked a joke, but he was completely, even sometimes overwhelmingly, loyal.

Hamidi waited until his GPS unit settled down and displayed a latitude and longitude in a box below the map screen which showed they were twelve hundred meters out, on a correct track. Providing the Russian they were to meet was on time and at the correct meeting place, they would make the exchange and be on the way back home.

"A little over a kilometer," Hamidi said, pointing to the northwest.

"Good, because it's bloody well cold up here. And I'm getting damned tired of carrying this bloody bag up and down hills. Allah only knows where we are, but if I had to guess I'd say we've crossed into Turkmenistan by now."

"Another thousand meters," Hamidi said, starting up a stony path that led to the top of a low hill. "Just over the top. And take care with the bag because you're carrying one million in U.S. money."

Alani followed a couple of meters back, silent until he said something under his breath that sounded like a swear word. "Are we defecting then?"

"No," Hamidi said, but he was sure that if he'd told his sergeant exactly what they were doing he'd get some complaints but no objections.

At the top something large and dark like a mass of metal that had been burned lay half-buried in the sandy rubble. Up close it looked to Hamidi like the remains of a jet engine. And spread out below and for as far as he could make out in the darkness was a path of debris.

"An airplane crashed here," Alani said. "A big one by the looks of it and not so long ago. Is this where we're supposed to meet the Russian? Because if it is, something is wrong. And I never heard of a plane crash up here. Have you?"

"No," Hamidi said. The colonel had told him that the crash site was very near the rendezvous point, but he hadn't elaborated whose aircraft it had been, and how it had come to crash at this point. But it was obvious from the pattern that the plane had been trying to get out of Iran not, into the country.

"The crash is none of your concern, Lieutenant," the colonel had told him. "And believe me, you're better off not knowing about it."

"The locals must have seen or heard something."

"That problem has been dealt with. Leave it alone. Just do this mission and get back with the drive. You have no other concerns."

"This is no coincidence," Alani grumbled.

"Only because it's near the border where we're to meet," Hamidi said, and he headed down the hill, where if the topographic map he'd studied was accurate, the Russian would be waiting on the other side of a jagged outcropping of rocks that rose thirty or forty meters above the floor of the valley just across the border.

The highway that ran all the way to Ashgabat, Turkmenistan's capital, was just ten kilometers farther north, making this a perfect spot for the handoff.

About twenty meters from the rocks, Alani pulled out his ZOAF 9mm pistol, which was a knockoff SIG-Sauer P226, and motioned for silence as he headed off to the left.

Hamidi pulled out his own pistol, the hairs at the nape of his neck standing on end. Something wasn't right . . . he could feel it, and not merely because Alani was reacting to something.

He headed slowly to the right when a thin, almost emaciated-looking man came around from behind the rocks, his jacket open, his head bare, and his hands in plain sight.

"I'm not armed," the man said in Russian. "No weapons."

"Did you bring the drive?" Hamidi asked in Russian, stopping about five meters away. Alani was to the left about fifteen meters out.

"*Da*. I will take it out of my coat pocket. Don't shoot."

"Carefully," Hamidi said. He guessed the man was young, possibly still in his teens, and he was obviously frightened.

The Russian took great care to reach into his pocket and take out a small envelope. "It's actually a Zip drive."

"Lay it on the ground and step away."

"Not until I have the money."

Hamidi motioned for Alani, who came forward cautiously, his pistol still at the ready. He laid the bag on the rocky ground one meter from the Russian and backed off.

The young man got down on his knees and opened the bag. He riffled through the stacks of hundred-dollar bills for a few seconds and then looked up, practically licking his lips. "I won't count it here. But if it's short, I will send a signal to erase the Zip drive's memory the moment it is placed in any computer. Am I clear?"

"What's to stop me from simply shooting you? We would have the money and the Zip drive."

The young man got to his feet and hefted the bag to his shoulder. He shrugged. "In certain online circles I'm well known. My absence would be noticed within twenty-four hours, probably sooner, and believe me, Lieutenant, there would be repercussions."

"As there will be for you if the information on the drive is not what we paid for. My friends and I have a very long reach, and an even longer memory."

The Russian nodded. "Then we have a deal," he said. "But tread with very great care. Wars have started for much less than what is contained on that drive. Make sure that your superiors know that there could be consequences." He turned and walked away.

Hamidi got the envelope and was stuffing it in his pocket, when the side of the Russian's head erupted in a spray of blood and the young man was violently shoved to the side off his feet as the sound of the distant rifle shot reached them.

Alani reacted first. "Move," he shouted urgently, and he sprinted to the left.

Hamidi turned as a bullet whistled past his head so close he could feel the shock wave and the heat. Alani had already started up the hill in a broken field run, and Hamidi started after him.

This had been a trap, which meant that the leak had come from the Russians. Hamidi could not believe that someone in VEVAK had leaked the mission details, because it would mean that he could never go home.

Alani reached the top of the hill and disappeared on the other side, seconds before Hamidi made it to his sergeant's side and flopped down on the gravel next to him.

"Fucking Russians," Alani said. He pulled out a pair of binoculars and cautiously rose up over the crest and glassed the spot where the Russian kid was down.

"Anything?"

"Not yet."

"That wasn't a Dragunov," Hamidi said. "I would have recognized it." The 7.62mm Dragunov (SVD) was the standard sniper rifle used by all Russian Special Forces, and it had its own sound that was distinctive, unmistakable.

"Americans?"

"It wasn't a Barrett, either, too light a caliber." The .50in Barrett was the sniper rifle of choice for American forces.

"Who then? Not one of ours."

"No, thank Allah," Hamidi said.

"There they are," Alani said. "Two of them, in white parkas."

Hamidi took the binoculars and, keeping as low a profile as possible, glassed the valley floor. One of the men had laid his long-barreled rifle on the ground, the muzzle raised above the dirt by a fairly long tripod just forward of the receiver, and was going through the dead Russian's pockets.

The second man was looking directly up the hill, slowly panning the scope of his rifle left to right, and Hamidi ducked down for a second.

"Who are they?" Alani asked.

"I don't know yet. But I think they're carrying FR-F2 sniper rifles."

"The fucking French?"

Hamidi rose up again, at the same time the man scoping the hill pushed back the hood of his parka and raised his scope directly at the crest of the hill.

Alani rose up before Hamidi could stop him, and the sniper fired, the shot catching the sergeant in the left eye, the entire back of his head disintegrating as he was flung violently backward.

The sniper jacked another round into his rifle as the second man jumped to his feet and grabbed his rifle.

Hamidi pulled back below the crest of the hill, his heart thumping. Sergeant Alani was dead, and no power on earth could save him. Nor was it possible for his body to be brought back to Mashad, not yet, perhaps never. He carried no identification—neither of them did—linking them to VEVAK. When his body was found and stripped, he would just be another cross-border poacher or trader who was murdered in a deal—probably for drugs—gone bad.

He scrambled backward a few meters below the crest and then got to his feet and headed in a dead run back the three kilometers to where they had left their nondescript Toyota pickup, sick at heart that he had to leave Ali's body behind, and dreading how he would break the news to his sergeant's parents.

But failure had not been an option. He had the Zip drive and as long as he could reach the pickup before the shooters caught up with him he would make it back, though how he was going to convince the colonel that the snipers who'd killed the Russian and Sergeant Alani were Chinese was beyond him.

PART ONE

THE FIRST PROBES

Thirty Days Later

1

MINNEAPOLIS WAS COLD, snow still on the ground, the trees bare. Like Moscow, no spring buds here yet. Former Spetsnaz Captain Yuri Makarov, a nephew of Nikolai Makarov who designed the 9mm pistol that had been universally used in the Soviet military, got off the Delta flight from New York's LaGuardia a few minutes before eleven in the morning, nodding to the two first-class attendants, and headed down the Jetway into the Lindbergh Terminal. A man in no apparent hurry.

Traveling under a British passport with the work name Thomas Parks, he'd brought only a small leather carry-on bag which he slung over his shoulder and turned left at the gate and headed to the main terminal. It was a weekday and the airport was busy mostly with business travelers, and no one paid any particular attention to him.

He was fairly short, under six feet, slender, with dark hair, wide dark eyes, glasses, a pleasant demeanor, and an easy almost shy smile, and at thirty-five he'd often been mistaken for a soccer player, or former soccer player for some British team. His accent was as impeccable as was his grooming and dress—lightweight tailored blue blazer, open collar shirt, and gray slacks. He carried a Burberry over his arm, and wore Italian handmade half boots.

Parks appeared to be a gentleman, perhaps in banking, probably old family credentials. In fact he was a contract killer, whose real name and actual background were known to only a few people inside Russia, and even they had no idea where he had disappeared to almost eight years ago. But he could be reached by the right people, mostly people working at fairly high levels for some government intelligence service, who had need of skills such as his. And who had access to a great deal of money. Makarov never failed and that expertise came at a hefty price.

He followed the signs to the car rental desks on the second level and stopped at the Hertz counter, the line fairly short. When it was his turn he presented his British driving license and American Express platinum card. "Thomas Parks."

"Good morning, Mr. Parks," the attractive young clerk said, smiling. "Good flight?"

"Yes."

She brought up his reservation on her computer screen. "I have you for a Chevrolet Impala, but I can upgrade you—"

"The Chevy will be just fine."

She nodded, ran his credit card and driver's license through the system, which spit out a rental agreement, which Makarov signed and five minutes later he was in the car and heading away from the airport.

For this assignment, which was almost ridiculously simple by his standards, he'd been contacted the usual way through a secure e-mail account that was routed through several remailers, ending with a large but discrete service in New Delhi. He'd met with his client at a booth in the back of a small pub just off Trafalgar

Square at noon fifteen days ago. Both of them carried the day's edition of *Le Figaro*. And twenty-four hours earlier Makarov had gone around to the back of the building to make sure that it had a rear door in case something went wrong.

"Good afternoon," he said, laying his newspaper on the table and sitting down.

The man across from him was older, perhaps in his mid to late fifties, with steel-gray short cropped hair, a square almost Teutonic face, and broad shoulders and thick chest that strained against the light jacket he was wearing. He was not smiling, and Makarov got the impression that he never smiled.

"What do I call you?"

"For the moment, Mr. Schmidt will do," Makarov said, a slight German accent to his voice. "You contacted me and I'm here. What do you want?"

"Do you want to know who I am?"

"You're Colonel Luis Delgado, SEBIN. What does Venezuelan intelligence want with me?"

Delgado's left eyebrow rose. "A small job of work at first."

Makarov said nothing.

"In western North Dakota, it's in the upper Midwest of the United States."

"Continue."

Delgado told him what the job involved. "We'll book your air, hotel, and car reservations, as well as provide you the proper equipment—"

Makarov raised a hand to stop the man. "I'll make my own arrangements. But there must be a better way of striking back after Balboa." The operation shortly after Christmas had been a U.S. strike on five of Venezuela's forward air force bases—the most important to Chavez. And the remark got to the colonel, because he was suddenly curt.

"Do you want the job or not?"

Makarov handed him a business card that contained only two series of numbers, one with nine digits which was a bank router and the second of ten which was his account number. "Five hundred thousand euros now and an additional five hundred thousand when the job is completed to your satisfaction."

The colonel nodded. "Time is of the essence," he said, but Makarov had already gotten to his feet and was heading for the door.

The half million had shown up in his Channel Islands' account twenty-four hours later and he'd spent the last eight days arranging with the Russian Mafia in New York for his equipment to be purchased and put in place, his British documents and credit card secured, and the first-class flight reservations from Heathrow to New York and from there to Minneapolis arranged. He would fly to Paris under a different set of documents when he was finished here.

He picked up Interstate 494 west which was part of the ring highway system around the Twin Cities and seven miles later turned off at one of the exits for the suburb of Bloomington, where he pulled in at an E-Z Self Storage facility. He entered the four-digit code and the gate swung inward so he could drive back to a small unit in the last row.

No one was around at this hour, and Makarov unlocked the roll-up door with the key that had been left for him at LaGuardia taped under seat 2A aboard his Delta flight. Inside, a duffle bag was propped up against the rear wall of the unit. Making sure that no one was coming, he opened the bag and expertly checked the partially disassembled American-made model 90 Barrett sniper rifle, making certain that the firing pin was intact. Also included as per his orders were the Leupold & Stevens x10 scope, and one eleven-round detachable box magazine loaded with .50 in Browning ammunition. The 1,000-grain big-caliber bullet was 100 percent deadly from nearly a mile out, and could even penetrate the engine blocks of military vehicles, and aircraft.

Something blocked the sun and Makarov turned as one of the largest men he'd ever encountered stepped inside. At nearly seven feet the man had to weigh more than three hundred pounds and yet with tree trunk legs, an impossibly broad chest, huge neck, and massive shoulders, his baby face was disproportionately small. He was grinning like an idiot.

"Who are you?" Makarov asked mildly.

"Don Toivo. I own this place."

"Well, you scared the hell out of me, mate. Do you always go around sneaking up on people?"

"Only when I find something interesting in the units they rent from me," Toivo said and he glanced at the duffle bag. "And what's in there is definitely very interesting. Illegal."

"It's for sport. Target practice. I'm in a competition the day after tomorrow."

"Not with full-grain hollow points. That is a weapon for killing people."

"How would you know something like that?" Makarov asked, measuring distances and angles. The big man had been injured sometime in the past because he favored his left leg.

"I make it my business."

"Very well. What comes next?"

"You have two choices: leave the rifle, drive away, and never come back, or pay me what I think I can get for it on the open market. I know some guys."

Makarov smiled. "You weren't a footballer, too big. I suspect that you could never move fast enough. Weight lifter, shot putter?"

"WWF," Toivo said.

Makarov shook his head.

"World Wrestling Federation. Television."

"I see," Makarov said. "Actually neither choice will work. I can't leave my things here, nor am I willing to pay you anything."

Toivo's grin broadened. "I hoped you'd say something like that, because there is a third choice."

"Which is?"

"I fucking break you in two and take the gun anyway. How about that choice?"

2

D R. WHITNEY LIPTON walked into the press tent at the Dakota Initiative power station a few minutes past noon and took her place at the podium. Only a half-dozen media people had bothered to drive all the way out here—in the serious boondocks, as a *Minneapolis Tribune* reporter had once quipped—and except for the cutting-edge microbial science, Whitney wouldn't be here herself.

Weekly press briefings were held on Fridays at the station just south of Medora in the western North Dakota Badlands, but Whitney, the project's director who was thirty-three and slender, with the dark good looks of the Hollywood movie star Lara Flynn Boyle, with a near-genius IQ had never gotten used to the things.

Talking to the scientists and technicians on her new team was a piece of cake, because they all came from the same place, they knew the project, and she didn't have to explain everything from scratch. Einstein had once told a newspaper reporter that you didn't really understand relativity unless you could explain it to a kindergartener.

These briefings about the current progress at the project amounted to just about the same thing. And a couple of weeks ago she'd asked her press officer, Army Lieutenant Rudy Doyle, if the reporters ever read each other's newspapers. Especially the *New York Times* and *Washington Post* science sections. If they had over the past six months, ever since the top-secret project had been thrown open to the public, they would have had at least a basic understanding not only of what was going on here, but some of the technical problems that had come up and that Whitney and her team had solved.

"In the forties with the entire world at war, Roosevelt had created the Manhattan District Project to develop the atomic bomb which would put an early end to the killing," she'd explained to groups just like the one she was facing this morning. "And it worked. All-out global wars were a thing of the past."

"Yeah, MAD, mutually assured destruction, us versus the Russians with ten thousand nuclear weapons. Is that what you guys are really doing out here?"

"Stopping a war, you betcha," Whitney said. "That's what we're facing, only this time it's an energy war, because if we keep on going the way we're going—burning coal for nearly half our energy needs in this country alone—there is pretty strong evidence that we're facing a runaway greenhouse effect that could do irreparable damage to the entire planet. Irreversible damage."

"Don't lecture," Doyle had warned her early on. "They'll tune out. The TV folks need sound bites, and the print people want one-liners."

"I'm a scientist, goddamnit."

"It's your project, and that makes you the mouthpiece."

General Bob Forester, who ran the project through ARPA-E, the Advanced Research Project Agency-Energy, in Washington, had been directed by the president to open the Initiative's door.

"The project has proven itself," the president had said to a joint session of Congress six months ago. "Through the work of Dr. Whitney Lipton, formerly of the CDC, we have injected a colony of coal-eating bacterium that produces as a by-product relatively clean-burning methane gas to produce electricity."

The process was patentless—anyone could request the formula and method for controlling the bugs, and within ten years, even at worst-case scenario outputs, the level of carbon dioxide levels in the atmosphere would begin to significantly drop.

"I want to talk to you this morning about a couple of problems, one of which cropped up five days ago," she began. "For first several days, actually until yesterday afternoon, we thought we might have such a serious issue that the entire project would have to be either shut down or completely rethought."

She had their complete attention now, and despite the electric heaters stationed in the tent the air was still cold, but none of them seemed to mind, not even Doris Sampson, a reporter for the *Los Angeles Times,* who raised her hand.

"Another accident like before Christmas when there were casualties?"

Whitney shook her head. "Nothing like that, except among the microbial colony in the coal seam."

The station had been attacked twice just before and just after Christmas by a Posse Comitatus group of fanatics who, as it turned out, had been hired by an American contracting firm that had done business in Iraq, and who had been directed by Venezuela's intelligence service. A lot of good people had lost their lives in the two incidents, among them most of her scientific staff, most of the power plant personnel, the press director, and Jim Cameron, who'd been chief of security. His death had been the hardest to bear because she had been falling in love with him. And he had given his life saving hers.

"Would you care to explain?"

Sound bites and one-liners, Doyle had warned. She glanced at him, standing at the back of the tent, and he shrugged. At the mention of possible casualties the reporters had looked up with interest, but just as quickly they were bored again.

"Six hundred microbes were injected into a coal seam one thousand feet below us. As long as we could talk to them they ate the coal and excreted pure methane, which we pumped out of the ground and burned to produce electricity. Five days ago they stopped listening and started dying."

"What'd you do, Doc, give them a pep talk?" one of the other reporters asked, which got a few laughs.

"Almost exactly that. They were doing pretty good for us, producing methane. But they were just kids. Five days ago they became rebellious teenagers who told us in effect to stuff it. They weren't interested."

"You solved the problem, how?" Sampson asked. At least she was interested.

"I took away their cell phones, and threatened to take their cars."

Someone else laughed, but she had their attention.

"We learned their language early on, and with the gadget that we lowered into the coal seam through the bore hole we could talk to them in a chemical and electrical lingua franca that all six hundred different colonies could understand. 'Work for us, and you get to eat all the free coal you want.'"

"What happened?"

"They grew up and lost interest in sex. They wanted to eat coal and party but they didn't want to reproduce. We finally hit on the notion that teenagers hooked up with each other—if you want to call it that—by texting. And they even spoke their own language. You know stuff like LOL for laugh out loud, or PRL, for parents are listening. This sort of chatter had a different chemical signature than what we were using, so we merely found another chemical that neutralized that sort of talk. And still another series of instructional units that told them in effect that it was okay to go ahead and have unsafe sex, and that if they refused we would send a third series of electrochemical messages that would have hobbled them—made it impossible to travel."

She glanced again at Doyle but this time the expression on his round Irish face was unreadable. One-liners indeed, but she still had the reporters' attention. Sex did sell, even bug sex.

"And it worked?" Sampson asked.

"Like Viagra."

They laughed. "Couldn't have been easy," one of them said.

"It wasn't," Whitney said. "None of us got much sleep this last week. But you'll be given a briefing package before you leave which will explain our work both in technical and layman's terms."

"You said two problems, what's the other?" Sampson asked.

"What to do with the power we generate here."

"High power lines lead out of here heading east, presumably they connect with the electrical transmission grid."

"That's the problem. Because unlike just about any other energy resource, electricity cannot be stored. It has to be used the moment it's produced. And it turns out that we're talking about a very delicate and very precise balancing act. If a station like ours produces too little energy during a hot summer day when everyone's air conditioners are running then that extra power has to be routed from somewhere else. Immediately. But if we produce too much power, that nobody needs, we have to shut down."

"There always has to be a need somewhere," Sampson said, but Whitney could see that the woman had a fair idea what was coming. "Hell, Los Angeles is always running short."

"You're right, but we cannot export our electricity to California. There are simply not enough transmission lines from here to there.

In fact there are three distinct power regions in the continental U.S. The Western Interconnect, which it's called, that includes everything west of a line between the middle of Montana all the way down to a section of New Mexico. The Texas Interconnect, which is pretty much the state of Texas. And the Eastern Interconnect, which is us here all the way out to the eastern seaboard."

"That's a big chunk of the country," Sampson said. "So why does the East Coast have so many brownouts and rolling blackouts? There should be plenty of power to go around."

"It's more complicated than that, because mixed in with those three interconnects are ten regions that are controlled by organizations called North American Electric Reliability Councils, and one hundred twenty-seven different control centers where computers are used to make sure the system works as well as it should under the circumstances."

"What circumstances?" Sampson pressed. She was a petite woman with long blond hair who looked more like a runway model than a serious journalist with a major newspaper.

"I'm a microbiologist, not an electrical engineer. But I can tell you that there is no national electrical grid in the U.S. Very few power superhighways. Nothing like our interstate system for cars and trucks. What we have is mostly a hodgepodge of a few big, but aging, highways and a lot of dirt roads."

"What's being done about it?"

"In this economic climate?" Whitney asked. "Not much. In the first place building transmission lines is very expensive, and almost no one anywhere wants them to run through their backyards. And all of these corporations that control various runs of power lines are not much interested in having Washington nationalize the grid."

"That's incredible," someone muttered, but everyone caught it.

"I agree," Whitney said. But what was even more incredible,

even unbelievable—something that General Forester had briefed her on two years ago—was a virus that had been implanted into the entire U.S. system. It had been done either by the Chinese or the Russians, there was no way of removing the computer bug, and at any moment whoever controlled it could crash our entire system. The destruction of property and the loss of lives would be far worse than the Civil War. Nothing would ever be the same in the U.S.

3

IT WAS IMPORTANT in Makarov's business that his face was never seen in the actual conduct of a field exercise by someone who could later identify him. In meant he either wore a disguise or he killed anyone who could connect him.

To this point he'd come out of every mission absolutely clean. And this morning he was not in disguise, which left him only the one option.

"How are you going to explain a dead body to your employees?" he asked, pleasantly.

"This is my place, I work alone," Toivo said.

"No secretary? No one at the front desk to answer the phone when you're away?"

"Voice mail. But I'm tired of talking, you little fucker. What'll it be?"

Makarov smiled. "You're here all alone, you're expecting no one, and if someone calls it'll be rolled over to a voice mail. Could be awhile before someone comes looking for you. Which makes you even dumber than you look."

"You son of a bitch." Toivo grunted and he lumbered forward, batting a meaty fist at Makarov's head as if he was swatting a fly.

Makarov easily sidestepped the charge, slammed a fist into the big man's kidney once, and immediately a second time before he moved back out of range.

Toivo wasn't affected in the least and he turned on a heel, again favoring his left leg, and he was grinning like a congenital idiot because Makarov was backed into a corner next to the still open duffle bag. "I would have settled for five grand because it's no skin off my ass who you're planning to shoot. But we're fucking well past that now, aren't we, you limey son of a bitch. Payback time for 'ninety-eight when I lost in Birmingham. It was a fucking fix and everybody knew it."

Makarov pulled the Barrett's thirty-inch heavy barrel out of the duffle bag, and held it in his right hand like a policeman's night-stick. In Spetsnaz training they'd been taught to take down an opponent either by slamming the stick down on their shoulder blade, which would make that arm totally useless, or if the position was correct making the strike on the back of the man's leg halfway between his buttocks and knee. The hydraulic shock would knock the man off his feet, and if the hit was a good one could even send the shock through the bloodstream, stopping the heart.

Toivo was suddenly wary, moving slowly on the balls of his feet. But he was still smiling. "Maybe if you put your toy together you'd have a chance to get out of here alive."

"No need," Makarov said, watching the big man, timing his movements, watching his left leg. It had probably been a knee injury.

Toivo rose up and lunged from five feet out. Turning slightly to his left, his left arm extending, expecting the blow to come from that side, he wanted to shorten the distance so that when the rifle barrel hit he could easily deflect it.

But Makarov stepped away, switched the barrel into his left hand, ducked beneath the former wrestler's outstretched arm, and hit the man in the back of the right leg with every ounce of his strength.

Toivo grunted in pain but merely shifted his weight to his left leg which held for just a moment until he toppled like a massive bull in the ring, his huge head bouncing off the concrete floor.

Makarov straightened up and skipped backward toward the door and looked outside as the wrestler worked to get back on his feet. The man was no longer smiling.

As far as Makarov could see no one was coming, but this was a business establishment, someone would be showing up sooner or later.

He turned back as Toivo was just getting to a knee and trying to lever himself to his feet with one hand on the floor and the other on the wall. Blood trickled down the side of his neck from a gash in his skull.

"You should have minded your own business," Makarov said, stepping toward him.

"In any stand-up fight you have two objectives," the Spetsnaz instructors had drummed into their heads. "The first is to win, and the second is to make damned sure that the *pizdec* can't recover and come after you later. Kill him."

"Who the hell are you, and why was this shit brought here?" Toivo asked. He wasn't so cocky any longer, but it was clear that he was waiting until his enemy got within reach of his massive arms.

"Did you tell anyone else what you found?"

Toivo just watched.

"I asked you a question, and your answer will determine whether I kill you, or merely injure you badly enough to send you to hospital."

"I don't share my business with anyone else, and that's the God's honest truth. But come on, you fucker, let's talk it over like pals, if you're man enough. 'Cause I'm going to jam that barrel up your ass."

Makarov raised the barrel and brought it down as if he were intending on hitting Toivo in the head, and the big man reached for it. At the last instant Makarov hit the man in the larynx, driving him backward on his ass, his head bouncing off the concrete floor again.

Toivo could no longer draw air into his lungs, and as he struggled to sit up, his eyes began to bulge and his face began to turn red.

At the open door Makarov made sure that still no one was coming, and then came back and stood over to watch as the wrestler fought not to lose consciousness.

Toivo raised a hand and tried to say something, but then his chest convulsed a couple of times and he was still.

Makarov waited another couple of minutes and then placed two fingers on the man's carotid artery at the side of the neck, and he could feel no pulse.

Five minutes later he had repacked the duffle bag, put it in the Chevy's trunk, secured the storage locker, and was driving out the gate toward the ring highway that would take him to Interstate 94 west toward Fargo, North Dakota two hundred plus miles and then Bismarck one hundred fifty miles farther where he would spend part of the night.

Sometime in the early morning he would switch the Impala for a pickup truck that would be delivered to the Holiday Inn Express and continue west to a spot south of Dickinson where he would do his job and then leave.

To this point no one who had seen his face and who could connect him to the mission was alive. He meant to keep it that way. And he began to hum an old Russian folk song, the lyrics streaming in his mind, about a grandfather and grandmother; a favorite of his because his grandparents had raised him in Noginsk thirty kilometers east of Moscow.

> *Where are you about, my darling old man?*
> *Working in the garden, my darling grandma!*
> *What are we going to do, my darling old man?*
> *We will make homemade vodka, my darling grandma!*
> *They will put us in jail, my darling old man!*
> *We will bribe the police, my darling grandma!*
> *How are we going to bribe the police, my darling old man?*
> *You will kiss the officer, my darling grandma!*

4

I T WAS ONE in the afternoon when the phone on Whitney's desk in the Research and Development Center rang and she picked up.

The press conference was over with, thank God, and at the moment Donna Marie, which was what they called the power plant itself, was burning a steady stream of methane from the well, which produced .250 megawatts of electricity. All that needed to be done for the next six weeks or so, was monitor the rate of gas production, and perhaps tweak the colony from time to time. It was one of the unpredictable problems that always cropped up in any complex system. Among engineers they were called unk-unks—or unknown-unknowns.

And she had been trying to convince herself all week that the problem with the microbes was solved and that they were home free. But after the attacks over the Christmas holidays she and just about everyone else on the project had been tense, waiting for the next ten-ton weight to drop on their heads.

"Dr. Lipton," she said.

"You sound like you could use the weekend off."

It was Ashley Borden, the reporter from the *Bismarck Tribune* who along with Jim Cameron, now dead, and Billings County Sheriff Nate Osborne had been right in the middle of their troubles. If it hadn't been for them, especially Nate and Jim, the entire project would have been leveled, and even more people killed—herself included.

Coincidentally, Ashley's father was General Forester, who was the chief administrator of the project that had started out six years ago as a top secret government endeavor that was concealed as a new system to communicate with U.S. submarines anywhere in the world, even when submerged as deep as one thousand feet. The three of them had become good friends; Nate and Ashley had become a thing, and current talk in Medora, which was the county seat north of the project, was that they would probably get married soon. And Ashley had asked Whitney to act as a witness.

Ashley was a service brat, a tomboy most of her life, and a brash, cocky, take-no-prisoners, opinionated woman of twenty-seven, to whom it was impossible to say no.

"Got a ton of work on my desk, and we're still not sure about the output from the seam. Could seize any minute."

"It's not smart to lie to the press," Ashley said. "Anyway Nate figured that you were way overdue for a weekend off. We want you to come up here this afternoon—right now if you can manage to drag yourself away. He's making his special spaghetti and meatballs with homemade pasta."

Ashley hesitated. She needed the weekend, yet she was almost afraid to leave.

"A crusty baguette I brought from Bismarck this morning. A

couple bottles of really good Valpolicella. Fresh parmesan. Nice salad, oil and vinegar."

Whitney found that she couldn't help but laugh; it was one of the reasons she liked Ashley, the woman made her smile.

"I'll be out of here in twenty minutes."

"You're staying here, so pack an overnight bag. Nate's taking us up to the Roosevelt South Unit tomorrow. Weather's supposed to stay good, and the park's supposed to be spectacular this time of year."

"Make it thirty minutes," Whitney said. "May I bring something?"

"Just yourself," Ashley said. "And Nate says he'll have a special treat for us after dinner."

"Like what?"

"I haven't a clue. He wouldn't tell me."

"See you in a bit."

Ashley didn't hang up. "Things okay down there? No real trouble?"

"Nothing but a little science. But you're right, I do need a break."

THE TINY town of Medora, population just one hundred, was twelve miles as the crow flies directly north of the Initiative, but by dirt road east to U.S. 85, then north to the interstate, and finally back west, the highway distance was nearly three times as far.

Driving up, the entire western part of the state had from the beginning struck her as if it were the landscape on another planet where life was just possible but not easy. Yet just about every North Dakotan she'd met in her off and on six years here was friendly, though very often a little insular. Only the occasional rancher, especially the old bachelors, tended to be a little gnarly around the edges, but they generally didn't smile for anybody, and she'd gotten used to them, and just about everything else out here. But she did miss the hustle and bustle of Atlanta and her lab at the Centers for Disease Control in Druid Hills just outside of the city.

Yet thinking about the Initiative—the project—her project—that had taken six years of her life, she knew that it was finally coming to an end, at least for her. If this latest round of tweaks held the colony together the project would go into the next phase—that of development on an industrial scale. And she was excited but a little sad.

Lee Mulholland, tall, lanky, a twenty-seven-year-old self-confessed geek, one of her postdocs in microbiology from the University of Wisconsin, had suggested just yesterday after it had become clear that they had cleared another hurdle, that Whitney should be thinking: first about what her next big project would be—something Whitney had been pondering for nearly a year—and secondly, writing her acceptance speech when she won the Nobel Prize for Chemistry or Medicine. It was a foregone conclusion in a lot of people's minds because she had cracked the code for the quorum-sensing mechanism in which colonies of microbes could talk to each other to achieve a common goal—such as the six hundred different types in the human mouth that worked as a team to create plaque. She could actually talk to any type of microbial colony—and there were thousands, perhaps millions in the human body—with a lingua franca of her own design. Cure plaque which led to gum disease, or cure any of a myriad of other medical conditions.

The rumor was out that she would be on the cover of *Time* magazine as the scientist who had finally come up with the clean coal people had been promised for twenty years or more.

And all of that was just added pressure, away from which the coming weekend sounded very good.

The ranch Nate had inherited from his parents was just off the interstate about five miles east of Medora bordering the park they were going to see tomorrow. She'd been there once before and easily found her way to the dirt road that led back to the low-slung house, barn, and a few other outbuildings.

Ashley's Toyota Tacoma pickup truck with the *Bismarck Tribune* magnetic decals on both doors was parked behind Nate's Saturn SUV sheriff's radio vehicle, and Whitney parked next to them.

Ashley came out as Whitney walked up to the porch. Like Whitney, she was dressed in jeans and a sweatshirt, a big grin crinkling the corners of her wide dark eyes. She was five inches shorter than Whitney, who had to bend down a little as they pecked each other on the cheeks.

"Project's going to survive without you for a couple of days?" Ashley asked, ushering her inside.

"They know where I am if something comes up."

"So does my newspaper. But maybe we won't answer our phones."

The house was old-fashioned but neat, with chintz curtains at the bowed windows in front, floral patterned wallpaper, dark oak wainscoting and chair rails in the dining room, doilies on the arms of the easy chairs, and a lot of photographs of Nate as a boy all the way up to his Marine FORECON graduation just a couple of months before his parents were killed in a car crash.

Last time she'd been here he'd explained that he'd always been too busy to change things, and now he liked the way the house was set up. Reminded him of growing up here. Stability was important. It was something Ashley totally agreed with. As a service brat the longest she'd ever been on one military base and in one school was three years.

In the kitchen Nate was stirring the pot of spaghetti sauce, and he turned around, a big, happy grin on his broad farmer's face. At six-four he was built like a pro football player, and despite the titanium prosthesis on his left leg from the knee down he moved like a cross between the quarterback and a ballet dancer.

"Ash and I had a bet that you wouldn't come," he said.

"Who won?"

"I did," Ashley said. She took Whitney's jacket and overnight bag and brought them back to one of the spare bedrooms.

"How's it going down there?" Osborne asked. "Heard you had a problem. Anything serious?"

"Just a little science. Looks like we might be over the hump."

Osborne poured a glass of wine for her. A plate of torn-up pieces of baguette had been set out on the counter. He dipped a scoop of his tomato sauce from the pot, put it in a bowl, and brought it over. "Not quite developed yet, but it's getting close."

Whitney sat on one of the stools and dipped the bread in the sauce and drank wine. "Good," she said.

"You'll be going back to Atlanta soon?" Osborne asked.

Whitney nodded. "This was fun, but Atlanta's home and I miss my lab."

Osborne looked at her and shrugged. Something was bothering him, and it showed on his face, but he smiled.

"What?"

"We'll miss you."

"No, there's something else."

Ashley was at the door from the dining room. "Nate thinks that we're not out of the woods yet. There might be another attack, because of what we did in Venezuela."

Whitney didn't want to think about it. Her plate was already full with the science, and for the past month or so she had been nearly successful in blocking out Jim Cameron's image. He'd been shot by the Posse people who'd attacked the Initiative. He'd been trying to save her life, and the lives of Nate and Ashley, and the others back at the R&D Center and at Henry's, the restaurant and bar that had been built in the main part of the Initiative's compound well away from Donna Marie. And no science could bring him back, no matter how many times in her dreams she had fantasized about coming up with a controllable colony of death-eating microbes.

She shook her head. "Have you shared this with Rapid City?" The Air Force at Ellsworth down in Rapid City had a Rapid Response team on full-time alert 24/7, and crises security was their job.

Osborne nodded. "And with Ashley's dad. He thinks I might be right and so does the FBI. He's convinced the National Security Agency to position a satellite to watch over the facility, at least until the end of the year. It's the best he could do because according to him other plants are going to come online out here and in Wyoming and Back East starting in the Virginias."

"So if they haven't hit us by then, there'll enough methane-burning power plants to make Donna Marie not so important," Whitney said. She could feel her blood rise.

"Something like that."

"But what about the people here? Aren't they important, too?"

5

MAKAROV HAD MADE the new Holiday Inn Express just off I-94 last night around eight, had a hot pork sandwich with mashed potatoes and gravy at a nearby truck stop, and had taken a shower and gone directly to bed. Lying awake now just after four thirty in the morning, listening to the wind, he was brought back to his meeting in London with Colonel Delgado. The man's mood had seemed as bleak as the wind across the plains outside.

That image had stuck and turning it over in his head, Makarov decided that when he was back in Sweden he would conduct a little more research than he'd already done. This job was entirely too simple for the one million euro fee, and the colonel's exact words had been: *"A small job of work first."*

Which meant more to come, and Makarov wanted to have some idea of what might be heading his way, what was ultimately at stake, who was behind this—who was providing the money—and something of even more importance: Who were his enemies?

The dark blue Dodge Ram pickup had been parked in the hotel's lot last night, and he had transferred the duffle bag to it from the Impala's trunk, and after wiping down the Chevy had taken his bag, plus one containing a change of clothes and an iPad that had been left for him in the big vehicle, and brought them into the hotel.

He got up, went to the window, and looked outside. The truck was still there but the rental car was gone, the contract driver taking it back to the airport in the Twin Cities. His back trail was clean.

Within a half hour he was dressed in jeans, a well-worn sweater, denim jacket, and scuffed work boots, and was heading west, no clouds in the star-filled sky and only the occasional semi or farm truck on the interstate.

No one had been in the hotel's parking lot last night or this morning, and other than the desk clerk and the waitress at the truck stop he'd not come face-to-face with anyone else.

He switched on the radio and tuned it to a country-and-western station and let the music, which reminded him in many ways of the Russian folk tunes he'd grown up with, muffle the road noise from the knobby tires. The lyrics were just about the same—troubles and woe, sometimes with a comic punch line at the end, and simple, rhythmic melodies.

Early in one of his Spetsnaz training evolutions, he had managed to get the drop on the hand-to-hand combat instructor with a lucky move, knocking the veteran to his knees. A few of the dumber trainees watching had actually cheered, which had angered the sergeant who jumped up and decked Makarov with a simple round-house punch to the jaw.

"Yours was luck," the sergeant had said. "Mine was calculated. Now get your arse out of the dirt."

It would have ended there, except that Makarov got slowly to his feet and turned as if to go back in line with the others, but the sergeant had reached out to stop him. It was a mistake. The veteran had underestimated the student.

"I'm not done with you," the sergeant said.

Makarov turned back, grabbed the instructor's arm, clamping it under his left armpit while holding the man's wrist with his right, and he swiveled sharply to the right. The muscles and ligaments in the sergeant's shoulder were ripped away from the bones and Makarov released his hold and stepped away as the much bulkier man dropped to the ground.

None of the trainees were grinning now. But the sergeant gave no indication that he was in excruciating pain as he got to his feet and looked Makarov up and down. But he nodded.

"On the other hand that wasn't a bit of luck," he said. "That was balls."

Makarov said nothing. He'd made his point.

"I'm going to the dispensary. I want you to teach your fellow trainees that move until I send a replacement instructor."

It had been the beginning of Makarov's special treatment, an intensified training regimen, no holds barred, in which he'd suffered a slight concussion, many sprains and bruises, and several cracked ribs, but never anything as serious as what he had done to the sergeant—who by the halfway point of the initial two years of training wanted to be friends. But Makarov had been a loner then, as he was to this day. And that attribute had saved his life more than once.

AN HOUR before dawn Makarov took the Dickinson exit off the interstate and followed State Highway 22 south, through the town of about sixteen thousand, passing the regional airport five minutes later.

A few farm vehicles and delivery vans and trucks plus a few cars were on the road now, and a small Great Lakes Airlines passenger jet was parked at the terminal for its six o'clock flight to

Denver—the only destination by a commercial airline from Dickinson. The next flight out was at nine forty, on which Makarov's people had booked him a seat.

Two miles south of town the highway was deserted and remained that way four miles farther south where the 230 kv high-power lines that led from Donna Marie crossed the highway just above the meandering Antelope Creek.

Makarov parked at the crest of a hill and got the Barrett rifle out and quickly assembled and loaded the weapon.

The nearest steel pylon shaped more or less like a giant spidery inverted V was at the bottom of the hill about six hundred yards away. Three lines which dropped in graceful catenary curves carried the power from one twenty-five-meter pylon to the next to where it reached the nearest Eastern Interconnect transfer point somewhere near Bismarck. The energized lines were held clear from each other and from coming in contact with the grounded tower by cap and pin modular insulators consisting of fifteen glass disks, about ten inches in diameter and seven feet long. An easy target even in the dark.

Makarov climbed up on the lowered tailgate and propped the loaded rifle on its extended bipod on the roof. Nothing was coming in either direction and it took him just a couple of seconds to get a decent sight picture of the outside insulator hanging from one of the pylon's arms. When the line dropped it would short out, causing an immediate power failure.

He racked a shell into the firing chamber, steadied himself, and squeezed off one shot, the noise like a runaway train right on top of him.

Almost instantly a large section of the insulator exploded and a second later the line began to drop. A blinding flash lit up a section of the tower, sparks flying everywhere. Slowly the high-tension line drooped to within a few feet of the ground.

Makarov brought the rifle down from the roof, unloaded it, disassembled it, and stuffed all the parts back into the duffle bag.

Within eight minutes of parking at the side of the road, he had made a U-turn and was headed back to the busy truck stop he'd passed on the interstate at the Dickinson exit, the first and least risky part of the mission completed.

"MERELY SHOOTING out an insulator and interrupting the flow of power will not be enough," Colonel Delgado had explained. "You must make certain that there will be a fatality."

"Why?" Makarov had asked. He couldn't see the necessity of it, especially against the risk that the authorities would come to the site to investigate. And he said as much.

"We understand what you may be faced with, and *señor*, it is why you were selected. You never fail."

"It will be expensive."

"No doubt," the colonel had said.

Makarov pulled into the truck stop, parked out of sight from the front entrance, and once inside ordered a cup of coffee and the standard American breakfast of eggs, bacon, hash browns, and toast—a meal which he had learned to detest after only one year in Stockholm where breakfast was salmon, toast, and tea.

He was seated alone in a booth near the windows. Business was starting to pick up, but no one paid him any attention. By his clothes he was obviously blue-collar, a worker somewhere, maybe an oil field roustabout on his way north. Guys like him passing through were commonplace here.

While he waited for his food to come he powered up the iPad that had been left for him with the clothes. A FOX network morning news broadcast was displayed on the screen, but via the Bluetooth earbud he was connected to the nearest Mid-Continent

Power Pool control center in an anonymous bunker outside of Sioux Falls about three hundred miles to the southeast where the outage had been detected.

One of the dispatchers was talking to someone by the name of Tony Bartlett, who apparently was the Basin Electric Power Co-op lineman on call from one of the company's service centers just off the interstate about five miles east of Dickinson.

"Goddamned hunters using our insulators for target practice," Bartlett groused.

"Looks like it on my board," the dispatcher said.

Makarov heard a woman say something in the background. "I've got a call," Bartlett said. "Maybe one of these days some fool will get too close and fry his ass."

"Donna Marie was automatically taken down so the line is deenergized, but check in before you climb."

"Naturally," the lineman said. Two hundred fifty thousand volts got everybody's attention and respect.

"Give me an ETA."

"Twenty minutes, half hour tops."

"At least it's not snowing or blowing," the dispatcher said.

"Piece of cake," Bartlett replied.

Makarov removed the earbud.

6

OSBORNE STOOD ON the front porch of his house with a cup of coffee as he watched the sky to the east get progressively lighter. It was chilly, in the low to mid forties, but after the long, cold winter he was just fine in a pair of jeans, a battered old HOO RAH sweatshirt, and unlined Indian moccasins.

Ever since Marine FORECON in the mountains of Afghanistan along the border with Pakistan he'd been a very light sleeper, never making it all the way through an entire night. The possibility of a Taliban incursion into your post at any second day or night had a tendency to make a man a little jumpy. He had come to appreciate the dawn because it meant that he'd survived another night.

Ashley had understood when he'd warned her before she began spending weekends with him; she'd said that her dad had told her the same thing. A great-uncle of hers came back from Korea, and got married a month later. The first morning after their honeymoon his wife went upstairs to wake him for breakfast and to get ready for work.

"All she did was touch his shoulder and he instantly jumped up, hit her in the face, and broke her jaw. He'd spent two years in a foxhole and to him she was an enemy soldier standing over him."

"Did they stay married?" Osborne had asked.

"Oh, yeah. But after that she'd stand at the door and call his name."

Osborne had grinned. "I'm not that bad anymore, except I tend to get up a few times in the middle of night to make the rounds."

"No wonder, after all you went through," Ashley told him. "Even a lot of the reporters embedded over there say that they couldn't get the real feel for it. Except for the ones who got shot up or seriously hurt by an IED like Bob Woodruff."

Osborne had lost his left leg saving his platoon from an attack—an action he couldn't clearly remember—not until it was explained to him at the White House when the president clasped the ribbon holding the Medal of Honor around his neck. And he'd been embarrassed because what he'd done, though probably brave, was in his mind stupid. Necessary at the time, but dumb anyway.

His wife, Caroline, had thought it was stupid, too, but the worst part for her was sleeping with a one-legged man. Looking at his stump sometimes made her physically ill. That and the isolation out here in western North Dakota had finally driven her away.

With Ashley it was different. He was a hero. "My hero," she called him.

He did remember how he felt the day of the Taliban ambush, and the attacks on the Initiative around Christmas. He'd been spooked. The same feeling you got in the summer when the sky to the southwest went pitch-black, the wind died to nothing, and the air turned green. Storms were coming.

And he'd been feeling the same thing now for the past month. More trouble was coming their way. There were no shelters for this kind of a storm, and even if there was one he didn't think he'd be running down the stairs to hide.

Whitney came out of the house, her jacket over her shoulders. She'd got a cup of coffee from the kitchen.

"You're up early," Osborne said. "Couldn't sleep?"

"Roger called me, said Donna Marie went off-line, about twenty minutes ago." Roger Kohl was the power plant's chief operating engineer. He was a steady, no-nonsense man who'd been around coal-fired plants all of his life, working his way through college at one of them out east somewhere.

"More trouble with the science?"

"It wasn't us this time. Looks like a problem with one of the transmission lines just east of here. Most likely some rancher shot out an insulator."

"Doesn't happen every day, but it does happen."

"Why?" Whitney asked. She was a scientist, which meant she thought like one and could never understand mindless acts of violence or in this case simple vandalism.

"They probably fell asleep in the sixth grade because their teacher was a bore, and they never woke up."

"Plain stupidity?"

"And boredom," Osborne said. "And it's everywhere, not just here, or Montana or Wyoming." But something niggled at the back of his head, the hair on the nape of his neck wanting to stand on end.

She sipped her coffee and stared at the sun just edging above the horizon. "I guess you're right. I've seen some really bright kids— some of them grad students—pull some dumb stunts." She shrugged and looked at him. "Even scientists aren't immune. Hell, Carl Sagan supposedly did some of his best work while smoking pot. Talk about killing brain cells."

"He probably had plenty to spare," Osborne said absently.

Whitney nodded. "I guess."

"Do you want to go back?"

"Nothing I could do about it. The problem belongs to Basin Electric."

"What problem's that?" Ashley asked, coming outside with a cup of coffee. She was wearing a sweater and jeans, sneakers on her feet.

"Donna Marie had to be shut down a little while ago. Some sort of trouble with the transmission lines over by Dickinson," Whitney said.

"Looks like someone might have shot out an insulator," Osborne said.

Ashley's eyes narrowed as they always did whenever she was skeptical about something that she was being told. It was one of the traits about her that Osborne found a little irritating, and yet taken together with her entire personality made her unique and interesting to him.

"No one is taking a shot at us again," Whitney said. "No damage done. We're just off-line until the problem is fixed."

"Are you going back this morning?" Ashley asked.

"There's no need." Whitney managed a little smile. "Anyway this is my first weekend off in I can't remember how long, and I mean to play tourist and enjoy myself, if the offer to go up to the park still stands."

Osborne nodded, but just for a moment he was far away, back at the Initiative around Christmas and back to his forward position in Afghanistan. One of Murphy's laws in FORECON was: "If everything is going right, you're surely walking into a trap." And another was: "Incoming rounds have the right of way."

The point was that he had learned to listen to his inner voice.

"Nate?" Ashley prompted, a look of concern in her eyes.

"I made dinner last night, so it's up to you to organize breakfast. And I'm hungry."

"Are you going to call someone?"

"It happened down around Dickinson, so I thought I'd give Kas the heads-up," Osborne said.

"Do you want to drive down?" Ashley said.

"No need," Osborne said. "I want eggs and pancakes."

"Yes, sir. Whatever you say, sir."

Whitney laughed, but it was clear from her expression that she had picked up on Osborne's mood.

7

ON THE RISE above the Antelope Creek, Tony Bartlett saw the problem at once, and he drove down to the valley floor, eased his truck off the highway to within fifty feet from the base of the pylon, and got out. He was a stocky man with a thick neck, broad chest, but narrow hips, and a perpetual grin.

Pieces of insulator disks were scattered all over the place, and the air still smelled of ozone from where the line had sparked before the relays at Donna Marie had been tripped.

But it wasn't nearly as bad as it could have been. The insulator's caps and pin looked to be in decent shape, as studying the damage with binoculars he counted only five disks missing. It had been enough to make one of the three phase lines droop far enough to just brush the pylon's metal framework and nearly reach the ground.

Whatever happened here, though, hadn't been done by only one shot from a hunting rifle. Bartlett had repaired enough of these problems over the past fifteen years that he knew what sort of damage could be caused by a deer or elk rifle, even an H&H .375

he'd seen once. This time the bastard or bastards had probably used up half a box of ammunition.

Bartlett phoned Stuart Wyman, the Area Desk dispatcher in Sioux Falls. "Looks like hunters or somebody shot the shit out of one of the insulators."

"How long do you figure before it's back up?"

"Probably two hours, maybe three tops."

"Do you want me to call for backup?"

"Not unless the line is energized, Stu, which you say it isn't."

"I'm showing no back feed. That's an isolated circuit from Donna Marie."

"I'll check, but from here it doesn't look as bad as it could be. Looks like the caps and pin are still intact, so all it needs is replacing five of the disks, and raising the line so it can be reattached."

"Any burn through?"

"I can't see any from here. Looks like we caught a break."

"Give me a minute," Wyman said.

Bartlett leaned back against the truck and lit a cigarette, his fourth already for the morning. He had hunted this area a few years ago, and when Tad, his only son who had just turned five, got a little older he planned on taking him down to the Antelope for a little fly casting.

Juliette already had big plans for their daughter, Taffy, who would be ten in June, entering her in beauty contests since she was four, most of which she had won or placed. In a few years Juliette wanted to begin training their daughter for the big leagues—Miss Teen North Dakota, Miss Teen USA, and then Miss America, even Miss World.

And in Bartlett's mind, his daughter was just that pretty.

Wyman came back. "The line is still de-energized, and Donna Marie's relays are tripped. You're good to go. Keep me informed."

"Right," Bartlett said.

He flicked the cigarette away and got back in the truck and maneuvered it so that it was on the gravel right of way beneath the tower and just ten feet to one side of the damaged insulator.

He got a cup of coffee from the thermos Juliette had sent with him, and with one hand on the controls lowered first the forward outrigger jacks on the left and right side of the truck, and then the rear outriggers.

When he was certain that the truck was stable, he finished the rest of his coffee then climbed up to release the safeties holding the bucket in its fixed position above the cab.

All of his movements were slow and precise. Even with a deenergized high-voltage line, the mere act of going up in a doubleboomed bucket was in itself dangerous. He'd seen trucks tip over, buckets come apart sixty feet or more off the ground, and he'd even heard of incidents where linemen had reached too far and ended up falling out of a bucket when it capsized.

He'd take some heat from his last supervisor who insisted even on simple jobs like these when the lines were not hot, that a crew ride along. But Bartlett was a senior lineman with a lot of experience and fifteen accident-free years under his belt. In effect, whatever Bartlett wanted, Bartlett got.

But it had never made him smug. Right now he was outdoors doing exactly the kind of job he loved doing. Only thing better was hunting and fishing.

He pulled on a pair of heavy rubber gloves, his hard hat and goggles, then powered the bucket up from the cab's roof, swiveled it away from the truck, and slowly angled it to the downed line and made contact. Static electricity sparked then flowed from the bucket, down the arms, and showed up on the meter as ten amperes of current that quickly bled off.

He powered the bucket away from the line and set it on the gravel. Next he put in a grounding stick and a block and tackle which he would use to lower the insulator so that he could disassemble it, replace the broken disks, reassemble it, and then haul it back up to the cross arm. From that point he would attach a rope to the downed line and haul it back up to the insulator. Only grunt work.

He attached the bottom end of the block and tackle's nylon braided rope to a tow ring on the back of the truck with a bowline knot finished with a pair of half hitches.

Once he had his tool kit secured inside the bucket, he walked down the power line and carefully checked a five-foot-long streak of charred metal. But it was superficial.

He walked back to the bucket, humming a Randy Travis tune, climbed aboard, and slowly began raising it straight up at first and then angling a few feet to the right of the damaged insulator, paying out the rope as he rose.

The attachment point that held the high-voltage line in place had been destroyed, causing the line to fall, brushing the side of the pylon on the way down. Whoever had done it had taken a hell of a chance that the line could have fallen on them. In his opinion it would have served the bastards right. Maybe cut down a little on this sort of bullshit work—though the time-and-a-half looked pretty good in his paycheck at the end of the month.

He was of the same stripe as just about every other lineman he knew who figured their job was to maintain power to their customers no matter what. But they counted on fighting Mother Nature, not some liquored-up hunter or rancher with a grudge that power lines ran across his land.

He phoned Wyman at the Sioux Falls Control Center. "I'm up the tower at the insulator. It's worse than I figured."

"Repairable, or does it have to be replaced?"

"I can fix it, but it might take a little longer than I thought. I'll let you know when I get it down."

"What about the line itself?"

"Looks good. But I'll stick around for a power test. Let you know when."

"You wearing your Barehands?" Barehand conductive suits were made of fireproof Nomex material that was embedded with microscopic stainless steel fibers that allowed the lineman to work bare-handed on energized high-tension lines up to 765 kilovolts.

Bartlett had to laugh. He'd worked with Wyman for the past eight or ten years, and although it wasn't part of a control center dispatcher's job description to ask about a lineman's safety procedures, Stu was sometimes an old mother hen.

"No need."

"I think you guys have to be nuts," Wyman said.

"It helps," Bartlett said and he broke the connection and pocketed his cell phone.

For just a moment or two he stood in the bucket, attached to it by a safety harness and looked out along the river, decent weather for trout fishing not all that far away.

He angled the bucket a couple of feet out to clear the insulator and powered the rest of the way up to the cross arm, where he secured the big three-sheaved pulley with a U-bolt, and clipped the carabiner on the end of the line to the ring at the top of the insulator.

A slight breeze had picked up as often happened out here with the dawn, but it was no bother. Bartlett had lost count of the jobs he had worked in blinding snowstorms, or even heavy rain. This, as he'd told Wyman, was a piece of cake.

The two bolts holding the insulator had frozen tight, and he had to squirt the double nuts on each with penetrating oil and then wait for it to do its job.

Nothing or no one moved in any direction for as far as he could see. He glanced at the highway where it topped the rise, and considered the sight line. If he'd wanted to shoot out an insulator, up there would be a good place. With the right rifle and a really good scope it'd be a hell of a shot, but makeable.

He turned back to the insulator and studied the damage. Six of the disks had disintegrated, plus the attachment points for the power line had been destroyed. One shot maybe? But definitely it would have to have been something a lot heavier than a deer or elk gun.

This had not been done by an ordinary hunter.

Bartlett glanced at the crest of the hill, and the first hints that something else had happened here than simple vandalism began to form in his head.

8

STARK COUNTY SHERIFF Gerald Kasmir had a raging cold, with a fever of 102; and although he'd never missed a day of work growing up on a ranch or during his twenty years as a cop in the Army and the last twelve years here as the sheriff, today he was making an exception.

Every bone in his slender frame ached, and a knee injury he'd got during boot camp had flared up so for the past two days he'd been hobbling around like a cripple.

His wife, Grace, poked her head in the bedroom to see if he was awake. "How you feeling, sweetheart?"

"I think you're right, maybe I'll stay home for the weekend."

She came to his bedside and gave him two aspirins and a glass of water. When he was finished she held a hand to his forehead. "This doesn't get any better by this afternoon, we're going to see the doctor. In the meantime I'll call Don and tell him I'm keeping you in bed." Donald Christen was Kasmir's number one deputy and longtime friend.

"I'm not an invalid."

"No, but you're a fifty-year-old man with a serious cold that could easily turn into pneumonia."

"Nag," Kasmir, said and he coughed all the way from the bottom of his lungs.

"That's right."

"There was a call a little while ago, who was it?"

His wife eyed him critically. "It was Nate over at Medora, wanted to talk to you about something. Nothing earth shattering, he said, just wanted to give you a heads-up."

Kasmir sat up, his head momentarily swimming. He'd been in bed asleep since just after dinner last night and besides his fever and aches, he was logy. "About what?"

"He didn't say."

Kasmir reached for the phone.

"I'm sure that it can hold till Monday."

"Is there any coffee made?"

His wife nodded. "Forget the phone and I'll bring you a cup."

Kasmir picked up the phone. "Since I'm not going into the office today you can put a bit of brandy in it."

She turned and huffed out, muttering something under her breath and he could just guess what it was. They'd been married now nearly thirty years.

Kasmir glanced at the clock. It was coming up on seven as Osborne answered.

"Grace tells me that you've got a bad cold or the flu; you okay?"

"I've felt better. What's on your mind this morning?"

"Someone apparently shot out an insulator or something on the high-power lines that cross twenty-two just south of you."

Kasmir's gut suddenly bunched up. A few months ago there'd been trouble over at the Initiative, in Nate's county, that had spilled over to Belfield just inside Stark. A rancher and his wife had been brutally murdered in their own home. It had shaken up people even in Dickinson. Stuff like that almost never happened here.

"How'd you find out?"

"Dr. Lipton is spending the weekend with Ashley and me. Roger Kohl, the chief engineer at Donna Marie, called this morning to tell her about it."

Kasmir had half expected something like this to happen. "Some of the ranchers down there aren't exactly tickled to have a power line cross their property. It rankles, mostly because they had no choice."

"Maybe," Osborne said. "But I thought I'd just give you the heads-up. Considering all that happened a few months ago."

Kasmir held the phone away and coughed again.

"You sound like hell. I hope Grace is keeping you home."

"She's wants to. But what are you trying to tell me, Nate?"

The line was silent for a beat. "I don't know, Kas. Just a feeling."

"I'm listening."

"The last attacks were almost certainly directed by the Venezuelan intelligence service."

"I read the papers. Chavez denied it."

"But we attacked five of their air bases anyway, and there's still hell to pay in the U.N.," Osborne said. "We're the bad guys again."

"If you're thinking that this could be a retaliation, I'd say it was pretty weak. I suspect a power crew is down there right now fixing the problem. Maybe cause a couple hours' of outage, if that."

"You're probably right."

Grace brought in the coffee with a scowl, set it on the nightstand, and left.

"How's everything out your way?" Kasmir asked.

"I'm taking the girls up to the park, we're going to make a day of it."

Kasmir chuckled. "You're taking the weekend off, so you called to put a bee in my bonnet? That it?"

Osborne laughed, too. "Go back to bed and let Grace take care of you. Sorry I called."

"Me, too," Kasmir said and he hung up.

He threw back the covers and sat on the edge of the bed. The coffee was good and especially with the brandy hit the spot. Like his dad who'd had a shot of brandy every morning of his life, but never any other alcohol ever, Kasmir had his own ways.

"Been doing it since my Army days, and it hasn't become a habit yet," he liked to tell his friends.

The right thing to do now was finish the coffee and go back to sleep. Grace would have chicken soup or something for him around lunchtime, and if he felt up to it he might watch a little golf on TV here in the bedroom.

He phoned Anita Yardley, the dispatcher at the office. "I need you to look up a phone number for me."

"You don't sound so good, Sheriff. Your wife called a couple of minutes ago and left a message for Don. You're not coming in?"

"I don't think so. But I need the phone number for the MAPP dispatcher at the Sioux Falls Control Center."

"There a problem?"

"Looks like some idiot shot out an insulator on one of the towers down around Antelope Creek."

"Do you want me to send someone down to take a look?"

"The repair crew is already down there," Kasmir said. "You got that number?"

She gave it to him, and he made the call.

"Gerry Kasmir, I'm the Stark County sheriff up in Dickinson, heard you're having a bit of a problem with one of our power lines."

"Good morning, Sheriff, nothing big," Wyman said. "We've got a lineman on scene working on it. Should be back in business in a couple of hours."

"What happened?"

"Someone apparently shot out an insulator and dropped the line. One of your ranchers probably."

"I'll check it out, but I expect you're right."

Kasmir hung up and sat drinking his coffee. Nate Osborne was not a hothead in anyone's book. The man was about as steady as they came. And there was that Medal of Honor he won over in Afghanistan. He was definitely a local hero, and more importantly a man of action, who once told him that he always followed his hunches.

"Kept me alive over there," he'd said. "Just learned to listen to my inner voice."

"Pretty good inner voice, if you ask me," Kasmir had told him.

Osborne had smiled shyly. "Didn't save my leg, but that could have been a lot worse."

The man was modest, and it was another thing that Kasmir admired about him.

He finished his coffee then got out of bed to dress in his uniform. If Osborne had a hunch, in Kasmir's estimation it was worth a drive down Highway 22 to take a look.

The biggest problem he would have to face this morning was getting past Grace.

9

MAKAROV HAD DAWDLED over his coffee after breakfast, reading the *Dickinson Press* newspaper, a steady stream of truckers coming and going, the lot outside filled with big rigs, while he monitored the telephone traffic from the MAPP Control Center in Sioux Falls.

He'd wanted to make sure that a lineman, and probably a crew, were on site and working to repair the damage he had caused before he headed back down to finish the job.

A few minutes ago the Dickinson sheriff had talked to the dispatcher to ask about the outage, and Makarov had waited to make sure that he wasn't sending a deputy. It would complicate the issue, though not impossibly so. At least not yet. He'd faced worse odds before, but each time he'd known what he might be running into.

He wanted the same information now, the first piece of which was that only one lineman was doing the work. The man had no crew with him. It was a piece of good luck.

Paying his bill, Makarov went outside to the pickup, but before he headed out, he switched his iPad to the Sheriff's Department dispatch frequency, and sat for a while listening. It was a quiet morning in the county. Nothing concerning the problem with the power line was being discussed. No units had been dispatched.

Power outages happened all the time. And from what he'd learned from his preliminary research, shooting insulators was just about a regional sport out here.

He drove over to one of the gas pumps to top off his tank, even though he didn't need any fuel. But he wanted to waste a little more time to find out if the sheriff was heading down 22 or if he was sending someone. He didn't want to get caught parked at the top of the hill. That could get messy and a little complicated.

Just as he finished the sheriff called the dispatcher.

"Anita, this is Kas."

"Grace let you out of the house?"

"Yeah, but it wasn't easy. Listen, I'm in my unit on the way down to check out the mischief with the power line."

"You coming back to the office afterward?"

"Not unless I find something interesting, which I doubt. Anyway I promised Grace I'd come straight home soon as I was done."

"Where are you right now?"

"About two blocks from the office."

"Roger that," the woman said.

Makarov took his receipt and headed through town on Third Street which was Highway 22. Traffic had picked up, but once he'd cleared the city limits only the occasional pickup truck was on the road.

Which would complicate things a little, but not impossibly so. It would mean that he couldn't set up on the hill to take his shot for fear someone would come along at the wrong moment.

No one seemed to be in a hurry, and Makarov took his time, driving well under the speed limit, as he split the screen on his iPad and brought up another program which connected him to a totally untraceable number in Amsterdam.

It was answered on the first ring by a young man speaking Dutch. "*Ja.*"

"In English," Makarov said. "Do you know who this is?"

"Of course I do, what do you think I am, stupid?"

ACTUALLY MAKAROV thought exactly that. Although he'd never met the twenty-five-year-old computer hacker who went by the username of *swiftlightning,* he knew quite a bit about him from Vasili Sumskoy, one of his resources in Moscow inside the Federal Security Bureau, which was the renamed KGB.

They'd met at a bar in the Radisson Blu Royal Hotel in Helsinki's city center ten days ago. Sumskoy, a bear of a man who'd served in the Spetsnaz with Makarov, jumped up and they'd embraced like long lost brothers, though Makarov had never been able to feel much of anything more than toleration for anyone.

"You're looking fit," Sumskoy said.

Makarov patted the man on the belly. "And you've been sitting behind a desk for too long," he said in Russian.

They sat down across from each other at a small table in a corner of the soaring atrium lounge, but waited until their waitress brought Sumskoy a vodka and Makarov a sparkling mineral water on the rocks with a twist.

Sumskoy nodded to Makarov's drink. "So you are on a job, my friend, and you've come to me for information."

"*Da.*"

"Same rate?"

"Depends on what you can tell me," Makarov said. They'd almost always agreed on twenty thousand dollars U.S.

Sumskoy nodded. "Where is it you said that you're calling home these days? Paris again?"

"I need to know about a computer expert who goes by the username of *switftlightning*."

The smiled faded from Sumskoy's broad features, and he took a long time before he said anything. "Where did you hear this name?"

"He's to be my contact on a job I'm currently involved with," Makarov said. He showed no emotion.

Sumskoy was deputy chief of the FSB's First Chief Directorate, which was responsible for all clandestine activities outside of Russia—except those mounted by the GRU, which was the military espionage service, or by special operations run by Putin's personal intelligence unit. He was a man behind a desk who knew things.

"I need to know the job and who it was who hired you."

"No."

Sumskoy thought about it for another long beat, his vodka untouched in front of him. "I'll need double our usual rate."

"Done."

Still Sumskoy hesitated. He had a wife and a mistress, both of whom liked the good life, and he was hemorrhaging money. "Be very careful with what I'm about to tell you, my old friend. And understand something else, because beyond his identity and location, there is something else out of Iran that he's become involved with that I cannot tell you about."

Makarov's curiosity rose. "This something else, could it have an effect on what I've been hired to do?"

"I can't tell you that unless I know the nature of your assignment. Even in general terms."

"I can't do it, Vasili. You must know how it is."

"Watch your back, I know that much. Just as I must watch mine."

Makarov had waited.

"His name is Barend Dekker, and he's not just another computer whiz kid—he's only twenty-five, graduated with a Ph.D. from MIT when he was fourteen—he's possibly the most important and therefore most dangerous hacker on the planet. I don't know all of his background, but he only takes on two kinds of jobs. Those for very highly placed individuals—and governments—for obscenely huge amounts of money. And the others simply for his own amusement. But both have the same purpose."

"Which is?"

"To fuck the United States."

"So what?"

"Listen to me, this kid is a genius, but he's just as warped as he's smart. He and his girlfriend live in some dump in some kind of a hacker's commune somewhere down around Voorburg just outside of Amsterdam. And nobody bothers them, not the cops, not even the *AIVD*." The latter was the Dutch intelligence service."

"Why not?"

"Because he could destroy their entire computer system with a few keystrokes. Infect them with a virus as bad or worse than the Stuxnet bug the Israelis put in Iran's nuclear centrifuge system. As long as they don't kill anyone on Dutch soil they're left alone."

"What else?" Makarov asked.

"There's nothing much more that I can tell you."

"Is he working on something for you?"

"No," Sumskoy said a little too quickly.

"For the FSB, or for someone inside the building?"

"I've done all I can, my friend. Including warning you to take care. The rest is up to you."

Makarov paid the bar tab and got to his feet. "What I'm working on now has a good possibility of developing. If it does I'll need more information about this kid."

"*Nyet.*"

"Everything," Makarov said, and he walked away.

"I'LL GIVE the word in about fifteen minutes," he told the hacker.

"Why did you call me now?"

"So that you can be ready when it's time."

"Believe me, I'm ready anytime."

10

THE REPAIR WORK on the insulator went much faster than Bartlett figured it would; sometimes jobs went like that, but not often. And since he was working on the ground away from the downed line, he could work with only a pair of leather gloves and not the thick rubber ones.

One pickup truck passed on the highway, but Bartlett only glanced up as it crossed the bridge over the Antelope.

Six of the ten-inch in diameter ceramic disks had been almost completely shot away, but the central bolt that held them together had been pretty much undamaged, and in his estimation still serviceable. The most serious damage had been done to the connectors at the base of the insulator that held the thick aluminum power line in place. It looked to him like the shock from the bullet strike had been so great that they had been bent far enough for the line to drop.

He replaced those, checked the integrity of his work, and then took up the slack on the block and tackle and pulled the insulator back to its attachment point on the cross arm.

When it was fully raised he got back into the bucket and powered himself up, again humming a Randy Travis tune, "Forever and Ever, Amen," half under his breath.

Juliette, who never really liked country-and-western music, but who thought Travis was hot, had gone with her husband to an outdoor concert over in Fargo a couple of years ago. He'd never forgotten it, nor had his wife, who admitted that she sometimes listened to Travis's music on their Bose CD player while she did her housework.

At the top, Bartlett eased the insulator up a few inches, to where he could muscle it in position where the bolt holes lined up. Five minutes later, he had the bolts threaded and the double nuts on each tightened down.

Unclipping the carabiner from the insulator's lifting ring, he started to lower the bucket when a Stark County Sheriff's radio unit topped the rise and came down. Wyman had probably called the sheriff's office about this incident and they'd sent a deputy down to take a look. Though there wasn't a hell of a lot to see now.

By the time he reached the ground, the cruiser had pulled off to the side of the road, and the sheriff got out and walked the rest of the way down.

"Morning, Sheriff," Bartlett said. He'd recognized Kasmir from the re-election posters last year.

"Heard you had a bit of trouble down here. Thought I'd come take a look."

"Nothing much to see. Just another pissed off rancher, or a bored hunter."

Kasmir glanced over at the power line nearly touching the ground. "Not kids?"

"I don't think so."

"Why's that?"

"What they did was shoot out the insulator up there, and they did a damned good job of it."

"So?"

"That's a serious piece of construction, and it'd take more than a deer or elk rifle to do the damage I had to repair," Bartlett said. "Those kinds of guns cost a whole hell of a lot more money than I make. Don't think a kid would be running around shooting at power company equipment with a fancy piece of hardware like that."

"I get your point," Kasmir said. He glanced up at the insulator hanging from the cross arm. "Have you already fixed it?"

Bartlett nodded. "I'm going to raise the line now, so you might want to stand back a bit."

"Is it still carrying power?"

"No. The relays at Donna Marie tripped, and they'll stay that way till I'm finished."

Kasmir shook his head and coughed. "Do you ever get nervous up there?"

"No need, if you're careful." Bartlett shrugged. "But if you do something stupid and your number comes up, it'll happen so fast you won't feel a thing."

Kasmir coughed again and took out a handkerchief to wipe his brow.

"If you don't mind me saying so, Sheriff, you look like hell. Maybe you ought to go home."

"I'll just have a look around first."

"For what?"

"For a high-power rifle shell casing, and whatever else might be lying around."

Bartlett brought his grounding stick over to the downed line, but it drew no sparks, so he set it aside and tied a rolling half hitch around the cable. The hitch would stay in place and not ride up as the power line was raised.

Kasmir had walked halfway back up to the highway where he'd parked his cruiser when he bent down to pick something up.

"Cigarette butt's mine," Bartlett called. "Marlboro?"

"Yeah," Kasmir said.

Bartlett took up the slack on the block and tackle and slowly raised the line up to the insulator. This part was tricky only if the wind got up to around twenty miles per hour or more, or if the rolling hitch slipped so that the peak of the line wouldn't end up directly below the insulator.

But not this time, and when it was in place, he tied off the line. He went back to the bucket and climbed in.

Kasmir was up by his cruiser and was searching for something along the side of the road as he slowly headed toward the crest of the ridge.

Bartlett powered the bucket up, slowing as he reached the vicinity of the power line and stopping a couple feet away. He used his grounding stick again, but as before drew no sparks. The line was definitely de-energized.

Angling a little closer he eased the line up so that it was directly at the attachment hooks on the end of the insulator.

At that moment something caught his eye to the north, and he watched as a dark blue pickup truck came over a rise about a mile away and then dipped down into the valley directly behind the nearest hill, slipping out of view. It looked like a Dodge to Bartlett, which in itself was nothing unusual, though most ranchers out here used Fords or Chevy trucks.

But as he turned back to the power line he had the thought that it looked clean, the sun glinting off the polished chrome. Too clean.

11

FROM A DISTANCE Makarov had spotted the lineman at the cross arm in a bucket. Rather than park below the crest of the hill from where he'd shot out the insulator and walk the rest of the way, he kept driving.

The sheriff would be parked somewhere near the power line. But it was essential that the officer was not sitting in his radio unit, because once Makarov called Dekker in Amsterdam and gave the signal, Kasmir would immediately call for an ambulance and backup power company crew.

As he topped the rise, the sheriff was walking along the side of the highway up the hill about fifty yards from his cruiser. The lineman was manhandling the power line to attach it to the insulator, and no one was coming from the south, nor could he see anything in the distance in his rearview mirror.

He keyed Dekker's number into his iPad, and the hacker answered on the first ring.

"*Ja.*"

"Now," Makarov said, and he broke the connection.

For a second or two nothing happened.

Makarov had nearly reached the sheriff, who had stepped off the pavement, and considered driving past if Dekker was unable to hack the power company's computer system, when a tremendous flash lit up the bright morning sky.

A dramatic arc of electricity seemed to envelop the lineman's torso, sending his hard hat soaring into the sky as the top of the man's head was engulfed in flames, his left arm instantly burning in two, and sparks flying out of his chest.

The sheriff stopped in his tracks for just a moment, looking back at the lineman, but then he turned and sprinted for his cruiser at the same time Makarov pulled up at the side of the highway.

Still no one was coming from the south.

He grabbed his old but reliable 9mm Styer GB from where he'd laid it on the passenger seat and got out of the truck. "My God, did you see that?" he shouted.

"Get the hell out of here," Kasmir, still running, shouted over his shoulder. But then he turned, and spotting the pistol in Makarov's hand, reached for his weapon.

Makarov fired one shot, hitting the sheriff center mass and knocking the man off his feet and spinning him around, so he sat down hard on the blacktop, but still alive.

"Goddamn, you shot me," Kasmir cried weakly. He was still fumbling at the holster on his right hip.

Makarov reached the sheriff, who looked up at him, and he shot the man in the side of the head at point-blank range.

At that moment he looked up in time to see a mud-spattered yellow pickup truck cross the Antelope. It immediately began to brake hard when the driver spotted the sheriff lying on the side of the highway, a man standing over him.

Makarov held the pistol behind his right leg and frantically waved at the driver to stop. He gestured toward the dead lineman up on the pylon. A relay or something had tripped, so electricity did not continue to cook the man's body where it was hanging by a safety strap at the side of the bucket.

The driver slowed practically to a crawl.

Fifty yards out Makarov could see that the driver, a youngish-looking man, had a passenger. When they got closer he could see it was a young woman. Possibly the man's wife. Her mouth was open and she was frantically gesturing at the lineman's body.

Makarov remained standing, the pistol concealed, until the couple got closer.

"Have you folks got a cell phone?" he shouted.

"Yes," the man said, hanging out of the window.

"Have you called for help?"

"No," the man said. He pulled up to a halt about twenty feet away and turned to say something to his wife.

Makarov walked directly toward them as he raised his pistol and fired five times, the first three hitting the man in the upper chest and head, and one destroying the woman's neck, snapping her head back, the last shot entering her head just beneath her chin.

The pickup truck lurched to the left then bumped off the road and into a ditch where it stopped.

It was sloppy, Makarov told himself as he went back to his truck. An incredibly stupid waste of his time and talent. So much could have gone wrong, and nearly had. His only real breaks had come by happenstance because the stupid rancher hadn't the presence of mind to call 911, and that his image had not been picked up on the forward-looking dash-mounted camera in the sheriff's cruiser, and that he'd not spotted a rear-facing camera.

All luck, which he'd never allowed to a play role in his missions.

And he was going to need even more if he was to get free with-out any further trouble. If his pickup truck was spotted before he reached the airport and was connected to the mess on the highway, he would have to radically alter his escape plans.

He made a sharp Y-turn on the highway and headed back toward Dickinson, constantly checking his rearview mirror until he topped the crest of the hill and started down the other side. No one had been coming from the south. Another piece of luck in a shaky string.

When he got out of this he would make it his top priority to find out exactly why Venezuelan intelligence had been willing to pay so much money for this assignment—the real motives. What was it they wanted next? Exactly what part did a Dutch computer hacker, who according to Sumskoy, was among the best in the world, play in something so minor as killing a North Dakota lineman? And why had Sumskoy been frightened enough about something or someone coming out of Iran to warn an old friend to take care?

None of it made any sense, and in such situations Makarov had learned that invariably he was being told lies. And in each case he had covered his backtrack by eliminating the liars.

ONLY TWO cars passed him, but that was in town not out on the open highway. He turned off at the T-Rex Plaza, where he parked in the lot just opposite the main entrance. His flight to Denver left in about an hour, and to this point he was clean.

He hid the pistol under the seat, then grabbed his small overnight bag from the backseat, and took it inside the nearly deserted mall and found the men's room. In one of the stalls he changed into khaki slacks, a light turtleneck and dark blue blazer, and polished half boots.

When he was finished he stuffed the old clothes into his bag and dumped the work boots into a trash receptacle and left the mall. The few people in the main corridor paid him no attention as he walked to his pickup truck. The discarded boots would be found, but probably not until later in the day when the restrooms were serviced, and it could very well take several hours before any connection to the murders was made—if ever. By then he would be long gone, well on his way home.

Several other pickup trucks along with a scattering of cars were parked in the lot, and before Makarov got into his truck something struck him, and he looked around. His pickup was clean, but just about every other vehicle here was mud-splattered.

It was spring, the muddy season in the farm and ranch countryside. Hardly anyone here drove trucks to make a statement, these were mostly used for work. And his stood out.

One mistake after another, he thought as he got into his truck and headed over to the airport. The Russian Mafia people he'd hired to supply him with the weapons, the air reservations to Denver, and the pickup truck were based either in New York City or Minneapolis. Big cities. No farmers or ranchers.

But it had been his error not to have thought the assignment through, and insist on checking these sorts of details. Even turning down the assignment when it was presented to him in Paris, because it hadn't felt right.

"Trust your training, gentlemen," a Spetsnaz intelligence officer had drilled into their heads. "You're being given the very best that the ruble can provide. No other army's special force is better. Rely on that, and you just might survive to bounce your grandson on your knee."

Driving back to the airport just south of town, Makarov switched back to the Dickinson sheriff's dispatcher frequency, still quiet. Almost too quiet.

12

THEY LEFT EARLY, Whitney in the backseat of Osborne's Saturn SUV cruiser, Nate and Ashley in front, driving back to Medora and turning north on the National Park Road, the Little Missouri River that ran through the park to their left. The morning was crisp, not a cloud in the sky, only a very slight breeze; a perfect spring day, yet Osborne was having a serious case of the willies that he could not justify.

"Do we want to stop at the visitor center?" Ashley asked Osborne. She turned back to Whitney. "You've never been to the park, have you?"

"No. But I'll leave it up to you guys."

"I'll play tour guide," Osborne said. "I grew up here, remember. Spent half my life as a kid hiking the Maah Daah Hey, canoeing down the Little Missouri, and couple of years ago some hunting to cull the elk herds."

"The river and elk I've heard about, but what's the other thing?"

"The Maah Daah Hey trail, Mandan Indian meaning an area

that has been or will be around for a long time. Used for hiking. More than ninety miles of it."

"I'll pass."

"Me, too," Ashley said.

They drove past the visitor center and over to the main entrance, the ranger on duty stepping out of the gatehouse as Osborne pulled up. His name tag said PARKS, for which he'd once told Nate that just about every federal park employee he'd ever met gave him a hard time.

"Mornin', Nate. Planning on arresting someone this morning?"

"My day off," Osborne said. "You know Ashley, but you probably haven't met Dr. Lipton. She runs things down at the Initiative."

The ranger nodded. "Morning, Doctor."

"Thought we'd take the scenic drive, be back in time for lunch. Anything doing?"

"Couple of rough spots on the trail, but the road's good. Wind's supposed to pick up this afternoon so we've already issued a camp-fire ban. See anybody out there cooking breakfast, tell 'em to put it out."

"Will do," Osborne said.

The ranger stepped back and nodded again. "Ladies."

Osborne drove into the park, the narrow, blacktopped, winding road first looping east away from the river, passing through some low bluffs and slope-sided broad canyons, until five miles later they came back to the present-day course of the river and one of the campgrounds and picnic areas. A few travel trailers and a scatter-ing of tents were set up, but no one had started a cooking fire.

"Law-abiding citizens," Ashley commented as they passed.

"Wish they all were," Whitney mumbled.

Osborne glanced at her in the rearview mirror. She looked sad, maybe even a little dejected. "You okay, Doc?"

She looked at his image and managed a slight smile. "Don't get me wrong, but sometimes it seems like I've been out here on this project forever, and I'll never have a real lab again."

"Do you miss Atlanta?" Ashley asked.

"Charlie Donovan promised me that I could have my old job back anytime I wanted it." Donovan was the director of the Centers for Disease Control. "But that was six years ago. I don't think he expected to wait that long."

"You're just about finished, that's what you've been saying, isn't it?" Ashley asked.

"The basic research and start-up experiments are done, but—"

Osborne glanced at her again. "But what?"

"I don't know."

"A gut feeling?"

Ashley was looking at both of them.

"Like the sword of Damocles hanging over my head. All of our heads," Whitney said.

"Christ," Ashley said. "Nate's been feeling that way for the past couple of weeks. What's with you two, what am I missing?"

"Probably nothing," Osborne said, but he didn't know if he believed it, especially hearing that Whitney was having the same doubts. "Do you want us to take you back to the project?"

"Absolutely not," Whitney said. "This is just what the doctor ordered. I haven't had a day off, let alone a weekend, for as long as I can remember. You're going to show me the park, and when we get back I'm buying lunch, maybe a bottle of champagne or two. My going-away present."

"Nate will give us another concert tonight," Ashley told them. "My turn to cook."

Last night after dinner Osborne had brought out an old flat-top Gibson and had begun serenading them as they cleaned up the kitchen. Old country-and-western songs, mostly plaintive about love gone bad, all of them very good, his playing and his voice perfect.

It was a talent that Osborne didn't show many people. Caroline, his ex-wife, had told him the music was hokey, pure corn pone. Her tastes, he should have known, ran to chamber music and opera. And she had hurt him badly enough that he'd never played for anyone until last night because he'd been humiliated.

Ashley never suspected he could play, and at one point when she looked at him, a slight smile parting her lips, he knew that he had touched her, and he was no longer ashamed.

When he'd finally put the guitar away, over Ashley and Whitney's protests, they'd asked about the songs. They thought that some of the tunes sounded familiar, but they couldn't place them.

"You wouldn't," he'd said.

Ashley started to ask why, but then a look of pure joy lit up her round face. "My God, they're yours," she said. "You wrote them."

"When I was over in Afghanistan, mostly, and then later here."

"After Caroline left?"

Osborne nodded. Against all logic, his failed marriage still bothered him deeply. And sometimes he was afraid that the fault had been entirely his; there was some flaw in his character that sooner or later would drive Ashley away.

A couple of miles farther, they came upon what looked like an old cattle ranch on the river. Osborne pulled off the side of the road so they could all get out. It was quiet here, not even the sound of the river broke the silence, only the light breeze in the distant treetops faded in and out in whispers.

"Peaceful Valley Ranch," Osborne said. "Not a lot usually goes on around here between September and May, but in the summer the Tangens, who run the Shadow Country Outfitters, put together trail rides. Lots to see: pretty countryside, wild horses, buffalo, elk, mule deer and whitetail, eagles, coyote, a lot of prairie dogs."

The gate back to the old ranch house and barns was open and

Osborne supposed that a couple of hands had come over from South Heart to get the place ready for the season.

Whitney leaned against the hood of the SUV and lit a cigarette.

"When did you start that?" Ashley asked.

Whitney shrugged. She'd been far away for a moment. "A couple months ago. One of the new roustabouts at Donna Marie was outside smoking one morning when I drove over. And for the hell of it I bummed a cigarette from him. Told me it was a stupid habit, and I agreed, but he gave me one anyway."

"Does it help?" Osborne asked. He'd taken up smoking the first day he'd arrived in Afghanistan, and never started up again once his leg had been shot off and he'd ended up at Landsthul.

"Sometimes," she said. "I'll quit when we're fully up and producing."

"I thought you were there," Ashley said.

"We'll see how the latest tweaking works. Looks good, but these kinds of bugs have a collective mind of their own. Not so easy as Pavlov with his dogs. Maybe if he'd been working with a pack of angry pit bulls it might have been something like we're dealing with."

Osborne got back in the car and radioed his office. Rachel Packwood, their dispatcher, came back.

"Morning, Nate. I thought this was your weekend off."

"It is. I'm over at the park with Ashley and Dr. Lipton, just wondering if anything's doing?"

"They had a power outage down at the project, but Basin Electric is taking care of it."

"I heard about it. Anything else?"

"Quiet as a Quaker woman at Sunday service," Rachel said. "You expecting something?"

"Not really."

"Good, then stop bothering me, and say hi to Ash."

13

MAKAROV PASSED THROUGH security at the airport with no questions asked about the dirty clothes in his bag, nor was he required to take off his shoes or belt, though he did have to put his iPad, wallet, and a few coins in a tray which was handed through, and had to show his boarding pass and a Los Angeles driver's license under the name Edward Puckett.

"Will the flight be on time?" he asked the TSA agent who was an older woman with a pleasant smile.

"Just finished refueling, should get you down to Denver in plenty of time for lunch," she told him. "Enjoyed your visit with us?" She was small-town snoopy and she'd never seen him before.

"Just passing through from Billings with a friend, actually, when I got a call that a job was waiting for me Denver. So he dropped me off here."

"Well, the best of luck to you."

"Especially in these times," Makarov said, and he picked up his things and walked back to the gate area where the thirty-passenger turboprop Embraer EMB-120 was pulled up fifty feet from the terminal.

A dozen people, most of them men, a few in business suits, and one family with two kids, were sitting waiting. Only a couple of them looked up when Makarov took a seat nearest the exit door where if need be he could get out in a hurry.

"Don't get yourself in a situation where there is no way out," the instructor said. "There'll come a time when getting out with your hide intact is the most important part of your mission. Remember it."

The full gamut of Spetsnaz training, which only a small percentage of recruits ever completed, took five years. During that time there were casualties, sometimes even deaths. Makarov had easily made the five years, in part because he was smart, but in a large part because he was ruthless. He had faked loyalty to the state, to the service, and to his unit; his highest loyalty had always been to himself.

He and a small number of Spetsnaz advisers had been sent by Putin over to Afghanistan on a highly classified mission to talk to the American Special Forces who'd been on the ground for five years. As it was explained to them by General Viktor Kazin, who was the director of all Spetsnaz forces, it was to Russia's advantage to help the Americans get out of the mess they were in.

"The politicians think that if we can convince them to get out, the region will begin to stabilize so that we can resume with our interests there," he told them, though he'd never explained what those interests might be nor did any ask.

Inside the first month in country it became clear to Makarov that the Americans would never quit, especially not until they got themselves out of their other mess in Iraq. And it was about that time he came to the full realization that conditions back in Russia were never going to change except for the worse. The only interesting possibility that he could see was the Mafia. They had the muscle and they had the money through the rackets, but in his estimation they were little better than street thugs—rich, but street thugs with no manners.

"*Nekulturny.*"

They'd been working in pairs with the Americans near the border with Pakistan, when Makarov, who was a captain by then, killed his sergeant and slipped across the border. The next night he stumbled across a Taliban patrol of four men, and he managed to kill all of them. He hid their bodies at the bottom of a nearby ravine, after changing clothes with one of them.

From there he made his way to Peshawar, where he tracked down a businessman returning home from his office, killed the man, and once again exchanged clothes and identities.

One week later he was in a luxury hotel in Mumbai, from where he considered his options. He was missed by then, AWOL, but years ago—soon after his Spetsnaz training had begun and he'd been given the lecture about the importance of always making sure you had a way out—he'd taken a train down to Helsinki on one of his leaves where he opened a bank account with a fictitious ID.

It hadn't been much money at first, but he was a natural-born card counter and did well at gambling, along with smuggling whores and booze into basic training barracks, money which he sent to his Helsinki account. Individually the recruits didn't have much, but collectively they'd made him relatively rich.

And sitting in Mumbai he'd decided that he would become a businessman. First in Helsinki and then after a couple of years Stockholm, where he became a reasonably successful stock broker and money manager specializing in exotics from around the world: oil fields in Iraq, uranium fuel processing equipment for Iran and North Korea's programs, investments in weapons dealers supplying governments such as Cuba, Angola, and lately Venezuela, which was one of the reasons he'd come to the attention of SEBIN.

Nine years ago he'd married Ilke Sorenson, a woman he'd met in Helsinki, and though they'd never had children, they had a loving, intimate relationship. He left from time to time on scouting trips, to places he kept secret for business reasons.

But when he was home he was a devoted, loving husband who kept regular office hours where he treated his handful of employees—who did legitimate work on the floor of OMX, the Stockholm Stock Exchange—with understanding and kindness. His only quirk was his aversion to cameras. He never allowed a photograph to be taken of his face; no wedding pictures, none at the office Christmas party and summer picnics, and none when he and Ilke traveled on vacation.

In fact the only photographs of him were on the half-dozen passports and supporting documents he owned. He'd had his features slightly altered by plastic surgery in Berlin three months before he turned up in Helsinki, so that he could not be easily identified from his Spetsnaz files except for his brilliantly violet eyes. For all most Russians knew, Makarov had died somewhere in Afghanistan, his body never found.

A young woman dressed in a Great Lakes Airlines uniform showed up at the gate and opened the door for the pilot, first officer, and one flight attendant who went outside to the aircraft.

At nine she opened the door again, and announced that flight 7135 with service to Denver's International Airport was ready for general boarding. Makarov joined the line, handed the agent his boarding pass, and made his way back to the window seat of row nine on the starboard side, at the emergency exit. He stowed his bag in the overhead, strapped in, and watched out the window for any sign that he'd somehow been connected to the incident on Highway

22 and the unlikely possibility that he'd somehow been traced to this flight.

Nothing other than routine traffic announcements had been made on the Stark County Sheriff's frequency that he had been continuously monitoring. No police cars had shown up on the tarmac, nor did anyone sit next to him. And he began to relax as the forward door was shut, the engines spooled up, the cabin pressurized, and the oldish flight attendant with short, gray hair explained about electronic devices, seat belts, and emergency exits.

Makarov shut off the iPad and stuffed it in the seat pocket as they taxied out to the runway, where the pilot powered up even as they were turning off the taxiway and a minute later they were airborne heading south.

Almost immediately Makarov spotted the Basin Electric truck parked beneath the pylon, the bucket raised, but he could not make out the lineman's body, nor the body of the sheriff beside his patrol car, or that anything might be wrong with the people inside the pickup truck on the other side of the highway.

Incredibly no one else had shown up yet, though as they continued to gain altitude over the Antelope Creek he thought he spotted the glint of sunlight reflecting off something coming up the highway from the south.

He sat back and glanced at his watch. They would be touching down in Denver at 11:38, less than two hours. And within twenty minutes of that time—say noon at the very latest—he would be at the United gate in an entirely different part of the terminal and traveling under his Thomas Park identification, aboard the one o'clock flight to New York's LaGuardia, and from there to Paris, where he would once again switch passports for the trip home.

No law enforcement agency, especially not a rural sheriff's department, would make the connections in time to have the authorities waiting to arrest him when he got off the plane in Denver.

When the attendant reached his row and asked if he wanted something to drink, he almost ordered a Bloody Mary, but changed his mind. No matter how unlikely, the situation could change, and he was still on a job.

He looked up and smiled. "Just a glass of mineral water, with maybe a twist, if you have such a thing, luv."

14

IN THE SIOUX Falls Control Center Stuart Wyman came back to his station from his coffee break, and sat down at his desk to take a look at the three flat-panel computer monitors in front of him, and then up at the status board, showing the conditions on his AOR—Area of Responsibility—all 12,353 miles of high-voltage transmission lines.

Carl Nesbitt, the assistant area desk dispatcher, looked up from what he was doing. "Roger Kohl called for you a couple of minutes ago, wanted to know what the hell we were doing."

"What do you mean?"

"Beats me. Said he recorded a power spike on his board about an hour ago, but nothing like that showed up here."

A hollow feeling crept into Wyman's gut. "You checked our data recorders? No possible leakage from elsewhere in the system?"

"That's the Donna Marie special circuit. Most of the time it's isolated."

"Yeah," Wyman said. He phoned Kohl over at Donna Marie.

The chief engineer answered on the first ring. "Kohl."

"Stu Wyman. Carl said you called with a problem?"

"No problem here, but I showed a definite spike on the line at eight twenty-nine, lasted less than two seconds."

Wyman pulled up the electronic record of conditions throughout his entire AOR for several minutes before and several minutes after 8:29. "I'm seeing nothing on my monitor."

"Well it showed up here."

"Could it have come from you? Maybe a faulty relay that opened and immediately closed?"

"First thing I checked," Kohl said. It sounded like he was angry. "You've got a lineman down there, don't you?"

"Yeah," Wyman said, the very bad feeling in his gut worsening.

"Well I just hope the guy was protected."

"Me, too," Wyman said, and he broke the connection. He called Tony Bartlett's cell phone.

It did not ring, instead it flipped over directly to the voice mail service.

Wyman tried again with the same results. Tony should have been up on the pylon at the time of Kohl's power spike and the thought of it was hard to bear. All he could think was that Kohl had made a mistake, gotten a faulty reading from somewhere. MAPP's monitoring and control systems with safety systems around every turn were foolproof. They'd been in place for so long with nearly perfect results that it was impossible to believe that Tony was in trouble.

He tried a third time to contact his lineman, still with the same results.

He ran a quick diagnostic on his systems, but everything turned up normal.

Nesbitt scooted over. "Do we have a problem?"

"Got a lineman in the field on the 250 kv line from Donna

Marie, who probably finished early and didn't bother calling in before he headed home," Wyman said.

He lit a cigarette, though smoking was not allowed anywhere in the center, and called Bartlett's wife, Juliette, who didn't answer until after four rings. She sounded harried, out of breath.

"What?"

"Mrs. Bartlett, I'm Stu Wyman, the dispatcher at Sioux Falls Control Center. We sent Tony on a job south of Dickinson, and he doesn't answer his cell phone. It's probably on low battery or something, because it doesn't ring, just switches over to voice mail. He has shown up at home, hasn't he? Or called?"

"No. Is he in trouble? 'Cause it's not very likely. He's a very careful man."

"God no, it was just a real minor problem. Someone shot out one of the insulators down there, and we shut off the power to make it easier for him to get the line up and ready to go."

Juliette was quiet for a moment, and Wyman could hear the television or radio in the background.

"Mrs. Bartlett?"

"Don't lie to me, goddamnit. I've two kids to raise here, and I've worried about Tony night and day since he took the job. I never liked thinking about him up there in the air fooling around with all that electricity. It just isn't safe. At the very least it's bound to give you cancer."

"Trust me, everything is just fine."

"Then why'd you call here and scare me?"

"I need to talk to Tony to see how the job went, is all," Wyman said, not knowing what else he could tell her. Certainly not how gut-wrenchingly worried he was about it.

"You find my husband, and when you do send him home!"

The connection was broken and Wyman hung up. Carl and the other five guys were looking at him. He tried Bartlett's cell phone again with the same results, and then only reluctantly, looked up the telephone number for the Stark County Sheriff's office at Dickinson.

A woman answered. "Clark County Sheriff's Department dispatch, how may I help you?"

"I'm Stuart Wyman, area supervisor at the MAPP Control Center in Sioux Falls. I dispatched a lineman a couple hours ago to repair a break in a power line just south of you where it crosses Highway Twenty-two. I talked to him when he arrived on site, but now I can't reach him."

"Yes, sir," Anita Yardley said. "Could you stand by for just a second?"

Wyman stubbed out his cigarette in his half-full coffee cup and immediately lit another. The guys were still looking at him, and he gestured for them to get back to work, which they did.

A full minute later a man who identified himself as Deputy Don Christen came on. "Can you tell me what caused the outage?"

"Looked as if a rancher or hunter shot out an insulator holding the high-tension line from shorting out. It happens from time to time."

"Anything else?"

"I sent one of Basin Electric's linemen—Tony Bartlett—out to take a look and repair it."

"Was he working alone?"

"Yes."

"Don't you usually send a team out on something like this?"

"Sheriff, I don't have time for this. I'd like you to send someone down there to take a look. I'm worried about Tony. He's a senior man, knows what he's doing, and this is just not like him."

"I'm on my cell phone at my squad car, I'm going to head down there to personally find out what's going on," Christen said. "Sheriff Kasmir called earlier this morning, said he was on his way to investigate. And now we can't raise him."

"You might want to call for backup."

"What are you telling me, Mr. Wyman?"

"That line carries power from Donna Marie, the experimental generating station south of Medora. It was the subject of at least two attacks a few months ago."

"Yes, we know that."

"Could be nothing, but you might watch yourself."

"I hear you," the deputy said, and he broke the connection, leaving Wyman nothing to do except worry.

15

OSBORNE, ASHLEY, AND Whitney were standing at the base of a narrow, shallow ravine that snaked its way from the road down to where the Little Missouri turned sharply west, away from them. The breeze this morning had been light, from the west, but in the ravine it had picked up sharply.

"Why they call this place Wind Canyon," he told them. "Funnels between the bluffs and accelerates."

"Ever get rough?" Whitney asked.

"You wouldn't want to be here in a blizzard, something from the northwest."

Ashley was looking at the river where it curved away, finally lost in the distance across a combination of scrub brush at the water's edge, grasslands farther in, and all of it framed by buttes and low bluffs carved by wind and water from the living rock, and she shivered.

Osborne touched her shoulder, breaking her out of her thoughts and she turned to him.

"Just got cold there for a minute," she told them.

"It's spring now," he said.

Just after Christmas she had been kidnapped in a bid to force her father, General Forester, who administered the Initiative, to delay the start-up. He'd refused, of course, because the attackers had no intention of keeping her alive. Barry Egan, a nutcase Posse Comitatus radical, had kidnapped her from where she'd been staying at the Rough Riders Hotel in Medora while Nate was in Washington meeting with the president. He'd taken her down to the Initiative, where he'd wire-tied her spread eagle to the back fence, her parka hood off, coat unzipped in a blinding blizzard, leaving her to freeze to death.

But Osborne had returned early, had somehow found her, cut her down, and managed to get her to safety.

She was remembering that night right now, and she shivered again.

Whitney hadn't been out at the fence line, she'd been inside the Research and Development section of the Initiative when Osborne had brought Ashley in, both of them half-frozen and all but unconscious. "How you guys ever made it was beyond any of us."

"I had some help from FORECON," Ashley said. "Hoo-rah." And she laughed.

The horn on Osborne's Saturn SUV cruiser began beeping. It was a signal that his office was trying to reach him by radio.

He walked back twenty-five yards where he was parked at the side of the road and keyed the mic. "Osborne."

It was Rachel, and she sounded excited. "Am I ever glad I finally reached you. Tried your cell phone first."

"I turned it off. What's up?"

"Don Christen called a few minutes ago. They've run into some trouble over there." She wanted to swallow her words.

"Slow down," Osborne said. It was the power outage he'd talked

to Kasmir about, and the hair on the back of his head was standing on end. The Marines called it the *pucker factor*. When you
knew damn well that something big was coming your way your
sphincter tended to pucker up.

"Don's down on twenty-two where a power outage was reported. The lineman was electrocuted. Kas drove down to investigate, and he was shot to death, along with another couple."

Osborne was waving for Ash and Whitney to come back. "How
did Don find out? Somebody call it in?"

"A power company dispatcher tried to get ahold of his lineman,
and when he couldn't get through he called the sheriff's office."

"Call Don and tell him that I'm on my way, and make sure that
the BCI sends someone down there right away."

"Okay, Nate. Do you want any other backup?"

"Not at the moment."

"Something going on?" Ashley asked when she and Whitney
reached him.

"I'll explain on the way," Osborne said, and he got behind the
wheel.

As soon as the girls were in, he flipped on his siren and headed
the way they had come, which was the shortest way back to Medora and the interstate.

Whitney in the backseat was white faced. "Does this have anything to do with the downed power line?" she asked.

"The lineman working on it was apparently electrocuted."

"That's impossible. Our relays would have tripped."

"I called Gerry Kasmir, he's the sheriff over there, and gave him
the heads-up. He drove down and was shot to death, along with a
couple who'd probably stumbled into the middle of the situation."

"It's started again," Whitney said, and she got on her cell phone.

"She's right," Ashley said, reaching for her cell phone. "I have to
call Tom." Tom Smekar was her editor at the *Bismarck Tribune*.

"Let's get over there first and see what happened."

"I just want to give them the heads-up. Have a rewrite man standing by."

"Not yet."

"Goddamnit, Nate," she said, her temper flaring. "What about my dad?"

"Go ahead, I want to talk to him when you're finished," Osborne said.

Whitney had reached Kohl at Donna Marie. "Are you sure it wasn't us? Absolutely certain?"

The paved road was narrow with gravel shoulders and Osborne had to pay attention to his driving, especially around the curves, the beautiful scenery with its first spring greens meaningless for him, as he kept going back to the way Kas had sounded this morning. Grace, who'd always worried about him, would be devastated. They had a couple of grown children, one of them teaching school over in Fargo, he thought.

But he couldn't beat himself up over it. He'd called this morning purely out of professional curiosity. Had the tables been reversed he would have expected Kas to call him.

"My dad's in conference, but someone is getting a message for him to call me right back," Ashley said.

Whitney finished her call. "Roger is one hundred percent certain that our relays tripped. Whatever power was on the line definitely did not come from us. But he told me that he talked to the transmission control center dispatcher in Sioux Falls who said that his computer showed that the line was and still is isolated from the rest of the system."

"But the lineman was electrocuted," Osborne said.

A couple of minutes later they slowed a little through the gate, Parks standing at the side of the road, but Osborne didn't stop, and when they reached Pacific Avenue which was the I-94 bypass, he turned east and sped up again, the few cars on the road pulling to the side.

Dickinson was about twenty miles east, and Osborne figured they'd make that in fifteen minutes give or take, with another fifteen to make it to what he was already thinking of as the site of the latest incursion.

As soon as he was on the interstate and steady at ninety miles per hour, he radioed his dispatcher.

"Have whoever is dispatching in Dickinson let Don know I'm en route. Should be there in about thirty minutes."

"Just heard you pass by. I'll let them know you're coming."

"Check to see if a BCI team is on the way."

"They are."

"Good. Anything else, no matter what, comes our way, let me know soon as."

"Will do, Nate," Rachel said. "Watch yourself."

Ashley's phone rang. It was her father. She handed it to Osborne. "He wants to talk to you."

"What's going on, Nate?" General Forester demanded. He had been an Army brigadier general, who'd done work for DARPA, the DoD's Defense Advanced Research Projects Agency, before the president had asked him to head up the Dakota Initiative which was eventually administered by the ARPA-E—the new Advanced Research Projects Agency-Energy.

"Looks like someone is coming after us again."

"Son of a bitch. Has Ellsworth been notified?"

A Rapid Response team stationed at Ellsworth Air Force Base outside of Rapid City provided the primary security for the project in the event of a major attack—like those that had occurred just before and after Christmas.

"No need yet. Whoever it was hit a power line about twenty miles east of Donna Marie."

"Tell me," Forester said. He'd not forgotten his field command days during which it was expected that questions, answers, and orders be quick and concise. He'd raised his only daughter that way and he expected everyone around him to follow his example.

Osborne outlined the extent of his information, including his hunch that something was about to happen, and his heads-up to Sheriff Kasmir.

"Where are you now?"

"I'm on the interstate, should be on scene in under thirty minutes."

"Out of your jurisdiction."

"Yes," Osborne said.

"Keep me posted, Nate."

"Will do," Osborne said and he handed the phone to Ashley.

"I want to call my newspaper," she said. "If this is the start of another attack it needs to get out there. Didn't do us any good last time to hold off."

Traffic was light, and when Osborne got past a semi, he reached over to the glove compartment and took out his 9mm SIG-Sauer P226 and holster and propped it beside him between the seat and center console.

"Okay, Daddy. But this time it's different, besides the sheriff there are at least three civilian deaths. I don't run with it, KDIX in Dickinson sure the hell will." Ashley broke the connection and pocketed her phone. "My father said it's your call."

"Let's get down there and take a look first, okay?"

Ashley nodded, but said nothing.

16

STARK COUNTY SHERIFF'S Senior Deputy Don Christen could not keep from looking back at Kasmir's body lying on the side of the road. A pair of Dickinson County ambulances had been the first on the scene, and one of the EMTs had covered the body.

At thirty, Christen, who'd played college football at North Dakota State in Fargo and still maintained his quarterback lean-and-mean physique and dark good looks, had worked for the sheriff's department for eight years. He wasn't married, though he never had trouble finding a date, and Kas and Grace had become almost like parents to him.

Nothing like this had ever happened in Stark County until around the holidays when all hell had broken loose over at the project in Billings County. And certainly he'd never expected in his wildest imaginings that he would become the lead investigator on what was shaping up to be at least a triple homicide.

A pair of highway patrol cruisers had set up roadblocks, one by the bridge, and the other at the top of the hill, stopping every car and checking IDs before the officers would let anyone through, warning them to drive with care but not to stop.

Basin Electric had sent out another cherry picker and three-man crew who were standing by their bucket in the lowered position. Two men would go up to retrieve Bartlett's body. They were waiting on word to go ahead. The third, a supervisor named Underhill, walked up to where Christen was standing by his patrol car.

"What's the word, Sheriff? We can't leave him up there."

"We're waiting for the BCI from Bismarck. Should be another twenty minutes."

"Come on, for Christ's sake. Tony doesn't deserve this."

"No," Christen said looking the man in the eye. "Neither did Sheriff Kasmir or the good people in the pickup truck."

The EMTs from the second ambulance were standing by waiting to remove the bodies from the truck where it had landed in the ditch across the highway. Christen had put crime scene tape around Kas's body, around the pickup truck, and around Bartlett's truck with strict orders that no one for any reason was to cross the lines.

Bob Olsen, the coroner from St. Joseph's in Dickinson, had shown up in his Chevy SUV and was waiting to examine the bodies.

"This is a crime scene, and I'm going to preserve the evidence," Christen told Underhill.

"Tony wasn't murdered, it was an accident."

"Are you sure about that?" Christen asked, holding his temper in check. He had the reputation of always being in total control: calm, cool, and collected, Kas liked to say. And some of the other deputies had taken it up, and had started calling him Cool Hand Luke, or just Luke.

But no one knew or even suspected that at times of high stress it took everything within his power not to lash out; tell the stupid son of a bitch to back off, or he'd end up in cuffs in the backseat of the patrol car.

"I know what you guys are going through, losing one of your own," he said. He glanced over at Kas's body. "It's the same for us. And if it means keeping their bodies here all day until we can figure exactly what happened, it's the way it'll be. I want to catch the bastards who did this."

Underhill nodded. "Sorry," he said. "It's just a little tough to see Tony hanging up there like that." He walked back down the hill to his waiting lineman.

Eddie Fritch, one of the younger Stark County deputies, who'd been parked at the top of the hill, drove down, pulled off the road behind Christen's unit, and walked over. "Just talked to Anita. Says the BCI team passed through town, should be here in a couple of minutes."

"That's fast."

"Her friend over in Bismarck said they got a call from the FBI in Minneapolis who told them to light a fire," Fritch said. He looked over at Kasmir's covered body, then up at the badly burned body of the lineman hanging from his bucket. "That's electric power from the project. I just hope to hell we're not going to have a repeat performance of what went down over the holidays, with the Bureau and military all over the place."

"Could be," Christen said. They all had the same fear, as did everyone in the small town of Belfield, just on the Billings County border where a rancher and his wife had been murdered by the same guy who'd hit the project. "Go back to the office, you're on standby."

"Yes, sir," Fritch said and he made a Y-turn and drove off.

People all across western North Dakota were uptight, figuring that none of this would have happened if the federal government hadn't put the project out here. Life would have gone on normally, nothing really big ever happening. They liked it that way.

And now this. But Christen couldn't make himself believe that the downing of the power line and the cold-blooded murders of at least Kas and the young couple in the pickup truck was done by someone from the county. Some disgruntled rancher who was angry that a high-tension line was strung across their land over their objections.

"Gives you cancer," was the generally held sentiment. "God only knows what the radiation will do to our cattle and horses—or our kids."

The BCI panel truck topped the rise and came down the hill, parking just above where the two Basin Electric trucks were set up below the pylon. Christen walked down as two investigators, one of them a slightly built woman, the other a tall, rangy man with a narrow chin and beak of a nose, both of them in blue BCI windbreakers and ball caps, got out and he introduced himself.

"Kathryn James," the woman said. "My partner, Lloyd Marks."

They shook hands.

"You the first on scene?" Kathryn James asked.

"Other than Sheriff Kasmir, yes, ma'am."

The BCI investigators did a three-sixty, and Marks nodded. "Good job securing the scene, except for the Basin Electric people. They should have been held back."

"I disagree," Christen said. "They provided the best clue so far."

"How do you see it going down?" Kathryn James asked.

"Someone came out here this morning, I'm thinking a lone gunman either somewhere up on the hill or maybe across the creek, shot out one of the insulators, which brought down the line and caused the power outage."

"Hell of a shot," Marks said. "But why not right down here?"

"The super said by the looks of the damage to the insulator it had to have been from a high-power rifle. But I've not found any shells other than nine-millimeter pistol casings close to Sheriff Kasmir's body, and on the road where the McKeevers—they're the ones in the pickup truck—were shot to death."

"Not one of your ranchers?" Marks said.

"I don't think so."

"Okay, Don, walk us through your scenario," Kathryn James said, "starting with why your sheriff was called out."

"He got a call from Nate Osborne, who's the sheriff over in Billings County, that there was a problem with the power line down here. Comes from the government project where we had that trouble last year. So everyone is still a bit touchy."

"So Sheriff Kasmir drives down, in the middle of the incident?" Marks asked.

"Kas would have called it in right away. I think he got down here, parked his car, and was talking to the lineman who was up working on the line, when the man was electrocuted. Then I think our shooter probably drove up and shot Kas once in the chest, and then a second in the head."

"The people in the pickup happened by and your perp shot them through the windshield causing them to run off the road," Marks said. "But it doesn't look like they were traveling very fast. Looks like they might have been almost stopped when they were hit and slowly left the pavement."

Christen nodded.

"So your shooter takes out the insulator, waits somewhere for the lineman to show up and then what?" Kathryn James asked. "He would have been taking a big chance hanging around like that. And you said the power was out. What makes you think that?"

"The lineman was electrocuted because he wasn't wearing protective clothing. Either he was told there was no power to the line, or he checked before going up there—or both. And he'd started to work on the problem, but at some point the power came back."

"Your shooter somehow got the power turned back on at the same moment the lineman was up there doing his work?" Marks asked. He was skeptical, and so was his partner.

"I don't see any of it," Kathryn James said. "We'll get to work, but I'd bet just about anything that we're talking about at least two guys—one with the hunting rifle, and the other with the handgun. And I'm thinking that they were local. Only reason Sheriff Kasmir let them get close enough, and why the people in the pickup truck stopped. The guys were somebody they knew. Neighbors."

17

T HE MOMENT OSBORNE topped the rise and slowed down for the highway patrol officer motioning for him to pull up, he had a good idea that the Initiative had come under attack. Again.

The state cop was John Watcznak from right here in Dickinson, and Osborne had worked with him a couple of times when blizzards stranded truckers, and last year after an eighteen-car pileup in a heavy fog just across the county line. He was an otherwise good man except for the cynicism he'd developed working for a couple of years on a street crime unit in the Twin Cities.

Osborne stopped and powered down his window. "Looks like we're finally going to get spring."

"Mornin', Nate, ladies," Watcznak said, tipping his hat. "You're little out of your jurisdiction."

"Don asked me to come over and take a look. And Kas was a friend."

"And the press already?"

"You have a problem with that, Officer Watcznak?" Ashley asked. She'd become peckish ever since she'd talked to her father.

The state cop gave her a hard look, but then glanced at Whitney in the backseat.

"This probably involves the power plant over at the project," Osborne said. "And Dr. Lipton is the chief scientist."

Watcznak nodded. "Your call, Nate," he said and stepped back to allow Osborne to continue down the hill.

He parked behind Christen's radio unit, and they got out as Don came over from where he'd been talking to the BCI people who were pulling their evidence kits and photo gear from the back of their van.

Three men stood around the Basin Electric truck, its bucket on the ground. The body of the electrocuted lineman hung from a safety strap. Yellow crime scene tape had been placed around Kas's covered body at the side of the road and around the pickup truck.

Whitney remained by the SUV, trying to avoid staring at the gruesome remains of the lineman, but Ashley was busy taking pictures with her iPhone.

"Glad you could make it, Nate," Christen said, shaking hands. He nodded to Whitney. "Dr. Lipton."

She nodded, the set of her mouth tight.

"I called Kas about the power outage," Osborne said.

"I sure hope that you're not going to run that picture on the front page," Christen said to Ashley.

"Not a chance, but I'm also working for the Initiative, and no way was this done by a disgruntled rancher. The Bureau will want to see this."

"The BCI will share whatever they come up with."

"ARPA-E is going to need it, too."

"Your dad," Christen said, and he wanted to take it further, but Osborne interrupted.

"What's it look like to you?" he asked, and Christen told him everything he'd told the BCI investigators.

"They didn't agree. Said it was probably a couple of agitated ranchers, someone the couple in the pickup truck probably knew otherwise they would have made a U-turn soon as they saw there was some trouble."

"It's possible," Osborne said. "Any sign that Kas tried to fight back?"

"His hand was on his holster. He was reaching for his gun."

"Tell that to the BCI?"

"Didn't have the chance," Christen said.

Osborne looked up toward the power line where the lineman had attached it to the base of the seven-foot-long insulator. "Take more than a deer rifle to knock out something that big." He looked over his shoulder to the crest of the hill where the highway patrol car was parked.

"What?"

"Did you happen to pick up one of the nine-millimeters from the side of the road?"

Christen nodded. "In an evidence bag in my unit."

Whitney had listened to it all. "Both of you think this was an attack on the Initiative?"

"I do," Christen said.

"So do I," Osborne said. "Let's take a ride to the top of the hill."

"I'll stay here," Whitney said. "Looks like Ash could use some help."

Ashley had walked down to where the coroner and the BCI people were starting with Kasmir's body, and it was obvious she was having words with them.

Osborne drove Christen back to the top of the hill and they got out.

Watcznak came over. "Forget something?"

"Tell you if we find it," Osborne said absently, and he walked farther up the road ten or twenty yards beyond the crest, to a point where he could just make out the pylon's cross arm where Bartlett's body still dangled from the bucket.

"What are we looking for?" Christen asked.

"If I'm right, and this was an attack on the Initiative, it was carried out by someone who knew his business. A professional. He shot Kas once, which probably would have been fatal, but fired a head shot for insurance. Be my guess he stopped around here somewhere, took out the insulator, then packed up and went somewhere to wait for the outage to be reported and for a repair crew to be sent out."

"To where?" Christen asked.

"I don't know. Someplace like T.D.'s up on ninety-four."

"He would have been taking a big chance, and Kas would have come as a big surprise."

"Not if he was monitoring your dispatch channel."

"Yeah."

Osborne spotted the fresh tire marks at the side of the road, the two outer wheels on the gravel, the inner two on the grass, which had not yet sprung back. "He parked here and took his shot. Shell casing would have been ejected to the right."

"Might take some help finding it in the grass," Christen said.

Osborne started down the hill. "Nope. It'll be too big to miss."

Five minutes later, nearly twenty feet down the hill Christen found it, and he called Osborne over. "Biggest damned shell I've ever seen. Looks like something from an elephant gun."

Osborne took a pen from his pocket and picked it up. "Sniper rifle. Fifty-caliber Barrett. Military. I fired it a couple of times in Afghanistan. Big son of a bitch, kicks like a mule. Our shooter stopped on the road, climbed up in the bed of his pickup truck or the tailgate of a SUV from where he could get a good bead on the insulator and to make sure no one was coming. He set up the rifle on the roof of the cab on its bipod, took his shot, and headed off. Probably took him only a couple of minutes."

"Damned good shot from all the way up here," Christen said.

"He's almost certainly ex-military Special Forces."

"One of our people?"

Osborne shrugged and they walked back up to the road where he lowered the tailgate on his Saturn and climbed up to take a look over the roof. From here he had a clear view of the pylon, maybe eight or nine hundred yards away. The rifle had been used in Desert Storm for a credited kill at just about eleven hundred yards. So this was not an impossible shot for a highly trained man. Definitely not the work of a hunter.

"Do you want me to ask the BCI people to come up here and take a tire cast?"

"He'll be long gone by now, but if he abandoned the truck in Dickinson someone will notice it."

"The sooner we find it the sooner we'll find fingerprints," Christen said. "Maybe DNA evidence."

"He didn't leave any, trust me. And the truck will be untraceable."

Watcznak walked down to them. "Find anything?"

"The guy took his shot from here," Osborne told him, getting down from the tailgate, the maneuver awkward because of the prosthesis on his left leg.

The state trooper climbed up and looked down to the pylon, and he shook his head. "Not a chance in hell, Nate. I don't know anybody around here who could make that shot from this distance."

"I could," Osborne said.

Watcznak jumped down and Nate and Christen drove back to the scene where the BCI pair were watching the tape from Kasmir's dash-mounted camera.

"Find anything we can use?" Osborne asked.

Kathryn James looked up. "And you are?"

"Nate Osborne. I'm the sheriff over in Billings County, and Kasmir was a friend of mine."

"Out of your jurisdiction, but okay." She nodded up toward the crest of the hill. "Find what you were looking for?"

Osborne took the shell casing he'd bagged out of his pocket and handed it to her. "Fifty-caliber Barrett sniper rifle. American made. They took the shot from up there."

"Not likely, but the lab will have a look."

"I've used the weapon, and I'm pretty well sure that no one around here has any need of something like that. No snipers in North Dakota."

"There was this time," Marks said, looking up from the images on the computer screen in Kasmir's car. "And whoever it was they were either damned smart or damned lucky, because they didn't step into camera range."

Kathryn James bagged the shell casing. "Thank you, Sheriff," she said. "If you come up with anything else let us know. In the meantime I'd appreciate you not contaminating the crime scene."

"You bet," Osborne said sharply, and he and Christen walked back up the road.

"They're just doing their jobs," the deputy said.

Ashley and Whitney had walked down to where the Basin Electric workers had gathered and were starting back up the grassy slope from the pylon. The morning was suddenly very quiet.

Osborne checked his watch. It was coming up on eleven thirty already, and he had the very distinct feeling that he was missing something here. That they were all missing something.

"So, after he shoots Kas, and the McKeevers, he turns around and drives off," Christen said. "Back to the interstate, and then where, east or west? Or if as you suggest he abandoned the pickup in Dickinson, he must have had another vehicle stashed in town or nearby."

"The airport," Osborne said.

"He could have rented a car out there. I'll call."

"Too easy," Osborne said. "Find out what flights left this morning. Sometime within the past hour or so."

Christen used his cell phone, and it took him only a minute. "Great Lakes 7135. Left at twenty to ten."

"To where?"

"Denver. Should be touching down any minute if it's on time," Christen said.

"Shit," Osborne said. "Call the TSA agent who handled the boarding passes and IDs for that flight. Find out if anyone stood out. Anyone out of place. Anything."

Christen got back on his cell phone and Osborne used his to call Deborah Rausch who was the FBI's Special Agent in Charge at the Minneapolis office. He'd worked with her on the incident over the holidays, and he had a great deal of respect not only for her intelligence, but because she had heart. She really cared about catching bad guys.

He got her after a couple of rings, and she sounded a little harried. She'd been expecting his call.

"Deb, Nate Osborne."

"I just talked to General Forester," she said. "He says you think shit is starting to happen again."

"I don't have time to explain right now, but I'm outside Dickinson where there've been four deaths. Looks like the work of a professional, probably trained in a Special Forces program somewhere, so this guy is going to be extremely dangerous. We think he could be aboard Great Lakes flight 7135 to Denver that should be touching down any minute now."

"Do you have a name, a description?"

"Should have something for you in the next minute or two."

"I'll call our Denver office now. What about TSA, or the airport cops?"

"Tell them to take care. If he's cornered he'll fight back."

"Not likely he got a weapon through Dickinson security."

"He wouldn't need one," Osborne said.

"Okay, stand by. I have Denver," Rausch said.

Christen was talking to someone and he was excited. "What'd he look like?"

Rausch was back. "They'll be rolling as fast as they can get to their cars. But they'll need something to go on. So will the airport cops."

"We're working on it," Nate said.

"I'll need something more than that," Christen said. "Anything you can give me. Anything even if you don't think it's important."

"What the hell do the bastards want?" Rausch asked. "The project works, so shutting down Donna Marie wouldn't do a thing to advance their cause. Or are they all just out of their friggin' minds?"

Christen thanked whoever he was talking to and he broke the connection. "Got his name and a pretty good description."

"Stark County Deputy Don Christen got a name and description from the TSA. I'll put him on," Osborne said. He handed the phone to the deputy. "FBI Special Agent Deb Rausch."

"Ma'am, he's traveling under the name Edward Puckett from Los Angeles. Didn't get an address, but the TSA agent at security said he was short, thin, hair and eyes dark, and he spoke with what sounded to her like a foreign accent, maybe British. Told her that he'd been riding with a friend from Wyoming when he got a call for a job interview in Denver, so he stopped here to catch a flight."

Ashley and Whitney walked over. "Anything?" Ashley asked.

"Got a name and a description. Guy's on the way to Denver."

"Yes, ma'am," Christen was saying. "The TSA agent said she

talked with the people who scanned his overnight bag. He was carrying nothing but some old clothes, which she thought was strange. In the first place he said he'd come from Wyoming, and he acted like a real gentleman, not some oil or gas field roustabout."

A moment later he handed the phone back to Osborne.

"You come up with anything else, give me a call right away," Rausch said. "Do you really think that it's starting all over again?"

"Yes, I do," Osborne said.

"Shit. I'll get this down to our people in Denver, and we'll talk later. I'm going to have to re-open the file."

18

A T DENVER INTERNATIONAL Airport, Makarov was among the first to get off the airplane. He nodded pleasantly to the attendant and flight crew, and inside the terminal walked down the busy corridor to the nearest men's room where he washed his hands and studied his face until a man in jeans and a dark zippered jacket came out of the last toilet stall and left.

Only two other men were the restroom, both of them using the urinals as Makarov walked back to the last toilet stall, went inside, and secured the latch. No one had paid him any attention.

A small gray wheeled suitcase, of the size that would fit in an aircraft's overhead bin, had been left for him. It had already passed through security and it was the last Mafia handoff that he'd ordered. From this point all the way to Stockholm he was on his own. And once he got home he would wire transfer the second half of the agreed-upon one hundred thousand dollars to an account number in the Caymans.

From the suitcase he took out a gray pinstriped suit cut in

European style, a white shirt and tie, and changed clothes, stuffing his old things, plus his small overnight bag of dirty clothes into the main compartment of the nearly empty suitcase, zipping it closed.

The man who'd brought the things had a full head of dark hair, streaked with gray. When he'd left, his hair was short, and nearly blond.

Makarov took the wig out of a zippered pocket and put it on. He checked through a crack at the edge of the door to make sure that the two men at the urinals were gone. At the moment no one was in the restroom.

He stepped out and went to one of the sinks where he quickly adjusted the wig in the mirror, straightened his tie, and went out. Rolling the suitcase behind him he headed toward the United gate at the other side of the terminal just as two armed airport security officers hurried directly toward him.

The corridor was busy but not packed, and the policemen were the only ones who seemed to be in a hurry. One of them was speaking into a microphone attached to his shirt on his right shoulder.

Makarov stepped to one side as they got nearer. It was highly unlikely that they were looking for him, but them being at this side of the terminal at this exact moment was too much of a coincidence for him to accept.

They were looking at faces and the one cop looked at him, his gaze lingering for just a moment.

Disarming the one talking on the radio would be simple, and using the cop's pistol to shoot both of them could be done in a matter of a couple of seconds. He would be forced to return to the Great Lakes gate where he could get outside, and then into the baggage handling area.

From there he would improvise, though he didn't think he would have too much trouble finding an airport employee who had an identification badge attached to his coveralls. He'd kill the man, switch clothes, and walk away.

Getting out of the airport where he could lose himself in the city could be problematic, but not impossible.

But the two cops passed him, and went directly to the Great Lakes gate, deserted for the moment.

Makarov headed toward the United gate. Once the cops talked to the flight crew, they would be coming to look for a dark-haired man wearing khaki slacks, a light turtleneck, and dark blue blazer, not a gray-haired businessman in a suit and tie.

But by then he would have reached the busier part of the terminal where he would merge with other business travelers like himself.

He was looking forward to getting home. The long Swedish winter was finally coming to an end, and he and Ilke loved biking in the countryside. Sometimes they would come upon a pleasant restaurant with tables outside during the good weather. Or walking along the paths in the Skansen or Tivoli on Djurgarden Island they would hold hands like young lovers.

And she adored shopping with him in Stockholm mostly, but whenever the press of his business wasn't so important she would make him take her to Paris, which outside of Stockholm and Helsinki was her all-time favorite city in the world.

Four years ago she had learned in secret to speak French. She was a bright woman and a quick study, and when they went to Paris for the first time, she'd chatted in French with the cab driver, the desk clerk at the Intercontinental, and with the concierge there for dinner reservations at the Jules Verne in the Eiffel Tower, delighting everyone. Including her husband.

At the time Makarov remembered being a little disturbed, because it had suddenly dawned on him that he was in love with his wife. He'd never felt that way about any other person in his entire life, and that day in Paris he'd never felt more vulnerable.

Since that time he never allowed himself to think that way about her until just this moment when he realized just how much he missed her.

19

AT FIFTY-TWO, STUART Wyman was one of the senior computer operators, not merely an area dispatcher in the Sioux Falls Center, so most of the other operators looked up to him. Steady Eddy. Old Mother Hen. Stickler for details. Nitpicker squared. But this morning, sitting at his board, he felt physically ill, as if he was the one who had killed Tony Bartlett. There wouldn't be a lineman anywhere who would ever trust his judgment again.

He'd turned over his duties to Nesbitt, whose console was next to his, and he'd spent the last two hours going over every computer record second-by-second from thirty minutes before the outage—when every indicator showed normal for that line—until thirty minutes after the accident. The line had not been energized, and he would bet everything he owned on it.

But none of that changed the fact that Tony had been electrocuted, and from what he understood Stark County Sheriff Kasmir and maybe a young couple from a nearby cattle ranch had been shot to death. All of it pointed toward another attack on the Initiative's Donna Marie generating station.

The other operators on duty left him alone, some of them working the dozens of issues that came up on every shift, including a pair of outages in central Nebraska, and a transformer issue in northern Wisconsin at the Superior distribution yard.

He'd been smoking all morning and his coffee cup was half filled with butts, but so far no one had challenged him, and there were other, bigger issues he would have to face when the shoe finally dropped.

Which it did a couple of minutes before one when the center's chief operating officer, Dick Remillard, phoned his console.

"Are you about finished with your diagnostics?"

"Yes, sir."

"Come up to my office, please."

"Yes, sir," Wyman said again and as he crossed the main control room he glanced up at the plate glass window where Remillard was watching him.

The COO was something of a legend in MAPP, working his way as a California lineman through MIT where he studied electrical engineering, and from there to Harvard where he earned his MBA. But instead of returning to California and setting up some sort of Silicon Valley high tech company, he'd gone directly to work for the Mid-Continent Area Power Pool right here as the number two man at the age of twenty-six two years ago. He was young (some of the old hands doubted if he had to shave more than once or twice a week), he was direct, and he was very smart and let everyone know it. All strikes against him, but he ran a tight ship and fairly soon, it was rumored, he would jump to a senior management position either at the Eastern or the Western Interconnect—the odds favored California, his home state. He was fond of complaining that he hadn't found a decent place anywhere in South Dakota to use his surfboard.

Remillard was six-two, much taller than Wyman, who he motioned to have a seat across the desk. Except for a wall filled with flat-screen monitors showing the overall picture of the entire system, and a wide-screen monitor on his desk, the office was spartan. Several photos of him skiing in Aspen, sculling on the Charles River in Boston, mountain climbing somewhere in Alaska, skydiving in Florida, and surfing in Hawaii and California, adorned the wall behind his clear acrylic desk—and in all of them he looked young, fit, and tan, just about how he looked now. Except in the pictures he was smiling, his teeth movie-star white.

An easy man to hate, Wyman decided.

"What did you find, Stu?"

"It's almost certainly the work of a terrorist or terrorists. The sheriff and a young couple who'd happened by were shot to death. And it was directed at the Initiative, just like the holiday attacks."

"But those transmission lines are not owned by the Initiative, they belong to us."

"Taking the line out shut down Donna Marie."

"But Mr. Bartlett wasn't shot to death. He was electrocuted."

Wyman looked away for a moment, but he nodded. "I know."

"How?"

"I can't find a trace, but my best guess is Donna Marie's relays somehow tripped, for just a second, energizing the lines just as Tony—Mr. Bartlett—was attaching the downed one to the insulator he'd repaired."

"I spoke with Donna Marie's chief operating engineer. I believe you've worked with the man?"

"Roger Kohl. Knows his business."

Remillard turned his computer monitor around so that Wyman could see the images on the screen. "These are four time/date stamped snapshots of his main board, showing the normal power level just before the line went down, immediately afterwards, and at the exact time of Bartlett's death and immediately after that unfortunate event. No power was coming from Donna Marie."

It was the same conclusion Wyman had come up with. "But the line was energized."

"Yes."

"Could have been a temporary malfunction of one of his programs. A shadow code or something like that. A line or two left over from one of their routine sweeps for viruses. A corruption of a code that somehow had unintended consequences before one of their safeguard programs kicked in."

Remillard held his silence for a beat. "Or an operator error?"

Wyman shrugged. He really didn't want to go in that direction. Kohl and his people were top notch. They'd been hired directly by ARPA-E, and like the Defense Advanced Research Projects Agency that had been there at the beginning of the Initiative, only the best of the best in the business had been hired. "It's possible."

"It's possible," Remillard said. "For an operator error at Donna Marie, you're suggesting."

"Yes, sir."

"Or an operator error here? A temporary lapse? Joking with a colleague? Distracted?"

"Anything is possible, but not likely. We have safeguards."

"Perhaps while lighting a cigarette?"

"I'm the only one who smokes," Wyman said, and it suddenly dawned on him that he was going to be the scapegoat. "No, sir, it's not going to be that simple. The problem could have been operator error—but that is the most remote possibility. I'm betting just about everything that it was a computer problem."

"Because?"

"Because of the timing. The line was not energized until the exact moment that Tony had his hands on it. Someone was right there, obviously. He killed the sheriff and the couple. Either he somehow manipulated a computer at Donna Marie or here, or he communicated with someone—a computer hacker somewhere—who did the thing."

"Now you're blaming the virus that either the Chinese or Russians have supposedly injected into the entire grid," Remillard said, his tone insinuating.

"That's more likely than an operator error," Wyman replied hotly.

"Your error," Remillard said. "Is that also possible?"

"Sure. But in that case I would have to be in league with the person or persons who shot out the insulator in the first place, then shot and killed those people out there."

"Exactly the conclusion we came to," Remillard said. He entered a few strokes on his keyboard, and the snapshots were replaced by the image of Teresa Dyer, the president of MAPP, whose offices were in Minneapolis. She wasn't smiling, the set of her eyes stern. Like Remillard she was young, attractive, and bright. She also had the reputation of being a shark.

"Good morning, Mr. Wyman," she said, and Wyman knew damned well what was about to happen. She was going to fire him because Remillard didn't have the guts to do it himself.

"Ma'am."

"Dick tells me that you've been working the problem all morning."

"Yes."

"A tragedy. The lineman left a wife and three children?"

"Two children," Wyman said. "But a police officer and two other people were shot to death out there."

"Their deaths, though just as tragic, are not a direct result of coming in contact with our equipment. Do you understand?"

"No, I don't."

"Doesn't matter," the woman said. "Our issue—actually your issue, Mr. Wyman—is finding out how and, perhaps more important, why the line became energized at the same moment the unfortunate lineman without the proper equipment was in contact with it. We don't believe it was an accident."

Wyman felt a glimmer of hope. "Neither do I, ma'am."

"No," the MAPP president said. "We will be conducting our own investigation, of course. Power was not coming from Donna Marie, but it was coming from somewhere within the system, and we will find out how it happened. As for the other, the FBI has been called. Their advice was to suspend you until this matter is straightened out. Your suspension will be with full pay and benefits, of course, but I want you to immediately leave the control center. I also suggest that you remain in contact with Dick to let him know where you are at all times until the FBI talks you, which I suspect will be much sooner than later."

Wyman found that he actually couldn't blame the company. A lineman had been electrocuted when he came in contact with a line that was supposed to be de-energized. It was someone's fault, and he had been the man in charge. The FBI had been called, because everyone agreed that whatever had happened out there had been another attack on the Initiative.

"Yes, ma'am," he said. "Will there be anything else?"

"Not this morning," the company president said.

Wyman left Remillard's office, got his things from his locker, and left the building. No one looked his way nor did anyone say anything to him, nor was he surprised to see that Nesbitt had moved over to the Area Desk Supervisor's console.

HIS WIFE, Delores, was out of the house, probably having lunch with one of her friends. She hadn't left a note, because she hadn't expected him to be home so soon, which was just as well. He needed a little time alone.

He got a Bud Light from the fridge and walked to his little office at the back of their ranch-style house, sat down at his desk, and powered up his computer. When he got online he double clicked the icon for the MAPP's Computer Analysis Center in Hibbing, Minnesota. When the home page came up, he entered his user name and password which brought up a directory, from where he found Arthur Tobias Lundgren.

He and chubby, geeky, pimple-faced Toby had gone to Denfeld High School together in Duluth, Minnesota—the school for the kids from the wrong side of the tracks. They went to the University of Minnesota at Duluth for their degrees in computer science, and Toby went on to the main campus in Minneapolis for his Masters and his Ph.D. But they'd kept up their friendship not only because they were in the same field—though Toby was much smarter—but because Stu had been his only friend through high school. In many ways they were like brothers.

"Twins," Wyman used to joke.

And Toby would laugh from the soles of his size twelves. "In your worst nightmare."

They'd had some good times together, and still talked by computer at least once a week.

Lundgren didn't respond, and Wyman's computer showed an error message. But a moment later the phone rang. It was Lundgren.

"There's some serious shit going down up here, and you're right in the middle of it."

"I'm at home now, they suspended me," Wyman said. "Have you any idea how it happened?"

"I know exactly how it happened," Lundgren said.

Wyman was relieved. "That's good."

"You weren't listening to me, Stu. I know exactly how it happened, because the order to override the shutdown, and allow a momentary back surge from the Bismarck Switch came from the Sioux Falls Center computer system."

"Impossible. I spent the last two hours looking for exactly that, and found nothing."

"The order came from your console."

"Goddamnit," Wyman said, but then he stopped. "But I didn't do it, I swear to God, Toby. And even if I did, the transaction would have showed up on someone's log."

"On mine."

Wyman sat back, his entire body slumping. Maybe he had done something wrong. Maybe he had been distracted. Maybe his head had been planted firmly up his ass as his ROTC instructor at UMD was fond of telling him and the other recruits. Most of them had made it through their four-year degrees into the service, but Wyman hadn't. Toby had talked him out of it: "Being a GI ain't in your future. No way, man. Not a chance in hell."

But he would never make such a mistake, no matter how distracted he was. And in fact he'd not been the least bit distracted this morning until after the accident.

"It wasn't me," he said.

"I know that," Lundgren said. "Which leaves a damned good hacker somewhere who wants to play games."

"Maybe it's another attack on the Initiative."

"I think that's exactly what's going down."

"Can you find him?"

Lundgren laughed. "Keep your pecker up, Stu. I'll get back to you."

20

OSBORNE GOT THROUGH to General Forester just as the BCI crew was finishing with Sheriff Kasmir's car, and the coroner gave one of the ambulance crews permission to remove the body to the morgue at St. Joseph's in Dickinson. They headed across the road to the pickup truck. The crime scene beneath the pylon would be the most difficult to sort out, so they were saving it for last.

"I've ordered the Rapid Response team back to the Initiative just until we get this new mess straightened out," the general said.

"I was going to suggest that you do just that, because this was no accident. But someone's going to have to figure out how the lineman could have made such a big mistake."

"The FBI's Cyber Crimes unit is on it. Best early guess is that someone hacked into the computer system either at Donna Marie— my people are checking on that—or at the transmission company's control center outside Sioux Falls."

"Something like that would have to be fairly sophisticated,"

Osborne said. He didn't know much on the subject, but after being around Whitney Lipton and some of her bright people, it stood to reason that plenty of safeguards would be in place. Passwords, security codes, probably encrypted programs, and he told Forester just that.

"I wish it were so. But the fact is the power grid is the weakest link. The Initiative proves that we can generate all the power we need from coal—which we have plenty of—without screwing up the atmosphere. But the grid is having a hard time accepting power from any new facility, including Donna Marie."

"I've heard some of that. Russian or Chinese viruses that can shut everything down. But what happened out here this morning is nothing like that."

"No," Forester said. "But maybe it was the opening shot."

"Of what?"

"I don't know, exactly," Forester said. "None of us do. We're just guessing."

"How about the CIA?"

"They're on it, believe me. In fact the president has been told repeatedly that a serious attack could come at any moment, with absolutely no notice."

"Nine eleven?"

"Worse. And the president will be told just that again this afternoon. He's called a Security Council meeting for two o'clock."

"Do you want Dr. Lipton to fly out?"

"Not necessary. We're thinking this is an attack on the grid—a test shot—and not necessarily at Donna Marie," Forester said. "But if she's still with you, I'd like you to have someone take her back to the Initiative. I'll feel better when she has some muscle around her. Just in case."

"I'll have one of my deputies come get her."

"What about my daughter? How's she doing?"

Osborne chuckled. "Well, she's pissed off just about everybody down here. But she has her story. And it looks like the TV people are on their way, so you might want to give her the go ahead. She'd be real unhappy if she were to be scooped."

"She can file her stories, but no mention of sabotage, computer hacking, or that this was probably a coordinated attack."

"The lineman's death could play as an accident, but how's she supposed to explain the shooting deaths?" Osborne asked.

"A random event," Forester said. "And I want your word that it'll be reported that way."

"I don't have any control over her."

"More than I do," Forester said.

Osborne phoned Dave Grafton, one of his deputies back in Medora, to drive over for Dr. Lipton and take her back to the Initiative.

"Trouble?"

"Some, so I want you to keep a sharp eye."

"I'm leaving right now."

Osborne walked back to where Whitney was smoking a cigarette, leaning against the hood of his SUV radio unit.

"Bad habit," he said. He felt sorry for her. She was a scientist, not a combat solider, and yet she'd been through hell the last few months. He'd smoked in Afghanistan to help calm his nerves. A lot of guys who hadn't smoked back in the World, had started soon as they stepped off the aircraft in country. He couldn't blame her for starting now.

"I think I should get back," she said.

"One of my deputies is on the way. Sorry about the weekend."

"Not your fault, but Jesus, won't they ever stop?"

Osborne had wondered the same thing, but the only answer he could come up with—and one that General Forester had agreed with—was that we were at war. An energy war, in which the battle lines weren't clear, nor were objectives, except we were taking casualties on American soil, and the purpose could be just as simple as the destruction of the U.S. Bring us down from being a super-power to just another western hemisphere country. But everyone, including Forester, was skirting around the possibility.

It was crazy, of course. More than crazy, even insane. But there were a lot of people in power around the world who wanted that to happen.

Ashley walked up from the Basin Electric cherry pickers, her eyes wide, her expression and demeanor bright. She was in the middle of a big story and she was loving it.

"Just talked to my dad, he says it's your call," she said. She nodded toward the crest of the hill where a remote truck from KDIX was stopped. "Cat's out of the bag in any event."

"It was an accident," Osborne said.

"And the bodies? They accidentally shoot themselves?"

"A random act," Osborne told her. "Someone shot out the insulator, that much we know for sure. When the lineman came out to fix it he was electrocuted. About that time another person or persons happened on the scene, and when Sheriff Kasmir tried to question them he was shot to death. As were the couple in the pickup truck."

Ashley looked at him for a long beat. "Bullshit. This is me you're talking to, Nate."

"Nevertheless that's the story you're going to file. You can take my car back to Medora to get your truck. I'll hitch a ride with Don soon as we finish here."

"I'll stick around."

"Don't you need to file your story?"

She held up her iPad. "Already have."

Osborne's anger spiked. "Goddamnit, Ash, you promised no story until I gave you the go-ahead."

"Relax, I reported it exactly the way you and my dad wanted me to. But all of us know damned well that this was no simple accident.

This was another attack on the Initiative. Most likely by Venezuela in retaliation for us hammering their important air bases. But it'd be the dumbest move Chavez ever made." She glanced at the lineman's body hanging from the bucket. "When are they going to take that poor guy down from there?"

"Soon as they're ready," Osborne said. And he thought that she was right about Venezuela on both counts; they were probably behind this attack, and they were as dumb as a box of rocks. Yet he didn't think it was going to turn out to be just that simple. Another dictator gone crazy.

"Whoever did this was a professional. Not another nutcase like the ones over the holidays."

"You're right," Osborne said, and Whitney shivered.

"Okay," Ashley said. "So what's next?"

"You're not even going to speculate on anything like that in print."

"I already got that. I meant what're they going to do next? Knocking out power for an hour or two, or even a day, from Donna Marie, doesn't do a thing to hurt the project."

"She's right," Whitney said. "It doesn't make any sense. The Initiative's a done deal. Permits for at least ten other coal-to-methane generating plants are already being fast-tracked right here in the U.S. And China will be on board pretty soon. Next month the Indian government is sending a team to talk to us."

Christen got out of Kasmir's radio unit and gestured for Osborne to come down.

"Question's still on the table," Ashley said. "What's next?"

"When we catch the guy who did this, I'm going to ask him just that," Osborne said. "Excuse me."

"I'm coming with you."

"Nope," Osborne said as he walked down to Kasmir's car.

"Get in, I want you to take a look at something," Christen said.

Osborne slipped in behind the wheel. "What is it?"

"It's Kas's dash cam," Christen said. He reached inside, past Osborne, and pushed a button. "I rewound it."

The image of Kasmir came up on the computer monitor. He was walking directly toward the camera and then passed it. His body had been found lying on the side of the road behind his patrol car.

"This is probably just before he was gunned down."

In the distance, a pickup truck was just crossing the creek bridge.

"The McKeevers," Christen said. "And there's nothing much after this. But look at it again, in slow motion and forget about what's happening outside, take a look at the reflections on the inside of the windshield."

Christen backed up the recording to just before Kasmir had walked past and out of camera range. A very faint image of something or someone moved across the screen and was gone. A minute later, the image of a man was reflected. He got into a pickup truck, made a U-turn, and was lost.

"Again," Osborne said.

Christen reversed the recording, and played it again. "I missed it at first, and the BCI people didn't say anything about it, so I think they missed it, too. But that's our killer. The sun was just right to make the reflection."

They replayed it a third time. "Can't make out the license plate, but it's a Dodge Ram, dark blue," Osborne said. "And the guy is short, slightly built, same as the man who flew to Denver."

"That's what I think, but I'm going to show it to the BCI people. They can take it back to the lab in Bismarck, maybe those guys can enhance it. I'd like to get the tag number."

"Won't tell us much, but have your people look for the truck. Be my guess it's parked at the airport, and you'll find the Barrett and the nine-millimeter pistol."

"Fingerprints?"

"Won't have left any," Osborne said. He phoned Deb Rausch in Minneapolis.

"We missed him by about ten minutes," she said, and she sounded bitter. "They're using your description to search the airport."

"I wouldn't bother."

"Our guys are pretty good."

"He's better. He changed his appearance, has a new ID, and by now he's on another flight, probably to Europe."

"You're guessing."

"Yes, I am. But if I were in his shoes, it's what I'd do. And there'd be no way you'd catch me. Leastways not in the short run. But this guy will be back, and now that we know what to look for we'll have a better shot at bagging him."

"We don't need any wild-ass assumptions, Nate. Let us do our jobs, you do yours."

"Fair enough, but this is just the start, you know."

"I hope you're wrong," she said.

Osborne rewound the recording and watched the faint images reflected off the inside of the windshield, and there was something just beyond his ken. Something about the man's build, about the cold-bloodedness of his acts, something about his professionalism.

21

WYMAN WAS IN his study working on his third beer and waiting for Toby to call back when his wife, Delores, came home. She stood at the doorway, concern written all over her face. They'd been married twenty-five years.

"Are you sick?" she asked.

He shook his head. "I've been suspended."

"Why?" she demanded, looking pointedly at the beer bottle in his hand, and the solitaire game in progress on his computer screen.

She was the same age as he was, and she'd managed to more or less keep her same good looks and slender figure since he'd met her. But while he had the reputation at work of being a stickler for detail, she was ten times worse. She had to know everything, and she had an opinion about everything. They were of like minds, and their marriage was stable. Neither of them liked surprises.

"It was a technical problem that Remillard is convinced was my fault."

"What kind of a problem? You're the best they have, and they know it."

"A line went down in North Dakota, so I sent a lineman out there to fix it. Told him it was safe. And it was. But he got electrocuted, and they think I was at fault."

"Oh, dear God," Delores said. She came the rest of the way into the study and put a hand on his cheek then on his shoulder. "But you couldn't have made such a mistake. They have to know at least that much."

Wyman was on the verge of tears. Earlier he'd been angry, but now he was incredibly sad that Tony Bartlett was dead and he felt as if the weight of the entire world was on his shoulders.

He looked up at his wife. "The order came from my console, but I can't find any record of it."

"Then how do you know where the order originated from?"

"I called Toby. He was the one who spotted it. And he's the only one other than you who believes I didn't screw up."

She nodded, some of the worry ebbing from her face. "He'll figure out what happened," she said. "Have you had any lunch?"

He held up the beer bottle.

"I meant to eat."

"No."

"I'll make us a couple of grilled cheese sandwiches. Do you want some soup?"

"Maybe later," Wyman said. "I want to get this straightened out first. Toby's supposed to call me back if he finds out anything."

"*When* he finds out what really happened," Delores said, and she went out to the kitchen.

Wyman felt a little better now that he'd told his wife. He had a tendency to blow things out of proportion when he was in a tense situation. He had a good imagination, and he could see the worst happening easier than he could see the best. Delores had a way of bringing him back down to earth.

He got back online and tried to get to the MAPP's website, but he was stuck on the home page. None of his passwords worked, and he started to get worried all over again.

TOBY PHONED just as Delores brought her husband a sandwich and another beer—this one in a glass.

"How're you holding up, Stu?"

"Okay, I guess," Wyman said. "I'm putting you on speakerphone, Delores is here." He hit the hook button and hung up the handset.

"Hi, Dee. You taking care of the old man?"

"So far so good, as long as you're working on the problem for us."

"This one's interesting, but I'm making some progress," Toby said. When something was *interesting* to him, it meant he was working on something very difficult. "Fringe," he sometimes liked to say, but he loved it.

"I tried to get on to MAPP's site, but apparently they've blocked my passwords," Wyman said.

"I did it, not only to keep you out of here, but to keep them from tracking your computer searches. Your firewall sucks."

"But why?"

"The FBI is taking a look at you, probably got your phone bugged, which doesn't matter because we're going to cooperate with them one hundred percent. We're all on the same team anyway, right?"

"Right," Wyman said, but he was stricken, and glancing at his wife he could see that she, too, was bothered.

"Okay, here's what I've come up with so far. First of all it wasn't a glitch in the system, but the order to re-energize did come from your board, but only after your program had been shut down for about a millisecond. Lets you off the hook."

"A hacker?"

"Yeah, but that's about the only good news so far."

"Who was it?"

"I don't know, but I'd say someone way off shore. Lots of remailers and blind alleys, just like when you're trying to peel an onion and every now and then you uncover a peach stone. But it's way cool, and I'm thinking it has the signature of a guy I knew back at MIT. Dutch or German, I think. Anyway, if it's the same guy last I heard he was part of some commune of superhackers who screw with any system they can get their hands on, mostly for the fun of it. Sometimes they do it for money, but mostly I think they just hack into bank accounts if they need cash."

"Just for the fun of it?" Delores asked. "How do you know?"

"Because I used to be just like them," Toby said.

"Do you know where they are?" Wyman asked.

"Amsterdam, last I heard."

"Can you get to them? Or at least prove it so the FBI backs off my case and I can have my clearance restored?"

"I'm on it," Toby said. "Not to worry, Stu. But if I'm right, and I usually am, this is something a hell of a lot bigger than merely taking out some poor lineman, or getting you canned. I don't know what yet, but I'm telling you, guys, this is damned interesting."

22

THE AIR FORCE Rapid Response team from Rapid City was already in place by the time Billings County Deputy Sheriff Grafton brought Ashley and Whitney to the Initiative's front gate. A pair of armed Air Policemen in combat gear had supplemented the lone civilian guard, and they refused Grafton entry.

"This is close enough," Ashley told him. "Thanks for the lift."

"Happy to oblige," he said.

Whitney was already out of the car but when Ashley got out, one of the APs, his rifle slung over his shoulder, stepped forward, blocking her way. His name tag read: YSTRIMSKY.

"Sorry, ma'am, but you'll have to leave with the deputy."

"We can either do this the easy way or the hard way," Ashley said.

Grafton just shook his head as he backed away, turned around, and headed down the long gravel road over to Highway 85, which connected with the interstate at Bellfield.

"Ms. Borden is our media rep, you do know that, don't you?"

Whitney asked. "She's been cleared, and in any event this place is no longer a classified site."

"Yes, ma'am, but we're in lockdown, and my orders are to allow only essential scientific and technical personnel through the gate."

"No cooks, no janitors?" Ashley asked. "Going to get a little hungry and messy in there."

"Call Captain Nettles, tell him that we're here," Whitney demanded.

Ystrimsky turned and went back inside the gatehouse. The second AP stood his ground, watching her.

Ashley phoned her father.

"Are you back in Bismarck already?" he asked.

"No, I'm at the Initiative with Dr. Lipton, but Ranger Rick's people won't let me in."

"You don't have any business being there. Especially now."

"Especially now is why I need to be here. If the project is going to come under attack I'm not going to miss it."

"At least go back to Medora, sweetheart," Forester said. "Please. I don't want you to get hurt again."

Ashley chuckled because she knew that she had won. "I got shot in the butt, not even worth a Purple Heart," she said. "I'm a newspaper reporter, Daddy. This is where I belong. Anyway, are you telling me that you expect another attack?"

"I don't know," Forester said after a longish beat. "I'm briefing the president this afternoon on what we know so far. And it's going to be up to him what happens next."

"Well let me know, please. I'll either be here, or walking back to Medora because I lost my ride."

"I'll call Captain Nettles," Forester said. "Try not to irritate the man, he's just doing his job."

"Promise."

Ystrimsky came back. "Sorry, ma'am. Captain Nettles has denied your request. He suggests that you phone someone for a ride."

He swung the gate open to admit Whitney, but she shook her head.

"I'll wait here," she said. "General Forester should be calling any minute, and Ms. Borden can ride up to my office with me."

The AP was clearly vexed. "Ladies, we're just trying to do our jobs here. Keeping you and this facility as safe as possible."

"And we're doing ours," Whitney said.

The civilian guard stepped out. "It's Captain Nettles for you, Pat."

Ystrimsky went back to the guardhouse and a half minute later came out again. "Doc, the captain says that Ms. Borden is your responsibility."

"Always has been," Whitney said. "Just like everyone else in this facility."

EXCEPT FOR the two airmen at the front gate the rest of the Rapid Response team was guarding the perimeter in Hummers, plus two helicopters in the air out a couple of miles doing lazy circles around the project. Nettles and his staff worked from a command post set up in front of Donna Marie.

The Administration and Research and Development Center, housed in a two-story concrete block building, was in the personnel compound two miles from the power station. In addition to the R&D building were a clean room where Whitney had done the bulk of her on-site microbial research, a machine shop, several housing units and a sick bay, a dining hall, and Henry's, which was a bar and restaurant modeled on a restaurant on Manhattan's Upper West Side.

It was spring and after a tough winter a lot of the postdocs and technicians sometimes played softball on the quad, but it was empty when Whitney and Ashley, riding in one of the project's golf carts, pulled up in front of R&D and went inside.

Lieutenant Rudy Doyle, the project's new press officer, came out of his office, a sorrowful look on his long, lean face. He'd played basketball for Northwestern and still looked like a teenager who'd just stepped off the court, all arms and gangly legs.

"Am I ever glad you're back, Doc," he said. "Hi, Ash."

"What's the problem?" Whitney asked.

"I think we've the makings of a mutiny on our hands. Rog just left a couple of minutes ago soon as he got word that we could bring our generator online, but no one in your staff wanted to listen to him. He was trying to calm them down, but as soon as Captain Nettles and his people showed up all hell started to break loose."

"Who can blame them after Christmas?" Whitney said. "I'll talk to them."

"They're in the lab. Do you want me to come with you?"

"No. Just keep Nettles and his people out of here."

"The ball's in your court," Ashley told her. "But if you need me I'll be with Rudy. I think I should bring him up to date."

Whitney nodded and headed down the hall to the main lab and computer center from where the scientific and technical work had been accomplished over the past six and a half years. As soon as the final bits of microbial tweaking were sorted out and their bacteria talker—the gadget—had settled in for the commercial production of methane and the bacterial scrubbers in the chimney which separated the carbon from the CO_2 were fully up to speed, the function of the lab would become mostly a quality control station.

Once everything moved into its final mode, Donna Marie's operation could be controlled by a handful of people. The only real work would be drilling new wells into the coal veins, introducing the bacteria and talkers, and running pipelines back to the power station.

Ashley followed Doyle into his office where he offered her a cup of coffee, but she'd been ready for a picnic in the park with Nate and Whitney; they'd packed sandwiches, fried chicken, a six-pack of beer, and a bottle of pinot grigio. She wasn't ready for coffee.

Doyle perched on the edge of his desk. "All I've been told is that a lineman was electrocuted over by Dickinson, and the team suddenly showed up," he said. "What's next?"

Ashley took off her jacket and sat down. "I don't know for sure, except that something is definitely heading our way again. Nate thinks it's some sort of an opening shot for World War Three, and exactly what that means is anyone's guess. But it's my story and no one's dragging me off it."

"You got past the gate guards, that's something," Doyle said. "Don't keep me in the dark."

Ashley told him everything including the Basin Electric Co-op supervisor's opinion that it was nothing but a stupid accident, caused by some idiot in the Sioux Falls Control Center.

They'd been standing beneath the pylon, the dead lineman's body so gruesomely mutilated that no one wanted to look up at it, but couldn't help themselves.

The image was burned into Ashley's mind, a sight she knew she'd never forget.

"The bastard should be stood against a wall and let the firing squad finish the job. And I think Tony's wife would be the one to give the order to fire."

"But it wasn't an accident," Doyle said.

"No," Ashley told him. She nodded toward the door. "What's going on in the lab?"

"They want to quit. The experiment's done, and anyway none of them think it's worth getting killed for."

Ashley used to think like that, but not anymore. Not after all they'd gone through. Not after Nate putting his life on the line for her and the others. "Maybe it is worth just that," she said. "Maybe it always will be."

23

FORESTER'S CHAUFFEUR-DRIVEN CADILLAC limousine came up East Executive Avenue where it was admitted through the gate, the guard immediately recognizing the general. This entrance to the White House was the least likely to attract any notice from the media, and the president wanted his people to come this way today.

In his fifties, the retired Army two-star was a short, slender man with the erect bearing of a career officer, and always in crisp dress even now that his uniform had been exchanged for sharply tailored suits. But getting out of his car and mounting the steps, he felt more like a man ten years older. He was worried about his daughter, about the project, and how the latest attack was going to affect the extremely volatile relations with Venezuela and with Hugo Chavez who, after we'd struck his air bases just after the first of the year, had promised a total oil blockade against us—which he'd done—and total war, which everyone had taken as nothing more than the rantings of a crazy man.

The president's portly, always charming chief of staff Mark Young was waiting for him when he checked in with the Secret Service agent on duty.

"You're giving the briefing. Did you bring any notes?"

"No need, there's not much yet, but what we do have is worrisome."

"He's not in the best of moods," Young said as they walked down the hall to the Situation Room in the West Wing.

"It's understandable. Has there been anything from Caracas?"

Since we had recalled our ambassador to Venezuela our interests in the country—where a lot of American citizens still lived and worked—had been handled from the Swiss embassy. In situations like this very often responsibility was claimed by some group or another.

"Nothing yet from the Swiss," Young said. "But it might be too soon."

"They've got nothing strategic for us to go after, and Chavez knows that we'd never invade, so if he directed this thing, he could thumb his nose at us and we'd do nothing."

Just before they reached the Situation Room Young stopped. "There's more to this, isn't there?"

"I think so," Forester said. "Are Walt Page and Ed Rogers here?" Page was the director of the CIA and Rogers ran the FBI.

"Yeah, and they'll have something to add."

"Let's hope so," Forester said and they went in and took their places around the long conference table.

In addition to Page and Rogers the others at the meeting included Secretary of State Irving Mortenson, the president's Adviser on National Security Nicholas Fenniger, Secretary of Defense Nicholas Trilling, Secretary of the Department of Energy Wayne Hathaway, Chairman of the Joint Chiefs Air Force General Robert

Blake, and Director of the National Security Agency Air Force Lieutenant General Samuel Voight.

Everyone around the table knew Forester and they understood what kind of news he was probably bringing them. Most of them seemed resigned, and there was very little talk.

Two minutes later President Robert Thompson walked in and everyone got to their feet.

"Good afternoon, Mr. President," Forester said.

Thompson looked more like a small-town banker than the president of the United States, meek, almost a milquetoast. And despite the fact that he was actually decisive, a lot of people had begun calling him Herb—for Herbert Hoover. He didn't like it.

He took his seat, and nodded to Forester. "What do we know so far?"

"Not as much as I'd like, but it does look as if the Initiative has come under attack again, to this point apparently by a lone gunman hired by a person or persons unknown."

"Take us through it from the beginning. All I have are the bits and pieces, and from where I sit what happened out there had only an indirect effect on the project."

"At approximately six fourteen this morning, a power line failure was recorded at the Mid-Continent Power Pool Control Center outside Sioux Falls, South Dakota, and a lineman for the Basin Electric Co-Op was dispatched," Forester began. He went through the rest of the scenario up to the point when Nate Osborne had telephoned him just twenty minutes ago.

"The Bureau has some information about how the line was re-energized," Rogers said, but the president held him off.

"What was the lineman's name?"

"Tony Bartlett," Forester said.

"A married man?"

"Yes, sir. Two young children."

The president was seething. "If this turns out to be another act of terrorism, and not just some hunter or disgruntled rancher shooting out an insulator as I was briefed earlier, then we will do something for his family, just as we do for the families of soldiers falling on the battlefield."

"Yes, sir," Young said.

"There's more?" the president asked.

"Yes," Forester said, "but Ed has something to add."

"That high-voltage line was carrying no power at the time the lineman began his work. But an order to temporarily restore electricity to the line was apparently issued from the console of Stuart Wyman, an area supervisor at the Sioux Falls Control Center, who dispatched the lineman. It's something he's denied, but he was immediately suspended and the investigation was turned over to our Cyber Crimes unit."

This was news to Forester and he said so.

"The situation is extremely fluid, and there simply was no time to keep you in the loop. Sorry, Bob," the FBI director said. "The supervisor went home from where he tried to get into the MAAP's Computer Analysis Center; we got an emergency wire tap order and were in time to get into his ISP account. But by then his passwords had already been blocked. Within less than one minute, Arthur Lundgren, who is one of the chief analysts for MAPP, telephoned him. They went to high school and the University of Minnesota together and apparently have maintained their friendship."

Rogers took a device about the size of an iPhone from his pocket. "Hansen confirmed that the energize order had indeed come from Wyman's console. And then we got this."

"It wasn't me."

"That was Mr. Wyman," Rogers said. "The next voice is Mr. Lundgren's."

"I believe you. Which leaves a damned good hacker somewhere who wants to play games."

"Maybe it's another attack on the Initiative."

"I think that's exactly what's going down."

"What's your take?" Thompson asked.

"My Cyber Crimes people were skeptical at first. Those computer systems are for the most part fairly well protected. But Lundgren called back, and this time the area supervisor's wife was apparently listening in. This is a version edited for brevity and clarity."

". . . the order to re-energize did come from your board, but only after your program had been shut down for about a millisecond. Lets you off the hook."

"A hacker?"

". . . I'd say someone way off shore. . . . and I'm thinking it has the signature of a guy I knew back at MIT. Dutch or German . . . if it's the same guy last I heard he was part of some commune of superhackers who screw with any system then can get their hands on, mostly for the fun of it. . . . sometimes they do it for money."

". . . How do you know?"

"That was Mr. Wyman's wife," Rogers said. "But the next part possibly has the most relevance to our problem. It's Lundgren first, then Wyman."

"Because I used to be just like them."

"Do you know where they are?"

"Amsterdam, last I heard."

"Can you get to them?"

". . . if I'm right, and I usually am, this is something a hell of a lot bigger than merely taking out some poor lineman, or getting you

canned. *I don't know what yet, but I'm telling you guys, this is damned interesting."*

Rogers switched off the device. "Our guess is that Wyman and Lundgren are telling the truth. And if that's the case we believe that someone is taking another run at the Initiative."

The president was grim. "But they hit a transmission control center, which would suggest a computer attack on our grid. The Chinese or Russian virus we've lived with since 'oh-nine, maybe earlier."

"Either that or Lundgren and Wyman are working together," Forester said. "Could be they said what they did because they knew their phones had been tapped."

"It's possible," Rogers said. "We're looking for any out-of-the-ordinary transactions to their bank accounts, or evidence that either of them have offshore accounts somewhere. But it still leaves us with who directed the operation."

"There have been several other minor outages in the past week," Hathaway, the energy secretary, said. "All of them due to unexplained minor computer glitches."

"Any other deaths?" the president asked.

"No, sir. But the other outages involved the Western and Texas Interconnects. This latest was on the Eastern Interconnect. Seems to me that our grid is being systematically probed."

"By whom?"

"Unknown," Hathaway said.

"Ed?" the president asked the FBI's director.

"I wasn't aware that our Cyber Crimes people were involved with the other incidents, but if they're connected it could point to a systematic testing of us."

"Nate Osborne telephoned me while I was on the way over here from my office," Forester said, even more worried than he had been before the meeting began. "He's convinced that this morning's attack was the work of a professional, who in all likelihood monitored not only the local law enforcement radio channels, but the communications with the MAPP Control Center in Sioux Falls."

Everyone in the room knew about Osborne because of his direct involvement stopping the attacks against the Initiative over the holidays. A few of them, including the president, had met him afterward, and they were all aware that he had won the Medal of Honor in Afghanistan. His opinions, even though he was only the sheriff of a very small county, were respected.

"Osborne gave us a fair description of him this morning, and we traced him to a flight from Dickinson to Denver," Rogers said. "But we missed him by ten minutes. And if he is a professional he's long gone by now, and the chances of finding him are nearly zero unless he strikes again."

"It could be him working with the hacker in Amsterdam," Forester said.

"Do you think these people will strike again?" the president asked.

"Osborne is sure of it," Forester said.

"If the attacks—if that's what they were—on the other two Interconnects are related, then I'd say this is just the beginning."

"Of what?"

"Of an all-out energy war," Forester said. "It was my first thought when I heard the news this morning, and Osborne agrees with me."

"Chavez can't be that crazy," the president said.

"He just might be," Walt Page, the DCI, said. "He promised to retaliate for Balboa. But it's possible he might not be working alone. Our people on the ground in Iran believe that Chavez met with Ahmadinejad again two months ago, but this time in secret. Though we don't know what was discussed at their meeting, we think it's possible Chavez was asking for help with his nuclear program."

"In 2010 he was asking Moscow for a pair of twelve-hundred

megawatt nuclear reactors plus a smaller one for research. And he's signed more than a hundred different letters of agreement," the president said. "I've been briefed."

"Yes, sir," Page said. "But Mr. Chavez has also visited North Korea."

24

MAHMOUD AHMADINEJAD'S AGUSTA-BELL 206A Jet Ranger flared over the landing pad and touched down lightly at his extensive personal palace outside the city of Amol just eighty miles northwest of Tehran. It was ten in the evening under a star-studded sky which matched the president of Iran's mood to a T.

Everything was going strictly according to the plans he and his friend Hugo Chavez had been working on since after the first of the year, and he effusively thanked his personal pilot and boarded a golf cart that took him to the main residence not fifty feet from the Caspian seashore. It was all he could do to keep himself from dancing across the rear courtyard, under the arches, and through the double-wide glass doors that one of the ground floor staff opened for him.

"Good evening, Mr. President," the servant said. Unlike Ahmadinejad who almost always wore western business suits but without a tie, the man was dressed in the traditional Persian Pirhan

Shalvar Jameh robes. It was something the president insisted on. It kept him in contact with his people's proud past.

"Has the colonel arrived? I didn't see his helicopter."

"He is in your study, sir. He ordered his helicopter to return to the city."

"Just as well," Ahmadinejad said. His chief of Special Operations, Colonel Pejiman Dabir, was as cautious as he was ruthless and brilliant. A combination of traits that had been useful to the State over the past few difficult years.

"Shall I serve tea?"

"It's not necessary. You may retire for the night."

"Thank you, Mr. President," the servant said and disappeared through a doorway on the left of the great hall.

Ahmadinejad walked back to his book-lined study in the east wing of the palace with French doors opening to a broad veranda that overlooked the sea. The room was large, with a soaring gold inlaid ceiling, several rare Persian rugs on the marble floor, and an ornate desk that had been used by the French king Louis XIV purchased five years ago in New York at a Sotheby's auction. A grouping of two antique couches and chairs and matching tables were backed by a hidden built-in liquor cabinet, the doors of which were open.

Colonel Dabir, a bear of a man who towered over Ahmadinejad, was dressed in civilian clothes. He rose from where he was seated, a brandy snifter in hand. "Good evening, Mr. President. I believe congratulations are in order?"

Ahmadinejad was only slightly peeved that Dabir had helped himself to the cognac, but overlooking such small indiscretions was worth the effort for the work Dabir did for the State but even more importantly for the office of the president.

"This is merely the beginning. I'm sending you to Stockholm this evening as you suggested."

Dabir nodded. "He might not want to return so soon, so he'll in all likelihood ask for considerably more money."

"Pay it," Ahmadinejad said. He poured himself a measure of an XO St. Remy brandy, which he'd always thought was top shelf, drank it down, then poured another and motioned for Dabir to have a seat.

Dabir had phoned earlier in the evening and outlined everything that Makarov had included in his preliminary report, plus what VEVAK's own agents and its Cyber Affairs section had managed to come up with concerning the final probe, this one in North Dakota. President Chavez had warned him just after the first of the year that their biggest enemy on the ground hadn't been the FBI or even the Air Force Special Operations team from Ellsworth. Surprisingly it was a one-legged local law enforcement officer who had served for the U.S. Army in Afghanistan.

"Before we proceed it might be wise to eliminate the man," Dabir had suggested.

"It can't be worth the effort," Ahmadinejad had said, vexed that such a small detail as one man had to be dealt with.

"I'm sorry to disagree, Mr. President, but I spoke with Colonel Delgado shortly after the operation was successfully concluded and it was he who recommended the contract. He warned me not to underestimate the man. And I have complete trust in the opinion of a SEBIN officer."

As well you should, Ahmadinejad had almost said. Iran's increasing isolation from most of the rest of the world had left with it with very few friends. But Chavez, in the same hemisphere as the Satan U.S., had proved to be loyal. On the same hand, however, the Venezuelan president had cancer and might possibly not last the year. It was the main reason that they had agreed to begin the operation so soon. They wanted to bring the U.S. to its knees; teach that smug President Thompson a lesson in humility, something that Americans hadn't felt since the attack they called 9/11.

That had been earlier in the day, but on further reflection, Ahmadinejad had realized that his colonel was correct, and that the only solution would be the elimination of the country sheriff.

"This needs to be taken care of within the next forty-eight hours before the next stage of our operation goes into full swing," he said.

Dabir nodded and sipped his brandy. "As you wish, Mr. President. There may be collateral damage."

Ahmadinejad waved it off. "He is to use whatever force he deems necessary. In fact, if he inflicts enough damage tell him that we will consider a bonus."

Dabir laughed. "He is too precise a man to do anything so sloppy. His only weakness is saving his own skin."

Ahmadinejad had wondered about such men. His own Colonel Dabir, for example, was married to a woman from an important family, and yet he had at least two mistresses on the side; one of them lived in Tehran, but the other lived in Paris. A special presidential investigative team had found this information and had brought it to Ahmadinejad's —Eyes Only. If his wife's family were to find out, the considerable money they showered on their daughter and her husband would stop instantly.

Dabir had a soft underbelly, he was vulnerable. So perhaps was Makarov.

"Find out more about him after he leaves Stockholm," Ahmadinejad said. "Perhaps he has a mistress or two. Information we might be able to use."

If the barely veiled reference to his own situation had any effect, Dabir didn't show it. "I don't think that will be terribly difficult, now that we know where he lives. I'll see to it."

"For the moment, whatever you come up with will not be shared with your SEBIN counterpart."

"I understand, Mr. President."

25

BEER IN HAND Osborne leaned against the railing on the front porch of his ranch house and stared at the sun still high in the west. Sunset this time of the year wasn't until after eight, and in the summer it wouldn't set until past nine thirty. Different place, different times than his ex-wife Caroline's life in Florida.

It was at the odd moments like these, when he felt that something was coming his way, and when he was alone, that he thought about his ex, and he was glad that she and their daughter were out of harm's way. Safe. He didn't have to worry about them.

But Ashley was at the forefront of his mind. Until just a few months ago, before the troubles over the holidays, she'd been nothing more to him than a pushy newspaper reporter from Bismarck. Their paths had crossed only once or twice, but now he cared deeply for her. And even though the prospect worried him, he was sure that he had fallen in love with her. But it had happened so quickly that he hadn't had the time yet to figure out what was supposed to come next.

And now this incident with the deaths along Highway 22. If it wasn't another attack on the Initiative, he didn't know what the hell it was.

He'd talked to Ashley a half hour ago. She was still at the project with Whitney but she'd promised to be back before dinner.

"It'll be just us. Whitney wants to stick around."

"How're things down there?"

"Tense. A lot of her people are kinda freaked out. Understandably so, but she talked them into sticking around until they collect the last batch of data—shouldn't be longer than a week, maybe ten days. And then most of them had planned on leaving anyway."

"Including Whitney?"

"Especially her," Ashley said. "You heard what she said last night and this morning."

Osborne went back inside where he looked up the home number of Army Lieutenant General William Welsh, who as a bird colonel had been his boss in Afghanistan. They had developed a mutual respect for each other on the battlefield, and had even become friends. Welsh had gotten his first star over there, and when he rotated Stateside he'd been promoted and right now his job was lead Army liaison for Air Force General Blake, who was the chairman of the joint chiefs.

Welsh's wife, Susan, answered after a couple of rings. "Hello, Nathan. It's been too long."

"That's the truth. How are you?"

"Fine. But if you want to talk to Bill you need to call his office."

"Something in the works?"

"The usual," she said. "The man doesn't know how to take a day off. Just like you."

"I'm learning."

"Fiddlesticks."

Osborne called Welsh's private number at the Pentagon, and it was answered on the first ring.

"I thought after all your excitement a few months ago you'd be taking a vacation. Or at least weekends off."

"I wish I could, Bill, but something's in the works."

"And incoming rounds have the right of way," Welsh said. "I'm all ears."

Osborne quickly ran through what had happened this morning, including his discussion with General Forester, and the fact that the Air Force Rapid Response team had once again taken over security at the Initiative.

"Not just a local operation? Some pissed off ranchers?"

"I wouldn't have called if I thought so."

"No," Welsh said. "But this guy's reflection in the sheriff's windshield, and the description you got from the TSA people at Dickinson is a little thin."

"He got to Denver and disappeared right under the noses of the airport cops, even though they'd missed him by less than ten minutes."

"They should have sealed the airport."

"I don't think they would have found him even then. This guy's a pro, and I think we might have met him in Afghanistan."

"One of ours?" Welsh shot back.

"I think he might be one of the Russians who came in on STAR-BRIGHT. I don't remember the name, but one of our patrols found a Russian sergeant's body shot to death outside of Achin just south of the Khyber Pass. His captain disappeared and never turned up. We reported him presumed KIA, and about six weeks later the STARBRIGHT group left."

"It was a lousy idea from the get-go. Nobody trusted each other to make it work."

"This captain was Spetsnaz, and he was damned good."

"They all were. But there are a lot of guys who fit your general description; what makes you think it's him?"

"Just a feeling."

"Come on, Nate. Give me something better than that bullshit."

"He fits the same general description. Knows military weapons. Unless I miss my guess he was hired by Venezuelan intel, for a lot of money considering the risk he took. He worked alone but had a support group. Someone to leave the weapons somewhere he could get to them. Someone who provided him the pickup truck with a totally untraceable registration—the VIN simply doesn't exist according to the FBI. The mess we went through over Christmas was a Posse Comitatus op, but the Bureau has picked up no indications that this incident was conducted by them or any other homegrown terrorist group—they would already have taken credit for it."

"Assuming you're right, what's left?"

"The Russian Mafia in New York and Jersey have the connections to put something like this together—the weapons, the truck, and the iPad we found with its memory totally erased. All of which points me back to the missing Spetsnaz captain."

Welsh was silent for several long beats. "Thin," he said.

"I don't have anything else."

"What do you want from me?"

"Access to classified FORECON records. STARBRIGHT. I want to know the name of the captain, and a photograph or two of him. DNA, fingerprints, hometown, relatives back in Russia, friends, fellow officers, Spetsnaz training records."

"You're dreaming."

"Can you help me?" Osborne asked.

Welsh hesitated again. "I might be able to get you a name, but as for the rest it'll be a stretch."

"I need it soon. Like this afternoon. I don't think we have a lot of time."

"I'll do what I can," Welsh said.

26

PRESIDENT AHMADINEJAD SAT on the veranda outside his study slowly sipping a glass of Krug champagne, watching the lights of boat traffic out on the sea, aware and comforted by the presence of his heavily armed bodyguards who watched over him 24/7. It was a little past three thirty in the morning, the evening soft, and he wasn't tired.

In many ways he missed the past he'd had with his wife Azam when their daughter and two sons had been little children. He'd been the unelected governor of Maku and Khoy in West Azerbaijan Province, and life had been simple, even sweet. Now the children were grown up, and in the press of business he didn't see enough of them or his wife.

All the sanctions by the U.N., all the troubles over the nuclear issue, the pressures from the people on the street who wanted to follow in the footsteps of what the infidel West was calling the Arab Spring and even the constant battles with Ali Khamenei,

Iran's Supreme Religious Leader, would become as nothing once Operation RIGHTFUL JUSTICE came to final fruition.

The day of Iran's ascendance would be long remembered when the true meaning of the nation's symbol was fully understood by the West; the four crescents meant nothing less than Allah, fitting for the assured rise of the old Persian empire to its rightful place of leadership.

He finished his champagne and got to his feet. "I am going inside now," he said.

"Yes, Mr. President," an unseen guard said from the darkness to his right.

Closing the door he went to his desk and powered up his computer. A minute later he got to his heavily encrypted Skype page and the call to Caracas, where it was around eight in the evening, went through.

President Hugo Chavez's image appeared, and although he was smiling, he seemed tired, his features pale and a little gaunt. It was the cancer of course, and although they'd never discussed who of his seven vice presidents would succeed him after death, Ahmadinejad had the most respect for Diosdado Cabello.

"Good evening, my old friend," Chavez said. "You called to report success with the latest probe."

"Yes, but I'm sure that your people have already brought you the details. I'm calling because we have a problem that I'll have addressed within the next forty-eight hours."

"The sheriff."

"Yes, he will be dealt with by our asset from Stockholm."

Chavez laughed, and stifled a cough. "Amazing, isn't it, that one man could create such problems for the combined assets of two sovereign nations. What do you have planned?"

Ahmadinejad told him.

"Then we begin the second stage of our little adventure; blackmail. It's something even the average gringo should understand very well. Threatening to hit them at the gas pumps wasn't enough, and our probes only showed the possibilities to their leadership, but now they will, as an entire country, experience a terror far worse than nine-eleven. That was an event witnessed by most only on television. This time no home or factory or shopping mall will escape. Every man, woman, and child will feel the effects—personally."

"Yes," Ahmadinejad said. "And this is only the beginning."

"*Sí*," Chavez said, stifling another cough.

Frailties. The thought crossed Ahmadinejad's mind. When he was a child he'd had a bout of pneumonia. He only had vague memories of the illness that his mother later told him had nearly been fatal. "Allah was with you, my son," she'd said.

"How are you feeling?"

Chavez shrugged. "I have my days."

"It's good that we are proceeding now."

Chavez raised a snifter of what looked like brandy or rum. "A very good thing," he said.

27

IN MEDORA IT was five in the evening when Osborne's telephone rang at the same moment Ashley walked in, her eyes bright as they always were when she saw him, her lips parted in a smile.

"Hi," she said.

He pecked her on the cheek, glad she was back here with him, and went to answer the phone on the third ring. It was Bill Welsh.

"If it's your guy, his name is Yuri Makarov, a nephew or something of Nikolai Makarov who designed the pistol. Important family. He fits the same general description and he was listed as KIA in Afghanistan about that same time."

"He came from an important family, there had to be photographs," Osborne said and he couldn't keep the excitement out of his voice. He was going to nail the bastard, if for nothing else than Kas's murder.

"Almost nothing shows up in any of the official databases I can access. Be my guess, if he is the pro you think he is, he went back and deleted as much of his past as he could. Probably long before he showed up in Afghanistan."

"Come on, there must be something," Osborne said. "At least one goddamned snapshot."

He'd taken the call in his small study. Ashley had pulled off her jacket and stood at the doorway watching him.

"That's exactly what I came up with. *All* I came up with. Is your computer online?"

"Yes."

"I'm sending it as an attachment now. Turns out one of your people took several photographs of our gun positions at Camp Foremost up near Khas."

"That's where I got my new leg."

"The shots were sent back to field ops and ended up in the record. In one of them three men were in the background, and probably didn't know they'd been caught on camera. And you're going to be surprised, buddy, believe me."

Osborne opened the e-mail, and then the JPEG attachment. The image on the screen was marked SECRET, the squad automatic weapons positions clearly labeled. Someone had identified the three men: FORECON Lieutenant Tommy Bronski, Russian Captain Yuri Makarov, and FORECON Lieutenant Nate Osborne.

It was his man, Osborne was sure of it. "I knew the bastard," he said.

"All you have is the reflection in the windshield and the description from the Dickinson airport TSA agent. And Makarov was listed as KIA not too long after this picture was taken."

"I want more. Anything you can get me. Because I know goddamned well this is my man. And it'd be my guess he's not done."

"I'll see what I can do," Welsh said. "But I can't promise you anything. Just watch your back."

"Will do."

Ashley came and stood over Osborne's shoulder. "That's you on the end," she said. "Afghanistan?"

"Yeah," Osborne said absently. He was staring into Makarov's eyes. He remembered the man, but only vaguely as an officer who apparently had no friends, not even his sergeant. A loner, aloof, sometimes almost disdainful as if he knew a secret he wasn't willing to share.

"The fucking Russians got their asses scragged and left with their tails between their legs, and now they're back telling us how to get it right," one of Osborne's troops had observed.

And it was true. But if the man in the photograph was the same one who'd engineered the death of the lineman and shot Kas and the couple to death, there'd be more to come. Makarov may have been disdainful and aloof, but he'd never given the impression of being a quitter.

PART TWO

BLACKMAIL

Eighteen Hours Later

28

JOGEL WIDMER, SPECIAL counsel to the Swiss ambassador, presented himself to the White House west gate at precisely one o'clock, where his credentials were checked before his limousine was passed through.

He was met at the west entrance by a marine sentry and by Albert Zimmerman, who identified himself as an aide to the president's chief of staff Mark Young.

"Good afternoon, sir," Zimmerman said. "May we check your attaché case?"

"Of course," Widmer said. He opened it on the table to reveal only an unaddressed plain white number ten envelope. "I was instructed to deliver this to President Thompson but I was not told of its contents."

"Unfortunately the president is away this afternoon, but Mr. Young will see you."

It was a lie, of course. Diplomatic deliveries, by protocol, should have been made at the State Department, and not directly to the president. That the president's chief of staff had agreed to meet with him was a mark of the favor the Swiss had with the U.S.

"Would you care to leave your attaché case here?"

"As you wish," the Swiss special counsel said. He took the envelope and followed Zimmerman down the corridor to the West Wing's first-floor reception area immediately next to Young's corner office.

Widmer had never been to the White House before, and he'd been told to keep his eyes and ears open, but to be discreet about it. He was to ask no questions, and only answer those he thought would not compromise his position. If he thought that was the case he was to say he could not respond without further instruction from the ambassador. He suspected that he was somehow bringing bad news, though he had no earthly idea what it might be.

"Consider this a diplomatic training mission, and you won't go far wrong," Ambassador Dreher had told him.

Young was seated at his desk. He looked up but did not rise. His expression was one of friendly neutrality.

"Good afternoon, Mr. Young," Widmer said.

After Zimmerman withdrew, closing the door, Young motioned for Widmer to have a seat.

"We were told that you had a letter for the president, sender and contents unknown," Young said. "Unfortunately the president is not available at the moment, but I personally informed him that someone would be delivering it. The president is as curious as I am."

Widmer couldn't think of a thing to say in response, so he merely handed the envelope across the desk and started to rise, but Young motioned him back.

"Please, give me a moment."

"I was told that the contents were for the president's eyes only."

"Yes," Young said, but he opened the envelope and took out the single sheet of paper. He read the message once, looked up, then read it again, slower this time.

Widmer thought that what he was witnessing was nothing short of extraordinary. In his training, diplomats did not act in this fashion. A for-your-eyes-only message was supposed to mean just that. But if the news was bad it was not reflected on Young's face.

At length Young folded the letter and laid it on his desk. He didn't speak for several beats, and his expression of friendly neutrality did not change, though Widmer was pretty sure that whatever was contained in the letter was not good news.

"I will see that the president is given this at the soonest possible moment," Young said. "Good day, sir. My compliments to Ambassador Dreher."

In four minutes Widmer was back in his limo passing through the west gate with absolutely no idea what he had just learned, if anything. Except that he felt slightly disturbed, as if he had handled something dirty.

YOUNG RE-READ the very short letter for a third time. They'd thought it was possible that something would be sent to them through the U.S. interests section in the Caracas Swiss embassy concerning the latest attack in North Dakota. But that it was under President Chavez's own signature was nothing short of extraordinary.

Pocketing the letter he walked down the corridor to the Oval Office, where Thompson, seated behind his desk, was talking with Jim Winston, his special assistant and aide, and Bob Towers, his press secretary.

"Pardon the interruption, Mr. President, but I wonder if you have a couple of minutes to spare?" Young said.

Thompson looked up, started to say something, but then nodded. "Hold my calls," he said.

Winston and Towers left, closing the door behind them.

Young handed the letter to Thompson and sat down. "This was just delivered from the Swiss embassy."

"Who's it from?"

"I think you'd better read it."

The president did, and when he looked up his expression was a mixture of anger and mirth. "The man has balls, you have to give him that much."

"It's a blackmail demand, that much is clear, but there's a lot more between the lines than demanding a public apology on the floor of the U.N. General Assembly for Balboa, and reparations, and demanding that you appear before the international court at The Hague. What's left out is the *or else.*"

"Also what's not mentioned is the latest incident in North Dakota."

"It's no coincidence," Young said.

"Of course not," Thompson said, glancing at the letter. "Assuming the Bureau's Cyber Crimes unit is correct and the system was hacked from someone or some group in Amsterdam, we have to face the possibility that they're working either with the Russians or the Chinese. A lot worse could happen to us."

"Yes, sir. But I can't believe it would be someone close to either Putin or Xi. Especially not the Chinese because of our trade and the U.S. debt they hold. An all out cyber attack on our grid would bankrupt us, something they simply cannot afford to let happen."

"Even bankrupt we still would have nuclear weapons and the means to deliver them," the president said.

Young lost his breath for just a beat.

"An all-out attack on our grid would be tantamount to a declaration of war. I placed my hand on the Bible twice and promised to preserve, protect, and defend the Constitution of the United States, and that's exactly what I intend on doing no matter the cost."

Thompson was fierce, and Young had read about these horrifying presidential moments in the history books, but had never believed he would be an actual witness to one.

"First we need to know where to place the blame, because Chavez could never do this on his own. No one in Venezuela has the technical expertise."

Thompson raised the letter. "The son of a bitch acts as if he does."

"He has to have help."

"Ahmadinejad."

"The Iranians don't have the technical expertise to create the virus, either," Young said.

"Then he had help, from the Russians."

"Possibly, but not from the government."

"The hacker in Amsterdam."

"The CIA has people on the ground over there trying to find him," Young said. "He's a problem, but very likely not our only problem. We have about two hundred thousand miles of high-power transmission lines crisscrossing the country. Impossible to guard them all, as we found out from the North Dakota incident. But worse than that are the big transformers which manage the system. When electricity is generated its voltage is stepped up into the tens and even hundreds of thousands of volts for transmission over long distances. More efficient that way, less heat and less loss. At the user end another set of very large, very expensive transformers step down the voltage to levels that can be used in factories, malls, and houses. The problem is that those transformers are not manufactured in the U.S. And the waiting list can be up to three or four years."

"Are these devices at least guarded better than the transmission lines?"

"For the most part, no. If a dozen or more were to be destroyed it would put us practically in the Stone Age."

"And you're saying that there is little or nothing we can do about it?" the president demanded angrily. He held the letter up. "This son of a bitch gets away with it?"

"No, sir. We'll find the computer hacker in Amsterdam, and it's very possible that the man responsible for the North Dakota attack, who has been identified as a former Spetsnaz officer, will be back for the second round, and we'll be waiting for him."

"That's what you're recommending?"

"For now, yes, Mr. President. Anything else, such as mobilizing the National Guard to physically patrol the transmission lines, or at least as many miles of them as humanly possible, and to mount guards on all the transformer yards would send Chavez a very clear message that we're taking him seriously."

"We are."

"But we cannot let him know that," Young said. "If we can capture either the hacker or the Russian shooter, we can find out who directed the attacks and why."

"Not Russia or China."

"It would not be in their best interest, sir."

"Leaves us with Venezuela and Iran as the best possibilities."

"Yes, sir."

"Have Walt Page come over. It's time for a full court press," President Thompson said.

Chavez had given them forty-eight hours, but Young didn't think it was enough time for what the president wanted to do—send more spies into Venezuela and Iran to gather the proof of their complicity.

29

THE FIRST HINTS of spring had finally come to Stockholm, and as Makarov stepped out of the three-story white brick building that housed his business, Trade Group International, TGI, a couple of minutes past noon, he took a deep breath of the sea-ladened air and felt truly at peace for the first time in months.

The assignment had been as complicated as he'd thought it might be, mostly because of happenstance: the storage unit manager in Minneapolis trying to shake him down, the county sheriff showing up, and the young couple stumbling into the scene. But the job was done, he'd gotten away free, and he'd been paid the balance Colonel Delgado had promised.

He headed along Regeringsgatan, just around the corner from the Royal Opera House, traffic busy, but without horns. The Swedes were, for the most part, a polite people, unlike Russians. And whenever he was at home he automatically took on their behavior. He smiled pleasantly and his pace became much slower than in Paris or Berlin or London.

But his attention to detail never changed; he noticed things, like the man in the dark trousers and tan car coat, no hat, who'd been studying something in a shop window across the street from his office, and who'd suddenly turned and walked away.

Probably nothing, Makarov told himself, but he was bothered. That someone should be here looking down his track so soon after an operation was in itself disturbing. But the why of it and the who made for some interesting speculation.

He'd planned on stopping by a small jewelry shop he'd used regularly to pick up the simple gold chain and diamond pendant he'd ordered for Ilke before he'd left for the U.S. It was something he'd been doing for a number of years now; coming home after a business trip, he brought her a small trinket, something to make up for his absence.

Afterward he'd planned on meeting her for lunch at the Operäkallaren, which was one of Stockholm's upscale restaurants located in the opera house building. It was her favorite in part because of its superb food and elegant surroundings, but also because it had become a tradition for them on his homecomings. He'd insisted in the beginning that he would pick up the regular routines of his life immediately after each assignment. No week or ten days' vacation to recover—no matter how difficult the task had been— but to the office first thing in the morning, to Petersen's for Ilke's gift on his lunch break, and then the Operäkallaren.

He turned and headed in the same direction as the tan car coat, though the man had disappeared in the group of people waiting to cross at the corner. When the light changed the man was there fifty meters ahead, crossing the street, and Makarov hesitated for just a second. Nothing else indicated that someone had tracked him to Stockholm, other than the fact that the tan car coat had been waiting across the street.

Coincidence? Makarov didn't believe in coincidences.

He made it to the corner just as the light turned against him, and he crossed with the green to the other side of Regeringsgatan, then across the avenue so that he was behind the man but on the opposite side of the street.

Within a few minutes he had reached a point where he had caught up with the tan car coat, and for half a block matched speeds, keeping a meter or so back. The man was tall, two meters, maybe a little less, and built like a wrestler, with broad shoulders and a thick neck, yet his walk was light, on the balls of his feet, ready for the starter's gun, for anything.

At the next corner the man turned and glanced across the street but then crossed with the light.

Makarov could think of no reason to suspect that anyone had traced him to Stockholm. All of his meetings had been arranged for elsewhere, usually Paris or London. His payment accounts were blind, as well as were his e-mail addresses. Nothing physically connected him here. And yet the son of a bitch had shown up in front of a shop window across the street from TGI's offices.

It was worth finding out who he was and what he wanted.

Picking up the pace, Makarov reached the next corner, the tan car coat twenty meters or so back, paid for a transportation ticket at the newsstand, and boarded a bus that had just pulled up. He didn't bother looking back as he took his seat.

For a long time, since he'd set up his business here and his home with Ilke, he'd contemplated a day such as this one, and what it might ultimately mean for his continued survival. If the tan car coat was someone who'd traced him here, he was almost certainly not from any law enforcement agency. Certainly not Interpol nor the CIA, who would have sent teams—several people on foot, more in cars or taxis. But he'd detected none of that, only the lone man in the tan coat.

His first guess would have been SEBIN, but the man didn't have the look of a Venezuelan. Beyond that he could only guess it was someone from his Spetsnaz past, except that the timing so soon after an assignment wasn't right.

Eight stops later he got off in front of the imposing National Library building in the Humlegarden, and took one of the walkways to what was the Swedish equivalent of the U.S. Library of Congress, as he phoned Ilke.

"I hope I caught you before you left the apartment," he said. A taxi had pulled up behind the bus, but he hadn't bothered looking to see if the tan car coat had gotten out.

"Just at the door now," she said brightly. The lunches were her tradition, too, and she never tired of the little presents he brought her.

"I might be a little late."

"Business?" she asked, her disappointment evident.

"An old, seriously fat man, who wants to make a very large investment."

Ilke laughed, her voice musical. "I always knew that I could be replaced. But by a fat man?"

Makarov laughed despite himself. "I'll call when I'm finished. Maybe we'll have dinner instead."

Their Swedish was passable, but they'd always spoken to each other in English, because Danish was difficult for him and she thought Russian was ugly.

"Erick's?" she asked. It was a first-class restaurant aboard a barge moored in the harbor. The cuisine was French and except in the summer when there were too many tourists it was another of their favorite spots.

"If I'm not home by then I'll meet you at seven."

"Take care," she said.

Pocketing his phone, Makarov continued up to the library, and inside bypassed the circular information desk and ambled to the

new annex, which held the microfilm reading room where all of
Sweden's newspapers plus those from a great many other countries could be viewed. Several dozen reading stations were stacked
in rows, some of them in alcoves near windows. Only a few were
occupied this morning.

He went to the rear of the large room and sat down at one of the
readers next to the exit. A minute later the tall man in the tan car
coat sat down at the reading station next to his.

Makarov looked at him. "I'm not armed, but believe me, I will
kill you here and now unless you tell me who you are, how you
found me, and what you want," he said, not raising his voice.

"My name is Pejiman Dabir. I am a colonel in VEVAK, and
President Ahmadinejad personally sent me to speak to you about
a matter of some concern to us and to our friends in SEBIN. As to
how I found out where you work, we've known about it since before you were hired."

"How did you come by that information?"

"We're very good at what we do."

"Not that good," Makarov said.

"A mutual friend, in Amsterdam, traced you through your OMX
trades, and from there to your offices on Regeringsgatan."

Makarov tried to think what mistakes he could have made, but
he could see none. "How?"

"You left a pattern, Mr. Makarov. Each time that you made a
profit from one of your secret arms trade deals the money always
showed up within ten days as an investment on the OMX."

He had guarded against just that, always assuming that the actual dollar or euro amounts from his arms deals were well enough
hidden that investing them in obscure stocks would be next to
impossible to detect. He'd been wrong. And now Stockholm as a
safe haven was ruined for him.

"Leave while you still can," he said, and he got up.

"We have another job for you in North Dakota."

"If you try to follow me I will kill you."

"The money will be enough for you to leave Stockholm and go to ground."

"No."

"Your wife's name is Ilke Sorensen, and if something untoward should happen to me, she would never reach Erick's."

Makarov was rocked. He wanted to kill the bastard this instant. He wanted to convince himself that having a wife and living an apparently normal life was just cover. Ilke was expendable. It was one of the reasons they'd decided not to have children.

"We want you to assassinate a man, nothing more than that."

Makarov's heart was aching. He promised that he would never get close to anyone, but Ilke's life hung in the balance now because he'd not been able to keep his word to himself. But he would kill Dabir, just as he would kill Colonel Delgado, before he and Ilke retired.

He sat down.

"His name is Nathan Osborne."

"Who is he?"

Dabir took a manila envelope out of his coat pocket and handed it across. "He's a county sheriff who's become far too involved in our business."

Makarov took out a brief bio, and after the first paragraph which described the man's war experience in Afghanistan, he suddenly knew who the bastard was and he looked up. "Why this one?"

30

"WHAT IS IT, Nate?" Ashley called from the open bedroom door.

Osborne, dressed only in sweatpants, stood at the living room window looking out toward the horse barn and beyond it to the north pasture, all of it bathed in silver moonlight. It was four in the morning and, unable to sleep, he'd gotten up, trying not to disturb her. "Just thinking."

"About the Russian?"

"Everyone believes I'm crazy."

Ashley came to him. She wore one of his old tee shirts. "I don't," she said.

"You're prejudiced."

"Yup."

She had made them planked trout from summer-caught fish in the freezer along with a big salad, and afterward they had listened to some Brazilian guitar music as they made love in front of the fireplace.

Having her with him was a good thing; it felt natural, as if she'd been in his life for a long time. For her part she continued to file stories for the *Bismarck Tribune*, going out on assignments during the day while he was busy at work, unless she was covering the most recent trouble involving the Initiative, in which case she was by his side. Like this moment.

"The Bureau doesn't want to believe that he could get back here," she said. "Nobody does. It'd mean that the TSA was doing a lousy job, and we're just as vulnerable as we were before nine-eleven."

"If he left the country. Could be he's still in Denver, waiting."

"For what?"

"That's the million dollar question."

Ashley put a hand on his cheek and turned his head to her. "Talk to me, Nate, 'cause you're starting to get spooky. Makarov is coming back—or he never left—but coming back to where? Here?"

Osborne had done nothing but think about what a professional contractor like Makarov would do next. The Bureau and airport cops had just missed him at the Denver airport. He would have been perfectly aware of the hubbub, which would have told him that someone in Dickinson was on his tail. It would be unacceptable to him, thinking that he'd left a loose end.

Double back the moment you realize that you are being followed. Take care of the situation before it takes care of you. Leave yourself options, none of which should include incoming rounds from your one-eighty.

"That's what I'd do," Osborne said. "Especially if he figures someone is coming after him, or is at least sniffing down his trail."

"If he does come back, it'll be because of you," she said. "You think you knew him from Afghanistan. Will he remember you?"

"If someone tells him my name, he will."

"You're going to use yourself as bait."

"Something like that," Osborne said.

Ashley shivered. "Christ, when will it ever end?"

"For now I'm just working on what's next," Osborne said.

BOB FORESTER was an early riser but he was surprised when he got the call from Nate Osborne a few minutes after six just as he was pouring his first cup of coffee, the *Washington Post, New York Times, Wall Street Journal,* and the latest edition of *Jane's Defense Weekly* stacked neatly on the kitchen counter.

"Good morning."

"Sorry for calling so early, General, but I need to ask you something," Osborne said.

"Okay, what're you thinking?"

"Assuming that the murder of the lineman was more than just an isolated incident, what have you heard?"

"You mean who's behind it?"

"That and why."

"So far as we can determine, it was not an isolated incident. Our national electrical grid has come under a series of probes over the past month, and that's classified information."

"The Venezuelans again?"

"With help, we think from Iranian intel, who may have gotten a copy of the virus from a Russian contact and passed it along to a hacker or hackers—unknown—who may or may not be living in Amsterdam."

"Do we have any proof?"

"Not directly, except for the latest development," Forester said. "And I'm serious, Nate, what I'm about to share with you, will stay with you. Not so much as a hint to my daughter."

"I'm listening."

"I want your word."

"You have it for the moment," Osborne said.

Forester heard the brief hesitation. "The president got an ultimatum from Chavez, through the Swiss embassy yesterday afternoon. I wasn't briefed until last night. They want the president to apologize on the floor of the General Assembly for Balboa and then appear before the International Court in The Hague for a reparations trial. Gave us forty-eight hours."

"Or else what?"

"Didn't say."

"The attack on the grid was just the start."

"It would appear so," Forester said. "Just as it would appear that there isn't much we can do about it."

"I might be able to help," Osborne said. "I know who the shooter out here was. He's a Russian, former Spetsnaz captain who I met in Afghanistan."

Forester was startled. No matter how high an opinion he and a lot of other people in Washington had of Osborne, he was beginning to realize how much they'd underestimated the man. "Does he have a name?"

"Yuri Makarov."

"You need to get out here this morning to brief the Bureau and the CIA. I'll send a plane for you."

"Sorry, but no, General. I have to do this on my own. He has to suspect that somebody knows who he is, otherwise we wouldn't have tried to catch him when he showed up at the Denver airport. I know his name, and I'm hoping that if he does his homework he'll know mine and realize that I could be his Achilles' heel."

Forester understood where Osborne was coming from but he asked anyway. "Why put yourself on the line for something that's Washington's problem?"

"Because this is my little part of the world, and Kas was a friend."

"Keep my daughter out of it as much as possible."

"Sorry, General, but I need her help."

Something cold clutched at Forester's heart. "Take care of her."

"You can count on it."

31

RACHEL PACKWOOD, THE stern-faced radio dispatcher for the Billings County Sheriff's department was already seated behind her desk when Osborne and Ashley walked in. It was Sunday and the office was closed on weekends over the winter. There wasn't enough money in the tiny county's budget, but like a lot of older widowed women, Rachel didn't mind doing extra duty for little or no pay, because she was a snoop.

"Getting a little busy around here, wouldn't you say?" she asked.

"It's heating up," Osborne said. "You don't mind pulling a few extra hours?"

"You couldn't keep me away," Rachel said. She and Ashley exchanged a hug. "Do you need David or anyone else?" David Grafton was one of the three deputies.

"Not yet. First I want you to reach Deb Rausch over in Minneapolis. She's probably at home."

Osborne had transferred the photograph he'd gotten from General Welsh to Ashley's laptop and she set up at one of the deputy's desks and got online with an advanced Photoshop program at her newspaper.

"My dad told you to keep me out of it, didn't he?" she said over her shoulder as she brought up the Afghanistan photo.

"Something like that but I told him I needed your help, and he just told me to take care of you."

She looked up and grinned. "Thank God for all the men in my life who're willing to take care of poor little ole me."

"He's your father."

"It's Ms. Rausch," Rachel said.

Osborne went into his office and picked up the phone as he was sitting down. "Sorry to bother you at home on a Sunday."

"Good morning, Nate. Actually I'm at the office. Got a call about your contractor and we're trying to find out if we have him in our database somewhere."

"Anything?"

"Not yet, but I was just about to call you. I was told that you might have a photograph of this guy."

"Name's Yuri Makarov," Osborne said, and he explained about the Spetsnaz presence in Afghanistan and about the snapshot in which his image in the background had been inadvertently captured. "He probably didn't know his picture was being taken."

"Send it to me, and I'll have my people enhance it."

"We're already working on it and soon as it's ready I'll e-mail it to your office."

The Minneapolis Bureau SAC objected. "This is a federal matter."

"You're right. The problem is I'm in that picture with him, and I'm going to need your help finding him."

"Like I said, it's the Bureau's job."

"I don't want to argue with you. But if you guys start a full-court press, he'll go to ground so deeply you'll never dig him out."

"I don't know, we're pretty good. Even Osama bin Laden couldn't hide forever."

"This guy is better, because until now he's apparently been on no one's radar. His name doesn't show up anywhere except on one Marine FORECON mission report, and the only photograph we've managed to come up with so far is the one from Afghanistan. I have a friend in Washington who's doing some checking for me."

"Yeah, General Welsh."

Osborne was sorry that Bill's name had surfaced, but it was too late now to change anything. "He's come up with nothing from Russian records. We know Makarov was Spetsnaz, but his service file was apparently erased some time ago."

"Okay, so if this guy is as good as you think he is how do you plan on finding him?"

"He's going to find me, and you're going to help him do it."

Deb Rausch was silent for a beat. "Silly me, but I thought you might say something like that."

"Can I count on your help?"

"I really do like you, Nate. I think that you're a hell of a good cop, so far as it goes."

"Western North Dakota."

"Something like that. No offense."

"None taken."

"Doesn't matter, I've been ordered to do what I can for you," Rausch said. "So where do we start?"

"Makarov comes out here—I'm guessing from somewhere in Europe—downs the power line, waits until the lineman shows up, and somehow manages to get the electricity turned back on. He had the means to at least listen to the power company's dispatch frequencies and access to a program or a hacker who could control that section of the grid."

"I understand all of that, but why did he take the risk to come back to the scene?"

"If the line had still been energized when the repairman showed up he would have used the special equipment that he carried on his truck that would have allowed him to work on it hot. Makarov had to make sure that the electricity wasn't turned back on until the poor man was in direct physical contact."

"It wasn't just about the power outage," Rausch said. "The bastard was making a statement."

"Kas and the couple in the pickup truck were nothing more than happenstance."

"He was ready for them. So again, Nate, what's next?"

"He went to Denver where he disappeared. West. Means it's likely he came here from the east. My guess would be that he landed in Minneapolis, where a rental car was waiting for him, and where his equipment had been stashed somewhere nearby."

"Wait a minute," Deb Rausch stopped him. "We're sure he flew to Denver where he disappeared. But why does that make you think he started here?"

"It's the way I'd do it."

"Come on, Nate. If you want me to help out, at least give me the courtesy of letting me know what's on your mind."

"I wouldn't take the same path out as I took in. Could have left bread crumbs. Witnesses. Maybe he ran into someone who got in his way. Maybe he got a traffic ticket. Maybe he hired a whore for the night somewhere between Minneapolis and here. Be my guess he headed west on ninety-four where he probably stayed the night at a motel. If I was doing it, my support team would have picked up whatever rental car I'd gotten in Minneapolis and switched it for the pickup truck we found in the mall in Dickinson."

"Did you find out who it was registered to?"

"No such VIN. Whoever was backstopping him were pros."

"Any idea who—assuming you're guessing right?"

"Russian Mafia, probably out of New York someplace."

"Brighton Beach. Might as well be on the dark side of the moon. Our people are having a hard time penetrating the organization. But most of those guys grew up with the KGB. Hell, a lot of them are ex-KGB officers."

Osborne had much the same thought. "I'll ask him when we meet."

"The last attack on the Initiative—assuming that this latest was another attack on the project—was backed by Venezuelan intelligence."

"Who backed the Posse Comitatus. This time it was a lone contractor."

"But why, can you explain it to me? He caused a power outage, killed four people, and walked away. The effect on the Initiative was nothing."

"It's something else I'm going to ask him," Osborne said. He wanted to tell her about the ultimatum the Chavez government had delivered to the president, but even if he hadn't been sworn to secrecy he didn't think it would help her understand the situation any better than he did.

"Soon as I get the photograph I'll get my people canvassing every motel, gas station, and restaurant between Dickinson and Minneapolis. But unless we get real lucky it's going to take some time."

Osborne had thought about that problem as well. "Let's say Makarov flew from Europe to New York or Washington. Check the times of arrivals to Minneapolis from those cities, and work the clock west. He showed up in Dickinson no later than an hour before dawn. He had to stop to get his gear—I think it would have been too risky to stash a weapon like a sniper rifle in the trunk of a rental car."

"If you're suggesting that we check every rental storage business in the area you're talking weeks not days."

"Let's say somewhere near the airport."

"Dozens of places—probably a lot more."

"It'll only matter if he ran into some sort of trouble. Someone saw his face and he had to do something about it. Find out if any storage rental places have reported trouble—any kind of trouble— during the last two days. Anything out of the ordinary."

"I understand where you're coming from. But what good will it do us even if we find out how he got his weapons and how he got to Dickinson? He's gone."

"Mention my name to everyone your people talk to," Osborne said.

"What?"

"He's looking over his shoulder, and he's looking real hard. If my name is mentioned often down his back trail, the word will get back to him."

"And he'll come after you?"

"I hope so," Osborne said.

"I have the photograph ready," Ashley called from the squad room.

"Send it to the FBI in Minneapolis," Osborne told her.

"That who I think it is?" Rausch asked.

"Yes," Osborne said. "We're going to start in Dickinson and head east this morning. If you come up with something let me know."

"You're nuts, do you know that? Both of you."

32

IT WAS NEARLY eight by the time Osborne and Ashley showed up at the Tiger Discount truck stop on the Dickinson Business Loop just off the interstate, and the place was busy mostly with truckers and ranchers. They showed the photograph to the manager who shook his head, but he called a couple of the waitresses over.

"You two were on duty yesterday morning," he told the women. "Either of you see this guy?"

One of them shook her head but the other one, Debbie, studied it for a long moment, before she nodded. "I think I served him. Bad picture, different hair, but I think it's him. Same eyes." She nodded toward one of the window booths. "Spent his time watching *Good Morning America* on his iPad."

"Say anything to you?" Osborne asked. He was wearing his uniform.

"This about the shooting yesterday?"

"He might have been involved. Did you talk to him?"

"Not much. He just ordered ham and eggs, whole wheat toast

and tea, which is a little odd for around here. The tea, I mean. But I could tell that he was foreign.".

"Foreign?"

"I pegged him for a Brit. Nice accent, good manners."

"Anything else?" Osborne asked.

Debbie shook her head, but then brightened a little. "Something on *GMA* got to him, 'cause I was bringing him another pot of hot water and a tea bag, when he looked up and told me that he wanted his bill."

"Did you hear what the announcer was saying?"

"No. He was listening on an earbud."

"Thanks," Osborne said.

OUTSIDE THEY climbed into Osborne's Saturn SUV. "It's how he monitored Basin Power's control center, and probably the Stark County Sheriff's dispatch frequency," he told Ashley.

"So he waits here until he finds out that the lineman is on site, and boogies out. But you pretty well know something like that had to have happened. He had to have holed up somewhere. What's next?"

"We head east. He probably stayed the night somewhere between here and Bismarck."

"That's a hundred miles. Lots of motels between here and there."

"I'm guessing Bismarck or Mandan, he would have figured that it was less likely someone might remember him in the busier places."

They got out on the interstate and Osborne had just passed an old pickup truck doing fifty in the left lane, when Deb Rausch called his cell phone.

"Where are you?" she asked.

"Just left Dickinson on ninety-four," Osborne said. He switched the phone to speaker so Ashley could hear. "Do you have something for me already?"

"He came in on a Delta flight from LaGuardia at eleven-oh-five Friday morning under the name Thomas Parks, British passport. He picked up a Chevy Impala from Hertz under the Parks name using a platinum American Express card."

"Someone recognize the photo?"

"No need, because we're pretty sure it's him. In the first place the British passport was a fake—no such number exists. And second of all the Amex card was listed to a fictitious business in the Channel Islands, which so far as we've been able to tell this morning is nothing but an accommodations address."

"Someone had to pay the bills."

"Never been used before," Rausch said. "But it gets better. The Chevy was rented for Parks from a New York branch of the business—North Sea Petroleum—which does not exist. And Friday afternoon the owner/manager of a self-storage facility about seven miles away from the airport was found beaten to death in a locked bay that had been rented three days earlier by North Sea Petroleum under the Parks name."

It wasn't adding up in Osborne's mind. "Sounds too sloppy for Makarov. From what I remember in Afghanistan he had the reputation of being precise. And everything he did in Dickinson and afterwards was neat. No loose ends."

"So maybe the Russian Mafia he used as his support group was sloppy," Rausch said. "But I'd just about bet the farm that Parks is your man. You said he was not very big, slightly built, maybe under six feet."

"I towered over him, and most of the other Spetsnaz guys."

"Well the owner/manager—a guy by the name of Donald Toivo— was a former professional wrestler, six-eleven, three-hundred-plus pounds. One of his employees who found the body said Toivo was

just as quick on his feet as he was mean. And the Hertz agent remembered him because of his cute British accent. But you said he
was Russian."

"Russians learn British English," Osborne said. "Where's Toivo's body now?"

"Minneapolis City Hospital morgue until somebody claims it."

"How about the storage bay?"

"Our people are on the way over to dust it for prints. But the city
cops were all over the place. Lead detective said that except for the
body it was empty."

"Have your people hold off for a bit," Osborne said. "And don't
let anyone claim Toivo's body until we get there. I'm going to turn
around and go back to the Dickinson airport and rent a light
plane. Should be able to make it to you by early afternoon."

"Nothing for you to do here, Nate."

"I want to take a look at the storage unit, and talk to the person
who found the body, maybe talk to some other people who knew
him; family, if he has any. Then I might claim the body."

"You're going to do what?" Rausch demanded.

"Claim the body. I'm going to tell anybody who'll listen that I
need to take a closer look at the wire he was wearing, and I'm going to make an official request to Interpol for records linking Yuri
Makarov to the murders there in Minneapolis and out here."

"We're going to do that as a matter of course."

"Go ahead," Osborne said. "But I'm going to stick my nose into
your investigation."

"As you wish," Rausch said and it was obvious from her tone
that she was dubious. "I'll send a jet for you, it'll be a lot faster that
way, and have a car waiting for you at the airport. But I suggest
that you drop Ms. Borden off."

"Nope, she has to tag along because she's going to write a series of
stories linking Makarov to me in Afghanistan and to the attacks

on the Initiative, and at least to the Venezuelan intelligence service."

"The Bureau will have no comment for now, unless I get orders to the contrary," Rausch said. "Nor did we ever have this conversation."

"Fair enough," Osborne said. "See you in a couple of hours."

He found a median crossing marked OFFICIAL VEHICLES ONLY, and took it.

Ashley held her silence until they were headed back to Dickinson. "If you're serious about giving me the go-ahead to file some stories, you'll have to get my dad's okay."

"I am serious, and I'll get your dad's green light, but in the end it'll be your decision."

"Come on, Nate, that's a no-brainer," Ashley said, and she was excited.

"This guy's good, and if he decides to come after us it could get dicey."

She was suddenly serious. "I've been there before, remember?"

"I remember," he said, and when he glanced over at her she was looking at him, her eyes wide, her cheeks flushed, and he thought he'd never seen a more beautiful woman in his life. And he was afraid.

33

SEBIN COLONEL LUIS Delgado was waiting for Makarov's Iberia Airlines flight from Madrid to touch down at Mexico City's Benito Juarez International a few minutes before eleven in the morning. The two men did not greet each other after Makarov had made his way through passport control and customs, and headed with his single carry-on bag into the main terminal.

He'd not been advised by the Iranian to expect Delgado, so the colonel's presence came as a surprise, and he didn't care for the closeness of it. In fact, since he'd returned to Stockholm he'd been making his escape plans; the only problem he'd not solved in his mind was Ilke. What would he have to tell her to justify their picking up and leaving Sweden with less than a moment's notice? And now, Delgado here lent an urgency to his planning.

He stopped at a newsstand and bought a bottle of Evian, before he turned around and went back to a waiting area at a gate where the next flight, this one to Rio de Janeiro, wasn't due to depart for another two hours. Only a few people were seated, and Makarov went to a window and looked out at the aircraft coming and going on the apron. The mountains in the distance ringing the city were lost in a brown haze.

Delgado walked over and stood next to him. "I'm glad to see that you've accepted the assignment," the Venezuelan intelligence officer said, keeping his voice conversational even though no one was in hearing range.

Makarov didn't look at him. "Why are you here?"

"To make sure you came this far."

"The money is in my account. I've accepted the assignment, I've read the file, I've made my excuses in Stockholm, and I'm *en train*."

"There've been some developments since Stockholm that you needed to know," Delgado said. "Osborne knows your name."

A little thrill of anticipation fluttered in Makarov's gut. "How?"

"I don't know. But it's possible that he remembers you from Afghanistan. Apparently he has an old photograph of you."

Makarov shook his head as he considered the possibility. His Spetsnaz record had been completely erased by Vasili Sumskoy for an appreciable amount of money all in U.S. hundreds within the year after Afghanistan. The only photos of him in the Makarov family albums were dated back to when he was just a kid. Since he'd gone AWOL from the service he'd never allowed any photographs of himself except when he was in a light disguise like now—black hair, contacts which darkened his eyes, and glasses—for his various passports and driving licenses, plus the little bit of plastic surgery to his nose and chin.

"That's not possible," he said. "There has to be another explanation."

"Be that as it may, he managed to trace you under your Parks' identification from LaGuardia to Minneapolis, and from there to a storage company where you killed the owner, then to a restaurant that caters to truckers outside Dickinson, and finally to Denver where you managed to disappear."

Makarov was astounded, but a part of him that admired intelligence and especially tradecraft, was intrigued. He only vaguely remembered Osborne as a bright, capable officer, though something of an American rube, who he'd heard later lost part of a leg for his heroics and had won the Medal of Honor.

"How do you know this?" he asked.

"It's on every police website in the country and even Interpol got your description this morning," Delgado said. "It's a wonder you got out of Europe."

The situation was worse than he'd faced in Denver, but not as bad as some corners he'd been in. "I'll need to go to ground here for a day or two, no longer, until I can change my appearance and arrange for new papers."

"There's no time for that," Delgado said and he took a small manila envelope, about the size of a paperback novel, out of his jacket pocket and handed it to Makarov. "Get rid of your contacts and glasses. Can't do much about your profile, but you can darken your skin with chemicals which will match your British Virgin Islands passport, under the name of Thomas van Houghton."

"How do I know that I can trust this?"

"It's to our benefit not to let you be taken. Besides, your Brighton Beach Russians are the ones who got you into this mess with Osborne. They rented the storage bay in your Parks name. Stupid, because they didn't give a damn. They cut corners to save themselves some extra work."

Makarov almost smiled even though he was bitter. The stupidity was all his. He'd never operated in the U.S. His work had almost always been confined to Europe and the U.K., so he had naturally used the Russian Mafia in the States. He decided that he wouldn't be burned again.

"What else do you have for me?"

"You're flying Aeromexico to Miami in one hour, your tickets are in the envelope. From there you connect to Atlanta, after which you're on your own, because I don't think you'll trust anyone but yourself the closer you get to Osborne. North Dakota is a ridiculously underpopulated state. I suggest you don't call any attention to yourself. The sheriff lives alone on a ranch he inherited from his parents. I've included a topographic map showing its location. "

"I suspect it's a trap."

"I suspect that you're right," Delgado said. "The point is with this new information, are you willing to continue? Eliminating Osborne is very important to us."

"How important?"

"Name a price, Señor Makarov. But within reason."

Makarov focused on the reflection in the window of the goings-on behind them. Steady streams of people, passengers as well as crew, moved along the broad passageway. An occasional cart to transport disabled people beeped past. A couple of airport security cops walked by, but they were not in a hurry. If Interpol had his Parks name and identification they would probably first concentrate their efforts in Europe. Osborne and the U.S. authorities would have already guessed he'd left the country.

But Osborne had set a trap by so openly sending up the hue and cry. The ex-Marine was taunting him to come back. The question was: Why? It had to be more than a simple sheriff's need to solve a crime that hadn't even happened in his county.

Taking out a high-tension line and causing the death of the repairman sent out to fix it, had made no sense in the first place, and it made even less sense now.

"The price depends, of course, on the importance to you. Explain it to me, please, because at this point the assignment you've offered me seems to have more at stake than you've let on."

"You don't need to know."

"Of course I do. It's become a high-risk assignment. Money aside, I need to know why I should take this risk."

"Be careful what you ask for, because knowing a thing can make you more enemies than you want or need."

Makarov held his silence. Two minutes, and he would go to ground somewhere here in Mexico City until he could arrange for Ilke to send him a sealed package that he kept in a wall safe at their home. She'd never asked him what it contained, or why it was so important to do exactly as she was told if and when the time ever came. She was in love, her husband was involved with international business deals, and she had to suspect that a time might come when a deal went somehow bad and he needed whatever was in the package.

And if and when the time ever came, he'd always known that he would have to kill her. He could not leave any loose ends behind.

"As you wish," Delgado said, and he told Makarov what was at stake and what was going to happen in less than forty-eight hours, and then what would happen after that.

It was all Makarov could do not to throw his head back and laugh out loud, for the sheer brilliance, and stupidity of the thing.

"One million euros," he said.

"We've already agreed on that amount."

"In addition," Makarov said, looking directly into the Venezuelan's eyes.

Delgado didn't flinch. "Done," he said.

34

DEB RAUSCH MET the Gulfstream bringing Osborne and Ashley from Dickinson a few minutes after noon. She had an Escalade SUV and driver waiting to take them wherever they wanted to go.

"We can go out to the self-storage business where Toivo's body was found, but there's nothing there," she told them.

"As long as my name's on the police wire I don't need to see it," Osborne said.

"At the head of the list. If Makarov has access, which I suspect a man in his profession would, he knows that you're looking for him, by name."

"Good," Osborne said. He and Ashley had had time to go back to his house outside Medora to pack a few things before they'd met the jet at Dickinson. They tossed the bags in the back of the Caddy and got in, Ashley riding shotgun and Osborne in back with Deb.

"Are you going to keep me in the dark?" the Minneapolis SAC asked.

"No, but first I'm going to need a phone number for the desk supervisor at the Sioux Falls Control Center who dispatched the lineman."

"I'm not going to ask where you heard about that," Deb said. "I'm not even allowed to go near him. Our Cyber Security people at headquarters are on it."

"Is he under suspicion for causing the accident?"

"His name's been mentioned."

"I want the number."

They had not moved from their parking spot in front of the General Aviation Terminal. Rausch got out of the car and walked a few paces away as she called someone on her phone. Osborne watched her.

"Why do we need to talk to him?" Ashley asked.

"He was on the front line, and if this was the work of a hacker he'd know about it."

Rausch seemed animated, and she glanced back at the car, but then turned away. A minute later she took out a notebook and wrote something down, then broke the connection and came back to the Caddy.

"They're not very happy."

"Who?"

"They," Rausch said pointedly, and she gave Osborne the phone number. "His name is Stuart Wyman. It's his home phone, he's been suspended."

Osborne called and Wyman answered on the first ring. "Yes."

"Mr. Wyman, I'm Nate Osborne, the Billings County sheriff. I'd like to ask you a question."

"You're out of your jurisdiction," Wyman said. "Don't bother me again."

"Gerry Kasmir was a personal friend of mine, and I'd like very much to find out who killed him, your lineman, and the young rancher and his wife."

"The FBI has already been here."

"It was the work of a computer hacker, we're pretty sure about that. But I want your opinion."

"You're goddamned right it was a hacker. Some sick son of a bitch somewhere in Amsterdam. And I told that to the FBI, too, along with a lot of other things."

"Like?"

"It's not over. This is just the start."

"Do you think it has anything to do with the virus that was planted in every control center along the grid?" Osborne asked.

"We know it does."

"Who's we?"

Wyman hesitated. "I don't think I should say anything else."

"Was it you who figured out about the hacker?" Osborne asked. "It's important to me to know how you did it."

"What the hell does a county sheriff have to do with this thing? Tell me that."

"I was caught in the middle of the attack on the Initiative over the holidays. So I'm personally involved. I know the guy who shot out the insulator and told the hacker just when to re-energize the line."

"When Tony was up in his bucket. Unprotected."

"Yeah. And the guy knows who I am and will probably come looking for me to settle an old score. I need your help."

"Toby Lundgren," Wyman said.

"Who's that?"

"A friend. He's the main analyst at our computer center up in Hibbing, Minnesota. I called him as soon as I was suspended and he found out that the accident was the work of a computer hacker in Amsterdam you talked about."

"Did he give you a name?"

"No, but he thought he might have known the guy at MIT. German or Dutch, and now a part of some kinky group that does this stuff for the fun of it."

"Have you talked to your friend today?" Osborne asked.

"The FBI ordered me to have no contact with him."

"I'm going up to see him," Osborne said. "And I'd like you to get word to him that I'm coming."

"Good luck, Sheriff," Wyman said. "And I sincerely mean it, because if Toby is right and this was just the beginning of something big—well, you can't imagine how bad it could be."

"Tell me."

"I'll let Toby explain it, if he'll talk to you. And you might tell him for me, that I'm goddamned scared."

ST. LOUIS COUNTY Sheriff's Deputy Jay Stromback, a round-faced man with a buzz haircut and wire rimmed glasses, was waiting for them at the Chisholm-Hibbing Airport. It was about three in the afternoon. Rausch showed her FBI credentials and introduced Osborne and Ashley.

"Long way from home, Sheriff," Stromback said, shaking hands. "Might be able to help out if I knew what this was all about."

"I'd like to talk to a man who works at the MAPP Computer Center."

"That's what Agent Rausch said on the phone. This concern my county?"

"Not directly."

They went out to the sheriff's radio unit. "Does he know you're coming to see him?"

"Yes," Rausch said. "This is official Bureau business but it won't show up in your log."

She and Ashley were in the backseat, and the deputy glanced at them in the rearview mirror but said nothing as they headed away from the airport. Fifteen minutes later they were on Highway 169 heading toward the tiny town of Kewatin and Stromback turned onto a narrow blacktop road into the woods that led to a gate in a tall chain-link fence topped with razor wire protecting a squat, windowless, one-story block house building that looked like a military bunker. The only notice on the gate was one forbidding entry by unauthorized personnel.

Stromback called on the intercom. "Your visitors are here."

A moment later the gate swung open and they drove through, parking in the small lot alongside a dozen other cars, and were buzzed into a small anteroom where they had to sign in with a security officer. Osborne and Rausch had to surrender their weapons, but Stromback was to wait outside for them.

Arthur Lundgren came to the door a minute later, blinking furiously behind his thick glasses. He was short, a little thick around the middle, and his face was scarred from acne as a teenager. He was dressed in jeans and a MIT hoodie.

"I was wondering when you guys were going to show up," he said when Deb Rausch showed him her FBI identification.

"Is there someplace we can talk?" she asked.

"Do I need a lawyer?"

"No," Osborne said. "Stu Wyman sent us, said he was scared, and he told me that you'd explain why we all should be."

"You're a G-man?"

"No," Osborne said.

Lundgren led them back to a small conference room, where Osborne explained who he and Ashley were and a little of why they'd come without mentioning Makarov directly.

"Holy shit, so you actually listened," Lundgren said. "But there had to be somebody with boots on the ground out there. The timing would have been all wrong with just my guy in Amsterdam."

"Yes, there was, but I want you to tell us how we're going to catch the hacker, and the sooner the better because I think he's not done."

"Not by a long shot," Lundgren said. "You ever read one of those doomsday novels, end of the world shit? This could end up just like that."

35

THE HAVEN, AS the area was known, was, in Barend Dekker's estimation, a slum. Just off the Westerstraat west of Amsterdam's city center the group of crumbling post–WWII apartment buildings at the edge of a run-down industrial park was home to squatters, some Roma who mostly stayed to themselves, and in one building the Group—more or less a dozen world-class computer hackers. The number varied as people tended to drift in and out, some staying a week or two, others much longer.

Dekker, thirty-one, was a small man, with narrow shoulders, long, delicate fingers, and wide, deep black eyes that under a high, frowning forehead made it seem as if he was always pissed off at the world. Which in a large way he was, though he'd never tried to figure out why.

Shit happened. It had always happened to him. When he was just a kid his mother had all but turned her back on him, and his father used to beat him with a leather belts, calling him the queer boy.

MIT could have been different, but he was too young—fourteen when he graduated with his Ph.D. in computer science—to fit in. So he'd been an outcast. A freak. A supernerd among nerds. His thesis had been Quantum Effects Encryption for Secure Computer Algorithms that even his major professor and advisor didn't fully understand, which had deepened the dissatisfaction he felt being the only smart guy in the room.

IBM and GE and Boeing Aerospace Division hadn't been much better, and finally one night he'd crashed the Cray Red Storm system at Sandia National Laboratories from a laptop in his bedroom in Brooklyn, just for the hell of it. That was in '07, and within a year he'd discovered the Amsterdam Group and Karn Simula, his girlfriend from Helsinki, who was just as pissed off at the world as he was.

But she had better reasons. From the age of seven until she'd stabbed her brother to death when she was fifteen, she'd been sexually abused by him, by an uncle, and by her father. The judge had sentenced her to two years in prison, after which she was supposed to undergo psychiatric counseling.

She did her prison time, but the day she got out she left Finland, finding her way to the Group, because like the nerds here she was a genius. But she fit in.

She was shorter than Barend, her breasts small, her hips narrow, her oval face and blond features Scandinavian-pretty and fresh. But she had a lot of tattoos—mostly of scenes depicting hell and the devil and the damned souls. And she had numerous body piercings; in her eyebrows, nose, tongue, nipples, belly button, and her shaved pudenda.

She'd learned enough about computers and programming from the Group so that she'd become an expert at broad-stroke planning. She advised them what they should do, and sometimes they implemented her suggestions.

It was her idea to use the Russian power grid virus to play with the U.S. Bring the arrogant bastards down a notch, while at the same time fulfilling their contract with the Iranians.

Dekker had been working on one of his ten-dimensional string theory war game programs and he looked up when Karn came out of the bedroom where she'd been doing a little acid while listening to *Madame Butterfly* and masturbating. She was naked, a petulant expression on her full lips.

He'd seen it before, especially lately and he was irritated. "If you're bored again don't take it out on me, I'm busy," he told her and he turned back to his game.

She padded into the dirty kitchenette, and came back with a couple of reasonably clean glasses and a bottle of Valpolicella. "Want a drink with me?"

Dekker turned away from his laptop. "Sure, why not." He couldn't stay mad at her.

She poured their red wine and then sat straddling his lap, her smell just then musky, her nipples erect, a thin line of sweat on her upper lip. "So what've you been thinking about the last couple of days?" she asked.

"Same shit, different day. But you got something stuck up your ass."

She sipped her wine, a few drops running down her chin and to her chest, between her breasts. "What are we waiting for?"

He knew exactly what she was talking about. They'd been cooped up here ever since he'd gotten the contract and the Iranian had delivered the flash drive almost two months ago. None of their friends had been over; his excuse was his string theory war game for which he still hadn't come up with a better title than 10-D. They'd not taken any drives into the country, or trips to the seashore, or down to Munich, a city he particularly liked. Even their sex had been off. Too much on his mind.

"They told me forty-eight hours, it's only been twenty-four."

She laughed, her voice husky, all the way from deep in her chest, and from smoking too much pot. "You gonna put that in your memoirs? Should make a whole chapter all by itself: The day the earth stood still and the Big D took orders from someone for the first time."

Dekker figured that he should be mad, she was teasing him, but he grinned. "What do you have in mind?"

"Make 'em squirm a little," she said. They spoke English as most international hackers did, and she especially had fun with sub-standard usage. It was, she said, like working crossword puzzles in a foreign language; speaking like real people did was the height of control.

"Send them a warning?"

"Like they know what's coming but nobody can do a thing about it. Like watching the tube on nine-eleven in west bumfuck Iowa. The buildings coming down. Helpless."

"The president sitting on a stool reading to the grade-school kiddies."

"Cryin' and prayin' to God for a miracle. But He wasn't home that day."

Dekker had worked hard at getting even for most of his life, but never with the kind of panache that Karn was suggesting. He'd always struck hard and fast, without warning. It was the main reason his handle was swiftlightning.

He glanced over his shoulder at the convoluted image of one of his ten-dimensional branes. He thought that he was close, but the complete image, the final breakthough had eluded him for months.

Karn followed his gaze and grinned. "You heard of three-dimensional chess? Three normal boards stacked one atop the other, with extra pieces on the two top boards? Deal is you can move certain pieces not just laterally across one board, but you can attack a piece from the board above or the one below. Position. Only this time you got ten dimensions. Maybe even a gateway or gateways to other universes. Hell, gravity is probably nothing but another universe's force leaking through a couple of the extra dimensions. You know, down around the Planck length."

She waved her wineglass toward the screen, slopping some of the wine on him.

"Send your extra-dimensional forces through the network. Cancel gravity. Turn it upside down. Hell, even make the universe expand faster than it should. Fuck with their heads, D. Loosen up. Have some fun."

He poured some of his wine on her chest then sucked it off her nipples. She arched her back in pleasure, just like a cat did when its back was scratched.

"We're drunk, so let's screw," she said.

"You think?"

IT WAS coming up on eleven in the evening when Dekker left Karn passed out on the bed. He'd covered her with a blanket, pulled on a pair of shorts and a sweatshirt, and got another glass of wine before he sat down at his computer and brought up the Internet. His connection came up through a series of re-mailers, two of them in India, and was totally secure. Untraceable.

Even in the middle of making love with Karn a part of him had been chewing on what she had suggested, turning the notion over in his head, loosening up, having fun.

He opened a Twitter account under the name How About Them Apples and piggybacked it on Jane Fonda's account. But he had another thought—have fun, Karn told him—and instead attached it to the White House Twitter account of Nicholas Fenniger, the president's adviser on national security affairs.

He'd love to be a little bird in the corner when the shit started to hit the fan.

ARMAGEDDON IS ABOUT TO FALL ON YOUR HEADS. ARE YOU READY, AMERICA?

He wrote in all caps which was the same as shouting out loud. A minute later he made another post.

24 HOURS AND THE LIGHTS START TO GO OUT. WHERE SHOULD WE BEGIN?

The Iranian who'd delivered the flash drive had told him to do nothing until he was contacted via e-mail. And he'd followed his instructions to the letter because he became motivated as soon as the five hundred thousand euros had actually been credited to his Luxembourg account. He'd never had so much money in his life. He'd never even thought about sums like that. And the five hundred Gs was only the down payment.

LET'S START IN L.A. AND HEAD EAST. SALT LAKE CITY. LAS VEGAS. DENVER.

People—actually in his estimation the vast majority of the population were sheeple—had to be led by the noses, step-by-step. Keep it simple stupid!

KANSAS CITY. CHICAGO. DETROIT. CINCINNATI. HOW ABOUT MIAMI?

Sometimes he wondered why he even bothered. Would they even get it? Not until the lights went out.

NASHVILLE TURN OFF THE MUSIC. PHILLIE CAN'T FIX THE CRACK IN THE BELL TILL THE JUICE IS ON.

He'd thought about making each message exactly 140 characters. But that'd be showing off. And why bother confusing the issue?

HOW ABOUT BOSTON?

He wanted to be there.

HOW ABOUT WASHINGTON, D.C.?

The newspaper and television and Internet headlines would be sweet—once they got their electricity back on.

HOW ABOUT NEW YORK CITY?

And this was just the beginning.

HOW ABOUT THEM APPLES?

36

WHITNEY LIPTON WAS at her desk when she got the encrypted video call from General Forester. It was a little after three in the afternoon and she'd finished briefing her staff less than an hour ago. The experiment was a complete success. The microbe talker—the gadget—which guided the coal-eating bacteria to not only continue to do their jobs, but continue to reproduce, was working well within its design parameters, and just about everyone on the research staff, her included, was about ready to go back to their university positions and new research projects.

Amidst all the hustle and bustle over the past several months— even during the attacks on the Initiative, and the horrible killings— she'd had time to think about what might be coming next for her. She'd been assured that she could have her old job back at the CDC, heading the pure research bacterial lab that she'd begun what seemed like a million years ago. It'd been from the lab where she'd developed the microbial Esperanto she used to train her bugs.

She'd thought a lot about training colonies of microbes to cure individual human diseases. Six hundred different species of bacterium in the human mouth worked in concert to produce dental plaque. Maybe if they were taught a different language they could prevent plaque.

Maybe a tailor-made army of microbes could cure a specific cancer in a specific patient. Open a blocked artery. Rid a joint of arthritis. Strengthen the bones in an eighty-year-old woman. And beyond that maybe the millions, even billions, of different species of bacterium already present in every human body could be taught different languages for different maladies.

When she'd brought that idea up with Lee Mulholland, her postdoc from UW, he'd tossed his head back and laughed out loud. "Way rad, Doc," he'd said. "You're talking about Dr. McCoy."

Whitney hadn't known who he was talking about.

"Bones, from *Star Trek*. He had a medical analyzer that he'd run over the patient's body, and voilà, the guy was cured. No barbaric cutting into a patient's body with a scalpel. All that was in the past, because his device was talking to the microbes, telling them to get to work."

"I don't think it'll be quite that simple—"

"Why not?" Mulholland had asked, and it had gotten her to thinking about some dazzling possibilities.

"How's it going?" Forester asked. "Have there been any security issues?"

"Nothing so far, other than the power line," Whitney said. "But Nettles wants to keep his people here for at least a week, maybe longer."

"I agree, because this isn't over by a long shot."

Something clutched at Whitney's gut. "Have you heard something?"

"Has Nate Osborne talked to you today?"

"No. What's going on?"

"I'm sorry, but you're on the firing line and you should have been told yesterday," Forester said, concern written on his face, and he told her about Chavez's forty-eight-hour ultimatum that had been delivered to the White House. "Leaves us twenty-four hours."

"Or what? What's supposed to happen?"

"No one knows, except that your downed power line was not the only attack on our grid. There've been others. Somebody has been systematically probing our system. And now that they're done with that phase something else is coming our way, but the tough part is that no one knows what that might be. And it's totally impossible for us to even begin to guard all of the high-tension lines, or even the transformer yards."

"Do you think they'll try to hit us here again?" Whitney asked, and she tried to read something in Forester's stern expression. "Are you warning me because you know something else? Something specific?"

"You're important."

"What are you saying?"

"Donna Marie no longer matters, but you're a national treasure we can't afford to lose."

"For Christ's sake, Bob."

"I want you here in Washington until this is settled. The FBI will set you up in a safe house with an armed guard."

Whitney was shaken. "What about my staff?"

"No one's going to come after them, or you probably, but if they'd feel safer they can sit tight and Nettles' people will provide security." Forester leaned closer to the camera. "Listen to me, Whitney, I may be acting like an old mother hen, but I want you out of there this afternoon, or first thing in the morning at the latest. And at least for now you're still working for me, so I'm going to insist."

"If I'm going anywhere it'll be to my lab in Atlanta."

"I talked to Charlie Donovan a half hour ago, and he agrees with me." Donovan was the director of the CDC's Druid Hills headquarters outside Atlanta.

"For how long?"

"At least another twenty-four, until we see what's coming, if anything. A lot of the president's advisers think it's just bluster."

"And then what, if nothing happens?"

"You can wrap things up out there, and go back to Atlanta a free woman, with the thanks of a grateful nation. There'll be a Rose Garden ceremony and you'll be asked to speak to Congress and there'll be television."

"I don't want any of it," Whitney said. And she sincerely didn't. She wanted the anonymity of her lab. She had started to fall in love with her chief of security here, only he'd been shot dead trying to save her and the others when they'd come under attack. It would be a very long time, she'd decided, before she could even begin to heal. For now she wanted to bury herself in work.

"I'll send a jet for you, and coordinate it with Captain Nettles. First thing in the morning, which'll give you time to pack."

Whitney wasn't happy and she let it show. "All right, whatever you say, General."

"Good," Forester said, and his image on her computer screen was gone.

WHITNEY WENT downstairs to the computer center where Mulholland and a couple of other postdocs were closing down the experimental links to the power station and setting up the much simpler monitoring parameters. They'd already installed and tested the complicated program that would take biofeedbacks from the microbe colony in the coal seam and automatically adjust the output of the gadget whenever it was needed.

"Which if you ask me is a nifty bit of engineering," Mulholland had told her.

"Makes the entire generating plant practically automatic," she'd said. "And that's the whole idea—or at least the last chapter."

The three of them were huddled around one of the computers and no one looked up when she walked in.

"Do we have a problem?" she asked.

Mulholland glanced over his shoulder. "Come here and take a look at this."

She joined them and looked at what was displayed on the monitor. At first it made no sense to her, and she said so.

They all looked a little pale, especially Mulholland. "We're waiting for the next Tweet, but this might be it," he said. He scrolled up several pages.

ARMEGEDDON IS ABOUT TO FALL ON YOUR HEADS.
ARE YOU READY AMERICA?

"This is the Twitter page of the president's national security adviser," Mulholland said. "A friend of mine out in Maryland was a poli-sci major at Wisconsin, now he works for a lobbyist, and he sent this to me about five minutes ago."

Something tugged at Whitney. A niggling fear at the edges. "That doesn't sound like White House chatter."

"No, but this does."

THE NEW POLICY BILL IS READY FOR THE SENATE.
WE NEED TO RALLY THE TROOPS.

Mulholland scrolled down past several more Tweets on the president's new energy initiative bill, until he came to another in the vein of the first.

24 HOURS AND THE LIGHTS START TO GO OUT.
WHERE SHOULD WE BEGIN?

"I don't understand," Whitney said.

"Somebody, somehow, has hacked into the NSA's Twitter account and interlaced these messages. Could be a joke, but it isn't."

"Not too hard to do," Pat Zobel, one of the other postdocs, said. At twenty-two she was the youngest on the team and she was their leading computer expert.

Mulholland scrolled down to the next message.

LET'S START IN L.A. AND HEAD EAST. SALT LAKE
CITY. LAS VEGAS.

Whitney's cell phone rang. "Yes."

"Get to a computer and log in to Nick Fenniger's Twitter account," Forester said.

"I'm there. What does it mean?"

"It means that the hacker we think was responsible for the death of the lineman isn't done. This is the next step I told you about."

"The one that some of the president's advisers think is just bluster."

KANSAS CITY. CHICAGO. DETROIT. CINCINNATI.
HOW ABOUT MIAMI?

"The same," Forester said. "Get your things together, a jet will be on its way to Dickinson in less than a half hour. But I'm going to tell Nettles to hold you there at the Initiative until it touches down, and then you'll be helicoptered over."

"He means to start rolling blackouts. Cut power to those cities."

"That's exactly what he means to do."

"But he's given us another twenty-four hours, and I've got to take care of my people out here first. Send the jet in the morning."

"I want you here."

"They're after the grid, not me. Anyway I'd actually be safer out here at Donna Marie."

"First thing in the morning," Forester said.

37

I T WAS A few minutes past four in Hibbing, and walking away from the forty-five-minute meeting with a man Osborne thought was among the smartest he'd ever met, he understood that catching the Amsterdam hacker was going to be next to impossible by ordinary means, and he voiced his opinion to Deb Rausch.

They were in the parking lot approaching the St. Louis County Sheriff's radio unit when Deb pulled up short. "Our Cyber Crimes people are pretty good," she said. "But what do you mean by *ordinary means*?"

"Our guys hunted Osama bin Laden for years, but it wasn't until we got some Pakistani intel on the ground right there, that we were able to find him and send SEAL Team Six in to take him out. We didn't ask for permission, especially not from the Pakistani military or intelligence service—we just went in, shot the bastard to death, and yanked his body out of there. In and out in a few minutes."

Sheriff Stromback got out of his car and was looking at them.

"Is that what you think needs to be done with this guy?" Rausch asked.

"You heard what Lundgren said: the Dutch federal cops and intelligence agency people haven't been able to shut the commune down."

"That's because these guys probably haven't committed any crime against the government," Ashley said. "They most likely even pay their taxes on time. And nobody wants to mess with them."

"I think that's exactly the case."

"You can't be suggesting that we send another SEAL team in to find him and take him out," Rausch said.

"We might have to," Osborne told her.

Rausch got a phone call and she stepped aside to take it, at the same moment Toby Lundgren came to the computer center's door and called to them.

"Hey guys, you gotta come back and see something."

"What is it?" Osborne asked.

"Your hacker has struck again, and this time it's way cool."

Rausch turned back, an even more serious expression on her normally severe face. "This was headquarters. They want to know what I'm doing up here. Something is going down in Washington."

"The hacker?" Osborne said, and Rausch nodded.

Lundgren, obviously impatient, waited at the open door.

"According to Lundgren he's struck again," Osborne said, and he walked back to the deputy. "You might as well go back to town, we'll find another ride to the airport. Something's come up we have to deal with."

"Anything I need to know?" Stromback asked. "It's not often we get the Bureau up here."

"Believe me, you'll be the first to know, you have my word on it," Osborne said, and he and the deputy shook hands.

"I'll hold you to it, Sheriff," Stromback said, and he got back in his patrol car and drove off.

LUNDGREN LED them back to his office instead of the conference room where they'd met earlier. A half-dozen large flat-screen monitors were arrayed on the front wall of the room that was about the size of a two-car garage. Desks and workstands on which stood a variety of monitors and keyboards enough to provide for a half-dozen workstations were arrayed in some random order. But this was Hansen's personal space; no one else worked here with him.

He sat down on the only chair and scooted over to one of the monitors on which was displayed a series of what at first looked like one-line messages.

"Looks like someone's Twitter account," Ashley said, looking over his shoulder.

"Exactly what it is," Lundgren said. "Belongs to the president's national security adviser, Nicholas Fenniger."

Osborne leaned in.

24 HOURS AND THE LIGHTS START TO GO OUT. WHERE SHOULD WE BEGIN?

"Is it him?"

"Yeah, and the dude is damned good, but he's made a big mistake this time."

"I don't understand," Rausch said. "Did he hack into the NSA's Twitter account?"

"That's exactly what he's done, and that's how I'm going to find him," Lundgren said. "He's interlaced his own Tweets in amongst Fenniger's. And he's given us a warning."

"Blackouts?" Osborne said.

"You'll see."

ARMAGEDDON IS ABOUT TO FALL ON YOUR HEADS.
ARE YOU READY, AMERICA?

"This was the first, just a few minutes ago," Lundgren said.
"Yesterday I set up a couple of search and recognize programs, to
look for any sort of a threat to our grid. I tried to think like this
bozo and I actually used the word *Armageddon*." Lundgren looked
up, grinning. "The guy's a bigger jerk than me."

"I need to call Washington," Rausch said.

"Hold on a minute," Lundgren said. "Anyway cell phones don't
work in here."

"There's more?" Osborne asked.

"Not a lot, but enough," Lundgren said and he scrolled down
several Tweets, past the twenty-four-hour warning to the next one.

LET'S START IN L.A. AND HEAD EAST. SALT LAKE
CITY. LAS VEGAS. DENVER.

"He's telling us that he's going to shut down electrical power to
those cities in that order."

"Can he do it?" Ashley asked, as Lundgren scrolled farther.

KANSAS CITY. CHICAGO. DETROIT. CINCINNATI.
HOW ABOUT MIAMI?

"I could," he said.

"From here—" Rausch began, but Lundgren shook his head.

"From my laptop. It'd be easy if you had the virus, which I think
this guy probably has. Could have gotten it from friends in Russia."

"I think that you've gone far enough for now," Rausch said. "I'm going to call this in, get a team out from Washington."

"Hang on to your panty hose, 'cause there's not much more to see, and anyway we're going to be damned busy coordinating with the other control centers around the country to see if we can head him off, or at least slow him down."

"What else is there?" Osborne asked.

Lundgren quickly scrolled through the remaining four threats, plus the last Tweet:

HOW ABOUT THEM APPLES?

"What's next?" Osborne asked. "You said he made a mistake and that's how you were going to find him."

"Might not be in time to stop the rolling blackouts he's warned us he's going to do, but I'll nail the bastard, because he's arrogant."

"What's his mistake?" Rausch asked.

"Piggybacking on an existing Twitter account, especially one that has more than a million hits every week. He's bound to have left crumbs. He's hiding behind a bunch of offshore re-mailers, so all we have to do is peel back the layers."

"I can get you help here," Rausch said. "We have some damned good people on the payroll."

Lundgren looked at her. "I know about your people. No disrespect, Agent Rausch, but I work best alone. And right now my first priority is protecting the grid from a total meltdown. Because if it happens, if even a little part of it happens, there're going to be a whole lot of people in this country who're going to find themselves in really deep shit tomorrow."

38

NICHOLAS FENNIGER RACED down the corridor from his corner office in the West Wing, his laptop under his arm, his jacket off, his tie loose, and burst into the Oval Office as the president was speaking to someone on the phone.

"It's begun," he practically shouted, though he was out of breath.

Mark Young, the normally affable White House chief of staff, turned around, a look of irritation on his round features. He came toward Fenniger. "He's talking to Xi. What the hell are you doing here like this?"

This morning Fenniger had urged President Thompson to call Xi Jinping, to update the Chinese president on the situation between us and Iran and Venezuela.

"Tell him to make his excuses," Fenniger said, keeping his voice low, but he couldn't hide the urgency he felt. The fear. He hadn't expected the situation to develop to this point. No one had.

"What the hell are you talking about?"

Fenniger opened his laptop and thrust it at Young. "Look."

The president, who'd had his back to them, swiveled around and glared at them. "I understand, Mr. President," he said.

Fenniger had brought up the first hacked Tweet:

ARMAGEDDON . . .

"What are you trying to show me?" Young asked.

"This is my Twitter account. The bastard's somehow hacked into it." He scrolled down to the other eight.

"It's not possible, is it?"

"That's what Jack Dorsey told me five minutes ago." Dorsey was Twitter's chief of security. "I finally convinced him that we weren't playing some kind of a stupid joke, and he said that he would look into it."

"I hope you told him to shut down your account."

"Yeah, but it's a little late now, don't you think?" Fenniger said. "But that's not the problem."

"Exactly what is the problem?" the president demanded, putting the phone down. He was angry.

"Sorry to barge in but it's something you have to see," Fenniger said, and he set up his laptop on the president's desk, and scrolled up to the ARMAGEDDON Tweet. "This was on my Twitter account about fifteen minutes ago."

"I don't understand, Nick."

"Someone hacked into my White House account—something that's supposed to be impossible to do—and inserted nine separate messages, this was the first."

"Who did it and why?"

"I think it's the hacker who's been probing our electrical grid," Fenniger said. He scrolled down to the next Tweet that gave the twenty-four-hour warning before the lights started to go out.

Thompson looked up.

"The son of a bitch has told us—and everyone else who logs on to my Twitter account—that he's going to shut us down. A series of rolling blackouts across the country starting in Los Angeles and ending here and up in New York."

"The message from Chavez gave us forty-eight hours, and this fits," Young said. "It's the 'or else.'"

The president went back to the top and slowly scrolled through the nine messages again.

"What do you want to do, Mr. President?" Fenniger asked.

"Do think this is a credible warning? I mean can he actually do this to us?"

"If he has the virus, yes, I believe he can. Or at least he thinks he can."

"He managed to bypass all the safety systems to electrocute the lineman in North Dakota," Young said. "So we have to consider the possibility that he has the means to do this and that he's not bluffing."

"I'm not going to the U.N. to apologize for Balboa. The Chavez government had it coming because of their hand in the attacks against the Initiative."

Fenniger knew what he would do, but he wasn't the president.

"I want to meet with my National Security Council as soon as possible. But no later than eight this evening."

"The full council?" Young asked.

"No," Thompson said. "Just the target members."

The entire council, which acted as a forum to advise the president on national security and foreign policy affairs, consisted of twenty principals that included, in addition to the president and vice president, Mark Young and Nicholas Fenniger, the secretaries of state, of defense and of energy, the chairman of the joint chiefs, the directors of national intelligence and of the National Drug Control Policy, plus others.

The target group whose existence was top secret included less than half of the full council whose identities were also top secret. The group's primary purpose was to authorize assassinations. They'd met to authorize the killing of Osama bin Laden. But its most sensitive job was to authorize the killing of U.S. citizens. There was no record of its existence or how it operated, nor were its infrequent meetings ever recorded, nor were minutes or even notes taken.

Only the handful of members knew exactly what role the president himself played in agreeing to or ordering the kills. And it was one of the things the sitting president briefed the president-elect on after the November election, usually between Christmas and New Year's Day. It was fairly common knowledge that the president-elect going into the meeting was a completely different, more solemn person afterward. Only presidents ever knew why.

"I'll see to it immediately, Mr. President," Young said and left the Oval Office to begin making the encrypted calls.

Fenniger gathered up his laptop and started for the door.

"Do you think that we'll be in time, Nick?" the president asked.

"I hope so, sir," Fenniger said. "But in case we can't find this guy and take him out, we'd better be prepared for the blackouts."

"He didn't say how long the outages would last."

"No, but even a few minutes in each city would play havoc with a lot of stuff. Computers, clocks, phones, even a large part of the Internet—a lot of servers don't have big enough backup generators."

"I hear a *but* in there," the president said.

Fenniger nodded tightly. The *Washington Post* called him the nation's cynic. A sobriquet he'd never denied. "It's what might be coming next. After the probes, after the blackouts. Because if this guy actually does have the virus he could do even greater harm."

The president had no reply.

"He could send us back practically to the horse and buggy days. And I mean it literally."

"I'll talk to the nation tonight."

39

MAKAROV DIDN'T HAVE the slightest qualm about flying back to Minneapolis, in part because the authorities would never suspect that he would return. In addition, he flew American Airlines, not Delta and not first class, and he rented a small car from Budget instead of a full-sized sedan from Hertz, and his look was different—light hair and pale eyes instead of dark, no glasses, darker complexion. He walked with a limp and he carried a different set of papers. People tended to see what they expected to see, and he was a completely different man, coming in contact with a different set of people.

Nevertheless he was as cautious as practicable under the circumstances. The risk to him here in Minneapolis where he was anonymous was only as slight as the speed he drove—too fast and he would be stopped and ticketed, or too slow and he would come under suspicion.

Once he had rented an anonymous dark blue Camry, he drove away from the airport but instead of heading west on I-94, he pulled off at a shopping mall on the way into the city and parked long enough to check his iPad first for any messages. Delgado had promised to warn him if something were to come up, and one message from the SEBIN officer was in his in-box.

This was not expected, Delgado had written, and he included a link to the White House Twitter account of Nicholas Fenniger, with the warnings presumably from Dekker in Amsterdam.

Delgado had also cautioned from the beginning that the power outage and the murder of the lineman in North Dakota were only the opening moves of something much larger. But this now, engineering a series of rolling blackouts across the country, made little or no sense to Makarov.

At the very least the power cuts would cause a lot of headaches for Americans, and probably even some accidents and maybe even a few deaths when home medical equipment without power backups turned off.

But the actions—especially so openly announced—could be a cause for an actual shooting war against Venezuela and against Iran. But the only way the U.S. could possibly come out ahead of the game would be all-out war. Maybe even using tactical nukes to take out some key targets in both countries—especially Iran's nuclear program and Venezuela's hydro power stations. Short of that, the U.S. would actually be losers in the sense that they had lost in Iraq and certainly in Vietnam.

And against all of that were his orders to find and assassinate Nate Osborne, a war hero, but nothing more than a small-town cop, which made even less sense to him. Unless he was missing something.

But two million euros—one million of which he'd already been paid, made perfect sense all of itself.

He pulled up a city directory for Minneapolis–St. Paul, finding the address of a place called Twin Cities Gun Emporium within a few blocks of the state Capitol. He took I-35 east across the river, finding the big gun shop just off Minnehaha Avenue. The place wasn't very busy, only a few cars in the parking lot and a handful of customers inside the store which was about the size of a Walmart.

He found the handgun section, and an old man with long white hair wearing bib overalls and combat boots came up to him.

"Help you with something?"

"I want a pistol. Ten-millimeter, auto load. I'm more interested in reliability and accuracy then I am with magazine capacities."

"Glock is a good pistol. The twenty is standard sized. Fifteen rounds." He walked down to the glass counter which held the Glocks, opened the drop flap in back, and took out the Glock 20.

"Doesn't jam, good accuracy, easy maintenance."

Makarov knew the pistol well, but he took it and felt its heft. "A little big."

"What's your most important purpose?"

"Self-defense."

"Conceal and carry?"

"Yes."

The old man returned the 20 and pulled out a smaller version. "Model twenty-nine. Same good features, fires a ten-millimeter round, smaller box magazine, ten shots."

Makarov took the pistol, hefted it, then checked the action. "This is about right."

"Two magazines? One or two boxes of ammo?"

"Two magazines, one box of ammunition," Makarov said.

"Let's do some paperwork," the old man said.

"Well, that's the problem," Makarov said.

The old man's eyes narrowed. "A felony conviction doesn't need to be a real problem."

"I'm not a U.S. citizen. British Virgin Islands."

"You're not allowed to carry a concealed weapon here or down there."

"I know," Makarov said, and he counted out two thousand in hundreds and laid them on the counter."

The old man pocketed the bills without hesitation, and grinned. "Like I said, Mr. Smith, let's do some paperwork."

IT WAS nearly seven P.M. Central Time before Makarov cleared the Twin Cities on I-94 just past where it merged with I-494 between Cedar Island and Fish Lakes. Traffic was light heading west, the weather was clear. He'd loaded the pistol and spare magazine, and although he was hungry he decided not to stop until much later.

Osborne lived alone on a ranch he'd inherited from his parents outside Fryburg just north of the interstate about five miles east of Medora. So far as Makarov had learned from his hasty researches, the spread was a nonproducing ranch, and therefore no hands worked the property. The place was relatively isolated, the nearest neighbors in Fryburg, which was not an incorporated town, only a listed as a populated place.

He phoned Osborne's home number, and after five rings an answering machine came on, and he broke the connection. Next he called the Billings County Sheriff's weekend and after-hours number, but he got a message advising the caller that if this was an emergency to dial 911, or telephone the Highway Patrol Office at Dickinson. He hung up before the message was completed.

Osborne wasn't home and his office was closed. Which could mean he was simply away for the evening; maybe in town for dinner, maybe out at the Initiative, or maybe even at his girlfriend's place in Bismarck.

He looked up the number for the Rough Riders Hotel where he'd been briefed Osborne often went for drinks and dinner. There'd been some trouble there with his girlfriend over the holidays.

A woman answered on the third ring. "Rough Riders."

"I'm trying to find Sheriff Osborne, he's not at home and his office doesn't answer."

"That right? Who's calling?"

"Special Agent Robert Banks, the FBI's Denver field office."

The woman backed off. "Oh, sorry. Nate's not here. I think he flew up to Minneapolis to speak to one of your people. I can get you the number."

"That's not necessary. Does Sheriff Osborne have a cell phone number?"

"I don't have it, but I'm sure you can reach him in Minneapolis."

"Thank you for your help."

"What'd you say your name was?" the woman asked, but Makarov hung up.

For just a moment he was convinced that somehow the Bureau knew that he was returning to Minneapolis, but that was impossible. In any event there would have been an increased police presence at the airport had they suspected. But he'd detected nothing out of the ordinary.

In any event Osborne was out of town, which was a piece of luck. If it held until morning Makarov would be at the ranch house waiting for him.

40

IT WAS AFTER five by the time Whitney had finished briefing her team, and they'd all marched over to Henry's where they had burgers, fries, and beers. She advised them to stick around at least until the damage the rolling blackouts were sure to cause had been straightened out, and they'd agreed accept for Pat Zobel and Pat's best friend, Cynthia Burgantz, who planned on heading to Boston in Cynthia's Lexus SUV first thing in the morning.

"Wouldn't catch me in a plane if some air-traffic-control facility or some airport on our route got knocked out," Cynthia said. She was a brilliant biophysicist, who came from a wealthy family, and she'd been used to doing things her own way most of her life.

"What if you run out of gas in one of the blacked-out cities?" Whitney had asked.

"They're warning about *rolling* blackouts. We'd just sit still wherever we were until the power came back on and we could pump gas."

"That's not what I meant. You guys saw what went on during

Katrina. Soon as the power went off, the looters came out of the woodwork. Even the cops couldn't handle it. I just don't want to see you two in the middle of something like that."

"I have a pistol in my glove compartment and I know how to use it," Cynthia said. She smiled. "We'll be okay, Doc. And I'll be looking for you in the journals."

"And the cover of *Time*," someone said and everyone cheered.

They were planning on throwing a big party in Washington next month courtesy of ARPA-E. They'd worked hard, under trying conditions—not one of them had hesitated to take over from the postdocs, some of who'd been murdered and some of the others who'd quit over the holidays—but the strain had been telling. They tended to be more snappish than most scientists, ready to party hard at the drop of a hat. And now they were just as ready to get back to their university positions and research projects, but they were also ready big time for next month in D.C., which had become a mantra lately.

Two of Nettles's off-duty sergeants were sitting at the bar drinking coffee and eating chili for which the New York transplant restaurant was famous. They looked over where Whitney and her postdocs were seated around a large round table, and glared. They didn't want to be here, none of the security team did. The last time they'd been too late to do much more than mop up after the civilians who'd taken out most of the bad guys and had prevented the serious damage that could have been done. And this time they'd done even less, because so far there'd been no direct threat to the project or its scientists.

Whitney got up and hugged all her postdocs, especially Cynthia and Pat. "If I don't see you in the morning before you take off, watch yourself."

"Where will you be?" Mulholland asked. They were all surprised.

"I'm going into town tonight and wait it out there."

Mulholland glanced over at the two men at the bar. "Do you think Ranger Rick will let you through the front gate?"

"They're doing their jobs, so don't let's make it any harder for them," Whitney said. "No one is going to arrest me."

Mulholland grinned. "Say hi to the sheriff and Ashley for us," he said.

IN HER quarters Whitney tossed a few things into an overnight bag. Most of the rest of her clothes and personal belongings were already packed and ready to be sent to the apartment the CDC had found for her outside Atlanta. All she had left were a last few things from her office.

Nate had told her on more than one occasion that anytime she wanted to get away from the project she should drive out to the ranch.

"Anytime night or day," he'd told her, and Ashley had agreed.

"Just call first, or honk your horn or knock or something, just in case."

And they'd all laughed.

Whitney had decided months ago that she was going to miss them. After losing Jim Cameron during the attack, the only man she'd ever known who she thought she could actually settle down with, she'd gravitated toward Nate and Ash. They were happy and in love, the way she'd envisioned her life would be with Jim.

She knew that she was a needy person, and that she was horning in on their relationship, but she'd told herself it was just tempo-rary. Sometimes North Dakota had been a very lonely place for her. She didn't know if Atlanta would be any better, but at least she would be surrounded with a lot more people—seriously smart and motivated people—and just maybe something would click for her. She hoped so. And it was a place and a routine that she was familiar with.

Her work was done, time to move on, and she felt as if she couldn't spend another night here. At least not this night, not until the attacks came to an end.

She looked at her image in the mirror over her bureau. Her features were gaunt, and her eyes drooped. It came to her that she was tired and more than a little frightened.

Grabbing her jacket and overnight bag, she left her room and went down to the lobby of the barracks, where Captain Nettles was waiting for her. Whitney was six feet tall, and Nettles was shorter than her, dark complected, with a mustache. He was dressed in camos, a holstered pistol strapped to his chest. The expression on his narrow face was not unkind.

"I heard that you were leaving tonight," he said.

"Any objections?" she asked.

"Yes, ma'am. General Forester asked that we keep you safe. He's sending a jet for you in the morning, and we're going to chopper you over to the Dickinson airport to meet it."

"That's tomorrow, in the meantime I'm going into town tonight."

"I don't think that's such a good idea, Doctor."

"Nevertheless that's how it's going to be unless you place me under arrest."

Nettles shook his head in exasperation. "Goddamnit, we're doing our best here to keep you and your people and this place intact. I'd like a little help."

"You heard about the rolling blackouts. Well, that's what they're going to do this time. They're not coming back here, and no one is gunning for me."

"I have my orders."

"Which doesn't include me," Whitney said. She stepped around him and went outside where she'd parked her government-issue Ford Taurus.

Nettles came to the door. "Keep your cell phone on, please. General Forester will want to talk to you."

"I'll tell him that you did your best, but that I slugged you."

41

THE BUREAU'S GULFSTREAM IV, with the military desig-
nator C-20F, touched down at Joint Base Andrews Naval Air
Facility across the river from Washington around seven thirty in
the evening local. On the flight out from Minnesota, Ashley had
worked on a series of stories which she planned on filing as soon
as she got permission from her father.

Osborne, Ashley, and Deb Rausch thanked the crew and then
walked across to where a black GMC Yukon with government
plates was waiting for them, two men wearing FBI blue windbreakers standing beside it.

"This time he's not going to say no," Ashley said. "Not with what
we've got coming our way tomorrow."

"I agree," Osborne said, and she looked up at him appreciatively.

"For once, so do I," Rausch said.

The two men identified themselves as Special Agents Mueller
and Johnson, and as soon as Osborne, Ashley, and Rausch climbed
into the back of the GMC they headed across the base to one of a

series of low-slung concrete buildings behind a tall razor wire–topped fence.

They'd come to Washington on Rausch's insistence so that Osborne and Ashley—but especially Osborne—could be debriefed. He'd thought they'd they be taken to the Bureau's headquarters downtown, and he said as much to Rausch.

"Change of plans in light of the Tweets on Mr. Fenniger's account. Twitter's been unable to shut the site down, and that alone has a lot of people interested in talking to you. To the both of you."

"Why me?"

"Because you knew about Hibbing, and you knew the right questions to ask."

"What's this place?" Osborne asked as they were buzzed through the unmanned gate after the driver stuck his head out the open window and submitted to a retinal scan.

"It's a debriefing center, for want of a better term," Rausch said.

"What better term?" Ashley asked sharply.

"It's an isolation center we share with the CIA."

"Hometown rendition," Ashley said.

"No. It's just your father and a couple of people—one of them from the Bureau and the other from the Agency—want to talk to you about what happened over the holidays, and what else Nate knows about the Russian he was stationed with in Afghanistan."

"We're not under arrest?" Ashley pressed.

"Good heavens, no."

"Then turn around now and take us back to the plane. I need to get to Bismarck."

"Easy," Osborne said. He placed a hand on her knee. "There's a lot at stake." He turned to Rausch as they came up to the entrance to one of the buildings. "We're not staying here tonight. You will take us back to Dickinson."

"It's out of my hands."

Ashley started to object, but Osborne squeezed her knee.

"It's not negotiable," Osborne said.

INSIDE THEY were ushered into a surprisingly done-up room with wood paneling, a few world cities posters on the walls, soft lighting, carpeting, and a conference table around which were six leather chairs.

General Forester, seated at the table with a stern-looking man dressed in an open-collar shirt and jeans, and a jolly-looking, almost grandmotherly woman in a print dress, got to his feet. "Here they are at last," he said.

He introduced the other two as Duane Urban, a Special Projects officer with the CIA's Directorate of Operations, and Dotty Hughes, a senior investigator with the FBI's Cyber Crimes division. She gave them warm smiles.

"We're going to give you folks one hour, and then we're going to leave and the Bureau is going to fly us back to Dickinson," Osborne said.

"We'll decide that," Urban said.

"Not if you want my cooperation. There's going to be a whole lot of frightened people tomorrow if this blackout actually occurs—which I think it will—and I'm going to be with the people of my county when it does. So let's make it quick and easy."

The CIA officer started to object but Forester held him off. "The president will address the nation at eight for the same reason you want to be back in North Dakota. So let's start with your Russian, Yuri Makarov. Tell us about him and how you figured he's involved."

Osborne did, succinctly, wasting no words as if he were giving a military SITREP.

"That's pretty thin, just from the reflection in a windshield," Urban said.

"It fit with what I knew about him, and the few people we could find who actually came in contact with him recognized him from the photograph."

"He's not done, is that what you're telling us?" Urban asked.

That had been a tough one for Osborne to figure out, and he admitted it. "If it's the same guy, simply shooting out an insulator so that he could cause the death of a lineman makes no sense. There's more."

"Do you think he's somehow involved with the rolling blackouts?"

"Toby Lundgren, the MAPP computer specialist in Hibbing, was sure the hacker was part of a commune somewhere in Amsterdam. He was pretty sure that the same person who was responsible for restoring the power as the repairman was working on the line sent the Tweets. So there is some connection."

"But neither you nor this Lundgren has any proof?" Urban asked.

"No."

Dotty Hughes, who'd sat silent until now, smiled pleasantly. "You've made it abundantly clear in public that you know for a fact that Yuri Makarov is involved. Can you tell us your reason?"

"I want him to come after me."

Urban started to say something, but the lady FBI agent held him off. "Why? Do you have a grudge, Sheriff Osborne?"

"Gerry Kasmir was a friend of mine. He didn't deserve this."

"No one does."

A console phone buzzed on the table in front of Forester and he picked it up. "Yes." He looked up. "A call is coming to your cell phone, Nate. From the Rough Riders Hotel. Do you want to take it? Cell phones don't work in here."

Osborne got up and went to the phone. "This is Osborne."

"It's Tina. I hate to bother you, but someone called here looking for you. Said he was with the FBI down in Denver. Robert Banks. But he sounded like a phony to me."

"Did he leave a number?"

"No."

Tina hesitated. "The president is coming on TV in a few minutes. Have anything to do with what you're up to?"

Osborne forced a chuckle. "The president doesn't consult with me. We'll be back in the morning," he said, and hung up before she could ask anything else. "Does Robert Banks still work with the Bureau's office in Denver?"

"I never heard the name," Deb Rausch said. She got up, took the phone from Nate, and made a quick call, mentioning the name and the Denver office. She hung up and shook her head. "No one by that name."

"Is it him?" Ashley asked.

"I think so," Osborne said. He phoned Whitney's cell number, and she answered after a couple of rings.

"Hello."

"Where are you?"

"I'm on my way to your house. If you don't mind a guest for a couple of nights until we get past this blackout thing."

"The general wants you in Washington."

"One of the blackout cities," Whitney said. "I think I'd be safer out here."

"Key's under the mat."

"When will you be back?"

"First thing in the morning, maybe sooner if I can swing it. In the meantime I'm sending one of my deputies to be with you."

"Do you think it's necessary?" Whitney asked.

"Just a precaution."

"Was that Whitney?" Forester asked after Osborne hung up.

"She's on her way to my place. So I need to get back right away," Osborne said. He phoned the home number for David Grafton, the youngest and brightest of his three deputies.

"Grafton."

"Dave this is Nate, I need you to do something for me. Could be trouble coming our way."

"Where are you? The caller ID is blocked."

"I'm in Washington, but I should be back before dawn. Dr. Lipton is on the way out to my place. She's going to stay for a couple of days, until this blackout thing sorts itself out."

"Holy shit, are we involved again?"

"Could be. Anyway I want you to stay with her until I get back."

"Take me fifteen minutes."

"And, Dave, I meant possible serious trouble. So take one of the thirty-thirties and an extra box of shells." The .30-.30 was a lever-action rifle that just about everyone in North Dakota owned, and that all the units in Osborne's office carried in a rack between the driver's seat and the computer. "Keep out of sight as much as possible. It's just for overnight."

"Gotcha," Grafton said, obviously impressed.

"We can send backup," Deb Rausch said, when Osborne hung up.

"He doesn't know where I live."

"Then why'd you send one of your deputies out there?" she asked.

42

WHITNEY STOOD ON the porch of Osborne's farm-house for a minute or two, listening to the distant sounds of what probably were trucks on the interstate highway. In the summer the cicadas and other insects were loud, and late at night sometimes the wolves or coyotes would howl. But at this hour, still daylight, the big bowl of the sky immense compared to what she could see in the Atlanta suburbs, she felt a deep sense of aloneness, and she shivered.

She found the key under the mat, and inside turned on the tele-vision to channel 7, the Dickinson NBC station, then dropped her jacket and overnight bag in the back bedroom. She went into the kitchen and poured a glass of red wine.

She felt at home here, and safe because of Osborne and even more so because of his and Ashley's relationship. But in the living room, the president had just come on and he looked serious, and her mood instantly deepened. The blackout thing was certainly no joke, but seeing the president on television brought it up-close and very personal.

"My fellow Americans," he began. He was speaking from his desk in the Oval Office rather than the press briefing room. He looked alert if careworn. "Those of you who follow my national security adviser's Twitter account are already aware that United States has been threatened by a person or persons unknown. While many of you may have considered the messages a hoax, they are not."

Whitney sat down.

"We have been warned that sometime within the next twelve to eighteen hours a series of rolling electrical blackouts will sweep across the nation. Although we don't know the exact timetable, or how long the loss of electrical power will last, we believe that the outages will be brief.

"Beginning in Los Angeles, the outages will spread east to Salt Lake City, Las Vegas, and Denver. The power may fail in ten other metropolitan areas as well, including Kansas City, Chicago, Detroit, Cincinnati, Miami, Nashville, Philadelphia, Boston, here in Washington, and finally New York City."

The president looked directly into the camera. "The outages will cause some inconvenience, but there is no need for panic. I repeat, there is no need for panic. The United States is not under direct military attack, this is just an act of computer terrorism."

Someone knocked at the front door and Whitney practically jumped out of her skin.

"The Emergency Operations Centers in each of these cities have been alerted, as have the local, county, and state law enforcement agencies, the National Guard units, along with hospitals and other important elements in our infrastructure that will need to go on backup power."

Whoever it was knocked at the front door again. "Ma'am, it's

Deputy Grafton, the sheriff wanted me to come out to make sure everything's okay."

The president was saying something about computers, cell phones, and clocks as Whitney went to a dining room window and carefully parted the curtains.

A youngish-looking man in a Billings County Sheriff's uniform was standing on the porch. She vaguely recognized him as one of Osborne's deputies and went back out to the living room and unlocked the door as he knocked a third time.

"You gave me a fright," he said, stepping back.

"Me, too," Whitney admitted. "Are we expecting trouble?"

"I don't know, Doc, but the sheriff asked that I hang around until he shows up. Said he'd be here sometime in the morning."

Whitney stepped aside to let him in, but he shook his head. "I'm going to wander around out here for a while. So you just go back to whatever you're doing."

"Do you want something to eat?"

"Already had my dinner, thanks," Grafton said. He looked beyond her to the television set. "Looks like they're trying another nine-eleven on us. But it won't work this time."

"Why's that?" Whitney asked, despite her bleak and deepening mood.

"Because it's no surprise this time."

Whitney didn't know what to say to that, and Grafton touched the brim of his cap, turned, and headed in the direction of the barn. He was carrying a rifle, and that bothered her.

"Deputy," she called out.

He stopped and turned. "Doc?"

"Should I be worried?"

"About what the president is saying?"

"About why you're here tonight."

"Far as I see the sheriff has a great deal of respect for you and the work you're doing. He just doesn't want a repeat of what happened over the holidays. Not that something like that is likely to happen out here again, he's just being cautious."

"Okay," Whitney said, again not knowing what else to say. But she was spooked, and she felt like she was becoming a paranoid old woman hearing rats in the attic.

The deputy disappeared in the darkness and Whitney closed and locked the door.

The president was just finishing and he was smiling now. "To quote a predecessor of mine: The only thing we have to fear is fear itself."

"Right," she muttered, and she went around inside the house to check every window and door lock then went to see if she could find where Nate kept his guns.

43

U RBAN WAS NOT impressed and he said as much. "I think Dotty will agree with me, that Makarov, if he's the contractor you think he is, wouldn't have anything to do with the rolling blackouts."

"That'd be something the Amsterdam hacker could manipulate through the long-distance transmission-line control centers," Dotty Hughes said. "Lundgren is right so far as that goes, but the Dutch federal police are not interested in helping us until or unless some local crime is committed. As far as they're concerned the people in the commune can do anything they want to do."

"So as you see it, Sheriff, why would Makarov come after you?" Urban said. "Assuming that he is working for someone, what would they have to gain by eliminating you? You're just a small-town sheriff. No offense intended."

"None taken," Osborne said, and it came to him that they were frightened. Very possibly their jobs were on the line because the White House was deeply concerned. No one wanted another 9/11.

"If you're talking about Venezuela's SEBIN and Iran's VEVAK, I don't have the answer. But for Makarov's sake he needs to maintain his anonymity."

"Traipsing out to North Dakota and assassinating you would hardly keep the man anonymous."

"We only have one photograph of him, the rest of what we know is in my head."

"You've given us your report, we have a copy of the photograph, and we have eyewitness accounts from Delta Airlines and Hertz in Minneapolis, plus the truck stop waitress in Dickinson. Killing you wouldn't make all that go away."

Forester sat forward. "I think what Sheriff Osborne is talking about are his gut feelings. He was stationed with the man in Afghanistan. They fought together presumably."

Osborne nodded, but didn't amplify.

"Fight together in just one battle and you get to know things about each other that can't be learned in any other fashion," Forester said. "Were you with him before you lost your leg?"

"He and his sergeant disappeared about two months earlier."

"What's your point?" Urban asked. He was irritated.

"Might give us an advantage if Makarov doesn't know that the sheriff is . . ."

"Handicapped, you can say it," Osborne said. "But the Makarov I knew was thorough. Never went into a situation he wasn't prepared for. He knows about me."

"Where you live, too?" Urban pressed.

"That's a matter of local records, a lot harder to hack into because they're on paper, but he knows the town."

"Phone, IRS?"

"Phone's unlisted, the IRS and everything else by mail comes to a PO box."

"You're saying that a thorough guy like Makarov hasn't found out exactly where you live?"

Osborne had given some though to that as well. And he'd come to the conclusion that in a way he'd been hiding out on his parents' ranch since Afghanistan.

"A slight post-traumatic stress disorder, but nothing debilitating," the military shrink at Bethesda had told him. "With time that'll fade, especially if you stay away from high-stress environments."

Which for the most part he had; being sheriff of Billings County was hardly a high-stress position, and living outside Medora—itself a town of only one hundred people—was even farther away from the battlefield. After less than a year his wife, Caroline, had not been able to stand the isolation, and she'd taken their daughter to Orlando, where before long she'd sent divorce papers.

Afterward he'd burrowed even deeper, nesting, going to bed and pulling the covers over his head. He'd never even bothered transferring the ranch out of his parents' names. As long as he paid the property taxes on time, no one out there cared if every *i* was dotted and every *t* crossed.

In fact it wasn't until Ashley showed up in his life a few months ago that he had begun to come out of his shell.

"Maybe."

"And you're betting a scientist's life that you're right, and that either your deputy will stop this guy, or Makarov won't be able to find out where you live," Urban said. He looked at the others around the table. "Yet you don't want the Bureau's help. Pretty fucking shortsighted—arrogant—if you ask me."

Osborne had thought of almost nothing else. He got up. "I didn't ask you," he said. "Your charter is ops outside the U.S., so go catch the hacker." He turned to the FBI Cyber Crimes agent. "The most likely way to stop him will be online. I suggest that you people get together with Lundgren. He's the only one who seems to know what the hell he's doing and not bothering to cover his ass in the meantime."

Ashley got up and stood next to him.

"Now if you people don't mind, I'd like to get back to my county, and to Dr. Lipton who figures she's safer out there than here where you're facing a blackout sometime tomorrow."

AIRBORNE OUT of Andrews aboard the Bureau's Gulfstream, Osborne used the aircraft's phone once they reached ten thousand feet to call Dave Grafton's cell. His deputy answered on the first ring.

"Sheriff?"

"What's your situation?"

"It's been quiet. I'm in the hayloft. Good sight lines on the driveway and the house."

"I'm on my way back in an FBI jet. We're making a stop in Minneapolis but then we'll continue on to Dickinson. I'll be there before sunrise. Did you talk to Dr. Lipton?"

"Briefly. Seems like she can take it."

Grafton, in Osborne's estimation, was just a kid. He'd never served in the military, but like a lot of guys his age he had a distrust of anyone over thirty. And especially if it was a woman. He'd once explained that his mother, who'd dabbled briefly as a rodeo cowgirl and then a stunt pilot, had set the bar pretty high for him when it came to judging women. *Seems like she can take it* was a pretty good compliment.

"Keep your eyes open."

"Will do," Grafton said.

Osborne phoned his own home number, and Whitney answered after only two rings. She seemed breathless, as if she had just finished a fifty-yard dash.

"Yes?"

"It's me. How're you doing?"

"Other than being just a little freaked out that you sent one of your deputies to ride herd—I think that's one of the terms you guys out here use—I'm just dandy. Next question?"

"His name's Dave Grafton, and he's a great shot. Right now he's in the hayloft riding herd, as you say, to make sure no one sneaks up on you."

The line was silent for just a moment or two. "Sorry, I'm just a little bit uptight after listening to the president."

"I didn't see it. What'd he say?"

"We're under attack, but not to worry, don't panic, we know it's coming and we're dealing with it," Whitney said. She was brittle.

"We're on our way. Shouldn't be more than a few hours, so try to get some sleep, okay?"

"Okay," Whitney said. "Is Ashley with you?"

"Here she is," Osborne said and he handed the phone to Ashley. "She's scared."

"No shit."

44

FOUR AND A half hours later, but well before dawn, Makarov pulled off the interstate onto a dirt road that led north, the opposite direction from Fryburg, making sure that no one was coming from either direction before he doused his headlights.

The morning was crystal clear, and once he got his night vision he had no problem seeing well enough to keep on the road, and pulled up just below a shallow rise a quarter-mile from the turnoff to Osborne's ranch.

Earlier, just before he'd reached Fargo, a program on his iPad had intercepted two phone calls; one to Osborne's deputy hiding in a hayloft, and the other to Dr. Lipton waiting at the ranch, and he'd heard everything Osborne had said to them.

It was a stroke of luck. Dr. Lipton was not on his hit list, but her presence out here made it certain that Osborne would come directly home to her. And knowing about the deputy was also a piece of good fortune, though it had never been his intention to simply barge in.

Even allowing for favorable tailwinds and a quick turnaround in Minneapolis he figured he had at least one hour, probably two, before Osborne and presumably Ashley Borden, the newspaper reporter, showed up.

He got out of his car, stiff after the long nonstop drive, and trotted on an angle toward the ranch, keeping below the crest of the hill until the land began to flatten out. A shallow creek, not much wider than a drainage ditch, meandered from the northwest, clumps of tall grasses and a few willow trees along its banks.

At the top he dropped to his hands and knees from where he had a good line of fire to the house about three hundred yards to the southeast and the barn, its hayloft door open. The deputy had parked his F150 out of sight, but Dr. Lipton's car was in front alongside a Toyota pickup.

No lights shone from any of the windows in the house. Presumably the scientist had taken Osborne's advice and had gone to bed.

Makarov had given himself forty-five minutes to take out the deputy, secure the woman, and bring his car to the ranch where he would wait for Osborne to show up. With any luck at all he would be back on the interstate and halfway to Minneapolis before anyone trying to reach the sheriff got suspicious.

Even then nothing would connect Thomas van Houghton, driving an anonymous dark blue Camry, with the crime scene.

Keeping low he crawled through the tall grasses along the creek bank until one of the outbuildings was between himself and the barn then he splashed across to the other side, and still keeping low, ran directly to the back of the house.

The night remained silent, no noises and no lights from any direction.

At the corner he could see the rear of the barn, its big service door open, the deputy's pickup parked inside. Osborne was expecting him, and his deputy had laid the trap. The open hayloft door in front would give a good view of the house and out toward the dirt road, though not as far as the interstate. Anyone driving up to the ranch would be spotted once they topped the rise, the headlights even farther.

Makarov pulled out his Glock, though he had no intention of actually firing it, unless he was cornered, and sprinted across the thirty yards of open space to the barn, where he held up at the open service door, for just a moment, before glancing back at the house, and then ducking inside.

He stood stock-still in the deeper shadows listening, all of his senses alert for any sound, anything out of the ordinary, any movement, a cough, footsteps, anything.

Almost immediately a dim light up in the hayloft switched on for just a couple of seconds then went out. A few moments later he smelled cigarette smoke. The idiot deputy had actually lit a cigarette.

It was something a man of Osborne's caliber and training would never have done, and Makarov was surprised and even a little disappointed that the sheriff hadn't trained his deputy better than that.

The hayloft covered the front half of the barn. Waiting another minute for his eyes to fully adjust to the deeper darkness, Makarov silently went to the ladder and slowly climbed up, rung by rung, until his head just cleared the floor.

A few bales of hay were stacked up in the far corner, and couple of others just a few feet back from the open door where a man was seated, his back to the ladder, his figure silhouetted from the dim starlight. A Winchester .30-.30 was propped against one of the bales, a pistol in a holster at the man's left hip.

With great care Makarov climbed the rest of the way up, and moved a couple of feet to his left.

Grafton, sensing something, suddenly looked over his shoulder, dropped his cigarette, and reached for the rifle.

"I will shoot you," Makarov warned.

Grafton's hand stopped inches from the gun.

"If you think that Dr. Lipton will hear the shot and call for help, you're wrong. She won't."

"You son of a bitch."

Makarov moved closer. "I won't kill her, it's not why I'm here."

"What do you want?"

"I'm here to assassinate your sheriff, of course," Makarov said, taking another step.

"Means you'll have to kill me, too," Grafton said, and he grabbed the rifle.

Makarov moved in on the deputy's left side and slammed the butt of his pistol into the man's temple.

Grafton was rocked back with a grunt, blood instantly filling his left eye socket, but he continued to try to bring the rifle to bear, the fingers of his left hand fumbling for the trigger. But like just about every law enforcement officer Makarov had ever come up against, this one did not have a round chambered. The philosophy was that the sound of a long gun being racked was intimidating enough to give the bad guy pause.

Ignoring the Winchester, Makarov slammed the butt of his pistol into the side of the deputy's head again with every ounce of his strength, knocking the man to his knees, where he lost his grip on the rifle.

Makarov wiped the butt of his pistol on the back of the deputy's jacket, then shoved it in his belt.

Grafton grunted again and started to rise, but Makarov stepped around the hay bale, shoved a knee into the younger man's spine, yanked his head sharply to the left breaking his neck, and let him slump to the floor.

The deputy looked up, trying to bring air into his lungs, but it was impossible, and he knew that he was going to die.

Indifferently Makarov dragged the still-convulsing deputy off to the side, then went back to the open loft door and looked out toward the driveway. The night remained dark.

Grafton's cigarette butt was smoldering on the floor and Makarov considered letting it lie. It was possible that the barn could catch fire, and with any luck spread to the house. Might leave an interesting message for whoever investigated the scene. But he ground out the butt under the sole of his shoe, and went back down to the rear service door where he held up again.

Still no lights shone from the ranch house windows and he darted across to the rear door, which not surprisingly was locked.

A sloping metal door was set against the foundation in the far corner of the house, and it was not locked. Inside, the only light came from the open door but it was enough for Makarov to make his way across what probably had once been used as a root cellar. A few jars of preserves with thick dust on them still sat on wooden shelves along the wall. A gas-fired furnace was tucked in one corner alongside of a water heater, also gas fired.

Taking great care not to bump into anything, or make the slightest bit of noise, he reached the stairs and at the top the door into the kitchen had been left unlocked.

He stood for a long time, listening for any sounds, but the only thing he could hear was the refrigerator motor. He walked out into the living room beyond which a short hallway led to the west wing of the low-slung house where he found a bathroom and the open door to a bedroom where a figure was bundled under a quilt in a twin bed.

"Dr. Lipton," he said softly.

Whitney stirred.

"Time to wake up," he said a little louder.

Whitney came awake with a start. She fumbled with her covers, but then sat up and reached for the bedside light.

"No lights, please."

"Who are you?" Whitney demanded.

"I think you know," Makarov said. "Certainly Sheriff Osborne knew I was coming tonight. That's why he posted a deputy in the barn."

"Are you here to kill me?"

"Not unless I have to, which I won't if you cooperate."

Whitney was fully awake now. "What do you want?"

"I'll be happy to discuss it with you, but first do you have any idea where the sheriff might keep his duct tape?"

Whitney shook her head.

"Well, then get out of bed and we'll go looking."

"If I don't?"

"Then I'll have to kill you after all."

"You don't have a gun."

"I don't need one, Doctor," Makarov said.

45

IT WAS FOUR thirty in the morning, local, when the Bureau's Gulfstream lined up for landing at the Dickinson Regional Airport, after the pilot first requested that the runway and taxi lights be switched on. Ashley had dozed in a seat near the rear of the main cabin for the last couple of hours, since before they'd decided not to stop at Minneapolis, but Deb Rausch had been almost continuously on the phone for most of the flight, leaving Osborne with his own thoughts leading back to Afghanistan.

He'd thought it more than odd at the time that a handful of Russian advisers had been sent supposedly to help the American forces to avoid some of the pitfalls that had kept them in country for ten years.

"It was our Vietnam," they kept saying.

Though exactly what that meant from a Russian point of view was anyone's guess, except that the brass in Kabul, presumably on orders from Washington, had permitted the Spetsnaz teams—one officer and one NCO—to be embedded with a few of the forward units around Kandahar in the south, Mazar-e Sharif in the north, and in the mountains outside Narang along the border with Pakistan.

It had been a top-secret, highly sensitive operation that had lasted less than six months before the Russians had been ordered home. And no one that Osborne had ever spoken with had the slightest idea what had been accomplished, if anything.

Deb Rausch was seated across from him, her eyes red. "Nettles is sending a helicopter for me. I'm going to hang out at the Initiative to see what happens if and when the attack on the grid actually develops. Do you want to come along?"

"They're not going to hit the project again," Osborne said.

"Probably not, but I've been asked to monitor the computer system at Donna Marie to see what effect shutting down parts of the grid is going to have on its output. Might give us a clue."

"From what Whitney told us, most of her scientists and technicians have already left or are in the process."

"We're not interested in the research and development team this time, only the folks running the generating station, and the power connection with the grid."

"And who's controlling it," Osborne said.

The hacker in Amsterdam, or wherever, had already shown them who was in charge. And if he pulled off the rolling blackouts, any last doubts would be completely erased. If it happened in just a few hours we would learn in no uncertain terms just how vulnerable the U.S. really was.

Shortly after 9/11 Secretary of Defense Don Rumsfeld was telling people that we had entered a new age in which all the might of the United States, all of our nuclear weapons and submarines and aircraft carriers and missiles could not have protected us from the strikes on the World Trade Center towers, the Pentagon, and what probably would have been a hit on the White House except for the heroes who had brought the fourth aircraft down in a Pennsylvania field.

We were in the same situation now, only instead of hijacked airliners filled with passengers and fuel, this time we were faced with a cyber attack. It was something anyone who used a home computer understood very well; someone hacking into your system, into your bank accounts, identity theft, crashed hard drives, e-mails suddenly irretrievable—the feeling of total helplessness in the face of a technologically superior bad guy. An alien in many ways.

"If we can pull up enough data from a sufficient number of locations we might be able to pinpoint his location," Rausch said.

"Your Cyber Crimes people come up with that idea?"

"No. It was Lundgren's suggestion."

They touched down with a bark of tires and a slight lurch, which woke Ashley, and she came forward. They taxied over to the terminal building and stopped about thirty yards from where an Air Force Blackhawk helicopter was parked.

"Do you want to go back to Bismarck?" Osborne asked her.

"I can file my stories from your place, if you don't mind," she said.

Actually he did mind. In Bismarck she would be safe. But out here—no matter how unlikely that Makarov would have gotten this far so soon—she could be in some danger. "Do I have any choice?"

She grinned. "Nope."

The door was opened and they headed forward. Dick Keating, the pilot, turned in his seat.

"We've been ordered to head back to Andrews if we can get a fuel truck out here in time," he said. "All air traffic across the country will be shut down in less than eight hours."

"I'm going to stick it out here," Deb Rausch said.

"Good luck," Keating said.

"To all of us," Osborne said. "Thanks for the ride."

Captain Nettles had walked over from the helicopter. He was

dressed in BDUs, his slacks bloused in his desert khaki boots. "Good morning, folks," he said. "Are all of you coming back to the Initiative?"

"Just me," Deb Rausch said.

"Mr. Kohl is expecting you, though it doesn't look as if this thing is going to start till noon on the West Coast."

"Unless whoever is doing it was lying about the timing," Osborne said.

Nettles looked at him. "You know something I don't?"

"Nothing that would have any effect on your operations at the project. Have your people noticed anything out of the ordinary?"

"We're running regular air patrols out twenty klicks. Infrared at night. There's been nothing but animals, and a little bit of traffic on the interstate and on eighty-five down around Amidon, but nothing heading our way."

"I don't think they're after the project this time."

"Neither do I, but I've been ordered to remain on scene until someone figures out what the hell is going on."

"You have my cell phone number," Rausch told Osborne. "Anything comes up let me know."

"You, too," Osborne said.

Deb Rausch followed Nettles over to the helicopter, and Osborne and Ashley walked around to where he'd left his Saturn SUV radio unit. Only a few other cars and a pickup were parked in the lot, and just then Osborne had a strong feeling that he wanted all this business to be over with and to get back to the generally peaceful life of a small-county sheriff.

He glanced at Ashley. A small-county *married* sheriff.

She was looking at him, a little smile on her lips. "What're you thinking, Nate?"

"Later," Osborne said, and as they headed out of the parking lot he phoned his deputy.

46

GRAFTON'S CELL PHONE rang softly. It was something Makarov had counted on. He moved to the edge of the hayloft door and looked out in the direction of the dirt road from the highway, but no lights were headed this way.

The deputy had spoken with a flat Midwestern accent, and fast. Makarov answered on the third ring, but positioned a finger so that it was partially blocking the microphone. "Sheriff?"

"David? I can barely hear you."

"How about—" Makarov turned his head away. "Now. Can—you—?"

"We're on our way from the airport. Is everything okay?"

"Yes," Makarov said, and he hit the end button.

Almost immediately the cell phone rang again, and he answered it. "Here—" and he hit the end button again.

Presumably Osborne was coming from the Dickinson airport. But he'd said *we* were on the way. Possibly another deputy, or possibly the FBI agent from Minneapolis Dr. Lipton had told him was involved in the Cyber Crimes investigation.

It hadn't been necessary to cause her much pain before she'd begun to cooperate. She'd been trussed head to toe on the bed, her ankles taped to her wrists. He'd found a long, slender fish-trimming knife in a kitchen drawer, and holding her mouth open with one hand had poked around several of her molars with the tip of the blade until he'd found a sensitive spot.

After less than a minute she'd told him about Special Agent Deborah Rausch, and General Forester and the flight to Minneapolis and then Washington.

"I was supposed to go, but Nate said I could stay here," Whitney had sobbed.

But there'd been no real tears.

Makarov shoved her head into the pillow and brought the tip of the blade to within a half inch of her left eye. "Much of your work involves looking through a microscope," he said.

She tried to struggle away, but he tightened his grip.

"Quiet now, we don't want me to make a mistake, because it would be a tragedy for a scientist such as you to be blind in one eye."

Whitney didn't move a muscle, but this time real tears began welling up in her eyes.

"More of a tragedy if you lost both of your eyes. Blind so young, at the height of your career."

"They think the blackouts will be caused by a computer hacker living in Amsterdam."

This was a surprise.

"They know it was you who shot out the insulators and killed the sheriff and the couple in the pickup truck."

"How do they know?" Makarov asked gently.

"Nate saw your image in the sheriff's dash cam. It was a reflection inside the windshield. And he managed to get your photograph."

"Impossible."

"From Afghanistan," Whitney said. "Nate was there. He knows you."

It had taken everything within Makarov's power not to plunge the knife all the way through her eye, and into her brain. Instead he taped her mouth shut and made a quick survey of the house.

He found her cell phone in her purse on the hall table and pocketed its battery. Next he cut the wires to the three landline phones he found—one in the master bedroom, one in the kitchen, and the other in the sheriff's study. The laptop computer there was not plugged into an Ethernet connection, so he went looking for the Wi-Fi router which was in the hall closet. He cut all the wires including the AC and emergency battery leads.

A gun cabinet was in the living room. He smashed the glass front and took out the three rifles and one 20-gauge over and under shotgun and field stripped them, taking the trigger mechanisms from all of them except for the Weatherby Mark V, which was an excellent long-range weapon. He found the scope and a box of .338 Lapua magnum rounds.

Before he went out to retrieve his rental car and drive it back to the barn he checked on Whitney, who'd managed to wiggle herself off the bed.

"If you prefer to lie on the floor that's fine with me," he'd told her. "But if I come back and find you anywhere except in this room, I will kill you. Do you understand me?"

Whitney glared at him, but she nodded.

"Do as you're told and the chances that you'll come out of this alive are very good."

———

IN THE barn Makarov set up another pair of hay bales just inside the hayloft door. He mounted the scope on the Weatherby and loaded the two-shot magazine and chambered one round.

Coming out here for the assassination he'd figured to find the sheriff asleep in his bedroom and take him out with an easy head-shot with the Glock. But the deputy waiting in the barn and Whitney Lipton asleep in the house had complicated the situation.

Grafton's cell phone rang again, and Makarov answered it, his finger partially covering the mic. "Yes."

"If you can hear me get on your police radio," Osborne said.

Makarov pressed the end button, then took the battery out and tossed it aside.

He hurried down to the deputy's pickup truck next to his Camry, backed it out of the barn and drove a hundred yards up the drive-way, and parked it at an angle across the road. He switched on the headlights, jumped out, and leaving the door open, raced back to the barn and up into the hayloft.

Two scenarios were likely. Either the sheriff would come up the driveway, see the deputy's truck parked in the middle of the road and get out to investigate, in which case the shot from the hayloft would be easy. Or the sheriff would suspect that he was running into a trap, and would circle around and come in from the west side of the property and across the creek. If that were the case, Makarov would go back to the house and use Whitney as a hostage.

Either way he would leave no witnesses and with any luck he'd be back out on the interstate heading west into the blackouts and disappear in the confusion.

From the Dickinson airport it was about twenty miles. Osborne would be showing up within a few minutes. If he came all the way up the driveway his headlights would be visible for a long ways off.

Makarov checked his watch. In ten minutes if there were no headlights, he would go back to the house to wait.

47

J UST OFF THE interstate, Osborne tried the radio in Grafton's police unit again with no response. Bracketing the mic he slowed down and switched off the headlights.

"What's the matter?" Ashley asked.

"Maybe nothing, but Dave's phone was cutting out and he hasn't answered the radio in his pickup."

"Do you want to call for backup? Nettles could have a chopper out here in ten minutes."

"Not yet," Osborne said absently. He didn't want the cavalry swooping down without knowing the exact situation. In the distance he spotted a light or lights. But they weren't from the ranch.

Ashley saw them, too. "Headlights?"

"Maybe," Osborne said.

The dirt road dipped down into a low valley then started back up to the crest of the last hill before his property began. Just before the top Osborne stopped. "I'm going to take a look, I want you to stay here," he said, and before Ashley could object he grabbed a pair of binoculars from the glove compartment, jumped out of his car, and trotted the rest of the way to the top.

Just at the crest he dropped to all fours and cautiously made his way just to a spot where, lying flat, he could see Grafton's truck parked at an angle across the road, its headlights on, the driver's side door open.

Resting on his elbows he glassed the truck and the field toward the east for any sign of his deputy. Something had happened out here to lure Grafton from the barn, drive to this spot, and then, leaving his headlights on, get out and head away from the road.

But nothing moved now in any direction as far as Osborne could see, and the night was very quiet and, except for the stars under a partly cloudy sky, very dark.

He followed the dirt track the rest of the way to his house where Whitney's government-issued Taurus was parked in front next to Ashley's pickup. No lights shone from any of the windows, and nothing seemed out of the ordinary.

Turning his attention to the barn, he studied the open hayloft door for any sign that Grafton had for some reason abandoned his truck on the road and had gone back on foot. But nothing moved up there, either, though he thought he was seeing a couple of hay bales stacked just inside, something Grafton would have set up to use as a firing stand.

But the situation wasn't right. It didn't smell legitimate to him.

He rose up on one knee for just a moment to get a better snapshot angle on the open hayloft door, and then dropped back. If this was a trap he'd given a shooter up there an invitation. But nothing happened.

He glassed Grafton's pickup again then followed a probable path out into the field, looking for something, anything lying on the ground. Grafton's body. Again there was nothing.

Lowering the binoculars he eased back ten feet then got up and went back to his car where Ashley was waiting at the side of the road with the shotgun. She was spooked.

"Well?" she demanded.

"Its Dave Grafton's truck, parked in the middle of the road, lights on, door open."

"No sign of him?"

"No."

"Could be a trap?"

"I think so, and I think Dave is probably already dead."

Ashley was alarmed. "We need to get some help out here right now, Nate. If Makarov is here Whitney could be next."

"He came for me. And if he has taken Dave out, it means he's monitored my calls and knew where to look. Calling for help now won't do us any good. He'll know they're coming."

"We can use my cell phone."

"No telling if he can monitor yours as well. Maybe he can monitor everything coming out of the local tower."

"So what if he does? If he hears us calling for backup maybe he'll just run."

"He has Whitney as a hostage. Unless I show up he'll just take her with him and kill her once he's clear."

Ashley wanted to argue, but she just shook her head in frustration. "Okay, you sneak in, flush him out, and if he comes my way I'll take him down." She raised the Ithaca 12-bore.

"Not a chance," Osborne said, though it was about what he thought she would say.

She started to object, but he cut her off.

"You're going to take my car and drive back to Tiger Discount in Dickinson and make a landline call to the project, and tell Nettles and Rausch what the situation out here probably is."

"Goddamnit, Nate, that's just going to take too long."

Osborne glanced back toward the crest of the hill and the head-lights stabbing the night sky. "I need the time, Ash," he said. "This is personal."

"Yeah, I know, your county."

"My house," Osborne said. He got his Kevlar vest from the back of the SUV, and put it on under his jacket. "Get going. And don't turn on the headlights until just before the interstate."

Ashley hesitated, but finally she nodded. "I'm not used to tak-ing orders."

"I didn't know that."

Ashley got back in the car, re-racked the shotgun, made a Y-turn, and headed south.

When she was finally out of sight, Osborne stepped off the dirt road and headed west toward the creek from where he could reach the rear of his house, out of sight from the barn. Probably the same way Makarov had come.

ASHLEY HAD never run away from a fight in her life, and just before she reached the interstate she stopped Nate's SUV and glanced at the shotgun. Ever since she was a teenager, and convinced that instead of a military career like her dad's she was going to be a newspaper reporter she'd modeled herself after the gutsy Nellie Bly—whose real name was Liz Cochran.

Nellie, who worked for the *New York World,* had taken a trip around the world just like Jules Verne's character Phileas Fogg—but this was in the late 1800s when things like that weren't done by women. She'd also gotten herself declared insane so that she could be committed to an asylum to gather material for an article.

The girl had guts, plain and simple.

Ashley looked in her rearview mirror. The man she loved was

humping his way across the prairie, in the dark, with one prosthetic leg and armed only with a pistol to take on a professional killer who knew that he was coming.

She touched the barrel of the shotgun.

But the bastard didn't know about her.

She made another Y-turn and headed back to the base of the hill where'd she'd left Nate.

48

STANDING IN THE shadows a few feet back from the hayloft door Makarov continued to watch the crest of the hill through the Weatherby's scope for a full five minutes. But Osborne had suspected the deputy's car on the road was a trap. Right now he was coming overland on foot. Probably from the west across the creek.

Only four calls had been relayed from the Medora cell tower in the past twenty minutes, none of them from Osborne. Nor had his iPad program picked up anything from the Billings or Stark County police and sheriff's radio channels.

Shoving the tablet in his jacket pocket he shouldered the rifle by its strap, climbed down the ladder, and held up just inside the rear service door, from where he looked outside. Nothing moved.

Unslinging the rifle he trotted across to the rear of the house, and at the west corner took a long look across the field toward the line of willows and the creek at the same moment a dark figure, hunched over and moving fast, dropped down behind a heavy clump of prairie grass.

It had to be Osborne.

Makarov switched the Weatherby's safety catch off, braced the rifle against the corner of the house, and studied the open field between here and the creek. But after several minutes nothing moved, and he got the feeling that the sheriff remembered his lessons from Afghanistan. If you reconnoitered from one direction today, you changed tactics the next day. Never do the obvious. And, if you seemed to be making progress you were probably heading into a trap.

He scoped the line of trees along the creek to the northwest where it blurred to a low smudge against the horizon a couple of miles out. Osborne was out there, circling, biding his time, maybe even until morning. And going out there to try to find the sheriff would be suicide. This was Osborne's land. He knew the place intimately.

The odds were the sheriff's. For now.

Makarov went back to the root cellar and hurried upstairs to the bedroom where Dr. Lipton had managed to tear the duct tape connecting her bound ankles with her bound wrists by rubbing against the doorframe.

She looked up, her eyes wide and tried to back away.

"Don't worry, Doctor, I'm not going to kill you just yet," he said.

He set the rifle aside, pulled the skinning knife out of his belt, and cut her ankles free so that she could walk.

"Sheriff Osborne has shown up to rescue you," he said, and he cut the tape from her wrists and pulled the tape from her mouth.

Whitney backed up a pace, unsteady on her feet. She was dressed for bed in an old sweatshirt, her legs bare. She rubbed her wrists to get the circulation back.

"You and I are going outside, and I'm going to offer him a deal he won't be able to refuse," Makarov said. He turned to pick up the rifle where he'd propped it against the wall, and Whitney rushed him.

She was several inches taller than him, and for just a moment she had him pinned against the doorframe, but he easily shoved her aside, and backhanded her so hard she was slammed against the wall, momentarily dazed.

"Let's not disappoint the sheriff," Makarov said. "I wouldn't want to offer damaged goods to him."

He grabbed her arm and hustled her out of the bedroom and down the hall to the back door off the kitchen, which he unlocked and opened, holding Whitney in front of him.

There was no sign of Osborne yet, but Makarov was certain that the sheriff had moved closer in the last minute or so.

"Nate, as you undoubtedly can see from your concealed position, I have Dr. Lipton here with me."

"He wants to kill you," Whitney shouted. "Call Nettles."

"This is just between you and me," Makarov said. "Teammates just like at the FOBs in Afghanistan."

"Leave the woman alone, or have you turned into a total pussy?" Osborne said from somewhere to the right, toward the barn, and very close.

"Do you want to trade? You for the doctor?"

"It'll be morning soon," Osborne said. "Maybe I'll just wait a bit."

"Maybe I'll kill her in the next ninety seconds."

"Don't," Whitney shouted. "He'll kill us both."

"There's no need to kill the good doctor. My contract is for you."

"Let her free and I'll step out," Osborne said.

He was in the barn, just inside the service door. "As you wish," Makarov said. He shoved Whitney the rest of the way outside, and fired the Weatherby from the hip at a spot in the barn's wall just to the right of the open door and about four and a half feet above the ground, at what he figured was Osborne's center mass. Immediately he bolted another round into the firing chamber.

A woman screaming something came rushing at him across

the kitchen from the front hall, and he turned just as she was two feet away, a short-barreled shotgun pointed at his head, her finger on the trigger. She was Ashley Borden, the sheriff's girlfriend.

He stepped into her, grabbed the barrel with his free hand, deflecting the muzzle into the ceiling the moment she fired, and yanked the weapon from her hands. He tossed it aside and brought the Weatherby to bear as she tried to scramble away from him.

"Bastard," Whitney screamed and crashed into his back, shoving him to the left, the rifle going off, the heavy round plowing into the refrigerator door across the room.

Before he could react she grabbed the rifle out of his hands.

"Run," she screeched, and she sprinted out the kitchen door.

Makarov turned and started after her, but reared back. He got a snapshot of Osborne lying on his back half out of the open service door, apparently dead or dying.

Whitney was fumbling with the rifle, and as he drew his pistol, Ashley was right behind him screaming like a madwoman and she clubbed the gun out of his hand with the stock of the shotgun's barrel.

Again he grabbed the shotgun from her, but she didn't try to run.

"The choppers are on the way from the project," she screamed.

"Nate is down," Whitney shouted from outside. "You've killed him. You bastard, you bastard!"

"My God," Ashley said and she shoved past Makarov, who turned to let her go, and she raced outside.

Whitney was still fumbling with the Weatherby when Makarov stepped outside as he racked a round into the Ithaca. It was obvious she wasn't going to succeed, so he started toward where Ashley had reached the downed sheriff.

She was on her knees by his side, and she suddenly turned, a big

9mm SIG-Sauer in her hand, and she fired, grazing Makarov in his left arm.

He raised the shotgun but before he could fire, Whitney was behind him, clubbing him in the back with the Weatherby.

Ashley got up and fired another shot, this one going wide because Whitney was so close.

The sheriff was down, he'd accomplished his contract. There was no need to stay here any longer. And Osborne's girlfriend just might get off a lucky shot.

Ashley was circling around to the left, and Makarov shoved Whitney that way and then turned and sprinted to the corner of the house, firing one shot over his shoulder, and headed in a dead run toward the deputy's car a hundred yards down the driveway.

49

ASHLEY AND WHITNEY propped Osborne up against the barn wall as color slowly began to return to his face, but his eyes were still out of focus, and his breath was fast and raspy. He was dazed and mostly out of it, but he could see Ashley's face in front of him, and hear her voice as if from a long ways off.

"You okay?" he managed to croak. His chest was on fire from where the rifle bullet had slammed into his level IIIa Kevlar vest, and as his awareness began to return he could feel that he had at least a couple of ribs broken.

"Yes," Ashley said, tears streaming down her cheeks. "But I thought you were dead. He shot you with a deer rifle, right through the wall."

A shot of adrenaline pumped into his blood and he tried to sit up. "Where is he?"

"Gone."

"I think I wounded him," Whitney said. "He turned around and ran away."

Osborne reached for his pistol but the holster was empty. "My gun?"

Ashley handed it to him. "He's not coming back, Nate. He thinks that you're dead."

The night was swimming back into focus and as it did Osborne's pain increased. He gave the pistol back to Ashley. "Go around front and see if you can still see Dave Grafton's lights."

"Okay."

"But be careful, Ash. This guy's going to take out anyone who tries to get in his way."

She got to her feet. "Watch him," she told Whitney and she headed around to the front of the house.

Osborne managed to fish his cell phone out of his jacket pocket and he dialed Deb Rausch's number. She answered on the second ring.

"Yes."

"He's been here," Osborne said. "But he's gone now. On the run."

"Shit. Are Ashley and Dr. Lipton okay?"

"Shook up, but he didn't get the chance to hurt them."

"How about you?"

"I took a round in my vest. Knocked the wind out of me. But you have to get on this right now."

"Not many places he can get to in any kind of a hurry. I'll get Nettles's team on it, and call out mine in Minneapolis. We'll put out a nationwide APB."

"I suspect that he's in disguise, so your people are going to have to go on a general description. And he may be wounded."

"Left arm," Whitney said.

"Left arm," Osborne repeated.

"What's he driving, or is he on foot?"

"Just a minute," Osborne said as Ashley came around the corner.

"The truck is gone," she said.

"He's taken my deputy's pickup truck. Yellow Ford F150 extended cab, with a light bar on the roof and Billings County Sheriff's Department logos on the doors. He's out on the interstate somewhere, but he hasn't had time to make miles. If you can get Nettles to put up two of his helicopters—one east one west, we can get this guy."

"Is he armed?"

"I'm not sure. Maybe Dave's shotgun in the truck. But tell Nettles to go with care, this guy is good. Russian Spetsnaz. He's had some of the best Special Forces training anywhere."

"Nettles is somewhere down at Donna Marie, I'll round him up and get right back to you."

"Hurry."

"Do you need an ambulance?"

"No," Osborne said and he hung up.

"Are Nettles's people on the way?" Ashley asked.

"Deb is working on it," Osborne said. He glanced inside the barn toward the ladder to the hayloft. "I think Dave is up there. Go up and check on him, please."

She handed back his pistol and climbed up into the hayloft.

Whitney had been holding the Weatherby so hard all this time that her knuckles were white.

Osborne struggled to his feet, holding onto the doorframe for support, and he couldn't help but grunt.

Whitney looked stricken. "If you have a broken rib you could puncture a lung."

He managed to smile. "I know. But if you don't put that rifle down, you might shoot me with it."

She looked down at the gun in her hands, and gave a little hysterical laugh. "I hit him with it when we thought he had killed you," she said. "I couldn't get it to shoot." She walked over and propped the rifle up against the barn.

Ashley came down from the hayloft, her face white. "He's dead. I'm not sure but I think his neck is broken."

Osborne's jaw tightened. He'd underestimated Makarov; he wouldn't do it again. His phone rang. It was Deb Rausch.

"I called out my people in Minneapolis, and I contacted the highway patrol and the acting sheriff over in Dickinson, and he promised to send units as quickly as possible. But Nettles needs authorization to move off station. His orders are to guard Donna Marie and until he's told differently there's nothing he or his people can do."

It was about what Osborne figured. "There's a dark blue Camry parked in my barn that he probably rented somewhere. You might try Minneapolis and Denver." He gave the license number. "We haven't touched it, so get your forensics team out here as soon as possible. Maybe we'll get lucky this time with some actual physical evidence we can use."

"But you doubt it."

"Yeah. Where are you?"

"On my way."

THEY WENT to the house where Ashley put on a pot of coffee while Osborne phoned for an ambulance to pick up his deputy's body. Grafton wasn't married, but he had a couple of sisters and his parents outside Minneapolis who would have to be notified later this morning.

Whitney went back to the bedroom where she got dressed, and the three of them sat at the kitchen table drinking coffee, none of them much in the mood for breakfast, though Ashley offered.

"Are we going to catch up with him this morning?" Ashley asked.

"Probably not without Nettles's help. Dave's truck is four-wheel drive, so he could have headed out across country in just about any direction."

"It's pretty empty out there," Ashley said. "And he's going to want to get to a big city where he can lose himself. If he makes Minneapolis or Denver or Kansas City he's as good as gone."

"He's going to be limited with what he can do if the blackouts actually happen," Whitney said.

"So will we be," Osborne said. "So will the Bureau. Everyone will have to hunker down and ride it out. But this isn't done. He'll be back. Maybe not back here, but back somewhere. And once he finds out that I'm not dead I'll become his top priority."

"But why?" Whitney asked. "I mean that's just stupid."

"Because he thinks he's smarter than me. Which he possibly might be, but that makes him arrogant which will be his undoing."

Whitney looked away. "Over electricity," she said. "War."

"Yeah," Osborne agreed. "And it might be one we'll be hard-pressed to win. And no matter what we're going to get chewed up a lot worse than nine-eleven."

50

IN TOM RESSO'S estimation Los Angeles was nothing but a giant shithole. After five days here in exploratory talks with Venture
Capital West to lend his company Circle Tool & Die a lousy five
hundred thousand—without luck—he figured the people were no
better.

When he got back to South Carolina, empty-handed, he was
going to have to face his fifty-five employees with the bad news.
Circle Tool—a company that his grandfather had started before
World War II—was closing. Permanently. They would lose everything, even their retirement accounts, which he had used to try to
save the place.

He was a large man, his doctor said obese, an opinion his ex-
wife had also held, but he'd always thought of himself as nothing
more than a big man with healthy appetites. And getting out of
bed late, he was hungry now. Starved in fact, but not for food.

His flight to Atlanta and from there Columbia didn't leave until six this afternoon. He had been granted a late checkout, but it still gave him a half day to kill.

Someone knocked at his door. It was one of the young Mexican girls who'd worked cleaning rooms on the twenty-fourth floor of the LA Live Hotels and Condominiums. Resso thought she wasn't bad looking.

"May I clean your room, sir?" she asked, her English badly accented.

"I'll be checking out shortly, darlin', but if you want to come in and start now it'd be okay with me."

She smiled. "No, sir. Later." She turned away and pushed her cart toward the end of the corridor, deserted at this hour, her legs nice, and ass great.

Resso pulled on a polo shirt, grabbed his room key, and hurried down the corridor catching up to her just as the service elevator door was closing behind her. He blocked the door and slipped inside, letting it close.

It was just noon Pacific Standard Time, and before Resso could hit the stop button, the power went out.

The blackouts that had been in the news. He smiled at her, and he could see in her eyes in the dim emergency light that had come on, that she knew what was about to happen. But before she could call for help, Resso smashed a meaty fist into her face, snapping her head back, and knocking her cold.

As she hit the floor, Resso was already yanking at the front of her blouse, ripping the material and tearing off her bra.

ALL AIR traffic across the entire continental U.S. had been grounded fifteen minutes before noon just as a precaution on orders from the FAA in case the rolling blackouts actually happened.

The lineup for approach to the arrival gates at Salt Lake City

International had been so long that at noon PST several aircraft including United's 3538 from Atlanta, forty-five minutes earlier than its scheduled 12:37 arrival was stuck on the tarmac with only three empty seats.

Lights all across the airport, including the modern terminal went out, and the passengers on that side of the aircraft sighed; the attack had really started, and a lot of them were frightened.

Donald Huberty, seated with his wife Madeline in 24A and B had always been a white-knuckle flyer, ever since he was a kid. And now at sixty-seven he was even worse. He'd argued with his wife before they'd boarded at Atlanta that they were cutting things close.

"I don't want us to get stuck up there until we run out of fuel and crash," he'd argued.

She'd patted him on the arm. "The airlines know what they're doing," she said. "They'll get us there in plenty of time. Anyway it's probably a bluff. No one can turn off all the electricity to an entire city."

"Fourteen cities," he'd corrected her. "Including Salt Lake."

The captain got on the intercom. "Sorry folks, looks like we didn't beat the rush. The airport is shut down, probably not for long. But the good news is we're here, and we'll just have to wait it out until the power comes back on and the Jetway can be moved out to our hatch. The even better news is that the attendants will break out the refreshments again, and everything is on the house for the duration."

"It shouldn't be too long," Madeline said to her husband.

A massive weight clamped onto Huberty's chest and a blinding pain, worse than anything he ever felt in his life, followed. He reared back in his seat, unable to catch his breath. Suddenly he was drenched in sweat.

Madeline was saying something to him, but he couldn't quite make out her words.

The lights in the airplane were growing dim, making it hard for him to see anything. At that point Huberty realized that he was having a heart attack and unless he got help right now he was going to die. Not in a plane crash after all. And he worried about how his wife would manage.

Someone was looming over him, shouting, he thought.

The last thing he remembered was the feeling of being lifted out of his seat and lowered toward the floor. But he never got that far.

IN LAS Vegas the traffic lights went out at precisely noon PST, but it took several minutes for the first fender-bender accident to occur. It wasn't until 12:15 when Doris Sampson, driving a Cadillac Escalade, her two-year-old twins strapped in the back in their booster seats, was T-boned by a loaded cement truck. She and the twins were the first fatalities in the city.

ROGER DHALBERG had just reached the second floor of his home up near Nellis Air Force Base when the electricity stopped. He was a paraplegic and went up and down the stairs on a chair lift. He was among a large number of people across the country who thought the threat of rolling blackouts was just talk, nothing more. But he damn well wasn't going to be stuck in the lift all day.

He eased himself out of the chair intending to scoot back downstairs on his butt, but he missed his hold on the rail and tumbled down, breaking his neck at the bottom.

In all, twenty-seven people died during the one hour the electricity was off in the three cities, including a pregnant woman carrying triplets in her eighth month, who was so nervous because of what was happening that she miscarried and died of a hemorrhage on the kitchen floor of her Los Angeles ranch-style house.

The power came back on at one P.M. PST, but the disruptions to telephone service, to radio and television stations, but especially to computers was massive.

AT THAT precise moment it was two P.M. Mountain Standard Time in Denver, when the power went out across the city. The first reports from the west had come in and people here were a little better prepared to deal with the inconvenience.

Except for twenty-eight-year-old Brandon Wilson, who'd fallen off his horse two years earlier and was paralyzed from the neck down. When he wasn't in bed attached to the machinery that breathed for him, he was confined to a special wheelchair that was equipped to do the same thing—keep him alive.

Unbeknownst to him or his sister, who he lived with in the suburb of Lakewood, and who had popped out to make sure her five-year-old was okay at the day-care center a half hour before the power was switched off, the battery pack in his wheelchair had developed a short circuit five days ago.

When the power went out, he stopped breathing. A few minutes later he lost consciousness, and long before his sister Susan returned home, Brandon Wilson, who'd always hoped for more, was dead.

By the time the power was restored at three P.M. MST, seven people in the Denver area were dead; some in car accidents, one electrocuted the moment the power was restored, and two who committed suicide because they honestly believed that this was the start of the End of Days.

IT WAS four P.M. Central Standard Time in Hibbing when Toby Lundgren watched the electricity fail in the three cities the hacker had warned about. He'd managed to get into the control center's system for Nashville Electric Service, which distributed power to more than three hundred thousand customers in middle Tennessee, and switch the electricity back on after fifteen minutes.

"How about them apples," he muttered.

But he wasn't in time to save the lives of three people, one of whom was a cop who tried to stop an armed robbery of a convenience store. The thief, who believed that the lights would go out, figured that it would be the perfect time to rob the store and get away.

Peter MacDonald, a ten-year veteran of the NPD, had just pulled up to get a cup of coffee and was getting out of his squad car when the thief, seventeen-year-old Ali bin Sharif, was coming out the door, the manager shouting something behind him.

Before MacDonald could react, Sharif raised his .38 Smith & Wesson and pumped three rounds almost point blank into the cop's face.

But Sharif was the second fatality when the enraged manager came out of the store with a short-barreled 12-bore shotgun and put one round into the thief's back. It took the young man nearly fifteen minutes to bleed out.

DEKKER HAD gone into the kitchen to grab a beer, pissed off that Karn had left a half hour ago to do some shopping, and when he came back to his computer he spotted the first glitch in his program. Somehow the lights in Nashville had come back on.

"Fucker," Dekker shouted, tossing the beer bottle across the room and sitting down at his monitor.

It took him less than a minute to realize that someone was screwing with him, and less than another minute to turn off Nashville's lights again.

The electricity came on again, and this time stayed on until five minutes later when Dekker placed a worm of his own design into the program. Whoever was interfering would get a nasty surprise if he tried again. His worm, which he called Brunhilde, the Valkyrie warrior, would infect the bastard's computer crashing its hard drive.

The lights in Nashville, along with those in Kansas City and Chicago, stayed out, and another fifty-three died—making a total of more than one hundred in the three cities.

IT TOOK Lundgren the rest of the afternoon and well past dinnertime before he could find and totally remove the virus from the backup computer he'd worked on. He'd expected something like that, so he'd used one of his old laptops.

Although he wasn't able to prevent the rolling blackouts in Detroit, Cincinnati, Miami, Philadelphia, Boston, Washington, and New York City, he did learn for certain that the hacker was Barend Dekker, the same guy he'd known at MIT, and pinpoint his approximate location outside Amsterdam.

THE LIGHTS in the seven Eastern Standard Time zone cities went out at six and stayed out until seven. Sections of each of those metropolitan areas became virtual war zones, the police versus the criminals who watched what had happened to the west, and were prepared for an all-out spree of looting, rape, murder, and arson.

In addition to several dozen traffic fatalities, a half-dozen industrial accidents, and from various other causes, two hundred nineteen people died—many of them police officers—during the crime spree.

———

BY MIDNIGHT the toll had reached three hundred ninety-seven dead and five times that many injured, some critically. The estimated cost of the damage and disruptions caused by the outages in the fourteen cities, plus the nation's air-traffic control system, topped the three-billion-dollar mark.

The president called a meeting of his Security Council for eight P.M. A council of war.

PART THREE

WAR

Forty-Eight Hours Later

51

IT WAS LATE in Amsterdam, nearly midnight, and Dekker was getting pissed off to the max. Karn had left around eight and wasn't back yet. No phone call, not a blast on his computer from the Internet café where he figured she'd gone to be with her friends, nothing.

He got up from his computer where he'd been doing some more work on his 10-D war games program and went to the window and parted the dirty blanket they'd nailed in place when they'd first moved in here four years ago. The apartment was on the tenth floor of the crappiest building in the complex. Only three other apartments were occupied, all of them on the ground floor where they figured they could bug out in case the cops ever showed up here.

From here he could just make out the spire of the Noorderkerk, which was built in the early 1600s, and which in Dekker's estimation was way cool, not because of the God thing, but because of the bird market every Saturday in front. Karn loved to go down there whenever they had a little extra money, and buy a few birds—canaries, doves, wrens—and set them free.

He supposed he was a little worried about her this evening, though he found it hard to admit. But he had come to depend on her, and not just for the sex, but for her sometimes really good advice. Like with his war game. He'd stacked up a 10-D board, and tonight he'd wanted to show her the game, and maybe figure out a rad name for it.

"Goddamnit," he said, half under his breath.

Nothing much moved in the huddle of the complex where no lights shone from any of the windows, and only a few small campfires from the Roma side. He and Karn had gone over there a couple of times to listen to the music and watch the dancing, but those people, in his estimation, were totally whacked out. Made him nervous.

From the start Karn had agreed with him that they would never snoop on each other.

"If it comes to that there won't be anything left for us," she'd said.

He went over to his iPad and brought up a GPS program that allowed him to track the SIM card he'd placed in her cell phone a couple of years ago. It not only showed her present location it also left cookie crumbs along each route she took.

At 8:07 P.M. she'd walked out of the building and headed north eighty meters toward the Roma encampment, where she stayed for nearly an hour, before she moved again, this time to the square in front of the church, where she stopped until 9:30 P.M. This time she moved very fast to the east, and then southeast. Too fast for her to be still on foot, at times nearly sixty kilometers per hour, but then slowing down and stopping for a minute or so.

She'd taken a cab, which had dropped her off at the Central Railway Station right on the waterfront. She'd not taken a train yet. She was still inside. But she was leaving him, and a blind rage threatened to blot everything else out of his mind.

Karn was leaving him, but to where? And more importantly to or with whom?

He threw on a denim jacket and slammed out of the apartment, taking the stairs two at a time to the ground floor and outside where he ran as fast as he could all the way to Westerstraat where he got lucky finding a cruising cab almost immediately and waved it down. The cabby was hesitant to stop for him because of his shabby dress and long, out-of-control hair, but Amsterdam law made it imperative that anyone who hailed a cab was to be picked up.

"The Central Station," Dekker said. He handed the cabby a one-hundred-euro note. "And hurry please."

The driver was impressed and he sped off, much faster than the speed limit.

Despite his anger Dekker had to grin. Having money was definitely better than not having any. And five hundred thousand euros was a lot.

One part of his mind had been thinking lately about getting out of Amsterdam, or certainly out of the slum building, to someplace decent. Maybe their own small apartment. Under assumed names, of course. Someplace just as anonymous as the Haven. And he had thought about discussing it with Karn—until now.

Goddamnit, just thinking that the bitch was up to something made him think about killing her. Throttling her goddamn neck, until her face turned purple and her eyes bugged out.

The nearly deserted station wasn't far, and it only took a couple of minutes to get there. The cabby turned around.

"Would you like some change, sir?" he asked.

"No," Dekker said. "And if you wait a few minutes to take me back there'll be another hundred for you."

"Yes, sir."

Dekker headed across to the main entrance as he opened the GPS program on his iPad. Karn was right here. He was almost on top of her.

He turned left in time to see her and a man in a dark jacket looking at him. They were seated on a park bench. Karn said something to the man and he shook his head, but they both got up.

Just before Dekker reached them, the man said something to Karn then turned on his heel and walked away.

Dekker was of a mind to go after the guy, but Karn was right there.

"What the fuck are you doing here?" she demanded, her voice strident.

"Is that guy fucking you?" Dekker shouted.

She noticed the iPad, its GPS program still running, and grabbed it out of his hand. "Spying? Are you a goddamned spy?"

"I asked you a question. Is he fucking you?"

Karn pushed him back. "If he was, so what?"

Dekker was shaken to the core. All he could do was step back and whimper like a beaten little boy. No one had ever stayed with him. Never in his life. But Karn had been with him for years; always there with her smiles, and good sex, and little kindnesses like sometimes washing his clothes, or once buying him a Myna bird from the market. He'd had to kill the damned thing because of the messes it made and because of the constant noise, but her present had been sweet. And she was a lot smarter than any other woman he'd ever met.

She stepped into him and touched his shoulder. "No, he's not fucking me. But he's come to help me—us."

"With what?"

"You're such a baby sometimes. With all this money I figured that somebody would come looking for us. Maybe wanting to figure out what we're doing. People in the Haven aren't exactly rich."

"Who is he?"

"A cop from Helsinki I used to date."

Dekker's gorge rose again.

"He's just a friend, Barend. Like an uncle, nothing more than that. Ever. I asked for help, he took the train down and when I tried to give him money he was insulted. He's going to look out for us."

Dekker breathed through his partially open mouth like he always did when he was worked up. "What's his name?"

"No," Karn said. "You start looking down his background he'll quit. We need his help."

Her *no* was like a red flag waving in front of his face. "Help? How?"

"Someone might be coming here."

"Why?"

"To stop you from interfering with the American electrical grid."

"They don't know who I am—" Dekker said, but then he stopped. The power in Nashville had come on briefly. Someone had tracked him down, or at least hacked into his program.

"There was a problem with one of the power outages," Karn said. "You fixed it, but it was there, and it makes—my friend nervous. He says that it could become a problem for us."

Dekker almost hit her in the mouth, but he held himself in check, just like he did when his old man used to whale on him. In those days he'd thought about the butcher knives in the kitchen drawer. And maybe getting up in the middle of the night and slitting the old bastard's throat. Maybe doing his mum as well.

"What is he going to do?"

"Watch our backs."

Dekker looked beyond her to the station entrance, but the guy in the dark jacket was gone. He turned back to her and looked into her eyes. If she was lying he couldn't tell. But there'd always been a secret part to her, just like a cat that was sometimes aloof but arched its back and purred when it wanted to.

He put his arm around her bony shoulder and pulled her close. "Okay, let's go home."

Karn handed back his iPad. "No more spying," she said. "I mean it." She grinned. "Maybe next time I'll bite your balls off."

52

OSBORNE DELIVERED GRAFTON'S body to his parents in Minneapolis. The governor had loaned him the use of the North Dakota Air National Guard's C-21 Lear jet and crew from the 119th Fighter Wing in Fargo for as long as he needed it, and Ashley had bummed a ride, getting her more than halfway to her next assignment, and saving her a lot of driving.

It was noon when they touched down and taxied over to a hangar on the Minnesota Air National Guard side of the airport.

"What's your plan?" Osborne asked her.

"I'm going to rent a car and drive down to Sioux Falls. I have a few questions I want to ask Stu Wyman, the guy from the control center where all this started."

"Can't you phone him?"

"Nope. I want to see his face. You can tell lot about someone that way."

Grafton's parents got out of a Cadillac Escalade, and were

waiting for the airplane to stop. A hearse was parked next to them, its rear door open, and two men in dark suits waited with a gurney.

"Do you want me to go with you?" Ashley asked.

"No, but just be careful on the road, okay? This mess is long from over."

"I know, but that goes for you, too. Your Russian got away, he's still out there."

"He thinks he killed me."

"When he, or whoever hired him, finds out differently they'll try again."

The jet came to a complete stop, and as the engines spooled down, the attendant, Staff Sergeant Bruce, opened the door and lowered the boarding stairs. A pair of Minnesota Air National Guard flight line technicians came across from the hangar, chocked the wheels, and opened the Lear's cargo bay hatch, as Osborne got out and went over to Tony Grafton whose wife, Susan, was holding his hand. He was an ER doctor at Abbott Northwestern Hospital and she was the chief ER nurse.

"Chapped their asses that I wanted to go into law enforcement," Grafton had told Osborne. "But they got over it. I think they were relieved that I took a job out in the boonies, where nothing much ever happens."

"I'm Nate Osborne and I'm very sorry to be here today like this."

Grafton shook his hand. "Thank you."

"David spoke often of you," Susan Grafton said, but then she watched the men from the funeral home pull the silver metal coffin from the aircraft. "I couldn't believe it until just this moment," she whispered.

Grafton was having a hard time as well, watching the men. "The services will be tomorrow afternoon. Will you stay for them?"

"I'm sorry, no," Osborne said. "I'm trying to find the man who did this."

Susan Grafton looked Osborne in the eye, a sudden grim set to her features. "You do that, Sheriff. You get the bastard, because I want to be there at his trial so I can look him in the eye."

As soon as the coffin was loaded into the hearse, the Graftons got back in their Caddy and left.

Ashley, carrying a small overnight bag and her laptop, got off the plane. She was going to get a ride over to the car rental counters in the main terminal. "Too bad for them," she said. "I know how devastated my father would be if someone delivered my body in a coffin to him."

"I wish you would go back to Bismarck and stay there," Osborne said.

"Can't stop me from doing my job any more than I can stop you from doing yours. Are you going home now?"

"Hibbing, I want to talk to Lundgren. In person."

"Then what?"

"I don't know," Osborne said. But he did know.

LUNDGREN WAS waiting for Osborne at the Range Regional Airport when the Lear jet pulled up at the Minnesota Army National Guard's 94th Air Cavalry operations center a few minutes before one.

"Any idea how long you'll be?" Captain Dan Gruder, the pilot, asked.

"Shouldn't be too long," Osborne said at the open door. "Grab some lunch."

"We'll refuel first."

Osborne walked across to where Lundgren was waiting. "Thanks for coming out," he said and they shook hands.

"You hungry?" Lundgren asked. He was wearing faded jeans, and a bulky turtleneck sweater. The wind was raw.

"I could eat something, but I thought we could go back to the computer center."

"Nope," Lundgren said. "I'm taking you to my place, the Bureau hasn't figured out how to bug it or my car yet, and what I have to say is for your ears only, okay?"

"Sure."

Lundgren gave him a hard look. "Afterwards it'll be your call if you want to share it with anyone."

"Why me?"

"I did some checking. You're straight up, something most people—especially in D.C.—are not."

Lundgren's car turned out to be a new or nearly new shiny black Mercedes S500, which he handled like a professional driver. "People up here are mad at anyone who owns a foreign car, especially German, for whatever reason. So I bought this beast just to piss 'em off."

"Does it work?"

Lundgren glanced over at Osborne. "Not usually. I'm an odd duck who has bags of money, so I'm pretty much left alone. But I found your hacker, and I can guarantee you that I pissed him off. Big time."

Osborne had gotten a call last night from Lundgren asking for a meeting up here, though he refused to explain why. "I'm here."

They headed over to Hibbing, a few miles west of the airport. The day was overcast, some patches of dirty snow still on the ground, and the vast craters of open-pit iron ore mines scattered through what was left of the pine forests looked like a giant's footprints.

"I turned the lights on in Nashville a couple of times," Lundgren said.

"That was you?"

"Yeah, and Dekker fell for it. The guy is a genius but he's as dumb as a box of rocks. Always was at MIT."

"You found out where he lives?"

"Yeah, but aren't you going to ask me how I did Nashville?"

"I suppose that you hacked into his program, but what about the rest of the blackouts?"

Lundgren was a little disappointed. "He sent me a virus, and by the time I got it cleaned up, the lights on the East Coast came back on. Do you understand?"

"I can turn on a computer, send an e-mail, and check a bunch of law enforcement databases, but that's as far as it goes," Osborne said.

Lundgren managed to grin. "I suppose that'll have to do. I find them because that's what I'm good at. And you can shoot them because that's what you're good at."

"I'm not a Neanderthal, Mr. Lundgren."

Lundgren laughed out loud. "Nope, and the name is Toby. He and his girlfriend live on the tenth floor of an abandoned apartment building outside of Amsterdam, in what's called the Haven with a bunch of other computer hackers, hippies, potheads, and a Roma camp that the Dutch police used to raid. But every time the cops cleaned out the place, their computer systems all crashed. They got the message a couple of years ago, and don't go back unless something serious happens, like a murder or something."

"The FBI knows about them?"

"Yeah, but the Dutch aren't interested in helping, because none of their laws are being broken. They'd just as soon leave well enough alone."

"Okay, how'd you find him?" Osborne asked.

"Thought you'd never ask," Lundgren said. "It was his really cool virus, which left a lot of calling cards if you know where to look. I do. Essentially what he did was cram all of my files onto a sliver of memory on my hard disk, and tried to download them to his machine. Before he got that far I found the cache, put a tracker on it, scrambled everything, and then followed the trail."

This time Osborne had to laugh, but he didn't think what Lundgren had told him was very funny. None of it was.

They pulled into the driveway of a three-story pile of a house with turrets and high-peaked rooflines, with huge bay windows and stone columns supporting a massive front porch. Though the house, which at one time had probably been the mansion of some wealthy man, had probably been built around the turn of the century—the nineteenth century—it looked to be in nearly new condition.

"Well?" Lundgren asked.

"Hell of a house."

"One of the Mesabi iron ore barons built the place, and after I bought it I put a ton of money into it," Lundgren said. "But I meant about Dekker."

Osborne shrugged. "You found him and I'm going to shoot him."

"Really?"

"I'm going to try."

"Way cool," Lundgren said.

53

A T THAT SAME moment it was two in the afternoon in Caracas and Colonel Delgado was at his desk preparing to report to President Chavez at a council of war meeting in the Miraflores Palace, when his secretary buzzed him.

"You have an encrypted Skype call from Tehran. Do you wish to take it now, or should I inform the caller that you have already left?"

"Who is it?"

"Colonel Dabir."

Delgado glanced at the clock. "I'll take it now, but phone Sr. Elizondo and tell him with my apologies that I may be a few minutes late." Edgar Elizondo was the president's chief of staff.

"Yes, sir," his secretary said.

He accepted the call, and Dabir's squarish frame appeared on the monitor. The VEVAK colonel was not smiling.

"I apologize for this call, my old friend, I'm sure that you have your hands full at the moment, but something has come up that must be dealt with."

"Yes, we all have our hands full, and it will probably get even busier around here if our presidents persist. So be brief."

They spoke English.

"We have a problem with Mr. Dekker, he's becoming unstable," Dabir said.

"I thought you had an agent in place for just that possibility."

"Her name is Karn Simula, and up until now she's been able to keep him on track, but he's told her that he means to crash the entire American electrical grid."

Delgado's stomach clenched. "Which he certainly can do because of the virus you supplied him with. Reckless. It's brought us to the brink of war."

"We're in no better a position, actually. But my analysts assure me that an attack by American military forces is unlikely."

"They assured us of that before Balboa, nonetheless we are still repairing the extensive damage their bombs did to five of our airbases, two of which may not be reactivated for several years if ever," Delgado said. "And if it's found out that it was you who handed over the virus to Dekker, Tehran could become the next Baghdad."

"That's not likely for a number of reasons, but we think the virus is Russian. The American CIA has known that fact for a number of years."

Delgado glanced at the grandfather clock in the corner of his fifth-floor office in El Helicoide, the building that served as SEBIN's headquarters. It was ticking down the seconds as it always did, but counting down to what?

"What do you propose we do about Dekker? Pay him more money?"

"Our agent doesn't think so. But we believe that his watcher may have become unreliable. Maybe she's fallen in love with the boy."

Delgado tried to work out the ramifications of what Dabir was telling him. He would have to bring it up with Chavez, along with his recommendations. A computer hacker with the means to completely shut down the distribution of electrical power all across the U.S. was in many ways an even more powerful weapon than a nuclear bomb. But if the kid had gone insane, he'd be no better than a terrorist, who the U.S. would hunt down and kill, after which they would come after the kid's paymasters.

"If we kill him, we lose the advantage for retaliation."

"I think we must do just that," Dabir said. "And in fact the order must come from your office. That way if it is discovered that Venezuela eliminated the threat, it will be seen by Washington as a conciliatory gesture from your president."

"Chavez is not in a particularly conciliatory mood in the best of times," Delgado said. "But I think you're right. Makarov is back in Stockholm. I'll see if he'll take the job."

"Good," Dabir said. "In the meantime I'll work with our asset to see if she can get the thumb drive away from Dekker."

"If I'm correct about computers, the program is already in Dekker's machine."

"You're probably right. Nevertheless I'll feel safer having the original back in our possession, just in case we are attacked."

"I'll need authorization," Delgado said.

"I suggest that you be quick about it."

DELGADO GOT his attaché case and on the way out had his secretary telephone Sr. Elizondo again to tell the president's chief of staff that he was on the way, and to ask for a brief private audience with Chavez. *Before* the council of war meeting.

Nearly to the palace on Urdaneta Avenue he got a call in his chauffeur-driven armored Hummer from his secretary. The president had agreed to the private meeting, but he would not wait forever.

"How did Elizondo sound?"

"Stressed."

Five minutes later they were cleared past the security checkpoint, and Delgado hurried inside to the Joaquin Crespo room, formerly the Hall of Mirrors, where formal meetings of the council of ministers was usually held.

Elizondo directed him to a small office across the ornate hall, where Chavez was staring impatiently out the window that looked down into the main courtyard.

"You're late, my friend," the president said, turning. He looked tired, but everyone thought it was the situation with the U.S. and not the return of his cancer.

"I'm sorry, Mr. President, but something of grave importance came up just as I was about to leave my office."

"Does it have a bearing on my council of ministers meeting?"

"Very much so, sir," Delgado said, and he repeated everything Dabir had told him about the situation with the hacker in Amsterdam.

Chavez smiled and rubbed his hands together. "I don't see the problem. If he wants to shut off the bastards' electricity, let him."

"This would be vastly more dangerous than simply engineering rolling blackouts."

"They want war—they've already made war on us—and so do I."

"It would be a war that we could not possibly win."

Chavez stopped smiling. "If you've no stomach for what must be done, then step down, I will replace you."

"It's never been that, *Señor Presidente*. I'm suggesting an option so that no matter what occurs we will come out as victors."

"Tell me."

"We eliminate the hacker and his girlfriend, who is an Iranian agent. We recover the thumb drive that contains the virus—and use it only if and when the U.S. moves its warships off our coast."

"It would cause them to attack with even more zeal," Chavez said.

"Not if the blame were to be placed on Iran," Delgado said, and his words hung in the air for a long beat.

"President Ahmadinejad is a personal friend."

"*Sí.*"

"Iran is an ally."

"*Sí.*"

Chavez bowed his head for a moment, then turned and looked out the window. "If Hitler had not allowed the British soldiers trapped at Dunkirk to escape back home, and instead slaughtered them on the beaches, and if he hadn't been so quick to open a front on the east he could have defeated the English and turned Great Britain into an island fortress before the Americans arrived. Maybe he would have gained the time for his scientists to build the atomic bomb and perfect the rockets to reach New York and Washington, D.C. History so often hinges on the slightest miscalculations."

The word *insanity* popped into Delgado's head, but he said nothing.

"I'll miss you at the meeting, but you have more important things to attend to," Chavez said without turning back. "Godspeed."

"You, too, Mr. President," Delgado said.

54

IT WAS VERY early in the evening, but Makarov and Ilke had gone to bed and lay naked under the sheet in each other's arms, listening to Dvorak's New World symphony playing on the B&O stereo in the living room. He'd come back from North Dakota, battered physically as well as emotionally, because he'd made a mistake.

He'd killed Osborne all right, he'd seen the man go down, but he'd left the women alive. They'd seen his face, even though he'd been in disguise. And the one who'd come up behind him in the house had looked into his eyes, some secret knowledge in hers. She would know him if they ever met again.

Ilke's head was on his shoulder, a hand on his chest. "A crown for your thoughts," she said. Her voice was husky as it always was just after they made love.

"I'm thinking about retiring."

She looked up at him. "Are you serious?"

SEBIN and VEVAK knew about his business here, and about Ilke, and it was no stretch to think that they knew where he lived, though how they had come by that knowledge remained a puzzle to him. But his life here was at an end, as he always knew it would be someday.

"I'm tired of working all the time, the being away, sometimes dealing with people who are—" He searched for the right word.

"Bad?"

"Who're only interested in money above all else."

She smiled. "Good, then we can take a long vacation. I've always wanted to see New York, and then Washington and Las Vegas. Will you take me gambling? I'd like to spend some of your money."

"It's possible," Makarov said noncommittally, though of course it would never be possible for them to return to the States, at least not as he looked now. And trying to explain why he would need to alter his face with plastic surgery would be next to impossible. One of the things she was most fond of saying was how she loved the line of his chin, and especially the furrow in the middle of his brow just above his nose.

"Makes you look like a professor," she'd teased. "All you need are a pince-nez and people would start to ask you serious questions." She'd laughed. "For which you would have all the answers."

When she got started like this he always let her finish before he brought her back down to earth. Sometimes she would cry, but in the end she would smile, sadly, and the discussion would be ended. But this time she had a fire in her eyes.

"Then when we come back we could buy a little house—doesn't have to be grand—and I would like to have a dog, and maybe cats. It would be in the country and we could take long walks. Make new friends who we could invite for Midsummer's Eve bonfires and maypoles."

To begin with she'd wanted children, but he'd convinced her otherwise, and their lives had been calm, except for his business. But she was hinting again about having a family.

Using the deputy's truck to get away from Osborne's ranch, he'd switched to the sheriff's SUV which he'd left on the eastbound lane of the interstate. By the time he'd crossed the median and flagged down two Walgreen drugstore managers in a Chevy Impala with Montana plates heading west, he'd heard the first helicopter a long ways to the south.

A little later that morning, he'd killed the two men, stuffed their bodies in the trunk, and had driven straight through to Seattle where he'd taken a Delta flight nonstop to Atlanta and from there Air Canada to Frankfurt, the train to Helsinki, and the train-ferry home, changing back to his Stockholm appearance between trains.

"I meant leaving Sweden. Maybe someplace warmer."

Ilke sat up, the sheet falling away from her small breasts, an uncertain look on her pretty round face. "Like where?"

"Spain, southern France, maybe Majorca."

"But why?" she'd asked, but the telephone chimed and before Makarov could reach it she answered.

"Yes?"

He could hear a man's voice, and then Ilke handed the phone to him, and got out of bed and padded into the bathroom.

"Who is calling?"

"You know," Delgado said.

Ilke had closed the bathroom door, but Makarov got out of bed, and took the handset into the living room where he looked down on the narrow street just off the busy Kungsgatan, but he could spot nothing suspicious.

"What do you want?"

"We have another assignment for you."

"I'm not going back to the States so soon, if ever," Makarov said.

"Amsterdam," Delgado said.

Makarov glanced over his shoulder at the open bedroom door down the hall. Ilke was still in the bathroom. Probably sulking. She was a Dane, and Helsinki was about as far south as she'd ever wanted to go. Majorca would be a trial for her.

"What's the problem?"

"It's Dekker, he's become unstable."

"You knew that from the beginning. Besides, you said that he had a minder."

"It's possible that she's become a part of the problem," Delgado said. "Both of them need to be eliminated and the thumb drive recovered."

"I've just returned," Makarov said. But the operation would be fairly easy. Down to Amsterdam in the morning, do the two of them, and return here the same day.

"This is important."

"They all are."

"One million euros. But it must de done immediately."

"Five million," Makarov said.

Delgado didn't hesitate. "Done."

The money would more than buy Ilke her house. Overlooking the Med on Majorca, he decided. "When half is in my account I will do it."

"It'll be there within the hour."

"How do I find these people?" Makarov asked, and Delgado gave him the specific details.

ILKE WAS sitting on the toilet when he knocked and went into the bathroom. She'd been crying, her face in her hands, and when she looked up her face was puffy and her eyes red.

"I love you," she said. "I'll go anywhere with you. Just tell me when and where."

He sat down on the edge of the tub next to her and took her hands. "Majorca, in the hills above the sea."

She smiled and half nodded.

"We will have a house, and you will have your dog and cats and maybe even some goats."

She brightened. "For sure?"

He nodded. "Absolutely. And maybe a llama or two, an ostrich, a milk cow, some chickens. We'll have a regular farm."

She laughed. "You're teasing me."

"Yes, I am. But after tomorrow there will be no more business, just pleasure. And if you want to spend some of *our* money on roulette or at the baccarat table, we'll dress up and play at the casino in Monte Carlo."

"What about tomorrow?" she asked.

"I have another trip, but this one just to Paris in the morning, and I should be back in time for dinner."

"Promise?"

"Yes. And then we'll fly down to Majorca, hire a real estate agent, and go house hunting."

"Just one last job?"

55

O N THE FOUR-HOUR drive down to Sioux Falls Ashley had plenty of time to think, and when the GPS advised her to turn right on Central Avenue, she came to the conclusion that being a newspaper reporter and being Nate Osborne's wife would never work. After this business was over with, and she'd filed the last of her in-depths on the attacks against the Initiative, she was going to quit and move to Medora.

The problem that had deviled her was what she would do with her time, and even more importantly, how she could keep herself occupied to a level where she wouldn't go cuckoo.

Pulling into the Wymans' driveway a little before five she'd finally accepted what she, and just about every journalist she had ever known, wanted to do was to write the Great American Novel. Or at least a novel. Maybe for children. A sort of modern-day *Little House on the Prairie*.

A short, somewhat pleasant-looking woman answered the doorbell. "You must be Ms. Borden, from the *Bismarck Tribune*."

"Mrs. Wyman?" Ashley asked.

"Yes. My husband has been expecting you," Delores Wyman said, letting Ashley in. "But he's been told not to talk to anyone from the press or television."

"Should I leave?"

"No. He thinks it's important."

"So do I," Ashley said.

She followed the woman to the rear bedroom that had been converted to a den or study where Stuart Wyman, dressed in jeans and a T-shirt, moccasins on his feet, was waiting. Her first impression was that he was a frightened man, and perhaps just a little angry. She'd gotten nothing of that from talking to him on the phone.

"Thank you for agreeing to see me," Ashley said, and they shook hands.

"I don't think anybody at MAPP is making any real progress. They're all working real hard just to cover their asses. And let me tell you that the rolling blackouts didn't do much for them."

"And you're the scapegoat?"

"Something like that."

The small room was pleasant; a desk stood in front of the windows, a pair of wingback chairs, a coffee table, and reading lamp between them, pictures of Wyman hunting and fishing, certificates of merit lining one wall, and two tall book cases along another. A can of Bud Light was on the desk.

"Would you like a cup of coffee, or something?" Wyman's wife asked from the door.

"Actually a beer would be good. I don't need a glass."

She went to get it and Ashley walked over to the bookcases, which contained a lot of books on electrical production and transmission, but several shelves held thriller novels by a lot of authors she'd read. *Hunt for Red October*, Ashley said. "I read it twice."

"So did I," Wyman said, and he motioned her to take a seat.

His wife returned with the beer and left again.

Wyman sat next to Ashley.

"So what do you think really happened to get your lineman killed?"

"His name was Tony Bartlett. Wife and two kids. Toughest phone call I ever had to make in my life, telling her that Tony was dead."

Ashley waited.

"A friend of mine at our computer analysis center in Minnesota is sure that it was the work of a hacker somewhere in Amsterdam. Same guy who caused the rolling blackouts."

"Does your boss know this?"

"Of course."

"But you're still on the hook."

"The energize order came from my console, and they need someone to blame."

Ashley took a drink of her beer. It tasted pretty good after four hours on the road. "Were you on duty anytime during the attacks on the Initiative over the holidays?"

"Almost continuously. We treated it the same as we would a natural disaster," Wyman said. "I never saw a woman drink beer from a can."

Ashley grinned. "I was a service brat," she said. "Do you think the attacks were connected to the murder of Tony Bartlett and the rolling blackouts?"

"Hell yes, especially if you eliminate the blackouts, just for a second."

"How so?"

"It'd be a pretty big coincidence—the attack on Donna Marie and then the sabotage of the transmission line coming from there."

"Who's behind it?" Ashley asked. "Other than the hacker in Amsterdam."

"I don't know."

"But you've heard things, you've got an opinion."

"Chavez. The Venezuelans. It's common knowledge, isn't it? Why we bombed their air bases."

"Heard anything about the Russians or the Chinese?"

"That, too, is common knowledge. Either of them, or both, has infected all one hundred twenty-seven of our control centers with a virus. In case of an all-out shooting war they could shut us down. But I don't think it's them."

"Why?"

"They'd have too much to lose. Hell, China would go bankrupt if we stopped buying their crap. And Russia has no reason that I can see to do something stupid like that."

"Do you think that Chavez would take such a risk, after we attacked his air bases?"

"He's crazy enough, I guess," Wyman said. "And if he did, what could we do in return? We sure as hell wouldn't put boots on the ground down there. It'd be a hundred times worse than Iraq or Afghanistan."

"But you believe it's possible that this hacker was hired by the Venezuelans to screw with us because of the air base attacks?"

"Toby thinks so. He says the hacker was just flexing his muscles with the blackouts. Showing us what he could do anytime he wanted to."

"Toby?"

"Toby Lundgren. He's a friend. In fact he called me a couple hours ago, said Nate Osborne, the sheriff who was involved in stopping the attack on Donna Marie, had just left."

"Did he tell you what they discussed?"

"The hacker," Wyman said. "Toby figured out where the guy lives and the problem could be solved in the next day or two."

Ashley was about to lift the can of beer, but she stopped. "How so?"

Wyman backed off. "Sorry, but that was supposed to be confidential. I'll tell you anything you want to know, but I have to ask that you don't use what Toby said to me. Could put the sheriff's life in danger."

"I know Nate Osborne," Ashley said. "In fact, he and I are engaged to be married, so there's no danger of me publishing anything that would put him in harm's way."

"I don't know."

"You have my word, Mr. Wyman. We're fighting on the same side. This guy in Amsterdam has to be stopped before the situation gets too far out of hand. A lot of lives are on the line. Already more than Tony Bartlett have died because of him."

"Osborne is going to Amsterdam, unofficially, to take care of the situation."

All the air in the room suddenly left, and for the first time in Ashley's life she was speechless.

56

IT WAS MIDNIGHT when the thirty-foot Bayliner with twin 350 horsepower Honda four strokes entered the Gulf Intracoastal Waterway at Port O'Connor southwest of Matagorda, Texas where the Colorado River emptied into the Gulf of Mexico.

Jesus Campinella was piloting from the fly bridge. "We're inside," he said.

Ignatio Gomez, out of sight with Ricardo Gomez just within the cabin, came to the open door. "Any traffic?"

"Nothing but the inbound tanker we've been tracking since eleven. She's still ten miles out."

They'd met their control officer, Major Pedro Ramirez, in a crappy hotel in Nuevo Laredo two days ago. All of them had flown up from Caracas the week before, and had taken different routes to reach the border town.

"We have a car outside with U.S. plates and the necessary paperwork for the three of you," Ramirez said. He was a short, narrow-faced special operations officer in SEBIN.

They'd worked for him before, and although Campinella had a great deal of respect for the man, he didn't trust him.

"You will drive to Corpus Christi where you will pick up the boat, go out into the Gulf at Port Aransas and from there back inside at Port O'Connor."

They'd studied the relatively simple in-and-out mission before they'd left Caracas, and the three of them, especially Campinella, had been chosen in part because of their good English, but also because they were expendable.

"Weapons and explosives?" Campinella had asked.

"Aboard the boat."

A nautical chart showing the Intracoastal Waterway and the first ten miles of the Colorado River was spread out on one of the beds.

Ramirez pointed to a bridge. "County Road 521. You will turn the boat around and tie up there. It's not likely there'll be any traffic at that time of the morning."

"How far to the transformer yard?"

"Two miles upriver, on the west side of the power plant," Ramirez said. "You can't miss it. It's protected by a twelve-foot-tall chain-link fence topped with razor wire."

"Is the fence electrified?"

"No, nor will there be any guards."

"*Estupido,*" Campinella had muttered.

"*Sí,*" Ramirez agreed. "Even after everything that has happened to them it hasn't occurred to anyone to take better care with something so valuable and so vulnerable."

They were to hike upriver, cut their way through the fence, and place explosives on three of the six high-voltage step-up transformers which increased the nuclear power plant's low voltage to two-point-five megavolts that was sent through the Texas Interconnect transmission lines. These huge transformers, each nearly as big as a Greyhound bus, were manufactured by Urja Techniques in

India, and couldn't be replaced in under two years. In Campinella's estimation it was another bit of American stupidity.

"What if we are caught?" Gomez asked. Like Campinella and Ricardo, he was slightly built and dark.

Ramierz had given him a hard stare. "Don't," he said.

When they had crossed the border without incident and were on their way over to Corpus Christi, one hundred sixty miles to the northeast, Campinella had explained what the major had meant.

"We're carrying nothing that could identify us as Venezuelans. We're Zeta soldiers from the Mexican drug cartel, pissed off that a fifty-million-dollar shipment of coke was seized two weeks ago by the border patrol. This is payback time."

"But after the attacks in North Dakota, and then the blackouts the FBI won't be that stupid," Gomez had argued.

"That's right. And it's why we can't be caught. Alive. Nothing must link us to Caracas."

"They will know anyway," Gomez said.

"But they won't be able to prove it," Campinella told them.

Except for the occasional lit ICW marker the night was dark. Port Lavaca well to the north showed up only as a faint glow in the sky, and the other small towns up the bay toward the port were only pinpricks.

At twenty knots Campinella figured to reach the bridge by two, the transformer yard a half hour later, a half hour to cut through the fence and place the thirty kilos of Semtex and acid fuses, and another twenty minutes to get back to the boat. By three thirty at the latest, when the explosions came, they would be on their way back to the Gulf and dawn by the time they dropped off the boat and got their car.

Unless something went wrong.

THE NIGHT was even darker upriver when they reached the high-way bridge. Campinella turned the boat around so that it was facing downstream, and backed it up into the much deeper shadows next to the riverbank where they tied it to a bridge piling. They were invisible from the road.

Each of them hefted a nylon rucksack packed with bricks of Sem-tex and acid fuses. They were armed with U.S. military standard-issue 9mm Beretta semiauto pistols, and slung over their shoulders were 5.56mm Colt Commando assault rifles, which were the short-ened version of the U.S.-made M16. Along with several magazines of ammunition for each weapon, and hydraulic bolt cutters for the fence, they carried nearly twenty kilos—more than forty pounds— on the forced march through the mud, rock riprap along the river-bank, and occasional tall grasses.

Units one and two of the South Texas Project Electrical Gener-ating Station were well lit, the nuclear plant's cooling towers rising into the night sky, red lights blinking atop them. There was no traf-fic here, but as they got closer they had a good view of the parking lot which was more than half full. It was a busy place even in the middle of the night.

A quarter mile to the left three strings of tall H-shaped towers led the high-power transmission lines away from the transformer yard, disappearing in the distance to the west, east, and north. They looked to Campinella like the Martian monsters from H. G. Wells's *War of the Worlds,* which was the only book he'd ever read in his life.

The yard itself was about the size of several tennis courts, and was jammed with six transformers, three for each unit.

They pulled up short about twenty meters from a rear corner of the yard, and hunkered down. They were a few minutes early, and Campinella wanted to use the time to make sure that no guards had been posted.

"Incredible," Gomez said softly.

They could hear the deep-throated rumble of heavy machinery somewhere in the distance toward the generating stations, but the sound was very low, almost inaudible.

"There is a lot of high voltage in there," Ricardo whispered.

"You'd have to climb a ladder to reach the connections," Campinella said, but he had a great deal of respect for the power contained inside the big machines.

They rose up on his signal and hunching low, ran to the fence, where they put down the rucksacks, and cut a man-sized hole in the fence, leaving one side attached like a door, and peeled back the fence so they could step inside.

Campinella hesitated for only a moment, but then pointed out the three transformers they were to take out and hurried to the center one in the line of three, and set up the ten kilos of Semtex at the base of the big machine that hummed as if it were a living thing.

When he was finished he reached out and brushed the case with his bare fingers and pulled back, startled. The metal fin was warm to the touch, and he could feel the vibration. It was alive. A monster.

They finished in under twenty minutes, climbed through the hole, and Gomez bent the chain link back roughly in place so that someone passing by in the night might not notice that anything was wrong.

Hunching down again they ran back into the darkness and made their way downriver to within thirty meters of the boat where Campinella motioned for them to hold up. Nothing moved in any direction, and from where they were concealed behind a stand of willows he couldn't see any signs that someone had been to the boat and were waiting for them.

Nevertheless he unslung his rifle and switched the safety off. Gomez and Ricardo did the same, and the three of them cautiously approached the boat expecting trouble at any second. But the night remained still, and within three minutes they had untied from the bridge pilings, Campinella had started the boat's engines, and they slowly headed downriver to the ICW, a full fifteen minutes earlier than they had planned.

THEY HAD just reached the pass at Port O'Connor out into the Gulf when the lights from Port Lavaca twenty miles to the north went out, and Campinella couldn't help but wonder at the stupidity of the Americans for not taking better security precautions, but at the even greater stupidity of his own government.

Chavez, *el mico mendante,* as some people had nicknamed him, was stark raving mad. It was likely that he was goading the U.S. into a shooting war that would end up terribly for everyone.

57

IT WAS NINE on another dismally overcast morning when Karn finally came out of the bedroom, her hair tied up in a scarf. She was wearing a GO BRAZIL sweatshirt and jeans, her feet bare, no makeup as usual. "You going to be a zombie for the rest of the day, or what?" she said.

Dekker had been sitting at his computer all night, switching between his 10-D game and the virus that would crash the entire mainland U.S. electrical grid. Just a couple of firewalls to get through, and a few keystrokes, maybe forty-five uninterrupted minutes or so, and it would be like a thousand nuclear bombs going off all at once. He looked over his shoulder.

"I can't launch the game."

She came to him, a sudden look of concern on her pretty round face, and used the mouse to get to the top level of the ten dimensions, where she hit the start button, and the first rockets came out of the battle star hanging in orbit above the earth. All of it was invisible to earthlings because everything at that level existed only in a superdimensional universe.

"Looks good to go to me," she said. "Send it out. It's going to blow their fucking minds."

"Not yet."

"You're such a baby, why not?"

"I don't have a name, and it's no good without it, they'd laugh their asses off at me."

Karn guffawed. "Not a chance, you'd destroy them if they did."

Dekker's anger spiked, but he held himself in check. Maybe the gamers, who knew about him and would be interested in matching wits with his game, might not laugh. But Karn did it a lot lately, just like the other night at the train station when he'd caught her with the guy she was probably fucking.

"Anyway let's go," she said. "I want to buy a couple of birds, and I need to find a decent pair of sneakers."

"Not this morning."

"Yes, this morning. And I'll make a deal with you. Buy me some lunch and I'll figure out a totally radical name. Ten-D wormhole. Black hole."

Dekker was suddenly interested despite himself. "Too plain."

"Okay. Hawking's Folly."

"Shit, shit."

"What?"

Dekker stared at the top-level images on his monitor, his brain suddenly racing. Something had been missing deep inside of his game, and it was one of the reasons he hadn't been able to come up with a good name—until now. But he'd held back because he hadn't been able to figure out what he needed to add—until now.

"I'm so goddamned stupid, sometimes," he groaned.

"You're anything but," Karn said.

"Hawking came up with the math for black holes. The event horizons, the ejecta—like light beacons—the swallowing of whole galaxies and the evaporation rates, and even when those big puppies begin to evaporate like ten to the hundred years from now. First the Big Bang and then fade to black."

He looked up at her to see if she was getting it, but she shook her head.

"Okay so it's a neat game," he said. "But it's way too easy."

"I don't think so."

"This one isn't for amateurs, this one's for the pros, the super-nerds. And you just helped me figure it out."

Karn spread her hands, mystified.

"I have the dimensions right, but the time frame is way too short. We'll speed it up, create black holes on every dimension; evaporate them, entropy in reverse, the universe clocking down to the big fade. Thing is, the player has to get to the goal before that happens."

"What's the goal?" Karn asked, and Dekker had to grin.

"The biggest prize of all, of course. Survival."

A LOW overcast had settled over Amsterdam, and it was at times like these when Dekker wished for a warmer, sunnier place to live. He had bought a pair of lovebirds for Karn on Westerstraat in front of the Noorderkerk, the plastic cage in her left hand as she prepared to release them.

"They won't survive," he said. "Weather's too cold."

"They'll live long enough to know freedom, so that their sprits will soar."

"Right," Dekker said, and a familiar face in the market-day crowd on the square caught his attention.

Karn opened the cage door and the birds immediately flew out

and up into the sky, at the same moment the man turned and disappeared.

It was the same bastard from outside the train station, and
Dekker's gut was instantly tied in a thousand knots, as if he'd suddenly come down with stomach cancer or something.

Karn was looking at him. "What's the matter?"

"I'm sick," Dekker said. "I need to lie down before I upchuck."

"I thought we were going to have lunch."

"First I have to go home."

"Do you want me to come with you, or do you want to meet me
somewhere?" Karn asked.

Dekker shook his head, his brain seething. "Help me get home
first. And then you can go—" He almost said to her lover, but he
bit it off.

"Okay," she said, and arm in arm they headed back to the Haven, not saying much of anything, until they got to their building.

"I'll need help upstairs," Dekker said. The elevators had never
worked as long as they had lived here, and consequently they both
were in pretty decent condition.

"Sure," Karn said, and they trudged up to the tenth floor.

She had been decent to him the whole time, but after the train
station Dekker had begun to wonder if everything she had said and
done, all of their lovemaking, had been nothing but a big lie. He
just wanted to tell her to get the fuck out, because he didn't need
her shit. But he couldn't. In fact he'd come to depend on her more
than he wanted to admit. And even now, heading up, he had to examine his own mind to make crystal clear what he intended doing.
But he could see no way out of it. In fact his logic was unassailable.

First he would deal with her.

Second he would finish his game, and send it out.

Third he would pull the pin on the Russian virus, and set it
loose.

"YOU OKAY, sweetie?" Karn asked when they reached their apartment.

"I'm going to lie down. Get me a glass of water."

"Sure," Karn said and she went into the kitchen.

Dekker slipped into the filthy bedroom, and waited just inside the door until she came back.

For just an instant she had no idea what was happening as Dekker slammed his fist into the side of her neck and shoved her forward, down onto the floor.

"Barend," she cried. But he clamped his hands around her throat, his thumbs pressing into the carotid arteries in her neck.

He'd searched the Internet last night for ways to best kill someone using only bare hands. Her face began to turn red and her struggles ceased in less than one minute, but still he pressed as hard as he could. Until at one point he peed in his pants and he reared back.

Karn was truly dead, no way of ever bringing her back.

Dekker went into the bathroom where he stripped and got into the shower. He figured that it would take him a very long time to get clean, but when he was fully cleansed physically as well as mentally, he would get on with his important work and then leave Amsterdam forever.

58

THE MOOD IN the White House Situation Room at nine in the morning was somber because the thirteen members of the National Security Council gathered for the emergency session knew what the president was going to ask them to consider. And waiting now for Thompson to show up, Mark Young couldn't help but feel as if they were all standing at the edge of a very deep precipice.

The dark mood was further deepened because the president had sent Vice President Lorraine Weiss out to the Cheyenne Mountain Directorate which was home to NORAD and buried deep within the Colorado mountains. The Speakers of the House and Senate had left earlier this morning for vacations somewhere unspecified. And security at a number of Washington's headquarters buildings had been quietly heightened.

To this point the press was dealing with the explosions in Texas as a non-nuclear accident in one of the transformer yards; an arc-over with no casualties. The public was being reassured that power would be restored in a matter of twenty-four to forty-eight hours. And this was an isolated incident having nothing whatsoever to do with the recent rolling blackouts that had been caused by the act of a terrorist group that had not yet identified itself, though al-Qaeda was being mentioned.

The president came in and took his seat at the end of the long table. The flat-screen monitors on the walls were blank, no tablets or pencils had been set out for the members, nor was there any coffee service. An aide closed the door.

"Good morning, Mr. President," Young said.

Thompson was a short, slender man, normally reminiscent of Truman with a pleasant if vacant expression. But this morning he looked like an angry pit bull on the verge of striking. "What's the latest on the ground in Texas?" he demanded.

"They may have come by boat, we're checking the marinas between Galveston and Corpus Christi, with no results so far," Edward Rogers, the FBI's director, said. "We have good cooperation with the Coast Guard, as well as the local police and Texas Highway Patrol. But we may already be too late."

"Tell me."

"Three men, who were identified as businessmen from San Antonio, rented a thirty-foot sport fisherman from Dugan's ICW Marina in Corpus, yesterday. They said they were going to do some offshore fishing for one week. But the boat was returned this morning, before the marina opened, and there was no sign of the men."

"No one saw anything?" the president asked.

"No. But we just got imprints of their driver's licenses, and we're doing a computer search with the Texas Department of Motor Vehicles."

"They'll be fakes," Thompson said.

"Possibly," Rogers said. "But we're continuing with our search until we're sure."

"SEBIN is behind this, just as it was behind the attacks on the Initiative," Thompson said and he looked away for just a moment. "Who the hell in Christ does the bastard think he's dealing with?"

"We're not entirely sure yet that it was Venezuela," Young said. What none of them needed was a president so angry that he went off half-cocked.

"Bullshit," Thompson said. He turned to his CIA director. "Do we still have assets in Caracas?"

"Yes, sir," Walt Page said. "But since Balboa and since we recalled our ambassador and all but a skeleton crew from our embassy, the city has been sealed tight. We've been getting very little hard information, and what we do have is conflicting."

"How about electronically? We can listen to their phone conversations, monitor their Internet activity."

"Nothing conclusive, Mr. President," Madeline Bible, the director of National Intelligence said. She was a short, somewhat rotund woman. With her hair done up in an old-fashioned bun, she could have been someone's kindly grandmother, except hers was one of the sharpest minds in the intelligence gathering business. "Our best guess is that SEBIN knows our capabilities and is hand-delivering important memos. Several high-ranking intelligence officers, including a man we've identified as Colonel Luis Delgado have been seen entering the Miraflores Palace at all hours of the day and night. Delgado is most interesting because we think he heads SEBIN's special operations department, which was almost certainly involved with the attacks on the Initiative."

"We have no one inside the palace who might have picked up something?"

"Unfortunately not," Bible said. "But although the information we do have is circumstantial, my analysts have a high confidence that President Chavez wants to strike back at us because of Balboa.

And he wants it done sooner rather than later, before his cancer kills him."

"Walt?" The president turned back to his CIA director.

"My analysts agree."

"Nick?" The president turned to his national security adviser.

"The *George H.W. Bush* is currently finished with her ninety-day turnaround," Fenniger said. "She should have her complete air complement aboard no later than noon today." CVN77 was the latest *Nimitz* nuclear-powered aircraft carrier in the U.S. fleet, currently stationed at Norfolk.

The room was suddenly cold.

"Sending her south would be nothing short of provocative at this point," Young said but he knew his would probably be the only voice of caution. Everyone in the room wanted this, no one more so than the president.

"Chavez didn't learn from Balboa, and if we can connect his intelligence apparatus with the Texas attack I won't hesitate to order a strike on him and his government."

"But we haven't established that connection without a doubt," Young said.

"No," the president said. "Can anyone here suggest to me an alternative? Someone else who wants to attack us?"

Young wanted to speak up, but despite his cautious nature he had no answer that made any sense.

"The strikes on the Initiative were ordered by Chavez," the president said. "The virus that the hacker in Amsterdam has used on us probably came from Russia via Iran's intelligence service. Chavez and Ahmadinejad are practically in bed with each other. What better time for them to strike again—first with the blackouts, and now this attack in Texas?"

"We should have something within the next ten or twelve hours," Rogers said. "Be my guess that the three fishermen used fake IDs and are probably on their way to Mexico. They won't get across the border. And once we have them in custody it won't take long to identify them."

"Good," the president said. "Whatever it takes, because I'm told that replacing those transformers could take as long as two years, crippling a lot of Texas industry. If this was a direct attack on us by a foreign government—Mr. Chavez's or anyone else's—we will strike back. Decisively. I won't ask for sanctions from the U.N., nor will I order the freezing of bank accounts or any other soft moves. I'll order our military to destroy hard assets on the ground. Perhaps the oil fields on and around Lake Maracaibo."

"There would be significant loss of lives," Young said.

The president looked at him. "Yes," he said, and he turned to General Robert Blake who was the chairman of the Joint Chiefs. "I want the *Bush* to sail immediately and head south at her best possible speed. They can recover the last of their aircraft while en route."

"Her mission, Mr. President?" Blake asked.

The Situation Room was deathly still. Thompson had not asked for a show of hands, he'd heard what he wanted to hear, and now the order was his.

"Reach Venezuela, where she will stand off shore between Caracas and Maracaibo and make ready for my order."

"This would be a conventional strike, Mr. President?" the general asked. "Not a nuclear one?"

The president hesitated for a couple of beats, which frightened Young more than anything else that had been said here this morning.

"We will meet any threat with the appropriate response."

59

ASHLEY LEFT THE rental car at the Sioux Falls airport and took the morning Delta flight to Washington National Airport via Baltimore. It was nearly noon by the time she arrived and phoned her father, the private number at his office ringing once and then flipping over to his cell phone.

"It's me, I tried to get you at your office. Something up?"

"Where are you?" General Forester said. He sounded strained, as if he hadn't been getting enough sleep.

"I just landed at Reagan, and I have to talk to you."

"Not here, sweetheart. Go back to Bismarck and I'll call you tomorrow."

"I need to talk to you about Nate, and it can't wait."

"Washington may not be the safest place in the world right now."

"What are you talking about?" Ashley asked, even more alarmed than she'd been all night.

"It's the thing in Texas. Could be the next strike, we just don't know for sure. But the president thinks he does."

"I haven't seen a newspaper yet this morning. What's happened in Texas, another blackout?"

"No," Forester said. "An electrical distribution yard that served a big nuclear plant a few miles from the Gulf was hit. Three of the big transformers were knocked out. It's hell of a mess, because everybody believes that Chavez was behind it."

"Is all that in the news?"

"Most of it," Forester said.

"Is there anything you've said to me that I can use?"

"Not yet."

"Goddamnit, Dad, I think that Nate might be getting in over his head, and I've got to talk to you about it. I think that he's on his way to Amsterdam to find the hacker. He has to be called back."

"Where did you hear about that?"

Ashley told him. "Did you know about it?"

Forester hesitated, and Ashley thought that she heard someone talking in the background. "Where are you right now?" she asked.

"Just leaving the CIA. Do you know where Turkey Run Park is located?"

"Never heard of it."

"It's on the parkway, about a half mile west of the Agency's driveway. I'm driving the gray Taurus. We'll give you twenty minutes to get here."

"Who's we?" Ashley demanded, but her father had rung off.

She got a *Washington Post* from a bookstore in the terminal, but there was nothing about any incident on the front page, and it wasn't until she was in a cab heading up the river on the George Washington Memorial Parkway that she found the story on the third page of the National section, under the brief headline: POWER TROUBLES IN TEXAS. The paper was treating it as an equipment breakdown; three high-power transformers had evidently failed and somehow burned out. Could be a matter of days, perhaps longer, before the full two-point-five megawatts of power would resume energizing the Texas Interconnect.

Nothing in the short article hinted at sabotage, nor was any federal official cited, which stank of a typical Washington coverup.

Ashley looked out the window. The scenery here was hilly and heavily wooded. Somewhere she had read something about there being more species of trees here than anyplace else in the country. Under normal circumstances she would have found this place comforting. She'd always liked the country, and living in North Dakota she missed the forests, so this was pleasant except that her gut was tied in a thousand knots. He father wanted to meet at some ridiculous location—not his office, not even a restaurant, a McDonald's or something. And talking to him on the phone she'd heard a voice in the background. And he and whoever was with him were coming from the CIA. And he was in his own car, not the limo.

The traffic was moderate on the parkway, and within less than a half mile after they'd passed the Agency's driveway the cabbie slowed for a road off to the right.

"This the road, ma'am?" he asked.

"So far as I know," she said, but then she spotted a gray Ford Taurus just inside the park. "Yes, right here."

The cabby turned in and pulled up behind General Forester's car. "Do you want me to wait for you?"

"I'll only be a few minutes, if you don't mind."

"Meter's running."

Ashley got out and walked up to the car at the same moment her dad and Nate got out. Neither of them looked happy to see her, but she felt an almost physical sense of relief. She wasn't too late.

"I'll share the cab with you back to the airport," she told Osborne. "We can go home."

"No, but you're going to do a one-eighty," Osborne said.

She looked at her dad. "You can't be serious. He's not going to Amsterdam. You can't allow this to happen."

"The CIA has a plane standing by for me at Andrews," Osborne told her. He seemed grim.

"For Christ's sake, Nate. You're a county sheriff, not a secret agent or spy or something. Going after some superhacker is a job for the CIA, or at least Interpol. Those guys are always busting groups like that."

"That's the problem," Forester said. "The Dutch government wants no part in it. They've refused to ask for Interpol's help until we can give them some concrete proof, which we don't have."

"That's stupid."

"Yes, it is. But they've got their hands full with their Turkish immigrant problems, and from what we were told this morning, the Dutch police no longer try to hassle anyone who isn't breaking a Dutch law. There've been serious repercussions in the past from the hackers over there."

"Send a CIA agent to take care of it."

"The Netherlands is a friendly country, and Walt Page doesn't want to burn any assets if there's another possible solution to the problem. The repercussions could be bad. Especially right now."

"So they're sending you." She turned on Osborne.

"No one's sending me, Ash. It was my idea, I just asked for the green light, which I was given because of the Texas thing, and what's about to happen next."

"What?" she demanded.

Osborne and Forester exchanged a look. "You might as well tell her," Osborne said. "She won't use it."

"She does and she'll go to jail no matter whose daughter she is," Forester said. "The president has sent an aircraft carrier to Venezuela."

Ashley stepped back. "That's more than stupid, Dad. That's nuts. Are we going to war?"

"That'll depend on Chavez, and the hacker. Because if our electrical grid—the entire grid—goes down, it'll be as bad as a massive nuclear strike. Thompson, no president, could hold back from making a measured response."

"Nukes on Caracas, is that what you're trying to tell me?" Ashley cried. She looked to Nate and then back at her father. "The Security Council went along with it?"

"I wasn't there. But according to Page the president promised an appropriate response."

"Whatever that means," Ashley said. She was not just frightened now, she was angry. "We didn't go to war over nine-eleven."

"No, but we finally caught up with bin Laden," Osborne said.

"And besides the fact that these attacks were directed by a sovereign nation, not some terrorist group, taking out our grid would be a thousand times worse than nine-eleven," Forester said. "It's the possibility that we're facing."

"Send the CIA to Caracas, take the bastard out. Better yet, send a drone to hit him where he lives, or in his limo, or in his office."

"Might not be necessary if I can get to Dekker first," Osborne said.

Ashley could hear the traffic on the parkway, and off to the left somewhere some birdsong. She looked into Osborne's eyes, but then she finally nodded. "Take care of yourself, Sheriff," she said.

She kissed him lightly on the cheek, and then her father, and without looking back returned to the cab.

"WHERE TO, ma'am?" the cabby asked.

"Dulles," Ashley told him. "I'll tell you the airline before we get there."

Ever since she was a kid she'd gotten into the habit of always carrying her passport. She called the Capital City Travel agent she usually worked with in Bismarck, and within fifteen minutes had a confirmed business-class seat on KLM flight 652 leaving at 6:10, and arriving in Amsterdam tomorrow morning at 7:45.

At nearly nine thousand dollars round-trip, her savings account was just about at zero, but besides being with Nate, she figured that she was going to get one hell of a story after all.

The problem was exactly what she was going to do once she got there; she had no idea where Dekker actually lived and she knew that Nate would get there well before she did. It could be an expensive trip for nothing. Still, it would be worth every penny.

60

MAKAROV HAD TAKEN one pass on foot from the Noorderkerk to the edge of the old Soviet-era slum buildings that housed the Haven and the Roma camp, and seeing the problem he might face backed off immediately. The Gypsies were likely witnesses.

That was earlier today. Now, a few minutes after seven in the evening, he waited in the Amstel Intercontinental Hotel's Spiegelzaal, the grandly ornate Hall of Mirrors, sipping a sparkling mineral water with a twist as he waited for his Russian FSB friend Vasili Sumskoy to arrive from Moscow.

Ilke had said she'd understood his delay when he phoned her at two, but he'd heard the disappointment in her voice. "How long then before your business is done and you get home?"

"I should be finished here sometime this evening, and I'll catch the first morning train."

"Call me if there is another delay."

"Of course," Makarov had promised her.

He wanted to extract himself from the relationship; it was a necessity for his safety—and hers as well—because at some point someone very good would be coming after him and anyone close to him. He knew too much that could potentially be harmful to too many people. But he could not do it. He loved her, and he was bound to do everything within his power to make sure that she stayed safe from harm even if it made him vulnerable.

"When I get back we'll go on a scouting trip for our new home," he'd said. "I don't think that I ever realized until just now how tired I am of the business world and the dreary people I have to deal with. After tonight, I'm officially retired."

"If I believed you, it would make me a very happy girl."

"Believe me," he'd told her.

The real problem, as Colonel Delgado had outlined it, was the timing. Dekker had to be taken out, but quickly and silently, before he knew what was about to happen to him.

"If he discovers that you're coming, and if you give him enough time to react, he will unleash the virus against the U.S."

"So what?"

"It would almost certainly mean war."

"You can't believe that the Americans would be that stupid. Not after their string of debacles from Vietnam to Afghanistan."

"That's exactly what we believe," Delgado had said. "Don't fail."

"I won't," Makarov had responded.

The hall was half full with early diners, a low hum of conversation like white noise making the venue safe from eavesdropping. Makarov looked up as Sumskoy, wearing an old corduroy jacket with leather patches on the elbows and an outrageous bow tie, followed the maître d' across the room.

The Russian was not smiling, but he'd come at Makarov's summons, which meant that he was probably broke again.

Makarov stood up. "Thanks for responding on such short notice," he said and they shook hands.

The waiter came and Sumskoy ordered a double Stoli neat, but he said nothing else until his drink came and the waiter was gone again.

"Here I am out of a warm bed, so it will cost you."

"Fifty thousand euros."

"One hundred," Sumskoy said.

"Done," Makarov said. "Is she worth it, Vasili?"

"You can't imagine. Now, this concerns Mr. Dekker, I assume. Unless I miss my guess he's done something to upset your employers—which I suspect is either the Venezuelans or the Iranians, or both—and you've been sent here to eliminate him and retrieve the thumb drive and the boy's computer before he causes even more havoc in the U.S. For which you need my help."

"I need his exact location," Makarov said, keeping the signs of any reaction off his face. Vasili knew entirely too much. By guessing that he knew about SEBIN's and VEVAK's connection he had signed his own death warrant.

"I could have given that to you over the phone."

"There's more."

"Of course. He and his girlfriend live in the tenth-floor apartment of a condemned building between the Jordaan and the Noorderkerk. There are actually three such buildings that were put up in the sixties, his is the one farthest west—on the other side from the Gypsy encampment."

"I assume that the elevators don't work."

"If they ever did. Russian contractors built the place. But the point is he probably likes it up there in his eagle's aerie. He'll have the stairs wired for visual, infrared, and motion so he'll know when someone is on the way up."

"You've done your homework since we last talked," Makarov said, which he'd expected.

"When you come to me for information on someone you're interested in, I find out what I can. It's a matter of self-preservation."

"And in this case?"

"From what a little bird told me just before I left to come down here, the VEVAK agent watching the kid did not make the usual contact schedule this morning."

"Who is this person?"

"Dekker's girlfriend, actually. She's a Dane the Iranians recruited about three years ago at Aarhus Universitet in Copenhagen. She was studying to be a sociologist, and was already a communist."

"Has there been trouble?"

"That I don't know, except my source said that her handler had become nervous over the past week or so."

"Who is he?" Makarov asked.

"Colonel somebody Dabir, I never knew his first name. In any event until you showed up it was none of my business."

"But now it is."

"Yes," Sumskoy said. "Once again, I'm here, what do you want?"

"I need your help to get to him before he can unleash your virus."

"Not mine—"

"If this actually goes down there'll be plenty of blame to go around. Something Putin, who's having enough trouble keeping the peace at home, doesn't want. You're involved now which puts your name at the top of a very small list."

"*Eb tvoiu mat.*" Sumskoy swore softly. "I've never had personal contact with the kid. He'd have no idea who I was—except that I'd probably pose a threat to him. As would you."

"Not if I called him first—he's talked to me on the phone—and told him that someone had come to kill him."

"Yes, you. But I don't see how that would help."

"Not me, Vasili, you. I would bring you to him up the stairs, at gunpoint. In the morning, I think would be best, when he's likely to be the least alert. Just before dawn, four or five."

61

THE C37B GULFSTREAM G550 on loan to the CIA from the Navy touched down at Amsterdam's Schiphol International Airport just before three in the morning, local. The pilot taxied across to the Dutch Coast Guard Station and parked in front of the Operations Building where a man in civilian clothes waited next to a Saab station wagon.

Tim Winkler, the CIA agent who'd been assigned to fly over with Osborne but for nothing else unless something unforeseen cropped up, looked out the window. "Just as we suspected," he said. He was an older man with a round head and thinning white hair.

"Police?" Osborne asked. He'd managed to catch a few hours' sleep on the way over, a trick that he and just about every GI who'd ever served in combat learned. But his mind had not shut off, and he'd replayed scenarios half dreaming, half daydreaming about just how he was going to get to Dekker. None of them had seemed workable to him. Improvise. It had been drummed into his head in FORECON.

"Worse. He's Major Andries DeJong. AIVD muscle. That's the Dutch intelligence service, whose main job is internal security. Anything that's not a military threat. Just about like our FBI and damned near as good."

"How'd they know I was coming?"

"We had to tell them, otherwise it would have been Ramstein first and from there by train or car. And frankly we didn't think there was enough time for that."

Jody Acers, the attendant, was busy with the front door.

"What about him, is he going to help or is he going to tell us to turn around and get out?"

"I don't know. But he'll at least listen to what we have to say," Winkler said. "I worked on an assignment in Oslo with him about five years ago. Had to do with a couple of diplomats—one of them Dutch, the other American—who'd received death threats. He's a tough guy, but he'll have his orders."

Once the door was open and the steps were down, Acers stepped aside to let the Dutch intelligence officer aboard. The man was lightly built, with sandy blond hair, a thin mustache, about fifty. He wasn't smiling.

"Good to see you," Winkler said, as he and Osborne got to their feet.

They all shook hands and Winkler introduced Osborne.

"Surprised to see you here, Timothy," DeJong said.

"We have a serious problem, some of which involves one of your citizens. But I think that you already know something about it."

DeJong scowled. "Have you brought me proof? My government would need that before we could take any action." He gave Osborne a pointed look. "Or allow any action to be taken."

"We don't have a lot of time, Mr. DeJong," Osborne said. "Either you're going to help me do what I came to do, or we'll just turn around and get the hell out of here and let the mess spill over your fence, which it'll surely do if this comes to a shooting war."

"You're nothing more than an obscure county sheriff; what do you think you can hope to accomplish here that my service cannot do?"

"What your service refuses to do," Osborne shot back. It would have been better if they had landed at Ramstein and he'd anonymously crossed the border by car, because he didn't think DeJong was even going to let them off the aircraft.

"Do you know anything of Sheriff Osborne's background?" Winkler asked.

"Yes, we checked on him. And he's an impressive man by all accounts, which is neither here nor there. The point is exactly what he's come here to do."

"To find Barend Dekker and take his computer and a thumb drive which contains a computer virus—probably Russian-designed— that was delivered to him probably by a VEVAK agent or agents."

"Probably, probably."

"As you know he's already caused serious trouble for us."

"Because of your intransigence with Iran's nuclear efforts, and your attack a few months ago on some Venezuelan military targets. Why don't you go to Tehran or Caracas?"

Osborne didn't know how much further he could take this and he looked to Winkler.

"As your people probably already know, President Thompson has sent one of our aircraft carriers to stand off Caracas," Winkler said.

"Yes, the *George H.W. Bush* from Norfolk. And I suspect that you have already given Israel the green light in case you come up with definitive proof of Iran's involvement," DeJong said. "My question stands: What are the two of you doing here?"

"To find Dekker and the virus before it's too late and the damage to our electrical grid is done," Osborne said.

"No. The *two* of you."

"I'm here to deliver the package," Winkler said, and it was what he'd warned Osborne would probably be the case.

"But not to babysit. Not to participate."

"It would make the operation easier."

"For you but not for us," DeJong said. "You will stay aboard the aircraft which will not be given clearance to take off until we know exactly what sort of damage Sheriff Osborne has caused."

Osborne was mad. "What the hell are you afraid of, Major?"

"Involvement in another American adventure," DeJong shot back angrily.

"It was different in the forties when we and the Allies came to save your asses from the Nazis."

"Seventy years ago. We live in a different world now."

"Yes, we do. But I hope it never comes to an all-out war again, or at the very least your Turkish immigrant problem doesn't rise up and bite you in the ass and you need help."

DeJong smiled faintly. "I hope that your field action is as sharp as your background suggests it is, or at least as to the point as your rhetoric is."

"The ball's in your court, Andries," Winkler said.

"We'll have your aircraft refueled and ready for turnaround by dawn. In the meanwhile Sheriff Osborne will come with me and I'll point him in the right direction, but I am ordered to do nothing more than that. Do you understand?"

"Yes," Osborne said.

They all rose and DeJong started for the door, but he stopped and turned back. "Are you armed? Have you brought weapons with you?"

"One pistol."

"Leave it here."

"What?" Osborne asked. He'd expected anything but this. "What the hell am I supposed to defend myself with, strong language?"

"As it has been explained to me, Barend Dekker is a computer hacker, not a trained soldier or operative. Use your strong language and he'll probably faint."

It wasn't the hacker who Osborne was concerned with, it was his girlfriend, the VEVAK agent assigned to watch him, or perhaps someone else in the neighborhood who might be interested.

"This is my government's condition. You will not bring a weapon onto Dutch soil."

Osborne unholstered his 9mm SIG-Sauer P226 and handed it to Winkler along with a spare fifteen-round magazine.

62

WHITNEY WAS AT her office. It was nine in the evening, and staring out her window the vague feelings of fear and even insecurity that had plagued her all day had grown stronger with the evening. She'd not been able to reach Nate, and his office said the last they'd heard he'd gone back to Minnesota to talk to the MAAP computer analyst in Hibbing. But when she called a spokesman said he was not there.

Nor had she been able to reach Ashley's cell phone, and she hung up after she reached the automatic voice message system.

Her old third-floor rear office at the CDC's headquarters in Druid Hills, a suburb of Atlanta, looked toward Emory University, the view in a colleague's estimation "industrial shit," with the smokestack, white trailer pods, electrical distribution yard, cars, trucks, and miscellaneous equipment parked seemingly at random. But as she'd told him, this was a working facility not a showplace, and who has time to look out their window anyway?

She'd spent the day arranging computer time on the center's

mainframe and setting the preliminary schedules for the half-dozen postdocs she'd selected from the nearly three hundred applications that had piled up on her desk since her work on microbial quorum sensing at the Initiative had been made public. She'd suddenly become a popular scientist and a lot of kids wanted to work with her.

Her office was organized, her lab would be up and running within a week, but the problem was she had no problem to work on. At least nothing specific beyond the broad, long-term goal of applying her research to animal subjects at first, and then to human trials.

The idea was fairly simple in concept: produce a mix of microbes that could be directed by her quorum-sensing language system to cure a very targeted ailment. Something so important as eliminating a cancerous tumor in a lung, or in a woman's breasts or ovaries. Or apparently simple as dissolving stones in a person's gallbladder.

But finding the correct mixture of microbes from a population that numbered in the hundreds of millions, and then coming up with the correct lingua franca that would cause them to work together to cure the problem instead of killing the patient was worse than finding the needle in a haystack by a factor of ten, or a hundred or a thousand.

That didn't matter as much as finding the starting point. Finding the correct mix of microbes and the language to make them eat coal, turn it into methane, and then reproduce more microbes to continue the process had been simple. Her failures had produced nothing but failures. No one died.

A sudden chill made her shiver. But people at the Initiative had died because of her work, and still more might. And now she'd been unable to reach Nate or Ashley.

Her phone rang, and it was General Forester. "Am I interrupting your work?"

"No," she said. "As a matter of fact I was just thinking about going home. It's been a long day."

"For me, too," Forester said. "You've tried to call my daughter several times today. Can you tell me why?"

It was more than a simple question. She could hear the strain in the general's voice. "I wanted to talk to her."

"About what?"

"We're friends, I wanted to see how she's getting along."

Forester held his silence.

"We haven't talked much since I left Medora."

"You've also tried to reach Nate Osborne."

Whitney bridled. "Your people have been monitoring my telephone, and I have a hunch you've looked at my e-mails. This facility is supposedly every bit as secure as yours, General. I don't like the intrusion."

"Yes, I'm sorry. But this is a matter of national emergency. And we are talking about my daughter. I don't know where she is, and frankly I'm very worried about her. She's a headstrong girl who tends to go off on tangents. You tried to reach her for something more than a chat. What do you think she's up to?"

"Do you know where Nate is at this moment?"

"Yes."

"That's where she is, and frankly I'm worried about both of them, because I think that we just might be at war. Undeclared, but war just the same. For energy. And it's been coming for a long time, and if it develops the way I'm afraid it will, we're all going to be in a lot of trouble."

"I'm afraid that you're probably right about Ashley, and everything else. It's been an energy war ever since they hit the Initiative."

"Where are they?"

"I can't tell you that."

Whitney started to protest but Forester cut her off.

"It's not what you want to hear, Doctor, but my hands are tied and it's going to get worse for you at least for the time being."

"What are you talking about?"

"The gentlemen are on their way up now," Forester said.

"Who?"

"The FBI. They're taking you into protective custody."

Her corridor door was open and she heard the elevator arrive. She jumped up. "Bullshit! I won't allow this to happen. I have work to do. My postdocs start showing up tomorrow."

"They'll have to wait," Forester said. "It's for your own good."

"We'll see about that," Whitney said, her anger spiking nearly out of control. "I'm calling Charlie right now." Charles Donovan was the director of the CDC, and his power in Washington had to be as great as Forester's.

"I've already talked to him, and he agreed that getting you out of the possible firing line was for the best. He doesn't want to lose you. None of us do."

Whitney felt trapped. Someone was coming down the corridor. FBI agents. And she simply could not believe that something like this could happen to her. She was a scientist, not a soldier or secret agent or even a politician. And yet in her heart of hearts she could understand their concern for her safety. In a *Scientific American* editorial two months ago the writer had called her a national treasure. It'd been embarrassing to her, yet standing behind her desk she couldn't help but think about the people at the Initiative who'd been murdered in cold blood simply because they'd been working on an alternative source of relatively clean energy. Scientists like her, some of them; others had been technicians, electrical workers, roustabouts.

And Jim Cameron, chief of security, who'd given his life to save hers and Ashley's and Nate's. She had been falling in love with him, and not a day went by she didn't see his face, his smile, his gentle good nature.

Two men, dressed in plain business suits, came to her door. One of them held up his FBI credentials.

"Dr. Lipton, I'm Special Agent Ian McAllister, and this is my partner Dan Herbert. I expect that you were told that we would be coming this evening and why."

"They're here," she told Forester and she put down the phone before he could reply. "I'll need to stop at my house to pick up a few things."

"It's already been done, Doctor," McAllister said.

63

DINNER ABOARD THE KLM flight to Amsterdam was finally winding down a few minutes past nine thirty by Ashley's wristwatch but she had passed on the salmon and on the steak and instead drank a couple of glasses of really good cabernet. She'd been way too uptight to eat anything, and already the wine had gone to her head, but she would get some sleep. Somehow.

Nate was going after the hacker, she knew that much, and she figured that it was a more than even chance that someone might know he was coming and would want to stop him. She was after the story, of course—the biggest in her career—but there wasn't a chance in hell that she was going to let the man she loved go into harm's way without her. No matter what she knew he was going to say when she showed up.

She had her speech rehearsed: they were a partnership, and it didn't matter what he had to say about that, because it was fact. "You and me, babe." Sooner or later he would have to accept it, and Amsterdam was a great beginning for both of them.

One of the male attendants from first class said something to a business-class attendant who turned and nodded toward Ashley, and he came back to her aisle seat.

"Ms. Borden?" he said, smiling pleasantly. "Ashley Borden?"

Ashley's heart thumped. "Yes?"

"Someone would like to have a word with you, if you'll just come forward with me."

"Who is it?" Ashley asked. But she unbuckled her seat belt.

"It's actually a telephone call from Washington."

An older man in a business suit looked at her curiously as she got up. She gave him a smile and followed the attendant forward where he took a phone from a cradle in the flight deck bulkhead.

"I have her here, sir," he said, and he handed the phone to Ashley.

She knew who it had to be. "How did you find me, Daddy?" she said.

"It wasn't easy," her father said, and he sounded more resigned than angry. "Why are you going to Amsterdam?"

"Nate's on his way there."

"Not good enough."

"I'm chasing a story."

"Not according to Tom Smekar, who told me he had no idea what you were up to, but when I mentioned Amsterdam he didn't seem surprised. He gave me the name of the travel bureau the paper uses and they gave me your flight information." Smekar was the *Trib*'s managing editor.

"Now what? You can't tell me that you'll somehow manage to have the plane turned around."

"What story?"

"Nate has gone to find the computer hacker who's been screwing with our grid and stop him before he crashes the entire system."

Forester was silent for a beat. "I'm not going to ask you where you got that, but you're right. I can't have the airplane turned around in midflight. But Amsterdam is still cold this time of year. What are you wearing? Something warm I hope."

For just a moment the question made no sense to her, and she almost told him that she had taken her blue blazer and she would be fine. But then it dawned on her what he meant. "I took a white turtleneck sweater and my tan Burberry. I'll be fine."

"Luggage?"

"I checked one suitcase."

"Fine. Someone will meet you at the baggage claim area and you're not to give him any trouble. If you do he'll have you arrested."

"He'd be interfering with the freedom of the press, and I'd scream bloody murder."

"You won't be on U.S. soil, and no is going to listen to a hysterical female."

"Goddamnit—"

"No, sweetheart, this is too important for you to stick your nose in it."

Ashley's anger spiked again. "You don't have the right."

"Nor do you have the right to possibly get someone killed for the sake of a story."

That stung. "But it's Nate."

"Especially not Nate, not now," Forester said. "I want your word that you'll cooperate."

"I can't," Ashley told her father, and she nearly hung up.

"It probably doesn't matter in any event. By the time you get there it'll be over with one way or the other. You'll be too late. And you'll be under arrest until you can be put on a flight back to Washington. I'm sorry, Ash."

"Me, too, Daddy."

64

MAKAROV, DRESSED IN jeans and a dark jacket, stood in the deeper shadows away from the traffic signals at the corner across from the condemned apartment buildings. No lights shone from any of the windows, but a hundred meters east, he could see the dim, flickering open fire at the Roma camp, and from somewhere in that direction he thought that he could hear a dog barking.

It was coming on three thirty in the morning, and the hum of traffic on nearby Westerstraat was nearly nonexistent. For all intents and purposes Amsterdam was sleeping and would not begin to come alive with work traffic for another hour or so. Only the delivery vans and trucks and the garbage collectors were out and about.

Sumskoy was right behind him. "Why have we stopped here?" he asked.

"Someone else has shown up."

"Where?"

"Just around the corner on the east side of Dekker's building. He must have come across from the Roma camp."

"I didn't see anything," Sumskoy said. He'd been nervous all morning, especially so after he'd handed over the large, thickly padded envelope he'd brought into Holland under diplomatic immunity.

They'd met in Makarov's suite.

"For God's sake, if you get caught none of this can be traced back to me."

"If *we* get caught, Vasili," Makarov said. He opened the envelope and took out the Austrian-made 9mm Steyr GB, two eighteen-round magazines of subsonic hollow points, and a suppressor. It was a very quiet weapon that Spetsnaz troops had used for assassinations of high-value targets in Afghanistan.

"I've had second thoughts."

Makarov loaded the pistol, chambered a round, fitted the suppressor, and pointed it at the Russian FSB officer. "Too late for that."

Sumskoy stepped back a pace, but then he nodded, resigned. "Okay, Yuri, but I'll need to get a couple hours of sleep, I'm fagged out, and I would be no good to you otherwise. And I'll need to change clothes. Something dark."

Makarov lowered the pistol. "Don't try to run, Vasili, because I will find you and when I do I'll put a bullet in your brain."

Sumskoy had been waiting in the rental Volvo parked around the corner from the hotel a half hour ago when Makarov had shown up and they had driven over here parking a half-block away.

The figure on the other side of the building appeared around the corner again for just a moment then ducked back. He was looking for something or someone.

"Let's go," Makarov said and he headed down the street to the end of the block, Sumskoy right behind him.

"Are we getting out of here?"

"No," Makarov said.

"What then?"

"I want to see who else is interested in Mr. Dekker, and why."

"Could be Dutch cops or maybe one of the AIVD people," Sumskoy said. "If it is, we're getting out of here."

Makarov turned. "If it is I'll kill him, and we'll proceed."

"My God," Sumskoy said softly, and he looked as if he were on the verge of bolting.

"Steady," Makarov said. "It'll be a lot easier with your help, but if need be I'll manage on my own."

Sumskoy understood immediately. "You'd really kill me?"

"Yes."

"Then let's get on with it, I want to be drinking vodka in Moscow tonight."

They had to hold up in the shuttered doorway of a small cellular phone shop as a taxi passed the intersection. When it was gone they crossed the street and hurried around the back to the east corner of the apartment building where Makarov once again pulled up short.

He took a quick glance around the corner, just as the figure of what he took to be that of a large man dressed all in black turned and started to the rear of the building.

"He's on his way back," Makarov said, pulling the pistol from inside his jacket. "But I don't think he's a cop." He held up a hand for silence. The man was just around the corner, and he'd stopped.

Sumskoy didn't move a muscle, but Makarov eased to less than an arm's length from the edge of the building and raised his pistol.

A man appeared and Makarov jammed the silencer's muzzle into his face.

"Move and I will kill you," he said. But then he recognized who it was and he lowered his pistol. "What the hell are you doing here?"

"Waiting for you," Colonel Dabir, chief of VEVAK special operations, said. He looked past Makarov. "Who is he?"

"A friend," Makarov said. He glanced over his shoulder toward the street from where someone passing might spot them, and then hustled them around the corner to the shelter of the east side of the building. "You were waiting for me to show up, otherwise you wouldn't have been so sloppy. Why?"

"We couldn't get in contact with you, and Luis called me with something that you needed to know about before you went in."

"It's your operative who was watching Dekker who went missing. I know about it."

"It's something else," Dabir said. "The Americans have sent one of their carrier groups out of Norfolk to the south, at its best possible speed."

"They're heading to Caracas," Makarov said. It explained the urgency of his assignment. "It'll take them two or three days to make it that far."

"Yes. But that's not the most immediate problem. Some serious mischief was done to an electrical transformer yard in southern Texas and the blame for that, along with the rolling blackouts, has been laid on President Chavez's doorstep."

"It's why we're here, to prevent Dekker from unleashing the Russian virus which your government provided him. What's the problem? Why else did you come here?"

"Moving the carrier south is provocative," Dabir said.

Makarov had to laugh. "So was causing the blackouts and damaging a transformer yard."

"Luis says that Chavez is dying, and there's no telling what the madman is capable of doing next."

"It sounds to me as if your President Ahmadinejad is trying to save his own ass. He's got trouble enough as it is with Israel."

Dabir nodded. "The aircraft carrier got his attention. He's seriously expecting another one to come into the Persian Gulf, and despite all his bluster he's finally realized that if he makes any sort of a military move it would signal the end of the regime. The

Ayatollah has taken him to serious task. A lot of unrest right now, and no one knows how this can possibly turn out for the good without your help."

"Maybe I should ask for more money."

"Anything. Name your price," Dabir said, and he was serious, as frightened men usually were.

"Later."

"The kid has a hair trigger."

"Is that what your watchdog told you?"

"I was here a few days ago, and she told me that she wanted out. She was afraid for her life."

"You should have told her to kill him first," Makarov said. "Would have saved us the trouble tonight."

Nothing moved in the apartment complex, and still the only light came from the glow of a fire or fires at the Roma camp. The dog that had been barking earlier was silent, and for just a brief moment Makarov wished that he could be just about anywhere other than here. It was a sentiment that had become increasingly strong over the past weeks. Time to move on, he told himself for the umpteenth time. Ilke was going to be over the moon.

"Is there any chance that Dekker has spotted you?" he asked.

"I don't think so. Karn said that his anti-intrusion devices were mostly centered on the area of the entryway and the stairs."

"How about the elevator shaft?"

"I'm not certain, though I don't think it would be such a good idea to climb that far."

"It could end up being necessary." Adapt. It was the mantra of every decently trained Special Forces around the world. Improvise.

"What is your plan?" Dabir asked.

65

AFTER PARKING ON a side street across from the Roma encampment, DeJong led Osborne past the one small oil barrel fire tended by a pair of men who watched them pass but said nothing. They stood now at the corner of the building on the east side looking directly across a parking lot to Dekker's building.

The figures of three people were huddled in the shadows on the near side of the building, just around the corner from the front entrance.

"It would appear that you're not the only one interested in Herr Dekker this morning," DeJong said.

"Most likely none of them carried weapons across the border," Osborne said with sarcasm.

"I can inform my office who will send a SWAT team to investigate. But if none of those men are armed, and they can present reasonable explanation for their being here at this hour, then you will have gained nothing."

"Your people could find something wrong with their identity

papers; that would give a reason to hold them until a proper investigation could be made."

"These guys are almost certainly professionals, their papers would be in order." DeJong shrugged. "I promised that I would take you this far as a service-to-service favor."

"You won't help me?"

"No."

In Afghanistan Osborne had worked as and with a team. But sometimes in the heat of a battle he, like many other soldiers, found himself cut off, isolated, and he'd had to operate on his own initiative. He'd lost his left leg below the knee charging a Taliban position. For that brief minute or so he hadn't been responsible for anyone's safety except his own. Ever since then he'd worked best alone. Lead, follow, or get the hell out of the way. He'd come to prefer the latter.

"Then get the hell out of here."

"I'll stay and observe," DeJong said. "Sorry, but those are my orders."

Osborne glanced around the corner at the three figures still huddled in the shadows across the parking lot. "A lot of guys are good at following orders, aren't they?" he said. He turned and trotted back to where the two Gypsies were sitting on overturned boxes in front of the fire.

They looked up at him with suspicion, but said nothing.

"Do either of you speak English?"

The two men held their silence. They were probably in their mid to late thirties, but they looked much older. Their scraggly hair was long and shot with gray, they had five-day growths on their faces, and their clothing was ragged and dark, except for brightly colored vests and orange sashes around their waists. They almost looked like caricatures.

"I need some help getting across the parking lot without being seen by the three men over there," Osborne said.

The Gypsies watched him curiously.

"I don't have much money with me, but I can pay for your help."

"You're an American," one of them said, his Eastern European Romany accent thick, almost Russian, but understandable.

"Yes. I've come here to help stop a war that no one could win."

The Gypsy nodded toward DeJong who had remained in the shadows, but was watching them. "What about him?"

"He's a Dutch cop, an intelligence officer."

"Ask him for help."

"He refuses."

"Why?"

"It is political," Osborne said. "I'm on my own. Will you help? It's important."

"To whom?" the other Gypsy asked, his English much cleaner.

"To me," Osborne said.

The two Roma spoke to each other in their own language for several exchanges then the one with the heavier accent switched back to English.

"What exactly do you mean to accomplish here?"

Osborne quickly explained what he knew about the computer hacker, and about the virus that had been brought here from Russia through Iran, and the harm that was about to be unleashed in the U.S. "The three over there mean to retrieve the computer virus and use it themselves."

"If there is trouble in the U.S. it is no concern of ours," the Gypsy said.

"War knows no boundaries," Osborne shot back.

The Roma nodded toward Osborne's left leg. "You were injured in a war?"

"Afghanistan," Osborne said and he lifted his pant leg so that they could see his prosthesis.

"There is a woman with the boy. Do you mean to kill her as well?"

"I think he's already killed her. She was sent by one of the men over there to spy on him for Iran's intelligence service."

"The girl of the birds?" the one with the better English asked.

"Yes," the other man said.

They spoke again in their own language for a long minute or so.

"Are you armed?" the one with the good English asked.

"No," Osborne said. "The Dutch wouldn't allow it."

"But the three men you mean to stop are."

"Almost certainly."

The Gypsy said something Osborne didn't catch, but he got to his feet. "Come with me," he said and he headed to the nearest building.

DeJong had watched the exchange but he said nothing as Osborne followed the Roma inside and down a flight of stairs into the basement to a steel door on the west side. Only a very dim light from outside filtered into the basement.

The Gypsy unlatched the door, which swung out noiselessly on well-oiled hinges. "All the buildings are connected by maintenance tunnels. This one leads directly under the parking lot. But there is no light, and someone could be guarding the door at the other end. Do you understand?"

"Will the other door be locked?"

"I don't know."

Osborne hesitated for just a moment. "Why are you doing this?"

"For the girl of the birds," the Gypsy said. "Go with God."

Osborne had to stoop to enter the low-ceilinged narrow tunnel and the Gypsy closed and relocked the door, the darkness nearly absolute.

66

DEKKER HAD BEEN expecting company for the past twenty-four hours and now that it was here he wasn't in the least bit surprised, except for the two men hiding in the shadows over on the Roma side. He didn't know who they were, though he thought they might be cops. If that turned out to be the case the bastards would be sorry they had tried again to stick their noses in other peoples' business.

He'd played *Hawking's Folly* and he was getting pretty sharp. Another week of practice and he figured he'd be ready to release the game. Only he'd have a head start and he'd blow his competition out of the water.

On the split screen to his left, which rotated to images from eight lo-lux cameras he'd placed in and around the Haven, including the front and back stairs and the elevator shaft of this building, he'd watched first the one man show up, and then two others who joined him on the east side of the building.

Something was wrong with one of the mics down there so he'd

only been able to pick up a few muffled words here and there, but nothing that his antisurveillance programs could make any real sense of.

Over on the Roma side one of the men had disappeared two minutes ago and he hadn't come back. It could mean nothing, and yet Dekker had always been a suspicious person. He didn't know why. But he'd been that way for as long as he could remember. He'd always had the darkest thoughts about people.

He got up and went into his bedroom where Karn's body lay on its back beside the bed. He hadn't bothered covering her face with a towel or anything, because he didn't want any surprises. It was possible that she was still alive, just faking it, and at any moment would get up and do something bad.

But her eyes, which had become milky, were open, her chest was not moving, and when he touched her cheek her skin was cold and firm. And there was a smell, and a spreading stain on the floor from her backside.

"Had an accident, did we?" he said, half to himself.

He'd packed his bag a couple of hours ago. Some underwear, a couple of shirts, a second pair of jeans, some money, and his three passports—one Dutch, one U.S., and one Canadian. Plus his iPad and a universal charging device that would work on all of his toys including the custom-built laptop which he used for his serious shit.

For a moment he stood, bag in hand, staring at Karn. It had been fun with her while it lasted. But she was a whore, like just about every other woman he'd ever known, including his two sisters. The fact that she was smart had hurt the most when he'd discovered that she'd cheated on him.

All things came to an end eventually, and over the past few months he'd started to get the feeling that the Haven was about done for him. No one was left here who was any challenge. A bunch of new kids had been filtering in over the past seven or eight months; squatters who wanted to party 24/7 and never make a contribution to the game worth crap.

He'd heard about some really good shit starting to happen in Bangkok, and maybe down south on the beach near Tha Chang. More stoners mostly, but he suspected that there might be a decent gamer or two among them.

"Here's looking at you, kid," he said to Karn. *Casablanca* was one of his all-time favorite movies, and he'd always wanted to use that line.

In the living room he put his bag down by the door and went back to his worktable. Time now, he figured, to set the virus loose. He almost wished that he was a little bird in some corner somewhere in the States, just to watch all the frantic people scurrying around when their lights went out.

The lone figure on the Roma side hadn't moved, nor had the second one reappeared, which was a little troublesome. But then the image from downstairs came up, and the three men were in the lobby. One of them was holding a pistol on the other two with one hand while with the other he held a phone to his ear.

At that moment Dekker's cell phone chimed the Lone Ranger's theme from the William Tell Overture.

The man with the pistol was looking up at the hidden camera, taunting him.

Dekker answered on the second ring. "*Ja.*"

"Do you know who this is?"

Dekker recognized the voice, though the man's face on the computer screen was unknown to him, as was that of one of the other men. But the third who'd just looked up was the VEVAK officer from Tehran who'd delivered the thumb drive.

"You're the North Dakota shooter. What are you doing here with Colonel Dabir?"

"We're here to protect you."

"From what?"

"This man," Makarov said. "We found out that he came here to kill you and retrieve his thumb drive."

"Who is he?"

"His name doesn't matter, what does matter is that he works for Russian intelligence. They want to stop you."

"Then shoot him and leave," Dekker said. "I'm busy."

"What about Karn?" Dabir asked. He seemed to be genuinely concerned.

"I'll send her down and she can go home with you. I know all about her."

"Yes, I understand. But I want to talk to her."

"I'll send her down," Dekker said, and he lowered the phone and was about to switch off when Makarov gestured to him. He raised the phone. "Yes?"

"We need to talk before you launch the virus."

"I have been paid, there is no need for talk. Kill the Russian and go home."

"We can take the money back," Dabir said.

Something clutched at Dekker's head. "You'll have to find it first," he practically shouted.

"Not so difficult as you'd think."

An image on the large screen caught Dekker's attention. A man was in the tunnel from the Roma building. It was a second hammer blow to his ego. He could fight the bastards, but only on a battle-field of his own choosing. Someplace far away, isolated. Thailand loomed large in his imagination.

He switched cameras to the one downstairs in the back stairwell.

The ground-floor door was blocked from the outside by construction debris, including a large mass of concrete that had apparently been accidentally spilled and left to harden. The important part was that no one was in that stairwell.

If they wanted a fight he'd give it to them, starting now.

"All right, come up," he said. "But you'll have to use the stairs, the elevator doesn't work."

"We know," Makarov said.

Dekker watched the three men go through the front stairwell door and start up. He brought up a program on his laptop and entered a few keystrokes which locked the tunnel door in the basement. Next he opened the valves from the building's rooftop reservoir which directed all of the water into the tunnel, and before he shut down he watched as the deluge began.

One down. The virus would have to come later, there wasn't enough time now.

67

NONE OF THE lights in the stairwell worked, and the climb to the tenth floor was mostly in darkness until near the top where the corridor door was open and a dim light spilled out. Sumskoy and Dabir were winded but for Makarov, who always was in good shape, it was nothing.

"Do you think he's waited?" Dabir asked.

"He has if he's interested in keeping his money," Makarov said, and he motioned for them to hold up a few steps down.

The building was absolutely still. No voices, no music, no machinery noises.

"Mr. Dekker, we're coming up," Makarov called softly. He motioned for Sumskoy to go first.

"I bloody well don't like this," the FSB officer said, but he went the rest of the way up, hesitated at the open door, then stepped into the corridor. "One light at the other end, nothing moving."

"Which apartment?" Makarov asked.

"First one on the right," Dabir said.

"That door is open," Sumskoy called from just around the corner.

"Damn," Makarov said. He pushed past Sumskoy and went to the open door where he held up for just a moment before he eased inside the apartment, his pistol at the ready. But he knew that the kid was already on his way downstairs the back way.

A computer monitor on a worktable in the front room showed images of the front stairwell, the lobby and elevator shaft, and other views including one of the Roma settlement on the other side of the parking lot. The small fire was still casting its glimmer into the night.

Sumskoy and Dabir had come in right behind him, and it was Dabir who found the body of Dekker's minder.

"She's been dead for twenty-four hours at least," he said at the bedroom door.

Makarov phoned Dekker, who answered on the first ring.

"Too bad."

"I'll find you sooner or later," Makarov said. "And when I do I'll kill you."

"You'll try," Dekker said. "But I'll be long gone."

The hacker appeared in the stairwell and he raised his middle finger at the camera and hurried the rest of the way down to the lobby and outside.

"You won't get far without money," Makarov said, but Dekker had already rang off.

"What now?" Sumskoy asked.

Makarov turned to Dabir. "That's your call."

"We have to find him."

"We'll be too late. He just has to go to ground, somewhere close to release the virus."

"That doesn't matter as long as we can get to him before the Dutch or Americans, kill him, and retrieve the thumb drive and his computer. Nothing can get back to Caracas."

68

OSBORNE REACHED THE steel door at the end of the tunnel, and it was closed, the very cold water already high on his chest and rising. Holding his breath he ducked under the surface and groping around in the darkness found the latching mechanism. It was a short handle in the middle of a pair of metal bars that slid into slots on either side of the door and could be retracted by pulling the handle to the left.

He pushed it first to the left and then to the right, but it didn't budge a fraction of an inch, and he surfaced to catch his breath, the water already a couple of inches deeper. The Gypsy hadn't known if the door on this end would be unlocked. But it was, and Dekker had opened some water valve somewhere to flood the tunnel.

Which meant there were probably cameras down here, and the bastard had picked his time, and by now was probably gone. It was also likely that he'd seen the approach of the three men who'd been lurking in the shadows on the east side of the building and had cooked up some nasty surprise for them as well.

"Or Moscow," Sumskoy said.

Another image on the monitor caught Makarov's attention.]
was in infrared. For a long moment or two he didn't quite under
stand what he was seeing until he realized that it was the view o
what probably was a maintenance tunnel beneath or between th
buildings. Water was pouring in from somewhere beyond the cam
era, and a man, already chest deep, was caught right there, his hea
against the ceiling.

"Who is it?" Dabir asked.

"I don't know, but in about five minutes he'll not be a problen
for us," Makarov said. "Dekker is."

"But where the hell did he go?"

Makarov stuffed the pistol in his belt and went into the bedroon
where he stepped over the girl's body and checked the closet and
the chest of drawers. A woman's clothes were there but one drawe
in the chest was empty and several hangers in the closer were bare

"He's gone," he said, coming back to the living room. "If wo
hurry we might still be able to catch him."

"Then what?" Sumskoy demanded. "I'm not getting into a gun
fight in the middle of Amsterdam even if we do catch up with him.'

"That's my job," Makarov said, stepping out into the corridor and
racing for the stairs. "Go home," he called over his shoulder. "Both
of you."

He'd underestimated Dekker. They all had.

Dark enclosed spaces had never really bothered him, nor had he ever been particularly afraid of drowning. And what little anxiousness he'd ever felt about either situation had been knocked out of him in FORECON training and out in the field behind enemy lines. But when he'd gotten out of the Marines he'd figured that all that was behind him. And nothing out in the North Dakota badlands was as difficult as the Marines, except for the winters.

He turned and looked back the way he had come. It was at least eighty meters to the Roma end of the tunnel, but there was no guarantee that even if he made it that far before the water reached the ceiling, that the steel door would be unlatched from his side, or that the Gypsy would be there to hear his pounding to get out.

Overcome, adapt; the basic principles had been drummed into the head of every FORECON recruit from day one. The RECON's creed had been just as simple:

Realizing that it is my choice to be a Recon Marine I accept
    all the challenges.
Exceeding beyond the limitations set down by others shall
    be my goal.
Conquering all obstacles I shall never quit.
On the battlefield I shall stand tall above the competition.
Never shall I forget the Recon Marine's principles: Honor,
    Perseverance, Spirit, and Heart.

A RECON Marine can speak without saying a word and achieve what others can only imagine.

He wanted to get mad at himself; it wasn't supposed to end this way, not with a job unfinished, not with Ashley and everyone else he would be letting down.

Overcome, adapt. The water was nearly up to his chin as he

started back to the Roma side, using his hands along the low ceiling to help propel him forward. And as it was he nearly missed the fact that the tunnel had grown a little lighter; almost light enough for him to see the rough concrete of the curved ceiling and the gray painted utility pipes that ran along its length.

He was suddenly at a narrow break overhead that led ten feet up to a steel grate that opened to the night. For a moment it made no sense, until he realized that the tunnel floor had been flanked by concrete drainage ditches. The grate was the opening to the storm sewer system, down which the water would eventually escape. But not fast enough in this case.

Within a minute or so the water reached the ceiling of the tunnel and Osborne rode it up until he was in reach of the grate. Bracing his back against one side of the storm sewer drain, his feet against the opposite wall to give himself leverage, he tried to push to grate out of the way, but his feet slipped away.

The grate had moved a half-inch but then had come up against something that held it from going any farther.

He braced himself better and tried again. This time the grate moved a little farther up, but again came up short.

The water was now within inches of the top of the sewer drain so that he had to hold his head back in order to breathe. The edge of a panic niggled at the back of his head; not strongly enough to make him lash out or flail around, but enough for him to understand that he was in a very bad spot from which he had only a minute at the most to get himself out of before he would drown.

All that was holding the grate in place was either a rusty steel pin or bolt. And it was ready to give. Nearly ready to give. He needed either time or more force, a tool or something, neither of which he had.

Except for his prosthesis.

The water already over his chin, Osborne reared back, took a

deep breath, and turned a somersault, his feet over his head. Bracing his shoulders against the side of the drain, and holding himself in place with his outstretched arms, he hammered at the grate with his titanium leg. Once, twice, a third time, every ounce of his strength into the effort.

"Goddamnit." The thought rebounded in his head. "Not like this! Not here! Not now!"

He kicked again and this time the grate came free from its restraint, and moments before he was about to pass out, he clawed his way upright, shoved the grate the rest of the way off and out of the way, and rose up out of the water into the clean night air.

69

THE BARREL FIRE on the Roma side of the Haven sent shadows flickering across the sides of the apartment buildings. Dekker held up behind a pile of broken concrete road barriers, looking over his shoulder toward the front door of his own building.

The North Dakota shooter hadn't come down yet, nor had the other two, but he didn't think they would be long behind him.

When he had crossed the parking lot water had been gushing out of the storm drain, but as he watched a figure rose up almost as if it were a sea monster coming out of the deep, and Dekker shrank back, his heart racing, his stomach so sour all of a sudden that he felt as if he were on the verge of throwing up.

The son of a bitch in the tunnel hadn't drowned. But he'd seen the bastard down there with no way out. No escape.

He looked back to where his lo-lux cameras had spotted the lone figure in the shadows on the north side of the Roma camp. The one who'd waited with the other. Dutch cops, most likely. But if he was still there Dekker couldn't make him out. Nor were the

Gypsies anywhere to be seen. But he had to count on them still being somewhere near.

The man who'd climbed out of the access tunnel headed in an oddly stiff gait across the parking lot, keeping low and moving in a zigzag pattern as if he thought that he would come under fire at any second.

Any minute now he would run into the three coming down from the tenth floor, and Dekker had half a notion to stick around to see what came next. Whatever, it would be interesting. The bastards shooting at each other would make for a nifty video game, as if a hundred others just like it weren't already out there.

Clutching his laptop under his left arm, his go-to-hell escape-kit bag slung over his shoulder, he worked his way to the south around the Roma camp, moving carefully from one shadow to the next, keeping low and as much as possible behind construction debris and other piles of garbage including the rotted-out hulk of a small riverboat that had been dumped here sometime in the past before he and Karn had moved in.

Within minutes he'd made his way around to Westerstraat which was deserted at this hour of the morning, as he expected it would be. Glancing once more over his shoulder he pulled out his cell phone and headed in the general direction of the Central Station where he might be able to find a cab.

He brought up an airline ticket search program and asked for any flight to Bangkok, coming up almost immediately with Lufthansa 2301 that left at ten until nine this morning. He booked a round-trip first-class seat, and entered an American express credit card under Wayne Hansen, the name on his Canadian passport, but before he submitted it he transferred the transaction to another program of his own design. Two simple voice commands aged the booking, making it look to the credit card and airline computers that he had bought the ticket eight days ago.

It was a minor next step but one that had become increasingly important since 9/11 where same-day bookings raised red flags in just about every airport in the world.

When he was finished he pocketed his phone and glanced again over his shoulder in time to see what he thought was the figure of a person ducking into a doorway half a block away.

He watched for a full minute but when nothing moved he put it down to nerves, and headed again down the street.

If Karn were here she would know the right words to calm him down. She'd been the only person in his entire life who'd had that power over him. She called it love, which was nonsense of course, because she'd played him like a fiddle. She'd been nothing more than a spy from the beginning, a whore for hire.

Nevertheless he wished that she was here with him right now. Bangkok would have been fun with her.

70

THE GROUND FLOOR lobby of the apartment building was in darkness, and nothing moved outside the open door. Makarov, his silenced pistol drawn, raised a hand for Dabir and Sumskoy to hold up. Something didn't feel right to him. Some inner voice was warning him to go with care.

"Is it Dekker?" Dabir asked softly.

"I don't know."

"Well if it's the Dutch cops we're in trouble if you insist on waving that gun around," Sumskoy said, not bothering to lower his voice. He stepped forward as if to go around to the door.

Makarov turned and shot him once in the forehead at point-blank range, driving him backward onto the filthy concrete floor. "Take his identification papers."

Dabir, unimpressed, bent over the body and went through the pockets. "We can't let the kid go to ground."

"We won't, but there's someone else out there," Makarov said.

"The police?"

"Maybe," Makarov said. He went to the door and cocked an ear to listen. Something was moving in the direction of the parking lot; it was something, not someone. Like flowing water perhaps.

From the tunnel.

He peered around the edge out toward the parking lot where water gushed from what was probably a storm drain. The man in the tunnel was dead by now, drowned. Whoever he was no longer posed a threat, though Dekker had thought he did.

"Anything?" Dabir asked from the darkness.

"No," Makarov said, but there was something out there. He could practically taste it.

"We're wasting time. If we don't catch up with him in the next few minutes, he'll be impossible to trace."

"He's not staying in Amsterdam. Our coming here along with his discovery of your spy has ruined it for him."

Dabir started to object, but Makarov cut him off.

"Check the airlines for bookings that have been made within the last twenty-four hours. My guess he's going to fly out sometime later this morning."

"Why twenty-four hours? Why not this morning when he found out that someone was coming here?"

"Because that's how long his girlfriend has been dead. He killed her and knew that her control officer or someone would be showing up. He wanted to wait to see who it would be."

"You're just going to let him waltz out of here?"

Makarov spotted the storm sewer grate lying at an odd angle. The man had managed to get out of the tunnel after all. "We don't have a choice now," he said. "Are you armed? Do you have a pistol?"

"Yes. What is it?"

Makarov glanced over his shoulder. "We're going to have company. A man was going into a maintenance shaft across from one of the other buildings. Before he left, Dekker flooded the tunnel but the guy got out."

"Who is he?"

"I don't know."

"Stay here, and cover my back," Dabir said, pulling out his gun. "I'll check the rear entrance."

"Yes, do that," Makarov said, and he looked outside once again as Dabir headed down the corridor to the rear door. Except for the water still bubbling up from the tunnel, nothing in the parking lot moved. Nor was anything moving across in the Roma camp except for the flicking light from a small fire of some sort.

The man Dekker had hoped to drown was coming here. To the rear entrance.

Makarov considered going after Dabir and warning him, but the alternative—one or both of them dead—would be for the best.

He slipped out of the building, and keeping an eye toward the open parking lot in case the man from the tunnel was hiding out there in the darkness, or in case someone else was watching from the Roma camp, he hurried to the east corner of the building and checked the side. Nothing moved.

For just that moment it seemed that the entire city of Amsterdam was deserted, and he was the only man left alive except for Colonel Dabir and the man who'd come out of the flooded tunnel.

71

OSBORNE HELD UP at the steel door at the rear of the apartment building and listened to the night sounds, but it was almost impossibly quiet.

Like the lull just before the battle when all hell would break loose. It was the same feeling from Afghanistan all over again, and he felt a great sense of calm, every thought except the here and now purged from his head.

Neither DeJong nor the Gypsies had come across to help when he'd managed to get out of the tunnel, which left him to face the three men, plus Dekker, alone. He suspected that at least one of them had been posted at the rear, to make sure that Dekker couldn't leave that way and that no one was coming up on their six.

And whoever it was would be armed. Osborne was counting on it.

Overcome. Adapt.

He pounded on the steel door and stepped back. "Mr. Dekker, it is Interpol," he shouted. "Come out with your hands over your head."

The morning remained silent.

"Mr. Dekker, we have been sent here to talk to you about a computer virus you received either from Iran or Venezuela. There is no way for you to escape this morning. All we want is to talk to you."

Someone was at the door.

Osborne took out his badge and held it up as the door opened.

"I am armed, but my pistol is holstered," Dabir said. He stepped outside, his Iranian diplomatic passport raised over his head.

"You're not Barend Dekker," Osborne said.

"My name is Pejiman Dabir, I am an officer of Iranian intelligence. Here apparently for the same reason as you."

"To retrieve the virus that you supplied Mr. Dekker."

"It was the Russians, and one of their agents is shot dead in the front lobby. But I'm afraid that Mr. Dekker has managed to escape."

Osborne pocketed his badge and held out his hand. "Give me your pistol."

"I'm traveling under diplomatic immunity."

"Your weapon will be delivered to your embassy once we have finished with our investigation," Osborne said. He turned his head to the left as if he were speaking into a hidden-lapel mic. "Come now."

Dabir's eyes narrowed. He reached inside of his coat.

"With care, sir," Osborne said. "We don't want trouble. Nor do we believe you do."

"I will lodge a complaint with my ambassador," Dabir said. He took out his SIG-Sauer and held it out handle first.

Osborne took it, eased the slide back to check for a round in the chamber, and popped the magazine to check the load. "Your passport as well, please."

"No."

Osborne raised the SIG, cocked the hammer, and pointed it directly at Dabir's face. "Your passport, please."

Dabir didn't flinch, but something suddenly occurred to him and his eyes widened slightly. "You're wet," he said. "You were in the tunnel when it flooded. You have no backup. And even if you did your radio was shorted out. No one is coming."

"Where did Mr. Dekker go?"

"You're not even Interpol. You're an American."

Osborne was certain that the man was stalling. "Where is Captain Makarov?"

Dabir backed up a pace and shouted, "He has my pistol."

Osborne stepped forward, grabbed Dabir, and spun him around at the same time someone around the corner of the building fired two shots—the first going wild and the second hitting the Iranian intelligence officer in the chest.

Osborne fired back, but no one was there.

Dabir's legs buckled and Osborne let the man crumple to the ground. He slipped backward inside the building's rear corridor.

For several long moments he held perfectly still, straining with all of his senses to detect any noise, any movement from outside, or from behind him in the corridor that led to the front of the building. But there was nothing.

"We know who you are," he called out. "I served with you at Camp Foremost. We even have a photograph of you, so there's no place for you to run. Sooner or later SEAL Team Six will come calling."

The night remained silent.

"They don't take prisoners."

"Neither do I, Sheriff," Makarov called from just outside the door.

"I want the virus whoever hired you gave to Dekker. If you give me that much I'll let you get out of here, and who knows, maybe you'll be able to go to ground somewhere. At least for a while."

"A question for you, Sheriff. I wonder which of us could reach Ms. Borden first? You or me? Care to make a friendly wager?"

Rats' feet walked across Osborne's grave, and he suppressed a shiver. Ashley was safely back in North Dakota, and because of the photograph it would be next to impossible for Makarov—no matter how good he was—to get to her.

Next to impossible.

"I think I'd like you to try it," Osborne said, careful to make absolutely no noise as he eased to the edge of the doorway.

"Perhaps I will do just that," Makarov said. "And by the way, Dekker is gone. With the virus."

Osborne reached around the door with the SIG-Sauer and pulled off three shots, immediately after which the pistol was ripped out of his hand and tossed away, clattering on the concrete service driveway.

Instead of rearing back out of the possible line of returning fire and trying to reach the front entrance to make his escape, Osborne lunged around the corner just as Makarov stepped forward, his pistol raised.

They collided, Osborne's heavier bulk driving the Russian backward. He batted the gun out of Makarov's hand, and for just a moment they stood facing each other, neither of them armed.

"You move like an old man, Osborne."

"The virus, or at least who hired you and supplied it to Dekker."

"*Pizdec*," Makarov said and he struck a blow with folded fingers at Osborne's Adam's apple.

Osborne moved sideways, the blow catching him low on his left cheek, and he kicked with his titanium leg, aiming at Makarov's crotch, but he was off balance himself and nearly fell.

Makarov laughed. "You should have stayed in Medora, cripple." He hooked a foot around Osborne's prosthesis and pulled it forward.

Osborne went down heavily, but before Makarov could stomp a boot into his face, he rolled left out of the way and managed to get to his feet. "You killed a friend of mine at the power line."

"He should have taken better care with his tradecraft," Makarov said, edging warily to the left, away from the building.

"And the lineman, and the couple in the pickup truck, and my deputy?"

Makarov shrugged. "They got in my way."

"And this morning?" Osborne asked. He was looking for an opening, but the Russian was light on his feet and remained out of arm's reach.

"I'm here for the same reason you are, to get the virus from Dekker. The man is unstable, and we wanted to get to him before he unleashed the thing. It wouldn't do anyone any good."

"Not the Iranian government."

"No."

"So now I'll go home and tell my government about what happened here tonight and let them deal with Tehran."

"Not if I kill you."

"Won't happen this morning, unless you can somehow reach your pistol before I break your neck, and I think you know it."

Makarov backed up a step. "I'll accept a stalemate for now. But unless one of us finds Dekker and soon, you won't be going back to much of a home. If he manages to cut your entire electrical grid, which I'm told he can do, think of the consequences. It'll push you back into the Stone Age. The death toll would be enormous, much worse even than your Civil War. There'd be no guidance for airplanes, no gasoline, no heating oil in the winters, no emergency generators at your hospitals once the fuel supplies dried up. It would be chaos many times worse than your country experienced when he caused the rolling blackouts."

Osborne had given that a lot of thought, as had Forester and just about everyone else in the know. It would take the U.S. years to fully recover if ever it did. But the immediate problem was finding Dekker and stopping him.

"If he's on the run can he do it?"

"I don't think so, but I don't know for sure. No one does. I was given a lot of money to find him and stop that very thing from happening. Only a madman would want such a thing."

"Chavez and Ahmadinejad."

Makarov nodded. "Perhaps," he said. "I'm leaving now."

"I could stop you."

"You could try, but the delay would give Dekker the advantage."

"Do you know where he went?"

"I have an idea," Makarov said. "But I'll promise you something. Once I find him, I'm going to ground, permanently."

"I'll come after you," Osborne said.

"Because of your friend Sheriff Kasmir and the others that day? Consider them casualties of the war."

Osborne said nothing.

Makarov glanced over his shoulder. "If I find out that you've come gunning for me, my first target will be Ashley Borden. And photograph or not, I think you know what I'm capable of."

Osborne wanted with everything in his body to end it with Makarov here and now. He wanted to smash his fist into the bastard's face, knock him down, grind him into the dirt. He wanted to feel the Russian's neck in his grip, and watch the man's eyes as the life was choked out of him.

At length ne nodded. "Good hunting."

Makarov nodded. "You, too," he said, and he brushed past Osborne and walked away.

Osborne didn't bother turning around to watch him go, instead he stood there for the longest time thinking about Kas and the lineman and the young couple in the pickup truck and Dave Grafton. And especially about Ashley.

She was his responsibility, everything else belonged now to the CIA and Interpol and the NSA. They'd found bin Laden, but this go-around the timing was supercritical. Once Dekker went to ground there'd be nothing they could do to stop him.

He headed back across the parking lot to the Roma camp to find DeJong and get back to the airport and report his failure here.

PART FOUR

ENDGAME

That Same Day

72

KLM FLIGHT 652 touched down at Schiphol Airport twenty minutes early and pulled up at the gate at half-past seven in the morning local. Ashley Borden, dead tired because she had managed to get very little sleep worrying about Nate and about her father tracing her here, walked through the Jetway and into the gate area where she was met by a stern-looking man in a dark blue blazer.

"Ms. Borden, may I see your passport please?" he said, his Dutch accent thick, but his English understandable.

Ashley reared back. She wanted to run, but there was nowhere to go. "You're not from my consulate."

"Actually no, I'm Major Andries DeJong and I received word a half hour ago that you would be aboard this flight."

"What do you want with me?" Ashley demanded, her heart in her throat.

DeJong took her arm and guided her away from the line of people coming off the aircraft. "As a courtesy to your government

I was ordered to break off what I was engaged with to meet you. Your father believes that your life may be in danger."

"Who the hell do you work for? Are you a cop?"

"No. But I have been ordered to make sure that you remain here in the airport, and that you board the next flight back to Washington."

Ashley pulled her arm away. "Not a chance in hell until I talk to someone I came here to meet."

"If you mean Sheriff Osborne, he's already here at the airport with the CIA officer who came with him. They'll be leaving Amsterdam very soon."

A profound sense of relief came over Ashley and her legs threatened to turn to rubber. He was safe. "Has he been hurt?"

"I'm told he was not seriously injured," DeJong said. He held out a hand. If you will give me the claim check for your luggage I will have it brought up to the gate."

"I didn't bring any," Ashley said. She took out her phone and speed-dialed Nate's number but the call wouldn't go through.

"Your American cell phone will not work here."

"I'm not going anywhere until I at least get to talk to him, and whoever the hell you are, you can manage it." The fear that had ridden with her across the Atlantic was turning into anger and frustration.

"There have been casualties this morning," DeJong said. "Two men were shot to death, and their killer has eluded arrest up to this point. One of his targets is you, Ms. Borden."

"Barend Dekker is nothing more than a hacker. He's just a kid."

"Not him, though he's disappeared as well. Osborne identified the killer as a former Spetsnaz operator he was stationed with in Iraq. Your sheriff is keenly interested in returning to the States to make sure that you're safe."

"Yuri Makarov," Ashley said. "He killed five people in North Dakota, including one of Nate's deputies."

"I wasn't aware of it."

"Has Nate been told that I'm here?"

"I don't know that, either."

"I demand that you take me to him immediately."

"Mr. Osborne is under orders to leave the country, and not to have any contact with anyone."

"Goddamnit," Ashley shrieked. "I'll leave with him."

The gate area and broad corridor were busy, and a number of people turned to see what the fuss was all about. A pair of airport security officers in uniforms headed over.

"Keep your voice down, you're attracting attention to yourself," DeJong ordered, and he tried to guide her back toward the open door to the Jetway from which passengers were still emerging.

"You're damn right I am," she shouted at the top of her lungs. "The man's name is Barend Dekker, and he's threatened to harm the U.S., but Dutch police are protecting him!"

"You stupid woman, we don't know where Makarov has disappeared to, but he could be here in this airport waiting for you."

Ashley was too angry to be frightened. Her father had warned more than once that her temper and big mouth were bound to get her into serious trouble sooner or later. Which it had over the holidays when the generating station, Donna Marie, had come under attack. But she couldn't stop now.

"Do you even know what he looks like? Do you have his photograph?"

The armed security officers reached them, and one of them, whose name tag read VAN RIJN said something in Dutch to DeJong, who produced his identification. They had a short conversation.

"You are creating a disturbance, Miss," Van Rijn said in passable English. He and the other officer were very young.

"And I will continue to do so, unless I can make a telephone call," Ashley said, lowering her voice.

The officer said something else to DeJong, who replied.

"We may be forced to place you under arrest, unless you cooperate with this gentleman," Van Rijn said reasonably.

"That's fine with me, but first I need to call my embassy."

Again the security officer and DeJong had a brief conversation in Dutch. Clearly exasperated because of the commotion they were causing, DeJong took out a cell phone and called someone.

He spoke in Dutch for a minute or so, but then broke the connection and made another call. This time he spoke in English.

"Timothy, it is Andries. Is Mr. Osborne with you? Someone here would like to talk to him."

A moment later DeJong handed the phone to Ashley. "Make it quick, they are on the taxiway and once they reach the runway their phone will have to be switched off."

"Nate?"

"Ash, I don't want to hear that you're in Amsterdam."

"I came to help you," she said, her relief sweet. "Are you okay, did you get it?"

"No. Dekker escaped."

"And I was told so did Makarov," Ashley said. "But it's okay now, they're going to put me on the next flight back to D.C."

"Do what you're told for once, and soon as you get home go to your dad's. I'll meet you there."

"He's not going to try to come after me in the States. He'd be a fool to try it."

"They want me to shut off my phone. Just go to your dad's."

Ashley looked up, past the two security officers, in time to spot a slightly built man in jeans and a dark jacket following a younger man, a laptop computer under one arm and a leather satchel slung over his other shoulder. Something about how both men moved attracted her attention.

Just as they passed where she stood the man in the jeans and dark jacket looked over at her, and she saw his eyes. They were violet, and a hint of recognition came over his features.

It was Makarov, she would have bet anything on it. And the younger man he was following had to be Dekker.

"It's them," she blurted.

"What are you talking about?" Osborne asked.

"Makarov is following Dekker. They just passed."

"Ash," Osborne shouted.

Ashley shoved the cell phone at DeJong. "It's them," she shouted. "The guy in the jeans and dark jacket."

The security officers turned to where she was pointing.

"Who are you talking about?" Van Rijn asked.

"Goddamnit, they're getting away," she said, and she bolted away from the three of them, just eluding DeJong, who grabbed for her.

"Ms. Borden," he shouted.

"Don't just stand there, come on," she screamed over her shoulder.

73

FOR JUST A minute Dekker paid no attention to the noise some woman was making at one of the gates he'd just passed. "It's them," she'd screamed. Or something like that. But it began to dawn on him that one of the *them* might be him.

He turned and looked over his shoulder. The broad corridor was very busy now, packed with people hurrying to or from gates in this terminal, but a great many of them had stopped and turned toward the direction of the hysterical woman.

His gate was only three away. He'd passed through passport control and the security check with no problem, and his flight to Bangkok was scheduled to leave in little more than an hour. He was practically home free.

During the cab ride out to the airport he'd gone online and transferred the entire five hundred thousand euros to an account in the Channel Islands, and from there spread the money in three portions to a bank in Luxembourg, one in Barbados, and one in Bangkok. All of the transfers were done under different identities, making it next to impossible for anyone, even a government intelligence service to ever find them. And before that happened he would cash out, and put the money in a mix of gold and diamonds, and maybe some cash for ready spending, though he'd never needed much, not even when Karn wanted to shop.

Makarov was suddenly there, less than ten meters away and moving toward him. Dekker backed up a step, then two, his heart racing. Somehow he'd been traced this far, and the North Dakota shooter he'd managed to get away from at the Haven was here now to kill him.

He turned and headed away, any thoughts of actually getting aboard his Bangkok flight and leaving the country completely impossible. The only two things he figured he had on his side were the thumb drive which contained the virus that he'd already loaded onto a Cloud memory in Germany, and the fact that the shooter would not risk a violent act with so many witnesses.

Looking over his shoulder, Makarov was right there, nearly an arm's length away, and the woman less than twenty meters farther down the corridor was being restrained by a man in civilian clothes while two uniformed cops were standing by. She was still screeching.

With a squeak Dekker broke into a flat-out run, knocking several people aside until he came to a gate whose boarding door was still open. He was across in a half-dozen steps, bowling a gate attendant off her feet as he entered the Jetway and pushed past the still deplaning passengers.

At the turn just before the aircraft's main hatch, Dekker slammed open the Jetway's service door and took the stairs down to the tarmac, the huge 747 looming overhead. A baggage handler driving a cart pulling two trailers filled with luggage came from inside.

Someone was coming down the stairs, and Dekker sprinted to the service door from which the baggage cart had emerged, but

Makarov was right on him, grabbing his arm and pulling him around.

"Give me the thumb drive with the virus and you just might live to reach Thailand and spend your money."

"How do I know you won't kill me?"

"You don't. But it'll be just a matter of a minute or less before Ms. Borden convinces the authorities that the both of us need to be arrested. I won't allow that to happen. The thumb drive. Be quick."

Dekker took the drive out of his pants pocket and gave it to the Russian.

"Your laptop as well."

"It's not on there. Only my games. The copy is on an encrypted Cloud memory in Germany that only I can access. I swear it."

Makarov was looking at him, gauging the truth, and Dekker found that he was almost mesmerized. He figured it was just like looking into the eyes of a cobra on the verge of striking.

But the Russian let go and stepped back. "Leave now while you can." He glanced toward the Jetway door. "Someone else will probably come after you, so bury yourself deep. Deeper than Thailand. And if you value your life, forget about the virus. If you use it they'll hunt you forever."

"I don't know where to go," Dekker said, and he was frightened. If only Karn were here she would know what to do.

"Go up to the baggage claim area, and from there take a taxi back into the city. Now. Fly away."

Dekker turned and ran toward the baggage-handling service door, when a woman screeched something from the top of the Jetway stairs, and a Gulfstream came right at them from the direction of the runways.

74

IN THE COCKPIT of the CIA Gulfstrean Osborne was in time to see Ashley heading toward a figure retreating into the baggage handling bay, DeJong along with two uniformed officers coming down the Jetway stairs.

"Stop here," Osborne shouted.

"We can't," Dennis Tate, the pilot, said. "Ground control is on my case right now."

Osborne reached around him and hauled the throttles back to their stops, then turned and went to the hatch, undogging it and shoving it open.

Tim Winkler tried to haul him away. "You son of a bitch, you're going to get us arrested. We're going to have to explain why a CIA operation took place in a neutral country."

The Gulfstream was nearly at a complete stop when Osborne lowered the boarding stairs. "*You* can explain everything, I'm going to try to save some lives." He turned back and yanked Winkler's pistol from its shoulder holster then hurried down to the tarmac.

A siren sounded from somewhere in the distance, a police car with blue lights flashing coming very fast directly across the taxiway.

Osborne ran under the 747's broad wing, and around the baggage cart past the two men loading luggage onto a moving conveyor belt into the belly of the big aircraft. They didn't stop what they were doing.

Ashley had disappeared inside the building, DeJong and the cops so intent in their pursuit that Osborne took them by surprise as he ran right past them.

"Seal off the airport," he shouted.

"Halt! Halt!" Van Rijn ordered.

Osborne ignored him, and raced inside past two baggage trains and toward the left where mounds of luggage were contained inside tall wire racks. Just beyond them, down a long row against the rear wall, were the baggage conveyor belts that went out to the claim area on the ground floor of the terminal.

Ashley had just ducked around one of the piles, and she shouted something Osborne couldn't quite make out. But it sounded as if she were in trouble.

He redoubled his efforts, DeJong and the security officers not far behind him. "Ashley," he shouted.

"No! Stay back!" she screamed.

"Halt, or I will shoot," Van Rijn warned.

At that moment Osborne rounded the baggage rack, and pulled up short. Ashley stood facing him, Makarov behind her, an arm around her neck.

"If need be I will kill her," the Russian said. It didn't seem as if he was winded, or in any hurry.

"Stay back," Osborne shouted over his shoulder. "We have a hostage situation here."

Winkler was somewhere back there. "What do you need, Nate?" he called.

"Seal the airport right now"

"It's being done," DeJong said.

"Osborne turned back to Makarov. "You might as well give it up, because you won't get out of here this morning."

"That's my concern, Sheriff. Not yours."

"Prison is better than a graveyard."

"Your concern is Ms. Borden. If you cooperate I will have no need to kill her. This time."

"Sorry, Nate," Ashley said. "I was stupid."

"What do you want?" Osborne asked.

Makarov took the thumb drive out of his pocket and tossed it overhand to Osborne, who caught it. "It's the virus from Dekker. Russian probably, but the thing is the kid says he made a copy and sent it to a Cloud memory somewhere in Germany."

"Did you believe him?"

"I had no reason not to. He was in fear for his life."

"He was here in the airport?"

"Yes. Heading toward Bangkok. I sent him back to the city, but if the authorities act quickly enough to close down the airport they might catch him. Which leaves you and me and Ms. Borden."

"You won't escape."

"As I said, that's my concern."

"What do you propose?" Osborne asked.

"Your word that you will stop following me for the next twenty-four hours. Take Ms. Borden and go back to the States."

"If you give me your word that you won't try to retaliate by trying to reach her again."

"There'll be no need," Makarov said.

"You have mine," Osborne said, and he lowered the pistol. "Go."

Makarov hesitated for just a moment, but then released Ashley and turned and disappeared down the long rows of baggage racks into the darkness.

Ashley half turned in the direction he'd gone. "You can't just let him walk away," she said miserably. "Not after everything he did to us."

"I gave my word," Osborne said. He took her arm. "Let's get out of here now. They'll catch him."

She looked up into his eyes, an odd set to her mouth, as if she was having a difficult time figuring out something that was just beyond her ken. "Just for me?" she asked in a small voice. "Grafton and Kas and the lineman and the people in the pickup?"

"They're dead, you're not."

"And you're in love with me." She said it as a statement, not as a question.

Osborne managed a smile. "Didn't you know?" he said. "We're coming out," he shouted.

More sirens were converging on the baggage handling bay, and Osborne realized that he'd not heard the sounds of jets landing or taking off for the past several minutes. Only the sirens.

75

C HINESE MINISTRY OF State officer Zhang Wei, a slightly built man dressed in a conservative Western business suit, doubled back through the terminal after Dekker came under pursuit and he waited in the baggage retrieval hall, the only possible avenue of escape for the young man.

His partner, Wan Xiuying, remained upstairs at the gate, which looked down at the commotion on the tarmac.

"I'm in place," Zhang Wei radioed from his Bluetooth headset.

"He went into the baggage loading bay as you thought he might."

"Is it likely that he will be apprehended?"

"Very likely," Wan Xiuying replied. "Mr. Makarov was behind him, along with the woman from the terminal, the Dutch intelligence officer, and two airport security officers. But there is another further complication."

"*Shi de.*" Yes.

"Sheriff Osborne got off the CIA's aircraft along with another man, and they also are in pursuit."

All things amazing, Zhang Wei, thought. From the near miss on the Iranian border, when the thumb drive had very nearly been theirs, to the events in the U.S., to the war fleet at this moment approaching Venezuela, and now this.

"If Dekker is arrested, he will almost certainly be led past your position," he said. "Stay in contact with him, no matter the circumstances, and do what is necessary if the chance arises. There are no other considerations."

"I understand. But it may not be possible to retrieve the drive."

"It will be of no concern if he is dead," Zhang Wei said.

The large baggage hall was crowded with people waiting for their luggage to arrive on the carousels. Nevertheless Zhang Wei spotted Dekker hurrying from the far end of the hall, where the two carousels were idle and no people were gathered. Somehow the young man had managed to slip away from his pursuers.

"I have him. I'll meet you at the car. Hurry."

"*Shi de*," Wan Xiuying said with a measure of relief. Unlike Zhang Wei, who did not pass through security, he was unable to bring a pistol into the gate area. If the chance arose to kill Dekker he would accomplish it with his bare hands. Not difficult, but his escape would have become problematic.

Zhang Wei turned and followed Dekker outside just as several airport security officers came down the escalators to seal off the baggage area.

Dozens of cars, several buses, and more than a dozen taxis were lined up along the curb, people exiting the terminal and loading their luggage for the trip into the city. Traffic streamed past in four lanes. The scene was busier and more chaotic than it had been inside the baggage retrieval hall.

For a moment or two Zhang Wei lost sight of the target, but then he spotted the young man stopped at the end of the taxi queue, hopping nervously from one foot to the other, obviously unsure of what he was doing.

Zhang Wei walked up behind him. "Mr. Dekker, I am a friend."

Dekker almost jumped out of his skin, and he pulled back. "What?"

"Come with me right now, or you will certainly be apprehended. Do you understand?"

"No," Dekker squeaked. He looked back at the baggage area doors and saw that people were being stopped by airport security officers.

"I have a car and I will take you to a place in the city where you will be safe. But you must make up your mind before it's too late."

Still Dekker hesitated.

Zhang Wei took his arm. "Come," he said, gently. "I will explain on the way into the safe house we have prepared for you. The Russian won't be able to get to you."

"He has the thumb drive."

It was a blow, but Zhang Wei did not let it show on his face. In any event it was Dekker who was the crazy one. So far as he understood Makarov was a professional, and would have no reason to unleash the virus in the U.S.

"We'll discuss that as well. I believe that I may be able to give you information that would allow the virus to be neutralized."

"No way," Dekker said, a glimmer of interest in his eyes.

"I'm sure that you've already thought about it," Zhang Wei said reasonably, and he led the young man away from the taxi line. "It's actually complicated, but for a man of your education and experience, it would be relatively easy. I'll show you."

They stepped out into the lanes of traffic and made their way across to the median, and then across the other three lanes of traffic, where in the shadows of a bridge abutment below the road that approached the main level of the terminal Zhang Wei pulled out his silenced 9mm Beretta 92F, the standard-issue pistol in the U.S. armed forces, stepped back a pace to keep out of the blood spray, and shot Dekker in the back of the head.

The young man went down hard.

Zhang Wei glanced over his shoulder to make sure no one in traffic or waiting outside the baggage hall had spotted anything. Satisfied that no one was raising the alarm, he turned back and fired four more shots into the back of Dekker's head.

He tossed the pistol aside, not worried about fingerprint evidence; all MSS field officers had their fingerprints surgically removed during training, and he walked away.

"Wan Xiuying, mission completed."

"I'm on my way to the parking garage, though I may be somewhat delayed by this lockdown."

"I'll wait for you."

"*Shi de.*"

76

IN THE WHITE House Situation Room it was four in the morning, and President Thompson, along with his closest advisers including Secretary of State Mortenson and Chairman of the Joint Chiefs Air Force General Blake were sitting on the edge of their seats, their eyes glued to the large-screen monitor.

The aircraft carrier *George H.W. Bush* and her entire Strike Group of Los Angeles–Class submarines, surface ships, and AWACS aircraft had threaded their way through the Antilles and were presently just over the horizon from Bonaire and Curacao, well within striking range of Caracas less than two hundred miles to the south. Real-time images were being transmitted from the carrier's Combat Information Center as well as from a Keyhole satellite that provided infrared images of Venezuela's north coast.

Until just a minute ago the city of Caracas had been lit up like a million jewels sparkling on a black backdrop. Most of the city was in darkness now. When the lights went out Thompson was breathless for just a moment.

"They know we're there," CIA director Walt Page had said. "But there's been no response."

The carrier group commander, Rear Admiral Horace Butler, came on screen. He was an unremarkable-looking man, a little rumpled this morning, but he was an extremely capable officer who never blinked. When he was pointed in some direction, he charged. He was Thompson's Sherman. "Mr. President, we're ready at this point. Do you have an order for me?"

"Are your targets set?" Thompson asked. He and Butler had spoken at length over the past twenty-four hours about the exact nature of the mission and the three main objectives.

"Yes, sir. We have six cruise missiles dialed up for Caracas—two on the Miraflores Palace, where because of the hour there should be a minimum loss of life, two on SEBIN's headquarters which under the circumstances may be fully staffed, and two on the Ministry of Defense which also should be well staffed. We have an additional four missiles which are targeted on four primary oil-loading sites in Lake Maracaibo. That will be our first wave."

"Any sign of their Navy or Air Force?"

"No, sir. But they're aware of us. We believe that they may be receiving real-time satellite information from the Russians."

"Have your aircraft or surface vessels been illuminated by radar?" General Blake asked.

"No, sir. Which makes us believe that they are getting satellite imagery."

"To this point you've encountered no resistance, nor have you come under any threat, real or implied," Thompson asked. He was wound up, as was everyone else in the room.

He'd draped a Medal of Honor around the neck of a SEAL, and afterward when they were talking the young man had jokingly told him one of the ten Murphy's Laws for combat soldiers: "If everything is going according to plan, you're probably running into a trap." He had not forgotten it.

"They have not yet fully recovered from Balboa, so we didn't expect much. The field is ours, sir. I just need the launch order."

"Standby," Thompson said and he cut the audio. "Discussion?" he asked his advisers.

"Our allies will look on this as an act of war," Mortenson said.

Thompson had hired the secretary of state precisely because he was a dove. "A measured response," he said.

"We accomplished Balboa."

"In retaliation for the attacks on the Initiative, with the loss of many lives. This morning is in response to the attacks on our grid and on the transformers in Texas. Perhaps they'll get the message that if they unleash the virus against us, I will order a nuclear strike on Caracas. Americans would demand nothing less of me."

Mortenson looked around at the others and he shook his head. "I'm sorry, Mr. President, but I cannot in all good conscience be a part of this." He started to rise.

"Are you resigning, Irving?" Thompson asked sharply.

Mortenson hesitated for a beat. "No, sir."

"Then sit down. This is still a democracy, and you've cast your vote."

Mortenson sat.

"Any other objections?"

"To a possible nuclear strike, yes, sir, I have objections," General Blake said. "But no, I am not resigning."

"The nuclear option is down the road, and very unlikely," Thompson said. "I'm talking about this morning. Diplomacy has failed, and sanctions have never worked, not even against North Korea. If our national grid goes down this country will face the most serious problem it's ever faced since the Civil War. The loss of lives and property would be staggering. You've all seen the reports."

No one said a thing.

"Discussion," Thompson prompted.

"What about the hacker in Amsterdam?" Nicholas Trilling asked. He was the secretary of defense and although unlike Mortenson he was no dove, neither was he a knee-jerk hawk. His philosophy was the same as Teddy Roosevelt's: Speak softly and carry a big stick.

"One of my people who accompanied Nate Osborne over there had heard nothing as of two hours ago. Osborne was disarmed, and a Dutch intelligence officer was to accompany him to where Barend Dekker was possibly barricaded."

"Which means unless Dekker is directed to stand down, he could be making ready at this moment to unleash the virus," Thompson said. "We need to give him pause."

Madeline Bible, the director of national intelligence, looked around the table, then back to Thompson. "I don't think we have any other choice this morning, Mr. President," she said.

The others all nodded their assent, and Thompson switched on the audio.

"What is the time to the various targets?" he asked Admiral Butler.

"We'll fire AGM-158s, which are medium-range subsonic JASSMs—Joint Air-to-Surface Standoff Missiles—which fly at eight hundred kilometers per hour. Time to target is in the thirty-minute range."

"Proceed on my orders, Admiral."

"Yes, sir," the admiral said. He turned and said something to the ship's captain, and moments later a camera view of the carrier's deck suddenly blossomed into bright white as the first missiles were launched.

"God help the poor bastards," Fenniger said half under his breath.

Less than two minutes later the admiral turned back. "All are away, and flying hot and normal."

An incoming call on the console was for Walt Page. The president motioned for him to pick it up.

"Page," the DCI said. He listened for several long moments. "Are you sure it's him? No possibility it was someone else?" He listened again. He hung up. "It's the computer hacker. He's dead. And Osborne has the thumb drive with the virus."

"Thank God," Mortenson said.

The relief in the room was palpable and Thompson sat back. "Any casualties?" he asked.

"Several, but none of ours. Osborne and the officer I sent with him are fine. They'll be leaving Amsterdam within the hour."

Thompson nodded. "The man has done it for us again. He'd needs to be here in Washington, with the Bureau."

"We've tried. He won't leave North Dakota," FBI Director Edward Rogers said.

"Try harder," Thompson said with an edge to his voice.

"Yes, sir."

Admiral Butler was privy to the conversation. "Shall we stand down, Mr. President?"

"The missiles can be self-destructed before they hit their targets?"

"Yes, sir. We can give the order now."

"Thirty minutes before they reach their targets?"

"Yes, sir."

Thompson smiled with satisfaction. "Send the self-destruct signal in twenty minutes," he said. "I want Chavez to swing in the wind to see what it feels like."

Epilogue

Fourteen days later
The White House

WHEN OSBORNE AND Ashley arrived in Washington a limousine was waiting to take them to the White House. General Forester was in the backseat. Ashley kissed her father on the cheek and they headed away from Reagan National, the day sunny and beautiful.

"I don't like this very much," Osborne said. He was dressed in a suit and tie, the first he'd worn since Kas's funeral, and he was uncomfortable. He didn't belong here, especially not now.

"When a president wants to give you the Medal of Freedom, with Distinction, you don't turn it down," Forester said.

"I don't deserve it."

"That's not for you to say. Anyway I don't agree. Without you this country would be in trouble. So like it or not your face is going to be on every network tonight and every newspaper tomorrow morning."

"Makarov is still out there someplace," Ashley said.

"He already knows what Nate looks like," Forester said. "And the chances are slim that he'd try to come after him. There'd be nothing in it for him. And from what I've been led to understand, the man is a professional, and doesn't need revenge."

Osborne let their conversation swirl around him. In a way it seemed to him that Ash and her father were talking about someone else; someone who was a complete stranger to him, a admirable man, a hero, but someone else.

Ashley took his hand. "It's over, Nate. They failed. And in a couple of weeks we're going to get married and you can go back to being a small-town sheriff."

He smiled, and wished with everything that the attacks against them were truly over with, but he couldn't. The same issues that had faced the Initiative were still on the table. Big oil, a multitrillion-dollar business was at stake. And like Whitney Lipton at her lab in Atlanta, he was about to become the poster boy in the struggle. The point man. His image front and center.

It wasn't about his personal safety, it was about Ashley's and the people around him who were in danger, and he felt as if he were helpless to do anything to protect them, and it was frustrating. Gun battles were easy by comparison, because they were almost always over in a couple of minutes. But for this now there was no end in sight.

They stopped at the east gate and when the guard saw it was Forester in the backseat, waved them through. They were met at the entrance by Mark Young, who shook Osborne's hand.

"The president is looking forward to this," he said. "Ms. Borden, welcome to the White House."

"Any possibility of me getting out of it?" Osborne asked.

"Nope. But you've been here before, you know the drill, only this time instead of a ceremony in the Oval Office we'll be using the Blue Room."

It was one of three formal parlors, this one on the first floor, and was normally used for receiving lines, receptions, and sometimes important state dinners.

"Why's that?" Ashley asked.

"The Oval Office isn't large enough," Young said and he led them upstairs to the Cross Hall, and to Blue Room, itself an oval about thirty feet wide and forty long, which this afternoon was filled nearly to capacity with media people, plus much of the president's staff, along with the secretary of state and others.

Osborne almost shrank back, but Ashley had a firm hold of his arm. "Easy," she said.

Inside they passed a reception line of well-wishers who shook his hand, and others who applauded. Whitney was near the head of the line and she kissed him on the cheek.

"This has to be better than being shot at, don't you think?" she whispered in his ear.

"No."

"Well, it'll be over in less than a half-hour and we can go have a drink," Forester said. "FORECON, hoorah."

Osborne had to grin. He was being an idiot, but there was more to come. He could feel it in his bones.

Young left them, and moments later at the door, he announced: "Ladies and gentlemen, the president of the United States."

Majorca

Makarov and Ilke lay in each other's arms after making love. It was early evening and a soft Mediterranean breeze ruffled the gauze drapes at the open balcony door of their royal suite in the Hotel Villa Italia.

After Stockholm they'd stayed here for nearly two weeks, sailing, walking the beaches, dinners in Palma, and right here at a small trattoria at Puerto de Andratx. They'd rented motor scooters and toured the island, and for the last two days they had looked at villas and houses with a German real estate agent, whose English was better than Makarov's.

"Is it really true, you're going to retire?" Ilke asked, stroking his chest with the tip of a finger. She was a slender woman, thirty years old, with short blond hair cut in a pixie style, and very wide, startlingly blue eyes. She was almost always smiling about something, but now she was practically bubbling over. She reminded him of a teenage girl he once knew a very long time ago.

"I've already turned over the business to Brant. He'll run it, and whenever possible he'll buy it from me." Brant Van DeHoef, a former South African Special Forces operator, had been in the company almost from the beginning. He knew the business well, and had developed many of his own contacts.

"Then what?" she asked.

"For starts, we'll buy a place here, and then travel."

"I meant about your secret life?"

Something very hard and painful clutched at his gut, but he didn't let his reaction show. Instead he smiled. "What are you talking about?"

"I know that you didn't go to Amsterdam on business."

"What then?"

"For that other thing. Another costume ball or something."

"You're making no sense whatsoever," Makarov said.

"Sometimes when you go away I know that it's for business. But other times you come back and your hair is different. Or sometimes your face looks as if you'd been out in a hot desert sun for weeks, cracked, red, and a little wrinkled. But by the next morning you look like you look now. Handsome."

"Sometimes I have to go in disguise."

"Why is that?"

"I do arms deals, and some of the people are less than honorable. I've never wanted to lead them back to Stockholm. To us."

"They know your business address," Ilke insisted.

"But not my home." His tradecraft had been sloppy, because all along he figured that he would have to kill her and move on. So it didn't really matter what she knew. But now it was different for him.

She looked into his eyes. "Then some of it was sometimes less than legal."

"Sometimes."

"And it's truly over?" she asked.

"Truly over."

"Because you love me, though you've never once said it."

Makarov pulled her down and kissed her lips. "Because I truly love you, " he said.

"Then I don't care whatever has happened in the past, only the now and the tomorrows."